Mistresses

LETHAL ATTRACTION

MELANIE MILBURNE JOSS WOOD KATHERINE GARBERA

Mistresses Collection

November 2016

December 2016

January 2017

February 2017

March 2017

April 2017

Mistresses

LETHAL ATTRACTION

MELANIE MILBURNE JOSS WOOD KATHERINE GARBERA

All rights reserved including the right of reproduction in whole or in part in any form. This edition is published by arrangement with Harlequin Books S.A.

This is a work of fiction. Names, characters, places, locations and incidents are purely fictional and bear no relationship to any real life individuals, living or dead, or to any actual places, business establishments, locations, events or incidents. Any resemblance is entirely coincidental.

This book is sold subject to the condition that it shall not, by way of trade or otherwise, be lent, resold, hired out or otherwise circulated without the prior consent of the publisher in any form of binding or cover other than that in which it is published and without a similar condition including this condition being imposed on the subsequent purchaser.

® and ™ are trademarks owned and used by the trademark owner and/or its licensee. Trademarks marked with ® are registered with the United Kingdom Patent Office and/or the Office for Harmonisation in the Internal Market and in other countries.

Published in Great Britain 2017
By Mills & Boon, an imprint of HarperCollins*Publishers*
1 London Bridge Street, London, SE1 9GF

MISTRESSES: LETHAL ATTRACTION © 2017 Harlequin Books S.A.

Uncovering the Silveri Secret © 2013 Melanie Milburne
If You Can't Stand the Heat... © 2013 Joss Wood
Sizzle © 2013 Katherine Garbera

ISBN: 978-0-263-92763-4

24-0417

Harlequin (UK) Limited's policy is to use papers that are natural, renewable and recyclable products and made from wood grown in sustainable forests. The logging and manufacturing processes conform to the legal environmental regulations of the country of origin.

Printed and bound in Spain
by CPI, Barcelona

UNCOVERING THE SILVERI SECRET

MELANIE MILBURNE

To my niece Bethany Luke – an absolute sweetheart who cares about everybody. xox

Melanie Milburne read her first Mills & Boon novel at age seventeen in between studying for her final exams. After completing a Masters Degree in Education, she decided to write a novel in between settling down to do a PhD. She became so hooked on writing romance the PhD was shelved and her career as a romance writer was born. Melanie is an ambassador for the Australian Childhood Foundation and is a keen dog lover and trainer and enjoys long walks in the Tasmanian bush.

CHAPTER ONE

IT WAS the first time Bella had been home since the funeral. Haverton Manor in February was like a winter wonderland, with a recent fall of snow clinging to the limbs of the ancient beech and elm trees that fringed the long driveway leading to the Georgian mansion. The rolling fields and woods beyond were shrouded in a thin blanket of white, and the lake shone like a sheet of glass in the distance as she brought her sports car to a stop in front of the formal knot garden. Fergus, her late father's Irish wolfhound, gingerly rose from his resting place in the sun and came over to greet her with a slow wag of his tail.

'Hiya, Fergs,' Bella said and gave his ears a gentle scratch. 'What are you doing out here all by yourself? Where's Edoardo?'

'I'm here.'

Bella swung round at the sound of that deep, rich, velvet-smooth voice, her heart giving a funny little jump in her chest as her eyes took in Edoardo Silveri's tall figure standing there. She hadn't seen him face-to-face for a couple of years, but he was just as arresting as ever.

Not handsome in a classical sense; he had too many irregular features for that. His nose was slightly crooked from a fist fight, and one of his dark eyebrows had a scar through it, like a jagged pathway cut through a hedge, both hoofmarks of his troubled adolescence.

He was wearing sturdy work-boots, faded blue denim jeans and a thick black sweater that was pushed up to his elbows, showcasing his strong, muscular arms. His wavy, soot-black hair was brushed off his face, and dark stubble peppered his lean jaw, giving him an intensely masculine look that for some reason always made the back of her knees tingle. She took in a little jerky breath and met his startling blue-green eyes, almost putting her neck out to do it. 'Hard at work?' she said, adopting the aristocrat-to-servant tone she customarily used with him.

'Always.'

Bella couldn't quite stop her gaze drifting to his mouth. It was hard and tightly set, the deep grooves either side of it indicating it was more used to containing emotion than showing it. She had once come too close to those sensually sculptured lips. Only the once, but it was a memory she had desperately tried to erase ever since. But even now she could still recall the head-spinning taste of him: salt, mint and hot-blooded male. She had been kissed lots of times, too many times to recall each one, but she could recall Edoardo's in intimate, spine-tingling detail.

Was he remembering it too, how their mouths had slammed together in a scorching kiss that had left both of them breathless? How their tongues had snaked around each other and duelled and danced with earthy, brazen intent?

Bella tore her eyes away and glanced at the damp dirt on his hands from where he had been pulling at some weeds in one of the garden beds. 'What happened to the gardener?' she asked.

'He broke his arm a couple of weeks ago,' he said. 'I told you about it when I emailed you the share-update information.'

She frowned. 'Did you? I didn't see it. Are you sure you sent it to me?'

The right side of his top lip came up in a mocking tilt, the closest he ever got to a smile. 'Yes, Bella, I'm sure,' he said. 'Perhaps you missed it in amongst all the messages from your latest lover. Who is it this week? The guy with the failing restaurant, or is it still the banker's son?'

'It's neither,' she said with a lift of her chin. 'His name is Julian Bellamy and he's studying to be a minister.'

'Of politics?'

She gave him an imperious look. 'Of religion.'

He threw back his head and laughed. It wasn't quite the reaction Bella had been expecting. It annoyed her that he found her news so amusing. She wasn't used to him showing any emotion, much less amusement. He rarely smiled, apart from those mocking tilts of his mouth, and she couldn't remember the last time she had heard him laugh out loud. She found his reaction over the top and completely unnecessary. How dared he mock the man she had decided she was going to marry? Julian was everything Edoardo was not. He was sophisticated and cultured; he was polite and considerate; he saw the good in people, not the bad.

And he loved her, rather than hating her, as Edoardo did.

'What's so funny?' she asked with an irritated frown.

He swiped at his eyes with the back of his hand, still chuckling. 'I can't quite see it somehow,' he said.

She sent him a narrowed glare. 'See what?'

'You handing around tea and scones at Bible study,' he said. 'You don't fit the mould of a preacher's wife.'

'What's that supposed to mean?' she asked.

His eyes ran over her long black boots and designer skirt and jacket, before taking a leisurely tour of the upthrusts of her breasts, finally meeting her gaze with an insolent glint in his. 'Your skirts are too high and your morals too low.'

Bella wanted to thump him. She clenched her hands into fists to stop herself from actually doing it. She wasn't going to touch him if she could help it. Her body had a habit of doing things it shouldn't do when it came too close to his. Her nails bit into her palms as she tried to rein in her temper. 'You're a fine one to talk about morals,' she threw back. 'At least I don't have a criminal record.'

Something hardened in his gaze as it pinned hers: diamond-hard. Anger-hard. Hatred-hard. 'You want to play dirty with me, princess?' he asked.

This time Bella felt that tingly sensation at the base of her spine. She knew it had been a low blow to refer to his delinquent past, but Edoardo always triggered something dark, primal and uncontrollable in her. She didn't know what was it about him that got her back up so quickly, but he needled her like no other person.

He had *always* done it.

He seemed to take particular delight in getting a rise out of her. It didn't matter how much she promised herself she would keep a lid on her temper. It didn't matter how cool and sophisticated she planned to be. He *always* got under her skin.

Ever since that night when she was sixteen, she had done her best to avoid her father's bad-boy protégé. For months, if not years, at a time she would keep her distance, barely even acknowledging him when she came home for a brief visit to her father. Edoardo brought out something in her that was deeply unsettling. In his company she didn't feel poised and in control.

She felt edgy and restless.

She thought things she should not be thinking. Like how sensual the curve of his mouth was, the way the lower lip was fuller than the top one; how his lean jaw always seemed to need a shave. How his hair looked like it had just been combed with his fingers. How he would look naked, all tanned, whipcord-lean and fit.

Like how he always looked at her with that hooded, inscrutable gaze as if he was seeing through the layers of her designer clothes to her tingling body beneath...

'Why are you here?' he asked.

Bella gave him a defiant look. 'Are you going to march me off the premises for trespassing?'

A glint of something menacing lurked in his gaze. 'This is no longer your home.'

Her look hardened to a cutting glare. 'Yes, well, you certainly made sure of that, didn't you?'

'I had nothing to do with your father's decision to bequeath me Haverton Manor,' he said. 'I can only presume he thought you were never very interested in the place. You hardly ever visited him, especially towards the end.'

Bella's resentment boiled inside her—resentment and guilt. She hated him for reminding her of how she had stayed away when her father had needed her the most. The permanency of death had made her run for cover. The thought of being left all alone in the world had been terrifying. The desertion of her mother just before her sixth birthday had made her deeply insecure; people she loved *always* left her. She had buried her head in the social scene of London rather than face reality. She had made the excuse of studying for her final exams, but the truth was she had never really known how to reach out to her father.

Godfrey had come to fatherhood late in life, and after her mother had left, he had not coped well with the role of being a single parent. Consequently their relationship had never been close, which had made her insanely jealous of the way in which her father had fostered his relationship with Edoardo. She suspected Godfrey saw Edoardo as a surrogate son—the son he had secretly longed for. It made her feel inadequate, a feeling that was only reinforced a hundredfold when she found out the way her father had left his estate. 'I'm sure you worked my absence to your advantage,' she said, shooting him another embittered glare. 'I bet you sucked up to him every chance you could, all the while painting me as a silly little socialite with no sense of responsibility.'

'Your father didn't need me to point out how irresponsible you are,' he said with that annoying, trademark lip-curl. 'You do a fine job of that all by yourself. Your peccadilloes are splashed across the newspapers just about every week.'

Bella simmered with fury even though there was some truth in what he said. The press always targeted her, making her out to be a wild child with more money than sense. She only had to be in the wrong place at the wrong time for some ridiculous story to come out about her.

But things would be different soon.

Once she was married to Julian, the press would hopefully leave her alone. Her reputation would be spotless. 'I'd like to stay for a few days,' she said. 'I hope that won't inconvenience you?'

Those intriguing eyes glinted dangerously again. 'Are you asking me or telling me?'

Bella put on a beseeching expression, her hatred of him tightening her spine until she could feel every knob of her vertebrae. It was positively galling to have to ask for permission to stay at her childhood home. That was one of the reasons she had turned up unannounced.

She'd figured he might not be able to turn her away with the household staff looking on. 'Please, Edoardo, may I stay for a few days?' she asked. 'I won't get in your way. I promise.'

'Do the press know where you are?' he asked.

'No one knows where I am,' she said. 'I don't want anyone to find me. That's why I came here. No one would ever dream of finding me here with you.'

His chiselled jaw was locked like a vice, a muscle on the left side moving in and out like a tiny heart beating under the skin. 'I've a good mind to send you on your way.'

Bella pushed her bottom lip out. 'It's about to snow again,' she said. 'What if I run off the road or something? My death would be on your hands.'

'You can't just turn up here and expect the red carpet to be rolled out for you,' he said with a look of stern disapproval. 'You could at least have called and asked if it was all right to stay. Why didn't you?'

'Because you would have said no,' Bella said. 'What's the problem with me staying a few days? I won't get in your way.'

The muscle tapped a little harder in his jaw. 'I don't want a bunch of voyeurs lurking about the place,' he said. 'As soon as the paparazzi turn up, you can pack your bags and leave. Got it?'

'Got it,' Bella said, inwardly seething at his overbearing manner. What did he think she was going to do—call a press conference? She wanted to escape all that and lie low until Julian came back. She didn't want any more scandals in her life.

'And nor will I tolerate you bringing friends here to party all hours of the day and night,' he said, drilling her with his diamond-hard gaze. 'Understood?'

Bella gave him her best 'I'll be good' face. 'No parties.'

'I mean it, Bella,' he said. 'I'm working on a big project just now. I don't want to be distracted.'

'All right, already. I get it,' she said, flashing an irritated gaze. 'So what's the big important project? Is she female? Is she currently sleeping over? I wouldn't want to cramp your style or anything.'

'I'm not going to discuss my private life with you,' he said. 'Before I know it, you'd be spilling all to the press.'

Bella wondered who his latest lover was, but there was no way she was going to ask. Asking would imply she was interested. She didn't want him thinking she spent any time at all musing over what he was doing and whom he was doing it with. He mostly kept his private life exactly that—private. His enigmatic, unknowable nature made him a target for the paparazzi but somehow he managed to keep his head below the parapet. Whereas Bella couldn't seem to step outside her house in Chelsea without attracting a camera flash from the lurking paparazzi, who always painted her as a professional party girl with nothing better to do than get a spray tan.

Her engagement to Julian Bellamy would hopefully put all that to rest. She wanted a clean slate, and once she was married, she would have it. Julian was the nicest man she had ever met. He was nothing like the men she had dated in the past. He didn't attract scandal or intrigue. He didn't party or drink. He didn't have a worldly bone in his body. He wasn't interested in wealth and status, only helping others.

'Would you bring in my bags for me?' she asked Edoardo with mock sweetness. 'They're in the boot.'

Edoardo leaned against the front fender of her car, one ankle crossed over the other, his arms folded against the broad expanse of his chest. 'When do I get to meet your new lover?' he asked.

Bella pushed her chin a little higher. 'He's technically not my lover,' she said. 'We're waiting until we get married.'

He laughed again. 'Holy mother of Jesus.'

She threw him a look. 'Do you mind not blaspheming?'

He pushed himself away from her car and came to stand close enough for her to smell the heat of his arrantly male flesh: sweat and hard work with a grace note of citrus that swirled around her nostrils, making them involuntarily flare. She took a prickly little breath and stepped backwards but one of her heels snagged on the crushed limestone and she would have fallen but for one of his hands snaking out and capturing her by the wrist.

Her breath completely halted as his long, tanned fingers gripped her like a steel manacle. An electric charge surged through her skin as soon as those calloused fingers made contact with her skin. She felt it sizzling all the way to the bones of her wrist; they felt like they were going to disintegrate to fine powder. She swept her tongue out over her lips as she tried to muster as much icy hauteur as she could, but even so her heart fluttered like a hummingbird behind the scaffold of her ribs as his eyes meshed with hers. 'What in God's name do you think you're doing?' she asked.

One corner of his mouth came up in a sardonic smile. 'Now look who's blaspheming.'

Bella's stomach dropped like an out-of-control elevator when his thumb pressed against her leaping pulse on the underside of her wrist. She hadn't been so close to him in years. Not since *that* kiss. Ever since that night, she had assiduously avoided any physical contact with him. But now her skin on her wrist felt like it was being scorched. It felt hot and tingly, as if electrodes had zapped the nerves. 'Get your filthy hands off me,' she said but her voice came out raspy and uneven.

His fingers tightened for an infinitesimal moment, his unusual blue-green eyes holding hers, sending a riot of sensations tumbling down the length of her spine. She could sense *him* so close to her pelvis, that essential part of him that defined him as a virile and potent male. Her body felt its primal magnetic pull just as it had all those years ago. What would it feel like to press against him now that she was no longer that gauche, inexperienced, slightly inebriated teenager?

'Say please,' he said.

She gritted her teeth. *'Please.'*

He released her and she rubbed at her wrist, shooting him a livid glare. 'You've made me all dirty, you bastard,' she said.

'It's good clean dirt,' he said. 'The kind that washes off.'

Bella looked at the cuff of her shirt below the sleeve of her jacket that now had a full set of his dusty fingerprints on it. She could still feel the pressure of his fingers as if he had indelibly branded her flesh. 'This shirt cost me five-hundred pounds,' she said. 'And now you've completely ruined it.'

'You're a fool, paying that for a shirt,' he said. 'The colour doesn't even suit you.'

She stiffened her shoulders in outrage. 'Since when did you become a personal stylist?' she jeered. 'You don't know the first thing about fashion.'

'I know what suits a woman and what doesn't.'

She scoffed. 'I bet you do,' she said. 'The less clothes the better, right?'

His eyes glinted as they did a lazy sweep of her form. 'I couldn't have put it better myself.'

Bella felt her skin tingle all over as if he had physically removed her clothes, button by button, zip by zip, piece by piece. She couldn't stop herself from imagining how his work-roughened hands would feel on the softer smooth skin of her body. Would they catch and snare like a thorn on silk? Would they scratch or would they caress? Would they...?

She pulled back from her wayward thoughts with a hard mental slap. 'I'm going inside to say hello to

Mrs Baker,' she said and swished past him to go to the front door.

'Mrs Baker is away on leave.'

Bella stopped as if she had suddenly come up against an invisible wall. She turned around to look at him with a quizzical frown. 'So who's doing the cooking and cleaning?' she asked.

'I'm taking care of it.'

Her frown deepened. 'You?'

'You have a problem with that?' he asked.

Bella blew out a little breath. She had a very *big* problem with it. Without Mrs Baker bustling about the place, she would be alone in the house with Edoardo. She hadn't planned on being alone with him. It was a very big house, but still…

In the past he had lived in the gamekeeper's cottage. But, since her father had left him Haverton Manor, he had the perfect right to live inside the house. He managed her father's investments and operated his own property-development business out of the study next to the library. Apart from the occasional business trip abroad, he lived and worked here.

He slept here.

In *her* house.

'I hope you don't expect me to take over the kitchen,' Bella said, shooting him another glare. 'I came to have a break.'

'Your whole life is one long holiday,' he said with a sneer that boiled her blood. 'You wouldn't know how to do a decent day's work if you tried.'

Bella gave her head a little toss. She wasn't going to tell him about her plans to help Julian fund his mission work with a good chunk of her inheritance. Edoardo could jolly well go on thinking she was a flaky airhead just like everybody else. 'Why would I need to work?' she asked. 'I have millions of pounds waiting for me to collect when I'm twenty-five.'

The muscle near his tightly set mouth started hammering again and his eyes turned to blue-green granite. 'Do you ever spare a thought for how hard your father had to work to make his money?' he asked. 'Or do you just spend it as fast as it's dropped in your account?'

Bella gave him another defiant look. 'It's my money to spend how I damn well like,' she said. 'You're just jealous because you came from nothing. You got lucky with my father. If it hadn't been for him, you'd be pacing a prison cell somewhere, not playing lord of the manor.'

His eyes glittered with sparks of acrimony. 'You're just like your gold-digging bitch of a mother,' he said. 'I suppose you know she was here a couple of days ago?'

Bella tried to disguise her surprise. *And hurt*. She hadn't seen or heard from her mother in months. The last time she had heard from Claudia was when she'd called to say she was moving to Spain with a new husband—her second since her divorce from Bella's father. Claudia had needed money for the honeymoon. But then, Claudia always needed money, and Bella always felt pressured into giving it. 'What did she want?' she asked.

'What do you think she wanted?' he asked, that hard gaze glittering with cynicism.

Bella gave him an arch look. 'Maybe she wanted to check you were still managing my assets properly.'

A frown suddenly pulled at his brow. 'If you want a blow-by-blow inspection of the books, then all you have to do is ask,' he said. 'I've offered to meet with you more regularly but you've always refused. The last three meetings, you didn't even have the decency to show up in person.'

Bella felt a little ashamed of herself. She had no question over his management of her father's estate. The profits had steadily grown from the moment he had taken over the share portfolio in the months before her father had died from cancer. His street-smart intelligence and clever intuition had saved her assets where other investors' had been lost during the economic turmoil of the past few years.

A couple of times a year he would insist they meet so he could go through the estate books with her. At first she had suffered those meetings, all the while sitting silently seething at how he was in control of her life. But even in that large, swanky London office he had seemed a little too close to her. The last meeting she had attended in person, her mind had wandered off into dangerous territory as she sat staring at the dark pepper of stubble around his mouth as he patiently explained the stocks and shares. She had tried to focus but within seconds she had started gazing at his hands as he had turned the pages of the meticulous report he had prepared. He had looked up at one point and locked gazes with her. She still remembered the throb of that silence. She had felt it deep inside her body.

She could still feel it.

'That won't be necessary,' Bella said. 'I'm sure you're doing all you can to keep things in order.'

There was a tight little silence.

'Are you expecting your boyfriend to join you?' he asked.

Bella tucked a strand of hair back behind her ear that the chilly breeze had worked loose. 'He's away on a mission in Bangladesh,' she said. 'I thought I'd come here until he gets back.'

'London nightlife losing its appeal?' he asked.

She gave him a brittle glare. 'I haven't been to a nightclub in ages. It's not my scene any more.'

'Prayer meetings more your thing?'

Oh, how she hated him for his mockery. 'I bet you've never got down on your knees in your life,' she tossed back.

His eyes slid to her pelvis and back with deliberate slowness. They seemed to burn with a secret erotic message as they met hers. 'Say the word, princess, and I'll be on my knees before you can say "heavens above."'

Bella's insides coiled and flexed with hot, traitorous desire. It simmered between her thighs. A flickering pulse that made her aware of every muscle and nerve and cell at the feminine heart of her.

He was the bad boy from the wrong side of the tracks.

She was the rich heiress with a pedigree that went back centuries.

She was about to become engaged.

It was forbidden.

He was forbidden.

Bella gave him a frosty look. 'I don't think there's a prayer on this earth that could save your soul,' she said.

'Why not try some laying on of hands instead?' he said with a bitter smile.

She felt that disturbing little flicker again. It made her hate him all the more. She hated that he could have this effect on her, even now. How could he make her body act so shamelessly wanton just by being near him? It annoyed her that he had so much sensual power over her. It shocked her that she couldn't control her reaction to him. It was even more shocking to know he was well aware of his impact on her. She could see it in those darkly brooding, indolent looks he gave her. The slow burn of his gaze made her skin feel like it was going to melt off her bones. 'Go to hell,' she bit out through tightly clenched teeth.

'You think I haven't already been there?' he asked.

Bella couldn't hold his gaze. It seemed to burn through her like a laser beam, touching her, stroking her, making her feel sensations she should not be feeling.

She turned on her heels and marched inside, closing the door with a satisfying clunk of metal and wood.

Edoardo let out a long hiss from between his teeth once she had gone inside the manor. He clenched and unclenched his fist a couple of times but he could still feel the tingling of where his hand had touched her wrist.

He should have frogmarched her back to her car and sent her packing. She was nothing but trouble.

And temptation.

He blew out another harsh breath. Yes, well, Bella Haverton was nothing if not tempting. She was a pint-sized little she-devil with an uppity attitude that stuck in his craw like a twig. He wanted her as much as he hated her. For years he had burned with lust for her. She was the temptation he had taught himself to resist, all except for that one night when she had pushed and pushed until he had snapped. He had kissed her roughly, angrily. The searing heat of that kiss had been building up for months and months. All those 'come and get me' looks she had been casting him, all those flirty little accidental touches as she had moved past him in the doorway had slowly but surely corroded his iron self-control. It had been like a massive explosion once their mouths met.

He still didn't know quite how he'd had the strength of will to pull back from her, but somehow he had. She had been only sixteen, young, passionate and way out of her depth. He was nine years older than her, but he was centuries older in terms of experience. He hadn't wanted to betray the trust Godfrey Haverton had placed in him. It had never been spoken in so many words, but he had always sensed Godfrey trusted him not to do the wrong thing by his young daughter.

It was different now she was older. There was no reason why he couldn't indulge in a hot little affair with her. She might fancy herself in love with some other man, but she couldn't hide the fact she still wanted him. He saw it in her eyes: the hunger, the wildfire passion she tried so desperately to hide from him.

He could *still* taste her.

All those years had passed, but he could still remember her hot, wet sweetness, the way her mouth had felt, the way it had moved against his. His body jammed with lust at the mere thought of driving into her, feeling her softness against his hardness, her arms tightly around him, her mouth on his, her tongue tangling with his in a sensual duel.

He had not touched her again until today. It had been like touching a live wire. His fingers still fizzed with the sensation. The ache to touch her again was like a pulse in his blood. It roared and screamed through his veins.

He *wanted* her.

He *lusted* after her.

There was a part of him that didn't *want* to want her. She was the one person who could make him lose control, and control was everything to him. He was not proud of the way he had grabbed her that night all those years ago. He had acted on impulse, not reason. She had that power over him.

She *still* had that power over him.

Bella always liked to play the haughty aristocrat with him. She looked down her nose at him as if he had just crawled out from a primeval swamp with his knuckles dragging along the ground. He could think of nothing better than taking her down a peg or two.

And she had played right into his hands by turning up unannounced.

He gave an inward smile. She might think she could flounce in and take charge, issuing orders as if he was nothing but a lowly servant paid to wait on her hand and foot. Had she forgotten how her father's will was written?

He was in charge now.

And he was not going to let her forget it.

CHAPTER TWO

As soon as Bella stepped inside the foyer, she felt a pang of emptiness that was like a hollow ache inside her chest. There was no hint of pipe tobacco. No sound of a walking stick tapping against the floorboards. No sound of classical music playing softly in the background.

There wasn't even the sound of Mrs Baker singing tonelessly in the kitchen. No homely sounds of pots and pans clattering. No delicious smells of home baking, just the sharp tang of fresh paint lingering in the air and a silence that was measured by the methodical ticking of the grandfather clock: Tick, tock. Tick, tock.

She wandered through the lower floor of the manor, noting the newly painted kitchen and conservatory. The formal sitting room, overlooking the garden, the lake and the rolling fields beyond, had also had a bit of a makeover. Edoardo had spent much of the past five years restoring the manor to its former glory. He did most of the work himself. It wasn't that he was short of money; he could easily have afforded to outsource to contractors but he seemed to enjoy doing hands-on work.

Bella had only been seven years old when he had come to live at Haverton Manor. It had been the year after her mother had left. Her father had taken Edoardo on as a project, presumably to distract himself from his own misery at being deserted by his young wife and left to care for a small child on his own.

Edoardo had been kicked out of every foster home in the county. At sixteen he had clocked up enough minor offences to put him in juvenile detention until he turned eighteen. Bella remembered a surly adolescent with a bad attitude. He had seemed to wear a perpetual scowl. He solved conflicts with his fists. He swore like a trooper. He didn't have manners. He didn't have friends, only enemies.

But somehow her father had seen behind the bad-boy façade to the young man with the potential to go places and achieve great things. And under Godfrey Haverton's steady and patient tutelage, Edoardo had managed to finish school and earn a place at university, where he studied commerce and business.

Edoardo had used the leg-up to good purpose. Godfrey had given him a small loan, and from that he had purchased his first property and subdivided it. He reinvested the profits in more property, which he subsequently restored and resold. His business had grown from those humble beginnings to what was now a highly successful property-investment portfolio that was constantly expanding. He also managed her father's estate, which was held in trust for Bella until she reached the age of twenty-five. With just one year to go until she could access her substantial inheritance, Edoardo was a thorn in her side she tried to avoid as much as possible.

Each month he dutifully transferred her allowance into her bank account. She had mostly kept within her budget, but now and again an extra expense would come in and she would have to suffer the indignity of contacting him to ask him to provide her with more funds. It infuriated her that her father had set things up in such a way, that he had chosen Edoardo as her trustee rather than appoint someone else—someone more impartial. Her father had trusted Edoardo more than he trusted her, and that hurt. It made the ill feelings she had always harboured against Edoardo all the more intense. To add insult to injury, her father had given him *her* ancestral home. She loved Haverton Manor. It was where she had spent the happiest days of her life before her mother had left. Now it was Edoardo's and there was not a thing she could do about it.

Bella hated him with a passion that seemed to become more and more fervent as each year passed. It simmered and boiled inside her. She could not imagine it ever abating.

He was her enemy and she couldn't wait until he was no longer in control of her life.

Bella moved through the upper floors, taking in the view from each window, reacquainting herself with the memories of the grand old house where she had spent her early childhood before she'd gone away to boarding school. Her nursery was on the top floor, along with a nanny's flat and a toy room that was as big as some children's bedrooms. The nursery hadn't been renovated as yet. She was surprised to find some of her childhood things were still there. She hadn't been back to pack them up since her father's funeral. She wondered why Edoardo hadn't packed them up and posted them off to her.

Going into that room was like stepping back in time to a period when her life had been a lot less complicated. She picked up her old teddy bear with his faded blue waistcoat. She held him to her face and breathed in the smell of childhood innocence. She had been so happy before her mother had left. Her life had seemed so perfect. But then, she had been very young and not tuned in to the undercurrents of her parents' marriage.

Looking back with the wisdom of hindsight, Bella could see her mother was a flighty and moody woman who was soon bored by country life. Claudia craved attention and excitement. Marrying a very rich man who was twenty-five years older than her had probably been enormously exciting at first, but in time she'd come to resent how her social-butterfly wings had been clipped.

And yet, while Bella could understand the frustration and loneliness her mother had felt in her sterile marriage, she still could not understand why Claudia had left *her* behind. Hadn't she loved her at all? Had her new boyfriend been more important than the child she had given birth to?

The hurt Bella felt still niggled at her. She had papered it over with various coping mechanisms but now and again it would resurface. She could still remember the devastation she had felt when her mother had driven away with her new lover. She had stood there on the front steps, not sure what was happening. Why was Mummy leaving without saying goodbye? Where was she going? When would she be back? Would she *ever* be back?

Bella sighed and looked out of the window. Her eye caught a movement in the garden below, and she put the teddy bear back on the shelf and moved across to the window.

Edoardo was walking down to the lake; Fergus was following faithfully a few paces behind. Every now and again he would stop and wait for the elderly dog to catch up. He would stoop down and give Fergus's ears or frail shoulders a little rub before moving forward again.

His care and concern for the dog didn't fit with Bella's impression of him as an aloof lone-agent who shied away from attachment. He had never shown any affection for anyone or anything before. He hadn't appeared to grieve the loss of her father, but then, she hadn't been around to notice all that much. He had been marble-faced at the funeral. He had barely uttered a word to her, or to anyone. At the reading of the will he had seemed unsurprised by the way her father had left things, which seemed to suggest he had a part in their planning.

She had flayed him with her sharp tongue that day. The air had rung with her vitriol. She had ranted and fumed and screamed at him. She had even come close to slapping him. But he had not moved a muscle on his face. He had looked down at her with that slightly condescending look of his and listened to her blistering tirade as if she'd been a spoilt, wilful child having a tantrum.

Bella moved away from the window with a frustrated sigh. She didn't know how to handle Edoardo. She had *never* known. In the past she had tried to dismiss him as one of the servants, someone she had to tolerate but not like, or even interact with unless absolutely necessary. But she had always found his presence disturbing. He did things to her just by looking at her. He made her feel things she had no right to feel. Was he doing it deliberately? Was he winding her up just to show he had the upper hand until she turned twenty-five?

He had always viewed her as the spoilt princess, the shallow socialite who spent money like it was going out of fashion. When she was younger she had tried her best to understand him. She had sensed the world he had come from was wildly different from hers from the occasional snippet of gossip from the locals, but when she had asked him about his childhood, he would cut her off with a curt command to mind her own business. What annoyed her more was that he must have spoken to her father about her probing him, as Godfrey had expressly forbidden her ever to speak to Edoardo about his childhood. He'd insisted that Edoardo deserved a chance to put his delinquent past behind him. It had driven another wedge between Bella and her father, making her feel more and more isolated and shut out.

Over the years her empathy towards Edoardo had

turned to dislike and then to hatred. During her adolescence she had brazenly taunted him with saucy come-hither looks in an effort to get some sort of rise out of him. His aloofness had made her angry. She'd been used to boys noticing her, dancing around her, telling her how beautiful she was.

He had done none of that.

It was as if he didn't see her as anything but an annoying child. But then, that night in the library when she'd been sixteen, she had overstepped the mark. With a bit of Dutch courage on board—compliments of some cherry brandy she had found—she had been determined to get him to notice her. She had perched on his desk with her skirt ruched up and with the first four buttons of her top undone, showing more than a glimpse of the cleavage that had begun to blossom a couple of summers before.

He had come in and stopped short when he'd seen her draped like a burlesque dancer on his desk. He had barked at her in his usual growly way to get out of his hair. But, instead of scampering off like a dismissed child, she had slithered off the desk, come over to him and tiptoed her fingertips over his chest. Even then he had resisted her. He had stood as still as stone, but she had felt empowered by the way his eyes had darkened and the way he had drawn in a sharp breath as her loose hair brushed against his arm. She'd pressed closer, breathing in the scent of him, allowing him to breathe in hers.

She could still remember the exact moment he'd

snapped. He'd seemed to teeter on the edge of control for long, pulsing seconds. But then he had finally grabbed her roughly—she had thought in order to push her away—and slammed his mouth down on hers. It was a kiss of hunger and frustration, of anger and lust, of forbidden longings. It had shaken her to the very core of her being. And, when he'd finally wrenched his mouth off hers and thrust her from him, she could tell it had done exactly the same to him...

Bella pushed back from her thoughts of the past. It was her future she had to think about now.

A future that could not happen without Edoardo's co-operation.

Edoardo was in the kitchen a few hours later preparing a meal. He knew the exact moment Bella entered the room even though his back was turned away from the door. It wasn't the sound of her footfall or even the fact that Fergus opened one eye and lifted one faded steel-grey ear. It was the way the back of his neck tingled, as if she had trailed her slim, elegant white fingers through his hair. His body had always felt her presence like a sophisticated radar tracking a target. He had spent years of his life suppressing his reaction to her. He had hardly even noticed her until she had reached adolescence. But then, as if a switch had been turned on in his body, he had noticed everything: her long, glossy brown hair and those big, Bambi toffee-brown eyes with their dark fringe of impossibly long lashes.

He had noticed the graceful way she moved, like a

ballerina across a dance floor or a swan gliding across the surface of a lake. He had noticed her porcelain skin, the way it was milky-white compared to his deep olive-brown. He had noticed her smell, that gorgeous mix of honeysuckle and orange blossom with a hint of vanilla. At just five-foot-five she was petite up against his six-foot-three frame. He towered over her. One of his hands could swallow both of hers whole. His body would crush hers if he took possession of her.

He *ached* to take possession of her. His body had been humming with it ever since he had grabbed her wrist outside. His fingers could still feel where they had come in contact with her skin. Her skin had felt like satin. He wondered if the rest of her body would be as silky-smooth.

How long before he caved in to the temptation? He had always been wary around her, distant to the point of rude. It wasn't just because of his sense of obligation to her father: he had a feeling she would do more than move him physically. He didn't want her to use him like she used the other men in her life. The men she dated were just playthings she picked up and put down again when her interest waned. He would allow no one—not even Bella Haverton—to use him for sport or entertainment.

'Dinner will be ready in half an hour,' he said.

'Would you like some help?' she asked.

Edoardo flicked the tea towel over his shoulder as he turned to face her. She looked young, fresh and innocent, yet worldly and defiant at the same time. It was a potent mix she had always played to her advantage. She was like a chameleon: a woman-child, a sexy siren and a doe-eyed innocent all wrapped in a knockout package.

Her clothes draped her model-slim figure like an evening glove on a slender arm. She could make a bin liner look like a million-dollar designer outfit. Her make-up was subtle and yet brought out the toffee-brown of her eyes and the lush thickness of her lashes. The lip-gloss she was wearing made her bee-stung lips all the more tempting and alluring.

She was playing her ice-maiden game now but Edoardo could see straight through it. She couldn't hide the way her body reacted to him. She was aware of him in the same way he was aware of her. There was a sexual energy in the air between them—a current, a force, that crackled every time their eyes met.

'You can pour a glass of wine for us both,' he said. 'There's a red open over there, or there's white, if you prefer, in the fridge.'

She poured a glass of red for them both and handed him one. He felt the zap of her fingers as they briefly met his around the stem of the glass. He saw the flare of reaction in her brown eyes. *'Salut,'* he said, holding her gaze as the blood thundered in his loins.

She gave her glossy lips a quick darting sweep with the tip of her tongue. *'Salut,'* she said and lifted the glass to her mouth. It always amazed him how sensual she was, seemingly without even trying. How could taking a sip of wine suddenly be so sexy? He couldn't stop staring at her mouth, how it glistened from the wine. How her lips were so plump and full, just ripe for kissing.

'So how did you meet this boyfriend of yours?' Edoardo asked as he dragged his gaze away from her mouth.

'He was serving meals to the homeless when I walked past from the tube station,' she said. 'I thought it was amazing that he was standing out there in the cold and wet, handing out food parcels and blankets. We got talking and then we exchanged numbers. The rest, as they say, is history.'

'How serious are you about him?'

'I'm very serious,' she said, setting her chin at a defiant height. 'I want to get married in June.'

He took a measured sip of his wine and then placed the glass back down on the counter. Bella married? *Not on his watch.* 'You realise you can't marry anyone without my permission?' he said.

She blinked. 'What?'

'It's clearly stated in your father's will,' he said. 'I have to approve your choice of husband if you choose to marry before the age of twenty-five.'

Her eyes widened and then narrowed. 'You're lying,' she said. 'It does *not* say that. You're in control of my money, not my love life.'

'Go check it out with the lawyer,' he said, turning back to his chicken dish on the stove.

Edoardo could feel her anger building in the silence. It made the air heavy, loaded with anticipation, like that tense period after lightning flashed, just before the thunder bellowed.

'You put my father up to this, didn't you?' she said. 'You cooked up this little scheme to get absolute and total control of me.'

Edoardo put the wooden spoon down on the spoon holder and turned back round, folding his arms across his chest and crossing one ankle over the other. 'So why do you want to marry this Julian guy?' he asked.

She put up her chin. 'I'm in love with him.'

He laughed and unfolded his arms. 'Now, that's funny.'

She sent him a gimlet glare. 'I suppose it is to someone who doesn't have an emotional bone in his body,' she said. 'You wouldn't recognise love if it came up and bit you on the face.'

Edoardo looked at her mouth again, at those lips he had fantasised about for years, remembering how soft and yielding they had been beneath the pressure of his. He had fantasised about them moving over his body, kissing and sucking on him until he exploded. A red-hot dart of lust shot him in the loins. He could just imagine her taking him to heaven with that sexy little mouth of hers. It would certainly make a change from her spitting at him like an angry little cat. 'Ah, yes, but I recognise lust when I see it,' he said. 'And you are positively simmering with it.'

She hissed in a little breath, her eyes flashing in fury. 'How dare you?'

'Oh, I dare,' he said, trailing a light fingertip down the length of her arm.

She pulled back from him as if he had scorched her. 'Don't touch me.'

'I like touching you,' he said in a low, growly tone. 'It does things to me. Wicked things. *Sinful* things.'

Her slim throat moved up and down agitatedly. 'Stop this,' she said. 'Stop this right now.'

'Stop what?' he asked. 'Stop looking at you? Stop imagining how it would feel to thrust inside you right to the hilt? To have you bucking and screaming underneath my—'

She raised her hand so quickly he almost didn't block it in time. He captured it within a hair's breadth of his cheek, his fingers clamping around her wrist with bruising force. 'I can do rough if you want, princess,' he said. 'I can do it any way you want it.'

'I do not want you,' she said, spitting the words out like bullets.

He felt her thighs bump against his. He felt the softness of her breasts where they brushed against his chest. He felt the drum beat of her pulse against his fingers. He felt his need race through his blood with an almighty primal roar.

It would be so easy to slam his mouth down on hers like he had done before. To taste her, to tempt her with the pleasure he could feel building like a dam inside him. She would go off like a firecracker. He knew they would be dynamite together. She needed someone strong enough to control her wild impulses and reckless behaviour. The men she dated danced around her like moths around a bright light.

He would have her. He knew it in his bones. He would have his fill of her, purging her from his system once and for all.

And she would enjoy every pulse-racing second of it.

Edoardo slowly released her wrist. 'Got that nasty little temper of yours under control?' he asked.

She gave him a fulminating look as she rubbed at her wrist. 'I pity the women you take to bed,' she said. 'They probably leave it bruised from head to foot.'

'They leave it panting for more,' he said with a smouldering smile.

She made a scornful sound. 'Why? Because you don't know how to properly satisfy a woman?'

His eyes mated with hers. 'Why don't you try me and see?'

She gave him a withering look. 'I'm about to become engaged, remember?'

'So you say,' he said. 'Has he asked you, or are you just clearing it with me in case he does?'

She gave him a reaction that reminded him of a bantam hen ruffling its feathers. 'The man doesn't always have to do the proposing,' she said. 'What's wrong with a woman asking a man?'

'That could work every four years, but this year isn't a leap year, so you've either got to buck the trend or wait.' Edoardo picked up her left hand. 'So where's the ring?'

She snatched her hand away. 'I'm having one designed specially.'

'Who's paying for it?'

She frowned at him. 'What sort of question is that?'

'So *you're* paying,' he said with a mocking look.

'I don't have to discuss this with you,' she said. 'It's none of your damn business.'

'Yeah, well, that's where you're wrong, Bella,' he said. 'It *is* my business to see that you don't get ripped off by some gold-digging sleazebag. That's why your father appointed me as your financial guardian. He didn't want you to be taken advantage of until you were old enough to understand how the world works.'

'I'm twenty-four years old!' she said. 'Of course I know how the world works. My father was old-fashioned. He was two generations older than my friends' fathers. You had no right to agree to this stupid scheme. You should've talked him out of it. I should've been given control when I turned twenty-one.'

'You were too young at twenty-one,' he said. 'I think you're still too young even now. You don't know what you want.'

Her hands were in tight little fists by her sides. 'I know I don't want you messing up my life,' she said. 'I love Julian. I want to be his wife. I want a family with him. You can't stop me marrying him. I'll fight you every step of the way.'

'Fight me,' he said. 'I'll look forward to it. But you won't win this, Bella. I will not allow your father's life's work to be frittered away by your impulsive choice of a partner. I'll put a hold on your allowance. I'll freeze your assets. You won't have a penny to buy a cup of coffee, much less pay for a wedding.'

'You can't do this!'

'How long have you known this man?'

Her cheeks blushed like a rose. 'Long enough to know he's my soulmate.'

He nailed her with his gaze. 'How long?'

'Three months,' she mumbled.

'What the—?'

'Don't say it.' She cut him off before he could let out his forceful expletive. 'It was love at first sight.'

'That's a load of crap,' he said. 'You haven't even slept with this guy. How do you know if you're compatible?'

'I don't expect you to understand,' she said. 'You don't even have a soul.'

Edoardo was inclined to agree with her. His childhood had bludgeoned his heart until he had hidden it away for ever. He had taught himself not to feel anything but the most basic of feelings. He hadn't loved anyone since he was five years old. He wasn't sure he *could* love any more. It was a language he had forgotten, along with most of his native tongue. He had taught himself not to need people. Needing people left you vulnerable, and the one thing he would never allow himself to be again was vulnerable.

'Let's leave me out of this,' he said. 'What I'm concerned about is you. You're doing exactly what your father was afraid you would do—you're letting your heart rule your head. It should be the other way around.'

'You can't choose who you fall in love with,' she said. 'It just...happens.'

'You're not in love with him,' he said. 'You're in love with the idea of marriage and family, of security and respectability.'

She flounced to the other side of the kitchen, taking her wine with her. 'I'm not going to talk about this any more,' she said. 'I'm marrying Julian, and you can't stop me.'

'Will he wait a whole year for you?' Edoardo asked.

She lowered her glass and sent him a furious scowl. 'You heartless, controlling bastard.'

'Sticks and stones,' he said, picking up his own wine and raising it in a toast.

She slammed her glass down so hard the stem broke and wine swirled in a red arc like a splash of blood. She yelped and jumped backwards, clutching her right hand.

'Are you all right?' he asked, stepping towards her.

'I'm fine.' She bit down on her lip.

He took her hand and unpeeled her fingers to find a little gash in the pad of her thumb. 'You silly little fool,' he said. 'You could've severed a tendon.'

'It's nothing.' She tried to pull her hand away but he didn't let go. She glared up at him. 'Do you mind?'

'You need a plaster on that,' he said. 'There's a first-aid kit in the downstairs bathroom. Come with me.'

She looked as if she was going to defy him but then she gave a frustrated sigh and allowed him to lead her to the bathroom next to the conservatory. 'I can sort it out myself,' she grumbled. 'I'm not a little child.'

'So stop acting like one.'

She flashed him a furious scowl. 'Why don't you stop acting like an overbearing ogre?'

'Sit on the bath stool,' Edoardo instructed as he pulled out the drawer where the first-aid kit was stored.

She sat and held out her hand with a recalcitrant look on her face. 'It's just a scratch.'

'It's just shy of needing a stitch,' he said as he checked the wound for traces of glass.

'Ouch!'

'Sorry,' he said.

She glowered at him. 'I bet you're not.'

'You know me so well.'

She gave him a lengthy look. 'Does anyone know you, Edoardo?' she asked.

He shifted his gaze to her thumb as he carefully placed a plaster over the wound. She had switched from spitting cat to gentle dove within a heartbeat. He had seen her work her lethal charm on others. He had seen grown men fall over like ninepins when she gave them that misty, doe-eyed look. She knew the feminine power she had and exploited it whenever she could.

But he was *not* going to let her manipulate him.

'What makes you ask that?' he asked casually.

'You don't seem to have a lot of friends,' she said. 'You don't seem to need people like other people do.'

'I have what I need in terms of companionship,' he said.

'Who is your best friend?'

He released her hand and moved to the basin to wash his hands. 'You should take care of that thumb,' he said. 'You don't want to get it infected.'

'Edoardo?'

He dried his hands on the nearest towel and then shoved it back on the rail. 'I'd better go clean up that glass before Fergus steps on it,' he said.

She bit her lip again. 'I'm sorry…'

He gave her a brief glance before he shouldered open the door. 'We all have our limits, Bella.'

CHAPTER THREE

WHEN Bella came back from the bathroom, there was no sign of the spill of red wine or any shards of glass. Fergus was still lying on his padded bed near the cooker. Edoardo was dishing up a delicious-looking chicken and tomato dish that smelt absolutely divine.

'Do you want to eat in here or the dining room?' he asked without looking up from what he was doing.

'Here's fine,' she said. 'Fergus looks like he's settled in for the night.'

'He's getting on,' he said as he set a plate in front of her. 'He's slowed down a lot just lately.'

'How old is he now?' Bella asked, screwing up her forehead as she tried to remember. 'Seven?'

'Eight,' he said. 'Your father bought him when you decided you weren't coming home for Christmas that year.'

Bella frowned when she thought of how she had behaved back then by choosing her social life over her father. It wasn't just an attempt on her part to avoid Edoardo after that kiss. Her relationship with her father had never really been the same after her mother had left. He had thrown himself into work, spending long hours in the study or going on business trips and leaving her with babysitters.

When he was at home he'd hardly seemed aware she was there. She had felt frustrated that she couldn't get close to him. She had been frightened he might leave her too and had perversely done everything she could to drive him away. She had blamed him for her mother leaving and had acted out dreadfully. She had thrown terrible tantrums. She had screamed, railed and deliberately made things difficult for him. The various nannies he had employed hadn't stayed long. In the end she had agreed to go to boarding school even though she hadn't really wanted to go. 'Was he lonely, do you think?' she asked. 'Did he miss me?'

'Of course he did,' he said, frowning slightly.

'He never said.'

'It wasn't his way,' he said.

Bella toyed with the edge of her plate. 'After my mother left...it was difficult to get close to him,' she said. 'He seemed to shut himself away. Work became his entire focus. I didn't think he cared what happened to me. I think I reminded him too much of Mum.'

'He was hurt,' he said. 'Your mother's affair totally gutted him.'

Guilt felt like a yoke around her shoulders. She had made it so much worse. Why had she been so selfish? Why couldn't she have comforted her father instead of pushing him away? She had ended up hurting him just as much as her mother. She looked at Edoardo again. 'You really cared about him, didn't you?' she asked.

'He had his faults,' he said. 'But basically he was a good man. I had a lot of respect for him.'

'I think he saw you as the son he never had,' she said. 'I was jealous about that. I never felt good enough.'

He frowned again. 'He loved you more than life itself.'

Bella gave a shrug. 'I was just a girl,' she said. 'He was of the generation where sons were everything to a man. He loved me, but I always knew that deep down he thought I was just like my mother. I suspect that's why he orchestrated things the way he did. He didn't think I had the sense to make my own decisions.'

'He was concerned you would be too trusting,' he said. 'He didn't want you to be hoodwinked by shallow charm or empty compliments.'

'So he appointed you as gatekeeper,' Bella said with more than a little hint of wryness. 'A man who never wastes time on charm or compliments.'

He took a contemplative sip of his wine. 'I can be charming when I need to be.'

She gave a little laugh. 'I'd like to see that.'

There was a little silence.

'You look stunningly beautiful tonight,' he said.

She shifted restively in her seat. 'Stop it, Edoardo.'

'I sometimes fantasise about you being in bed with me.'

She blushed to the roots of her hair. 'You're not being charming,' she said. 'You're being lewd.'

He leaned forward with his forearms resting on the table, his eyes locking on hers. 'I feel you in my arms,' he said. 'I feel your body wrap itself tightly around me. You feel it too, don't you, Bella? You feel me driving into you. You feel it right now: hard. Thick. Strong.'

She swallowed tightly. 'Why are you *doing* this?'

He leaned back in his chair and picked up his wine. 'I want you.'

She gave him a haughty glare. 'I'm not yours to have.'

His eyes challenged hers in a hot little tussle that had her spine tingling like high-voltage electricity. 'You've always been mine, Bella,' he said. 'That's why you hate me so much. You don't want to admit how much you want me. It shames you to think you lust after a bad boy with no pedigree. It's not done in your highbrow circles, is it? You're not supposed to slum it with the ill-bred. You're supposed to mingle your blood with the high flyers, but you just can't help yourself, can you? You want me.'

'I would rather boil in oil,' she said looking down her nose at him. 'You have no right to speak to me this way. I've done nothing to encourage you to think I...I fancy you.' *Or at least not since I was a silly little sixteen-year-old.* 'You have no place in my life. You never have and you never will.'

He leaned back in his chair with an indolent look. 'I'm at the centre of your life, baby girl,' he said. 'You can't do a thing without me. I could cut off your allowance right here and now if I thought it was warranted.'

Bella felt her heart slam against her ribcage. 'You can't do that.' *Please God, you can't do that.*

'You need to have another look at the fine print on your father's will,' he said. 'Why don't you check it out? I have the number of the lawyer in my phone.'

Bella looked at the mobile phone he was holding up. She swallowed once, twice. She suspected he wouldn't have said it if it wasn't true. Her father's will *was* incredibly complicated. She had read it years ago but it had been full of the sort of legalese that made it almost indecipherable. The financial-guardianship arrangement with Edoardo only made it a thousand times worse. 'What do I have to do to prove I'm old enough to make my own decisions, including choosing the man I want to marry?' she asked.

He studied her features for a moment, his gaze unnervingly steady on hers. 'I have no problem with you marrying,' he said. 'I just want to be sure you're doing it for the right reasons.'

She frowned at him. 'What other reason could there be other than I love him and want to spend the rest of my life with him?'

'People get married for lots of reasons,' he said. 'Mutual convenience, sharing familial wealth, arrangements between families—to name just a few.'

'Why is it so hard for you to accept that I'm truly in love?' she asked.

'What do you love about him?'

Bella found his direct look rather confronting. It made her feel as if he was seeing right inside her to where she kept her insecurities stashed away. She didn't want to be questioned on her love for Julian. She just loved him. He was perfect for her; he made her feel special.

He made her feel *safe*.

She shifted her gaze to the left of Edoardo's and answered, 'I love that he devotes so much of his time and energy to people less fortunate. He cares about people. All people. He can talk to anyone. It doesn't matter if they're rich or poor. He makes no distinction.'

There was a ticking silence.

'Anything else?' he asked.

She moistened her dry lips. 'I love that he loves me and he's not afraid to say it.'

'Words are cheap,' he said. 'Anyone can say them. The point is whether there's any truth in them in their actions.'

Bella gave him a direct look of her own. 'Have you ever been in love?'

His mouth cocked up at one side as if he found the notion amusing. 'No.'

'You seem very certain about that.'

'I am.'

'Not even a teensy, weensy little crush?'

'No.'

'So you just have sex for the physical release it offers?' she asked.

His eyes seemed to heat and smoulder the longer they held hers. 'It's the only reason I have sex.' He paused for a beat as his gaze continued to stoke hers. 'What about you?'

Bella felt a tremor of unruly forbidden desire roll through her like a bowling ball pitched down a steep descent. Her body shook and sizzled with it, every sensitive nerve suddenly awake and alert. She shifted in her seat, crossing her legs under the table, but if anything it concentrated the wicked sensations in the secret heart of her. It was as if he had a direct line to her womanhood by just looking at her. He was stroking her with his gaze, making love to her with his mind. She could see it in his expression—the knowing curve of his sensual lips and the slightly hooded gaze as it focused on her mouth.

She felt his kiss as surely as if he had closed the distance between them and pressed his mouth to hers. Her lips buzzed and tingled. Her tongue grew restless inside her mouth in its hunger to feel his mate with it. Her breasts felt full and sensitive behind the lace of her bra. Her knickers were damp. She could feel the moisture seeping from her and wondered if he had any idea of how much sensual power he had over her.

Of course he did.

'You haven't answered my question.'

Bella felt a blush steal across her cheeks. 'That's because it's none of your business.'

'You asked me first,' he pointed out. 'Fair's fair, and all that.'

She pressed her lips together for a moment. 'Sex is an important part of an intimate relationship,' she said.

'It's a chance to connect on both a physical and emotional level. It builds a stronger bond between two people who care about each other.'

'You sound like you just read that from a textbook,' he said, his mouth still cocked mockingly. 'How about you tell me what you *really* think?'

Bella felt her flush deepen. It seemed to spread all over her body. She felt hot. *Scorching hot.* She had never had a conversation like this with anyone, not even with one of her girlfriends.

Sex was something she'd had to work at. She had never felt all that comfortable with her body. She had spent most of the time during sex worrying if the cellulite on her thighs was showing or whether her partner was comparing her breasts to other women's.

As for her pleasure, well, that was another thing she wasn't too confident about. She had never been able to have an orgasm with a partner. She just wasn't able to relax or feel comfortable enough to let herself go.

That was why Julian had been such a refreshing change from her previous dates. He had never pressured her for sex. He had told her he was celibate and intended to stay that way until he was married. He had made a promise to God, and he was going to keep it. She had found that so endearing, so admirable, she had decided he would be the perfect husband for her.

'I think sex means different things to different people,' she finally said. 'What's right for one person might not be right for another. It's all a matter of feeling comfortable enough to express yourself in a...sexual way.'

'How do you know if you'll be comfortable with this Julian fellow?' he asked.

Bella picked up her wine glass for something to do with her hands. 'Because I know he'll always treat me with the utmost respect,' she said. 'He believes sex is God's gift to be treasured, not something to be dishonoured by selfish demands.'

He gave a little snort. 'You mean he'll pray before he peels back the sheets on your wedding night.'

She gave him a withering look. 'You are *such* a heathen.'

'And you are a silly little fool,' he threw back. 'You haven't got a clue what you're getting yourself into. What if he's hiding who he really is? What if this celibacy thing is just a ruse to get his hands on your money?'

'Oh, for pity's sake.'

'I mean it, Bella,' he said, his blue-green gaze suddenly intense and serious. 'You are one of the richest young women in Britain. It's no wonder men are beating a steady path to your door.'

Bella froze him with her stare. 'I don't suppose it has ever occurred to you that it might be because of my dazzling beauty and vivacious personality?'

He opened his mouth as if he was about to say something but then closed it. He let out a long breath and pushed back a thick lock of his hair that had fallen forward on his forehead. 'Your beauty and personality are without question,' he said. 'I just think you need to be a little more objective about this.'

She sat back in her chair with a thump. 'Thus speaks the man who measures everything by checks and balances,' she said, rolling her eyes. 'Don't you do things sometimes just because it *feels* right?'

His eyes remained steady on hers. 'Gut feeling doesn't cut it with me,' he said. 'It's too easy to allow your emotional investment in something or someone to cloud your judgement. The heavier the investment, the harder it is to see things and people for what or who they are.'

'How did you get so cynical?' Bella asked.

His eyes moved away from hers as he reached to top up their wine glasses. The sound of the wine making a *glock-glock-glock* noise as it poured out of the bottle was deafening in the silence. 'Born that way,' he said.

'I don't believe that.'

He met her gaze, his mocking half-smile back in place. 'Still trying to save my sorry soul, Bella?' he asked. 'I thought you gave up on that little mission years ago.'

'Have you told *anyone* about your childhood? About where you came from?' she asked.

A mask slipped over his features like a dust sheet over a piece of furniture. 'There's nothing to tell.'

'You must have had parents,' she said. 'A mother, at least. Who was she?'

'Leave it, Bella.'

'You must remember something about your childhood,' Bella pressed on. 'You can't have blocked everything out. You weren't born a teenager with authority issues. You were once a baby, a toddler, a young child.'

He let out a short, impatient-sounding breath and reached for his glass. 'I don't remember much of my childhood at all,' he said and drank a deep mouthful of his wine.

Bella watched his Adam's apple go up and down. Even though his expression was masked, there was anger in the action as he swallowed the liquid—anger and something else she couldn't quite put her finger on. 'Tell me what you do remember,' she said.

The silence was long and brooding, the air so thick it felt like the ceiling had slowly lowered, compressing all the oxygen.

Bella continued to search his features. The stony mask had slipped just a fraction. She could see the flicker of a blood vessel in his temple. The grooves beside his mouth deepened as if he was holding back a lifetime of suppressed emotion. His nostrils flared as he took a breath. His eyes hardened to granite. His fingers around his glass tightened until she could see the whitening of his knuckles.

'Why did you get kicked out of all those foster homes?' she asked.

His eyes collided with hers. They were dark with a glitter that made the backs of her knees go fizzy again. 'Why do you think I was kicked out?' he asked with a tilt of his lips that looked more like a snarl than a smile. 'I was a rebel. A lost cause. Bad to the core. Beyond salvation.'

Bella swallowed a thick knot in her throat. He was so intimidating when he was in this mood but she was determined to find out more about him. His enigmatic nature intrigued her. She had always found his aloof, keep-away-from-me manner compellingly attractive. 'What happened to your parents?' she asked.

'They died.' He said the words as if they meant nothing to him. He showed no emotion at all. Not even a flicker. His face was like a marble statue, a blank, impenetrable mask.

'So you were an orphan?' Bella prompted.

'Yeah, that's me.' He gave a little laugh as he swirled the contents of his glass. 'An orphan.'

'Since when?' she asked. 'I mean, how old were you when your parents died?'

It seemed like a full year before he spoke; Bella waited out each pulsing second of the long, protracted silence. It was a silent battle of wills, but somehow she suspected the battle was not between her and him. It was between two parts of himself: the aloof loner who didn't need anyone and the man behind the mask who secretly did.

'I don't remember my father,' he said with the same blank, indifferent expression.

'He died when you were a baby?' she guessed.

'Yes.' There was still no emotion. No grief or sense of loss.

Bella moistened her lips, waiting a beat or two before asking, 'What happened?'

At first she didn't think he was going to answer. The silence stretched and stretched interminably.

'Motorbike accident,' he finally said. 'He wasn't wearing a helmet. Can't have been pretty.'

Bella winced. 'What about your mother?'

A tiny, almost imperceptible spasm tugged at the lower quadrant of his jaw. 'I was five,' he said and twirled his wine again, his eyes staring down at the liquid as it splashed against the sides of the glass.

'What happened to her?'

'She died.'

'How?'

There was another silence before he spoke. A bruised silence. 'Suicide.'

She gasped. 'Oh, my God, that's terrible.'

He gave a careless shrug. 'It wasn't much of a life for her once my father died.' He tipped back his head and drained his glass, setting it down on the table with a little thump.

Bella frowned as she thought of him as a young motherless boy. She had been totally devastated when her mother had driven away that day, but at least she had known her mother was still alive. How had Edoardo coped with losing his mother so young? 'Your father was Italian, wasn't he?'

'Yep.'

'And your mother?'

'English,' he said. 'She met my father while on a working holiday in Italy.'

'Who looked after you after she died?'

He put his napkin next to his plate and pushed back from the table, his expression closing like a door that had been clicked shut on a sliver of a view. 'Fergus needs to go outside,' he said. 'He's too stiff to use the pet door now.'

Bella sat back with a frown pulling at her forehead as she watched him stride from the room. He had told her things she was almost certain he hadn't even told her father. Her father had said Edoardo had always refused to speak of his early childhood and he wasn't to be pressured to reveal things he didn't want to reveal. She, like her father, had assumed it had been because Edoardo was ashamed of his background, given that it was so different from theirs. His youth had been misspent on rebellious behaviour that had alienated him from the very people who had wanted to help him. He had used the very words the authorities would have used to describe him: a rebel, a lost cause, bad to the core, beyond salvation. Was he really all or any of those things? What had happened to make him so distrustful of people? What had made him the closed-off enigma he was today?

And why on earth did it matter to her to find out? It wasn't as if it was any of her business.

He was her enemy.

He hated her as much as she hated him.

She chewed at her lower lip as she looked at his empty chair. It shouldn't matter to her what had happened to him. He had been surly and uncommunicative for as long as she had known him. He had clearly inveigled his way into her father's trust and taken control of her life. He had done nothing but taunt and ridicule her from the moment she had turned up at what used to be *her* house. He was threatening to ruin *her* wedding plans. He was the spanner in the works, the fly in the ointment, the brick wall she had to climb over or knock down.

It shouldn't matter... But somehow—rather surprisingly—it did.

CHAPTER FOUR

EDOARDO waited for Fergus to sniff every tree and shrub in the garden as the moon watched on with its wise and silent silver eye. The air was cold and fresh; the smell of the damp earth was like breathing in a restorative potion.

It cleared his head.

It *grounded* him.

It reminded him of how far he had moved from his previous life—a life where he'd had no control. No hope. Only pain and miserable, relentless suffering.

Haverton Manor was his sanctuary, the only place he had ever called home. The only place he had ever wanted to call home.

He clenched his fists and then slowly released them. The past was in the past and he should not have let Bella get under his skin enough to pick at the hard crust that covered what was left of his soul. Inside him were wounds he would allow *no one* to see. The scars he wore on the outside of his body were nothing to the ones on the inside. He could not bear pity. He could not stomach people's interest in what he wanted to forget. He didn't want to be painted as a victim. He had no time for people who saw themselves as victims.

He was a survivor.

He would not allow his past to cast a shadow over his future. He had proved all his critics wrong. He had made something of himself. He had used every opportunity Godfrey Haverton had offered him to better himself. He was educated. He was wealthy. He had everything he had ever dreamed of when he had been that cowering child shrinking away from the drunken blows of a cruel and sadistic stepfather. He had pictured his future in his head as a way to block out what was happening to him: he had pictured the luxury cars, the lush, rolling fields of a country estate, the opulent mansion, the beautiful women and the designer clothes.

He had made it come true.

Haverton estate was his: every field and pasture, every hill and hillock, the lake, the woods and most importantly the manor—his very own regal residence, the ultimate symbol of having left his past well and truly behind.

No one would be able to take it off him. No one could toss him out on the street in the cold and wet. No one could deny him a roof over his head.

When he was a child he had dreamed of owning a place such as this. His very own fortress, his castle and his base. *His home.*

Godfrey had known how important the manor was to him: it was the first place he had felt safe. The first place he had put down roots. The first place he had discovered friendship and loyalty. Within these walls he had learned all he needed to learn in order to make something of his life. Before he had come here he had been close to giving up. He had gone beyond the point of caring what happened to him. But Godfrey had woken something in him with his quiet, patient way. He hadn't pressured him to open up. He hadn't bribed him or coerced him in any way. He had simply planted the seeds of hope in Edoardo's mind, seeds that had grown and grown until Edoardo had started to see the possibility of changing his life, becoming something other than a victim of circumstance and cruelty.

He was no longer that pitiful child with a constant fear of abandonment, with no one to turn to, with no one to love or be loved. He was no longer that brooding, resentful teenager with a chip on his shoulder.

He depended on *no one* for his happiness.

He had no need of anyone but himself. He was totally autonomous. He didn't want the ties and responsibilities that other people saw as a natural part of life. Marriage and children were not something he had ever pictured for himself. Life was too fickle for him to chance it. What if the same thing happened to him as had happened to his father—his life cut short in its prime and his wife and child left to fend for themselves as best they could, easy prey for the scurrilous, conscienceless predators out there who would do anything to get their hands on money for drugs and drink?

No. He was fine on his own; perfectly fine.

* * *

Bella was in the kitchen stacking the dishes into the dishwasher when Edoardo came back in. It was a domestic scene he wasn't used to seeing. She had never been one to lift a finger about the place. She had grown up with a band of willing servants to cater to her every whim. He had always thought her father had been far too lenient with her. She had never had to work for anything in her life. It had all been handed to her on a silver plate with the Haverton coat of arms emblazoned on it. She had flounced around issuing orders as if she was already lady of the manor, even as a small child. Not even as an adult had she ever considered the sacrifices Godfrey Haverton had made to provide a secure future for her. She hadn't even had the decency to be by his side as he drew his last, gasping breath.

He had been the one to watch Godfrey pass from life to death.

He had held his frail hand and listened to the sounds of the breath slowly leaving the old man's rail-thin body.

He had been the one to close Godfrey's eyes in final rest.

He had been the one to weep with grief at losing the one person on this earth who had truly believed in him. He had sworn on Godfrey's death bed that he would do the right thing by him and protect Bella. He would make sure she stayed out of trouble until the guardianship period was over. He would not let her waste her father's hard-earned money. And in the meantime he would continue to restore Haverton Manor into the grand old residence Godfrey had loved so much, thus keeping a part of his mentor and friend alive.

Bella closed the dishwasher and straightened, her tongue darting out to moisten her lips. 'I was going to make some coffee,' she said. 'Would you like some?'

Edoardo couldn't help a little lip curl. 'You mean you actually know how to boil water?'

She pursed her mouth and tossed the dishcloth she had been holding on the sink. 'I'm trying to be nice to you, Edoardo,' she said. 'The least you could do is meet me halfway.'

'Nice?' He gave a rough sound of derision. 'Is that what you call it? You're sucking up to me to get what you want.'

'I'm not,' she said. 'I've been thinking about what you told me about your parents—about being orphaned so young. I didn't understand how devastating it must have—'

'Cut it, princess,' he said savagely.

Her smooth forehead crinkled in a frown. 'But surely talking about it would be helpful?'

'There's nothing to talk about,' he said. He reached for the coffee grounds in the pantry and slammed them down on the counter. He filled the percolator with water, spooned in the coffee and switched it on, his hands clenching the counter until the tendons on the back stood out starkly against his tan. Was she never going to give this up? What was it about women that they had to *know* everything? To *talk* about everything? He wanted to block it out, not dredge it up all the time.

He wanted it to go away.

He *needed* it to go away.

The percolator hissed and spat in the silence.

Edoardo heard her move across the floor. She had such a light, almost silent tread but the hairs on the back of his neck lifted all the same. He felt her just behind him. He could smell her perfume. It danced around his nostrils. If she touched him, his control would snap. He could already feel it straining on its tight leash. It felt like a wild beast being held back by a thin, rusty chain. One of these days one of those fragile, corroded links would break.

He heard her draw in a small breath and then she spoke his name, softly and hesitantly. It was like a caress on his skin. It made every pore react as if a soft feather had brushed over him. 'Edoardo?'

He waited a beat before he turned around and looked down at her. Her beautiful heart-shaped face was uptilted and her big brown eyes were soft and dewy, her rosy lips full and moist. 'I know what you're doing,' he said with a cynical look. 'You always lay on the charm when you want something. I've seen you do it to your father hundreds of times. But you're wasting your time. It won't work with me.'

Her expression soured. 'Why must you be so...so *beastly*?' she asked.

'I won't be manipulated by you or anyone,' he said. 'I made a promise to your father and I'm going to keep it.'

'I want to get married here,' she said, throwing him

a combative look. 'I've dreamed of it all of my life. My father would have wanted it. You can't say he wouldn't.'

Edoardo thought of the highbrow, vacuous crowd she would have swarming around her like bees around a honey pot. The press would besiege the place. They would crawl over his private domain like ants at a picnic. His private sanctuary would become party central. And, if that weren't enough, he would have to watch Bella smiling up at some toffee-nosed man who—he could almost guarantee—only wanted her for her money. 'No,' he said. 'He wouldn't have wanted it, otherwise he would've left you the manor in the first place.'

She narrowed her eyes to hairpin-thin slits. 'You're doing this deliberately, aren't you?' she said. 'All that talk of wanting me was rubbish. You don't want me at all. You want the power. It turns you on, doesn't it? You get off on it. You just want the rush it gives you to have me squirming in the palm of your uncivilised hand.'

Edoardo captured one of her wrists and held her fast. The urge to touch her had been unstoppable. He had barely even realised he had reached for her when he heard the gasp of her breath. He saw the sudden flare of her pupils. He felt the rapid jump of her pulse. He brought her closer, inch by inch, watching as her brown eyes went wider and wider. 'Maybe I should show you just how uncivilised I can be,' he drawled silkily.

Her pulse went wild beneath his fingers as he tugged her against his swollen groin. She swallowed and then licked her lips, her gaze tracking to his mouth as it came inexorably closer. He felt the soft gust of her breath against his lips. 'If you kiss me I will scratch your eyes out,' she said in a breathless little voice that was at odds with her warning.

'Before or after I kiss you?'

Her eyes blazed with hatred. 'During.'

He held her gaze for a throbbing heartbeat. 'I'd better not risk it, then,' he said, stepped back from her and reached for his keys on the hook near the door.

She blinked a couple of times as if she had been expecting him to call her bluff. 'Where are you going?' she asked.

He tossed the keys in the air before deftly catching them. 'Out.'

'Out where?' she asked with another frown. 'It's close to midnight.'

'Can you let Fergus out before you go to bed?' he asked. 'I might not get back before dawn.'

She gave him an irritated look. 'Is that how you stay under the press's radar?' she asked. 'By keeping your liaisons the other side of midnight?'

'Works for me,' he said, shouldering open the kitchen door.

She threw him a caustic glare. 'You disgust me.'

'Right back at you, princess,' he said and let the door swing shut behind him.

Bella was too annoyed to sleep. She tossed and turned and counted sheep and sheep dogs. She got up and had a glass of water. She checked on Fergus three times. She couldn't stop her mind from conjuring up images of Edoardo with one of his anonymous women. It disgusted her that he could just go out like that and find someone to slake his lust with. She could just imagine the type of woman he would go for: someone brash and bold, someone who would be confident sexually. His lovers wouldn't agonise over their breasts or thighs, they wouldn't worry about bikini waxes and whether they weren't responsive enough in his arms. He would *make* them respond just by looking at them, just like he did to her.

'Grrrhhh,' Bella said as she threw off the covers yet again.

She was out in the garden waiting for Fergus to come back in when she saw the twin beams of Edoardo's car headlights move across the fields of the estate as he came up the long driveway. 'Fergus?' she called out softly. 'Come on. Hurry up. I'm freezing to death out here.'

There was still no sign of the dog when Edoardo's car purred its way back to the garage. Bella listened as his footsteps crunched over the gravel of the driveway. She slunk against the shadows of the manor, holding the edges of her dressing gown tighter around her body. She didn't want him to think she had been losing sleep over his nocturnal activities. She didn't want him to think she had been waiting up for him to return, even though—subconsciously, at least—she had.

It was unnaturally, eerily quiet.

The night sounds that had seemed as loud as an orchestra rehearsing just moments ago had stilled as if silenced by a conductor's baton.

Bella edged her way along the manor with her back against the icy-cold, hard stone. Her skin was pebbled with goose bumps and her heart hammered like a piston. She inched her way closer to the window of the morning room. She took a breath and started to climb the trellis, where the gnarled and twisted skeleton of some clematis was situated, when a pair of strong arms suddenly tackled her from behind. 'Oomph!' she gasped as she fell backwards against a strong male body.

'Bella?' Edoardo swung her around and gaped at her in shock. 'What in God's name are you doing?'

She put up her hand in a little fingertip wave and gave him a sheepish smile. 'Hi...'

His expression went from shock to furious. 'What the hell are you playing at?' he asked. 'I could have hurt you. I thought you were a burglar.'

Bella straightened her dressing gown, which had slipped off one shoulder in the tussle. Her body was still tingling from where it had pressed against his. Her heart was still jumping and her pulse as crazy as an over-wound clock. 'Do you normally wrestle burglars to the ground?' she asked with a wry look.

He scraped a hand through his hair. 'Not usually.' He let his hand drop back by his side. 'Are you all right?'

'I will be when I get my heart to get back where it belongs,' she said with an attempt at humour. 'You scared the living daylights out of me. I didn't hear you make a sound. I thought you'd gone the other way around the house.'

'What on earth were you doing?' he asked, still frowning darkly.

'I was taking Fergus out for a comfort stop.'

'Then why hide in the shadows like an intruder?' he asked.

She gave a little shrug, suddenly feeling foolish and gauche. 'I didn't want you to see me...'

'Why not?'

She waved a hand over her night attire. 'I'm not... um, dressed.'

'I've seen you in a lot less,' he said.

Bella was glad of the muted moonlight because her face felt suddenly hot. 'So, how was your date?' she asked.

A shutter came down over his face. 'Where's Fergus?' he asked.

'Good question,' she said as she made her way back to the kitchen door. 'I was trying to find him when you came home. He's not very obedient, is he?'

'He's deaf and practically blind,' he said. 'You shouldn't have left him on his own. He gets disoriented at night.'

'You were the one who left him while you went off sowing your wild oats,' she tossed back. '*You* find him. I'm going back to bed.'

It was mid-morning when Bella came downstairs the next day. She supposed Edoardo had been up since dawn, or maybe he hadn't been to bed at all—or at least not his own bed, she thought with a niggle of pique.

She was halfway through a cup of tea and a muffin when she heard a car come up the driveway. She went outside and watched as a slim, elegant woman of about thirty got out from behind the wheel.

'Hello,' the woman said with a friendly smile. 'You must be Bella. I'm Rebecca Gladstone. I moved into the area a few months ago.'

'Um…hi,' Bella said.

'Is Edoardo about?' Rebecca asked. 'I was passing and thought I should check on Fergus.'

'Fergus?'

Rebecca smiled. 'I'm the new vet.'

'Oh…' Bella pasted a stiff smile on her face. Was *this* Edoardo's latest lover? Beautiful, classy, educated, good with animals and probably children as well. She felt a tight pinching feeling close to her heart. Somehow she hadn't been expecting him to go for someone so…so likeable. Did this mean he would get married and fill Haverton Manor with a brood of kids and pets? He had stolen her house and now he had stolen her dream as well. It should be *her* children and *her* pets filling up the place, not his. 'Come this way,' she said. 'Fergus is asleep in the kitchen.'

Bella watched as Rebecca greeted the dog. Fergus, the old fool, practically gushed. His tail wagged like a metronome on steroids and he even gave a puppy-like wriggle of his hindquarters. Pathetic. Absolutely pathetic. 'He seems to really know you well,' Bella said.

'Yes, we're old friends, aren't we, Fergus?' Rebecca said, ruffling his ears.

Bella wanted to hate her but she couldn't quite do it. She decided to hate Edoardo a little bit more for choosing someone so damn perfect. Why couldn't he have a shallow, self-serving mistress she could really have a good bitch about?

After a minute or two, Rebecca stood up from examining the elderly dog. 'I'll leave some vitamins in case he's not eating properly,' she said, taking out a little bottle and placing it on the table. 'Irish wolfhounds don't live much longer than eight or so years. He's doing well for his age, but it's best to be on the safe side.'

Bella tried on another smile. 'Thanks.'

'So, how long are you staying for?' Rebecca asked.

'Just a few days,' Bella said. 'I haven't been home much just lately... Actually, not since my father's funeral.' *Not since he gave away my home to my worst enemy,* she added silently.

'I'm sure Edoardo will be glad of the company,' Rebecca said as she clipped shut her bag. 'He works far too hard, but I guess I don't have to tell you that.'

'I'm not sure Edoardo enjoys my company too much,' Bella said, pursing her mouth.

Rebecca looked at her quizzically. 'Oh? Why do you say that?'

Bella wished she hadn't been so transparent but it was a bit late to retract what she'd said. *In with a penny, in with a pound,* she thought. Anyway, why should she sugar-coat her relationship with Edoardo? He had probably derided her to Rebecca every chance he could. 'He thinks I'm a spoilt brat who hasn't grown up,' she said.

Rebecca studied her for a moment. 'You've known him a long time, then?'

'Since I was seven years old.'

'So you're like brother and sister?'

'Um...not quite,' Bella said, blushing in spite of every effort not to. She paused for a beat. 'We're not exactly bosom buddies.'

'He's your financial guardian, isn't he?' Rebecca said.

Bella felt like a fool. Who on earth had financial guardians these days? Kids under eighteen or elderly people with dementia, that was who. 'Yes,' she said. 'I expect Edoardo has told you all about it.'

Rebecca gave her a reassuring smile. 'It's all right,' she said. 'I didn't hear it from him. He never talks about you. I heard it from Mrs Baker. She told me your father set things up in a rather complicated fashion.'

'Very complicated,' Bella said, blowing out a breath. 'I can't do anything without Edoardo's approval. It's incredibly annoying.'

'I'm sure he would never stop you doing anything you really wanted to do,' Rebecca said. 'Anyway, it won't be long, and you'll be free to do what you like. I seem to remember Mrs Baker saying it's only until you turn twenty-five.'

'Or until I marry.'

'Are you planning on doing that any time soon?' Rebecca asked, glancing at Bella's left hand.

'It's not official as yet,' Bella said. 'I'm just waiting until he gets back from a trip abroad before we announce anything.'

'Congratulations,' Rebecca said. 'You must be so excited.'

'I am,' Bella said. *Or I would be, if it weren't for Edoardo standing in the way of my plans.*

There was the sound of firm footsteps, and Bella watched as Rebecca Gladstone's cheeks took on a pink hue as Edoardo strode in. He glanced at the dog in the basket before meeting Rebecca's gaze. 'What's going on?' he asked.

'I was in the area and thought I'd drop by,' Rebecca said. 'I've left some vitamins for Fergus. They'll boost his immune system.'

'Thank you,' Edoardo said. 'How much do I owe you?'

'Isn't it me who owes you?' Bella said with a pointed look. 'He was my father's dog, after all.'

'You don't owe me a thing, either of you,' Rebecca said. 'That's just a sample pack in any case.' She smiled up at Edoardo. 'Want to walk me to my car?'

His expression was as blank as a sheet of paper. 'Sure.'

'It was lovely to meet you, Bella,' Rebecca said. 'I hope you enjoy your stay.'

'I will,' Bella said with a smile that cracked her face.

'She's in love with you,' Bella said as soon as Edoardo came inside a few minutes later.

He reached for a glass and filled it with water from the tap. 'And you can tell that how, exactly?' he asked.

'She blushed as soon as you came into the room,' she said.

He turned from the sink to look at her. 'Just because a woman blushes doesn't mean she's in love,' he said. 'Take you, for instance.' He let his eyes run over her slowly but thoroughly. 'I could make you blush within seconds. Does it mean you're in love with me?'

Bella jerked her chin back against her neck in disdain, her cheeks feeling like they had been too close to a fire. 'I would never fall in love with someone like you.'

'That's very reassuring,' he said with a mocking slant of his mouth.

'Rebecca seems a very nice person,' she said. 'The least you could've done is said a proper hello to her.'

'I don't like impromptu visitors,' he said. 'If she wanted to see me, all she had to do was call me and arrange a time.'

'Maybe she doesn't like being called in the middle of the night to suit your needs.'

He gave a loose shrug. 'She's not my type.'

'No, because she's got a brain between her ears,' she shot back. 'I can only imagine what your type is like: big boobs, toothpaste-commercial smile, long legs and no conversation. Am I close?'

A half-smile kicked up the edges of his mouth. 'Close enough,' he said.

'Have you dated her?' she asked.

'We had a drink a few weeks back,' he said.

'Have you slept with her?'

'No.'

'Why not?' she asked.

He put the glass down on the counter. 'What's with all the questions?' he asked. 'Are you jealous?'

'Of course I'm not jealous!' Bella retorted. 'I just think you could really hurt her if you don't do the right thing by her.'

'It's not my problem.'

'It *is* your problem,' she said. 'You should nip it in the bud before she gets too involved. You shouldn't encourage her to just drop by if you're not serious about her.'

'I didn't encourage her to drop by,' he said. 'I've given her no encouragement, full-stop.'

Bella folded her arms across her chest. 'She obviously thinks you have,' she said.

'Then she's mistaken.'

'Is she who you went to last night?' she asked.

'No.'

'Who *did* you see?'

He leaned back against the counter in an indolent fashion. 'Are you sure you're not jealous?' he asked.

She rolled her eyes. 'How could I be?' she asked. 'I'm about to get engaged.'

'It's not official.'

'It will be soon.'

'There's been nothing in the press about your relationship with your preacher boy,' he said. 'Not even a whisper.'

'That's because Julian doesn't attract press attention,'

she said. 'Anyway, I want to wait until he gets back from Bangladesh before we tell anyone anything. I'm going to meet his family and then we're going to make a formal announcement.'

'You're assuming, of course, that I'll agree to this match.'

Bella unfolded her arms and clenched her fists. 'You can't prevent me from marrying the man I love.'

His blue-green eyes challenged hers. 'If you love him so much then why aren't you over there with him?' he asked.

Bella floundered for a moment. 'I...I have things to see to here,' she said. 'I'd be in the way over there. I need to learn the ropes a bit before I go with him on a mission.'

He made a sound of scorn in his throat. 'I just can't see you handing out trinkets to the natives.'

'That's not what missionaries do these days,' she said. 'They help to build schools and hospitals.'

'And what will you do when you do accompany him?' he asked.

'I'll support him in any way I can,' she said.

'It's what every man of the cloth needs,' he said with a curl of his lip. 'A rich wife to bankroll every do-good project.'

Bella glowered at him. 'You think I haven't got a clue, don't you? You think I'm too stupid to do anything but get my nails done.'

'You're not stupid,' he said. 'You're naïve. You've lived a sheltered life. You don't know how the other half lives. You don't know how desperate and ruthless people can be.'

'Like you, you mean?' she said with an arch look.

His eyes glinted as they locked down on hers. 'I can be very ruthless when I go after something I want.'

Bella felt the skin of her arms lift in a tiny shiver. 'You can't always have everything you want,' she said.

The corner of his mouth lifted in a devilish smile. 'Who's going to stop me?' he asked.

She quickly moistened her parchment-dry lips, her heart doing double time inside her ribcage. 'I'm not going to sleep with you, Edoardo.'

He picked up a lock of her hair and coiled it around his finger. She felt the gentle pull on her scalp; it made her backbone tingle and fizz like an effervescent liquid was being poured down its length. 'I'm not planning on us doing too much sleeping once I have you in my bed,' he said.

Bella's insides flickered and flashed with red-hot lust. She felt shocked at her involuntary response to his incendiary words. After years of keeping her distance, her body now seemed to have a mind of its own. It totally disregarded her common sense. Her body was drawn to him, lured into his sensual orbit like a satellite.

'Read my lips, Edoardo,' she said stiffly. 'I am *not* going to end up in bed with you, asleep or not.'

He slowly unwound her hair, his eyes meshed with hers in a sensual lock that felt like an intimate caress at the secret heart of her femininity. 'Want to put money on that, princess?'

Bella gave her head a toss as she stepped away from him. 'I don't need to,' she said. 'I already know who's going to win.'

'So do I,' he said and, before she could get in the last word, he left.

CHAPTER FIVE

BELLA kept out of Edoardo's way for the next couple of days. She caught up with some old friends in the village and ate out rather than spend time alone with him at the manor.

But as the week drew to a close, she felt increasingly bored and restless. She hadn't heard from Julian, as he had gone to a new mission in the mountains where the telephone signal was poor. With each day that passed without a message from him, she felt more insecure. She needed his reassurance and encouragement. She needed his enthusiasm and positive attitude to life.

A niggling doubt had started playing at the corners of her mind about how she would fit into his life of self-sacrifice. She admired his commitment and faith enormously, but she sometimes wondered if he could be passionate about anything other than trying to save the world. She knew it was selfish of her to want to be the central focus of his attention, but she couldn't help wondering if he truly loved her the way she wanted to be loved.

Her mother's desertion when she was so young had

made her insecure about intimate relationships. She loved too deeply and too quickly, only to be disappointed when the other party pulled away from her. Was Julian's trip abroad his way of distancing himself? She knew he loved her, but it wasn't a passionate all-or-nothing love.

It was a *safe* love.

A love she could count on to get her through the bad times as well as the good. A love that would be the solid foundation of a well-ordered family life.

It was what she wanted. What she *needed*. She didn't want to be like her mother, flitting off to somewhere exotic on yet another passionate fling that would only end in tears and heartbreak.

She didn't want the hair-raising, nail-biting, gut-twisting rollercoaster ride of passion. She wanted the smooth, predictable ride of a merry-go-round.

Bella was in the kitchen poking about in the fridge when Edoardo came in from outside.

'Eating in tonight?' he asked as he hung up his jacket on the hook behind the door.

She closed the fridge guiltily. 'I can get something later,' she said.

'I can rustle up something for both of us,' he said. 'You don't have to hide away in your room.'

'I'm not hiding away in my room,' she said. 'I've been busy catching up with friends.'

He grunted and moved across to wash his hands at the sink. 'Give me half an hour,' he said. 'I have to sort something out on my computer.'

'Who taught you to cook?' she asked.

He dried his hands on some paper towels and dropped them in the pedal bin. 'No one in particular,' he said. 'I didn't stay anywhere long enough to pick up more than the basics.'

'What was the longest you stayed with a foster family?'

Edoardo felt the familiar tension crawl over his skin like a cockroach. He hated thinking about his past, let alone talking about it. He wanted to forget it had ever happened. He wanted it erased from his brain. He mostly *had* erased it from his mind. Every time Bella pushed him for more information, it made his head ache with the suppressed memories. They felt like they were busting out of the shackles he had bound them with all those years ago. 'Can you quit it with the twenty questions?' he said. 'I'm not in the mood for it.'

'You're never in the mood,' she said. 'You're like a closed book. Lots of people come from difficult backgrounds. I don't see why you have to be so secretive about it.'

He stepped into her body space, watching as her big brown eyes rounded. 'You're playing with fire,' he warned. 'But I think you already know that, don't you?'

A silence throbbed between them.

'I've known you since I was a child, but I hardly know you at all,' she said in a husky tone.

He placed his hands on her shoulders and watched as the tip of her tongue snaked out to sweep over her lips. He had never seen a more kissable mouth. Desire twisted and tightened in his groin. He felt his body surge and swell. He wanted her so badly it was like a drug his system craved. The trouble was, he knew one taste would never be enough. He wasn't sure how long with her would be enough. For years he had thought of this moment, when she would come to him with that look of wanting in her eyes. He saw it: the need, the lust and the longing. It pulsed in the air in a hot, swirling current that was almost palpable.

Her eyes flickered to his mouth and back again to his. 'I want to know who you are,' she said. 'Who you *really* are.'

'This is who I really am,' he said.

'I want to know why you're so closed off emotionally,' she said. 'You push everyone away. Why do you do that?'

Edoardo gripped her shoulders a little tighter. 'I'm not pushing you away right now, am I? In fact, I'm about to bring you a whole lot closer.'

He felt her body brush against his. It engulfed his in a wave of hot longing that was like wildfire as he pulled her against him, male against female, need against need. His mouth came down slowly, giving her plenty of time to get away if she wanted to—but she didn't move. Instead, she parted her lips as his came down. He brushed the point of his tongue against hers, a teasing taste of the eroticism to come. He felt her whole body respond. She pressed close and whimpered in the back of her throat as his tongue teased her again, in and out, barely touching, just hinting at the sensual delight in store.

Her tongue flickered against his, flirting, daring, increasingly provocative. Her hands snaked up around his neck, her fingers weaving through his hair, her pelvis jammed against his. His erection became painful as it moved against her urgently. She rubbed against him wantonly, her body pliant and soft against his.

Edoardo devoured her mouth like a starving man does a succulent meal. He fed off her hot, sweet moistness, tasting the nectar of her; relishing in the answering dart and dance of her tongue as it met and mated with his.

She was everything and more than he had dreamed of: sweet yet sultry, shy yet demanding. He couldn't get enough of her softness. She yielded to his pressure, softly whimpering in delight as he drove deeper and deeper, demanding more and more of her with each thrust or flicker of his tongue against hers.

Her perfume danced around his nostrils, teasing him, tantalising him with the scent of hot summer nights. He was almost dizzy with it, intoxicated.

He moved his hands from her shoulders and splayed them roughly in her silky hair. Her slender hips moved against his, instinctively searching for him. Wanting him as a woman wants a man.

He ached to feel her surround him, to milk him of his essence with every tight contraction of her body. The need inside him built to fever pitch. Had he ever wanted someone as much as this? It was like a raging torrent in his blood. He could think of nothing but how much he wanted to possess her. His body was rigid with desire, hot and pulsing against her.

His right hand moved under her top to cup her breast through the lace of her bra, the softness and delicate shape of her thrilling him. That night in the library she had brazenly taunted him with her body. But it was her touch that had unravelled his control. The sexy little tiptoe of her fingers on his chest had been like throwing a match on a spill of gasoline. It had roared through his veins until he had finally snapped and grabbed her and shown her what a real man felt like instead of those pasty-faced adolescents she had surrounded herself with like a queen bee with drones.

He had wanted her then and he wanted her now.

He pushed her bra aside and bent his head to take her nipple in his mouth, swirling his tongue around and around until she was groaning in delight, her fingers digging into his waist for purchase.

He moved to her other breast, taking his time exploring it in intimate detail: the tightly budded nipple, the pink areola and the sensitive underside where thousands of nerves quivered and danced under his touch.

Her hands moved from his waist and danced over the front of him. His erection jutted proudly against her tentative touch, the blood thundering in him—the ache of need so intense he felt like a teenager at his first sexual encounter.

He reclaimed her mouth and backed her up until she was against the kitchen table. He lifted her onto it, and she opened her thighs and wrapped her legs around him, her arms tight around his neck as her greedy little mouth wreaked havoc on his.

The kiss went on and on, drawing him into a sensual whirlpool that was making it impossible to think of anything but possessing her totally. His erection was nudging her intimately, the damp barrier of her lacy knickers taunting him until he was fit to explode.

He blindly went in search of her slick wetness, pushing aside the cobweb of lace so he could slip one finger inside. He felt the tight grip of her body, heard her little gasp of pleasure. But then she jolted and pulled back from him, her cheeks fire-engine red, her eyes shocked and wide with horror. 'Stop!' she said.

He gave her a questioning look. 'Stop?'

She pushed at his chest with both of her hands. 'Get away from me!'

He stepped back and watched as she scrambled off the table and pushed her skirt down with shaking hands. She kept her gaze averted, her shoulders hunched as she wrapped her arms around her body. 'You had no right to do that,' she said.

'To kiss you?' he asked.

She threw him a blistering look. 'You shouldn't have touched me...like that.'

'Why not?' he asked.

She frowned fiercely at him. 'You know why not.'

'Because you fancy yourself in love with another man?'

Her cheeks fired up again. 'You went too far,' she said. 'You know you did.'

'So,' he said with a sardonic look. 'You're OK with me kissing you, but it's hands off below the waist. Is that it?'

She compressed her lips until they lost their rosy tint. 'That shouldn't have happened either,' she said, still frowning furiously. 'Although I accept it was partly my fault.'

'Partly?' He gave a scornful grunt. 'That was the biggest come-on I've had since you flashed your breasts at me when you were sixteen.'

'I wasn't giving you the come-on back then,' she said in a tight little voice.

'So what *were* you doing?'

She shifted her gaze. 'I was angry with you. You were always ignoring me as if I was just a silly little spoilt brat who was always getting in the way. I wanted to teach you a lesson.'

'You wanted me to notice you,' he said. 'Well, here's the thing, princess—I noticed you. I noticed everything about you. I just didn't follow you around with my tongue hanging out like all of your pimply suitors.'

Her eyes came back to his, the colour still heightened in her cheeks. 'Can we just forget this ever happened?' she asked.

Edoardo let the silence be his answer.

She swallowed a couple of times, an agitated look in her eyes. 'It meant nothing,' she said. 'It was probably just hormones or something. It happens to women as well as men, you know.'

'Lust.'

She gave him an irritated frown. 'Do you have to be so…blunt?'

'No point dressing it up in fancy euphemisms,' he said. 'You've got the hots for me. I'm gagging for you. The thing is, what are we going to do about it?'

'Nothing,' she said, folding her arms even tighter

across her chest. 'We're going to do nothing, because it's wrong.'

He gave her a wicked smile. 'I won't tell anyone if you don't.'

She flung herself away. 'I'm going to bed. Goodnight.'

He waited until she was almost out of the door before he spoke. 'If you can't sleep, you know where to find me. I'll be happy to be of service.'

She gave him an arctic blast with her gaze by way of answer and then disappeared.

Bella was still shaking with reaction when she got to her bedroom. She closed the door and wished there was a lock on it. Not for Edoardo, but for herself. She didn't trust herself not to wander down the long corridor to where his bedroom was and take him up on his offer to "service" her.

She groaned in self-recrimination. How could she have been so stupid to get so close to him again? He had danger written all over him; it was like a tattoo on his body only she could see.

His touch had set her flesh alight. She had not been able to control her reaction to him. It had taken over her common sense, her principles and morals.

She had wanted him.

She *still* wanted him.

The pulse of her blood was still reverberating through her body like a tiny bell struck by a sledgehammer. She could still feel where his long, thick finger had been. If she squeezed her thighs together, she could recreate the delicious sensation of him touching her so boldly, so possessively. And that was just his finger! What if he were to…?

No.

She slammed the brakes on her traitorous imaginings. She could not, *would* not, go there. He was off-limits for a host of reasons.

He was her enemy.

He only wanted her to prove a point.

She was a trophy he wanted to collect just like a big-game hunter. He would hang her up on his wall of sexual conquests. He would mock her as soon as he had finished with her.

He didn't have a heart. He was not capable of feeling anything for her other than lust.

Bella wrenched herself out of her clothes, tossing them to the floor as she stomped to the *en suite*. But showering did nothing to quell the aching, pulsing need of her flesh. If anything, it made it worse. She was hyper-aware of her body, of all its nerves and sensations and needs. It was as if her skin had turned itself inside out.

She wrapped herself in a towel and went back to her bedroom, but it was impossible to even think of sleeping. She looked at the bed, and her brain immediately conjured up an image of Edoardo lying there waiting for her. He was so tall he would have taken up most of the mattress. In his arms downstairs she had felt tiny and dainty, feminine and all hot, sensual woman.

She imagined him naked on her bed, his muscled body lean, cut, carved and *aroused*.

She let out a stiff curse, veered away from the bed and looked out of the window. The moon was high in the sky, casting a silvery glow over the rolling fields. She rested her forehead against the glass of the window and closed her eyes and groaned.

She heard a sound of a door opening and closing downstairs and opened her eyes. She watched as Edoardo took Fergus outside for his last comfort stop. He waited near the parterre garden, his tall figure so still and silent as the dog went about his business in the shadows.

Bella was transfixed.

The moonlight captured Edoardo's arresting features in relief. He looked like a dark knight or warrior fighting some internal battle of his own. His jaw was locked tight and his fists were thrust into the pockets of his trousers. His broad shoulders were fixed in position, the length of his spine straight and grimly determined. His brow was heavily furrowed, tense in fierce concentration.

Then, as if he sensed her watching him, he turned and locked gazes with her.

Bella felt the shock of the visual connection like a punch to her solar plexus. Her heart kicked like a horse's hoof against her breastbone. Her breathing stalled and her mouth went dry.

His eyes read her mind as surely as his hands and mouth had read her body only half an hour ago.

She jumped back from the window like someone leaping away from a roaring blaze. She clutched at her chest, sure her heart was going to flop like a goldfish tossed out of its bowl and land on the carpet at her feet.

What was *wrong* with her?

She wasn't a teenage girl experiencing her first crush. She was an adult, a mature, sensible adult who was about to become engaged to a man she loved and admired. She had no right to be lusting after a man she didn't even like.

It was shocking.

It was immoral.

It was *tempting*.

She grabbed twin handfuls of her hair and castigated herself. 'No. No. No.'

She heard the stairs creaking as Edoardo's firm tread came up to her floor. Her heart skipped another beat. She held her breath, her body poised, every nerve super-alert, her self-control and resolve gone to some far-off place she couldn't access even if she wanted to.

But then there was silence.

Nothing but an empty, hollow silence, apart from the lone hooting of an owl as it flew past her window, the sound of its wings moving through the air like a velvet cape being swished around someone's shoulders.

CHAPTER SIX

BELLA wasn't sure what woke her. She hadn't even realised she had been asleep, but she must have been because when she opened her eyes and checked the clock, it was close to four in the morning. She pushed back the covers and sat up, straining her ears in the eerie silence.

She didn't hear a thing for a full minute or so and then she heard a faint groan. Her skin lifted in goose bumps, as if a ghost's hand had touched her.

Don't be silly, she chided herself as she reached for her wrap. *Haverton Manor does not have any resident ghosts.* At least, none that she knew of.

She tiptoed out into the corridor and immediately noticed a sliver of muted light shining from beneath Edoardo's door at the other end of the passage. She chewed at her lip, wondering if it was wise to go any further. But then she heard the groan again, louder this time, and it was definitely coming from inside his room.

She pushed her reservations aside and padded down to his door, softly tapping on it as she leant her ear to the woodwork. 'Edoardo?' she said. 'Are you all right?'

There was a rustle of sheets being wrestled with. 'Go

back to bed,' he said, but his voice didn't quite have the stern authority she was used to hearing in it.

She turned the doorknob before she could change her mind and stepped over the threshold. Her eyes went to his figure lying in a tangle of sheets, the pallor of his face almost the same shade of white. 'Are you ill?' she asked.

He cranked open one eye and told her to get out with an expletive graphically sandwiched between the curt command.

Bella turned on the major light near the door but he immediately swore again and put his forearm across his eyes. 'Turn off the damn light!' he growled.

She flicked the switch off and came over to the bed where the light from his bedside lamp was shining with a pallid glow. 'What's wrong?' she asked.

'Get the hell out of here.'

'But you're sick.'

'I'm fine,' he said through gritted teeth.

Bella rolled her eyes and leaned forward to put a hand on his brow but he must have sensed her coming for him and blocked her by grabbing her wrist with his other hand. He opened his eyes to narrow squints and glared at her. 'I told you to get the hell out of here.'

She felt the bruising crush of his fingers around her wrist and winced. 'You're hurting me.'

He dropped her wrist. 'Sorry.' He let out a serrated sigh and covered his eyes again. 'Just leave me alone… please?'

Bella sat gently on the edge of the bed next to his thighs. 'Migraine?' she asked softly.

His whole body sank against the mattress. 'It'll pass,' he said on another weak sigh. 'They always do.'

'You get them often?'

'Now and again.'

'I've never seen you sick before,' she said.

He cranked open one eye again. 'Enjoy the show,' he said dryly.

She placed a hand on his brow, frowning at how clammy it was. 'Have you taken anything for it?' she asked.

'Paracetamol.'

'That's hardly going to do much,' she said. 'You need something stronger. What if I call an after-hours doctor?'

'No.'

'But—'

'No,' he said, glaring at her again. 'Will you quit it with the sweet little nurse routine and get the hell out?'

'I'm not leaving you like this,' she said. 'You could fall and knock yourself out or something.'

He flopped back down, but within a few seconds he suddenly reared up and, almost shoving her aside, stumbled to the *en suite*, not even stopping to close the door. Bella winced in empathy as he was violently, wretchedly sick. She gently pushed the door back, rinsed a face cloth under the tap and silently passed it to him where he was huddled over the toilet bowl.

'You don't give up easily, do you?' he said but there was no sting in it.

'I choose my battles,' she said and rinsed out another face cloth.

He took it from her once he had flushed the toilet. 'Thanks,' he said a little gruffly.

'My pleasure.'

He gave her a look. 'I bet you're enjoying this.'

Bella frowned at him. 'Why would I enjoy seeing you, or anyone, suffer?'

He hauled himself upright and took a moment to steady himself against the basin. She could see the outline of every muscle of his back and shoulders beneath the thin cotton T-shirt he was wearing. The boxer shorts left most of his long legs bare, the muscles strongly corded with regular and strenuous exercise. 'There are people in this world who would enjoy nothing more,' he said with a bitter twist of his mouth. 'It's sport for them. Cheap entertainment.'

'I hope I never meet someone like that,' she said, giving an involuntary shudder.

He looked at her for a long moment. She sensed he was looking at her but not actually seeing her. His eyes had a far-away look, a shadowed look. But then he blinked, turned away and moved back to the bedroom on legs that didn't seem all that steady.

Bella came up alongside him and put an arm around his lean waist. 'Here,' she said. 'Let me help you.' She led him back to the bed and, while he was still standing, quickly straightened the mangled linen.

He closed his eyes once he was lying flat. 'If you tell anyone about this, I'll have to kill you,' he said after a moment's silence.

She smiled, and before she could stop the impulse, she briefly touched the ends of her fingers against his where they were lying on the mattress close to her thigh. 'You'll have to catch me first.'

He gave a soft little grunt without opening his eyes. 'That will be the easy part,' he said and within half a minute he was soundly asleep.

Bella woke again as the sun touched her face in a golden slant from the window. She stretched her legs—and encountered a hair-roughened one. Her eyes flew open as she realised she was in bed with Edoardo.

You're in bed with Edoardo Silveri!

The words were like a neon sign flashing inside her head.

Had she *slept* with him? Had she actually *had sex* with him? She squeezed her thighs together and was momentarily reassured. But why, then, was she lying in his arms with her legs caught up with his?

OK, let's be sensible about this, she thought. There's got to be a perfectly reasonable explanation for why she was lying with her legs entangled with his. She was still in her piglet pyjamas. All the buttons were still done up. Maybe she'd just drifted to sleep and unconsciously reached for him. Or maybe he had reached for her. Why, then, hadn't she woken up and moved out of reach?

Could she somehow wriggle away and leave without him waking?

Before she could get her scrambled thoughts together, he turned and looked at her.

'So you slept with me after all,' he said.

'I did not!'

He smiled a smile that tugged on something deep inside her belly, like a small needle pulling on a tiny thread. 'You did too,' he said. 'I heard you snoring.'

'I do *not* snore.'

He picked up a lock of her hair and slowly wound it around one of his fingers. She couldn't help noticing it was the same finger he had slipped inside her the evening before. She felt her inner core give a little tremor of remembered pleasure. 'You snuffle,' he said.

'Snuffle?' She wrinkled her nose. 'That doesn't sound much better.'

He gave her hair a gentle tug, his eyes holding hers in an erotic lock. 'Come here,' he commanded.

Bella let her breath out in a fluttery rush that felt like the pages of a book being rapidly thumbed inside her chest. 'Don't do this, Edoardo,' she said.

His eyes read the message her mind was relaying, not the one her mouth had just uttered so breathlessly. 'You want me,' he said. 'You curled yourself around me during the night. I could have taken you then and there.'

'I'm about to become engaged to another man,' Bella said, but right at that very moment she wasn't sure if she was reminding him or herself.

'Call it off.'

She looked at his mouth, her belly turning over itself as she thought of how it had felt to have those sensual lips moving against hers. She forced her gaze back to his blue-green one. 'I can't call it off,' she said. 'I don't *want* to call it off.'

He tugged on the tether of her hair; it was part pleasure and part pain. But wasn't that just typical of what she felt for him—a confusing mix of emotions she didn't want to examine in too much detail? She hated him and yet her body wanted him as it had wanted no one else. His mouth came closer and closer, stopping just above hers. 'I could talk you into it,' he said. 'All it would take is one little kiss.'

Bella put a finger against his lips, the graze of his stubble sending a dart of longing straight to her core. 'I can't.'

He opened his mouth and sucked her finger into his mouth, gently snagging it with his teeth as his eyes held hers in a silent challenge that made her insides quiver like not-quite-set jelly.

A sweeping wave of red-hot desire coursed through her.

She felt her body gravitate towards him like a magnet attracting metal. Temptation was like a surging tide she had to swim against without the use of limbs. She felt the hard ridge of his erection against her belly and ached to hold it in her hand, to stroke him, to explore him, to *taste* him. Her hand moved forward but then she snatched it back, shocked at her own wantonness. 'Let me go,' she said, pulling at the lock of hair still tethered to his finger. 'Please?'

His eyes smouldered with unmet needs. She felt the echo of them like a drum beat in her body. He slowly unwound her hair until there was nothing connecting them but the desire that throbbed like soundwaves in the air.

He got off the bed and hauled the T-shirt he was wearing over his head.

'What are you doing?' Bella asked, pulling her knees up to her chest as she sat up on the bed.

'I'm going to have a shower,' he said and stepped out of his boxer shorts.

Her eyes widened at the sight of him so gloriously male and so potently aroused. She gulped and quickly covered her eyes with her hands. 'For God's sake, can you stop parading yourself around like a peacock?'

He gave a mocking laugh. 'Stop acting like a shy little virgin,' he said.

Bella didn't know why but she *felt* like a virgin when she was with him. His wealth of experience was so much broader than hers. She knew it just by looking at him. She *sensed* it in her body. He only had to look at her with those blue-green eyes of his and all her nerves and senses would go off like rescue flares.

She didn't open her eyes until she heard the *en suite* door close. She quickly scrambled off the bed and bolted, not stopping until her bedroom door was shut tight against the temptation of his touch.

Edoardo worked outdoors all day in spite of the freezing weather. He wanted Bella so badly it was like a persistent ache in his body. Lying next to her last night had been a form of torture. He had wanted to cover her body with his, to thrust into her softness and finally claim her as his. She had crawled all over him during the night, her soft little hands reaching for him, her warm, sweet breath dancing all over his chest as she snuggled close. It had been so hard not to peel those ridiculous pyjamas from her body and plant kisses all over her skin. He had wanted to explore her in intimate detail, to caress her breasts, to taste them again, to roll his tongue over those tight little nipples. He had wanted to slip his finger inside her hot moistness, to feel the delicious clench of her body, to taste her saltiness with his tongue.

But instead he had stared fixedly at the moonlight reflected on the ceiling as he had slowly run his fingers through the gossamer silk of her hair while she slept.

He never spent the whole night with anyone. It was a rule he had never broken. His nightmares were both terrifying and dangerous. He was always so frightened he might hurt someone by lashing out while he was reliving the horror of his childhood.

He loathed the weakness of his body. His migraines were not as frequent as they once had been but they more than made up for it when they came. Last night's had been the worst in a long while. The doctors had told him stress was a contributing factor. Bella pushing him for information about his childhood had been the trigger; he should never have allowed her to get under his guard like that. She had a way of slipping under his defences, ambushing him with her concerned looks and softly spoken words.

He could just imagine the shock and disgust on her face if he told her about his past. For all these years she had goaded him, taunted him with words about his background that were a whole lot closer to the truth than she probably realised.

He *felt* filthy. He had lived in filth so long he still felt dirty underneath his skin even though the outside was now clean.

He *felt* uncivilised. His childhood had been a black hole of despair. He had wanted to die at times rather than endure it. His anger and rage at the world had been like a cancer growing inside him. He had hit out at everyone. He hadn't trusted anyone to do the right thing by him. He could not afford to get his hopes up only to have them brutally dashed down again. It had been so much harder to summon the will to live after a let-down.

Bella had grown up with every privilege. She had never wanted anything she couldn't have had at the click of her finger. She had never had to fight to stay alive.

He was still fighting his demons. They plagued him when he was awake and they tortured him when he was asleep.

Sometimes he wondered if he would ever be free.

It was late in the afternoon before Bella saw him again. She was coming back from a walk to the lake when she saw him up on a ladder doing something to one of the second-storey windows. She would have walked past without acknowledging him but the ladder shifted as he reached for one of the tools on his work belt, and her stomach suddenly lurched at the thought of him falling to the icy ground below. 'Do you need me to hold the ladder steady?' she said.

He gave her a brief glance and turned back to the task at hand. 'If you like.'

She watched from below as he shaved some wood off the casement with a plane. The muscles of his wrists and forearms bunched as he worked. He looked strong and fit and every inch a man in his prime. She tried not to think about what she had seen that morning but it was impossible to rid her mind of the image of his aroused body. Her insides were still smouldering with lust. She had been trying to ignore it all day but it was like a switch had been turned on inside her and she had no idea how to turn it off.

The ladder started to shudder again as he came down. She leaned her weight into it and only stepped away once he was safely down. 'What was wrong with the window?' she asked.

'Water damage,' he said, wiping some wood dust off his forehead with his forearm. 'We had a big snowfall a few weeks back. The wood's swollen with moisture. It'll need replacing eventually.'

'Why don't you get a professional to do this sort of stuff?' Bella asked.

'I enjoy it,' he said as he gathered his tools.

'That's beside the point,' she said. 'What if you had

a fall? There would be no one around to help you. You could break your neck or something.'

His eyes met hers as he straightened. 'That would be quite convenient for you, wouldn't it?'

She frowned at him. 'What do you mean by that?'

'You'd get the manor back,' he said. 'That's what you'd like, isn't it?'

'It's my home,' she said, shooting him a resentful look. 'Generations of Havertons grew up here. I don't see why a blow-in like you should take it away from its rightful owner.'

'Not happy with your four-storey mansion in Chelsea and the millions of pounds in assets?' he asked.

She glowered at him. 'That's beside the point. This is where I grew up. This is where I expected my children to grow up. You don't belong here. I do.'

'Your father obviously thought differently,' he said.

'He should have consulted me about it,' Bella said. 'The least he could have done is put it in both our names.'

'Would you have been happy living with me here?' he asked.

'No, I would not,' she said. 'Would you?'

'I don't know,' he said with a glinting smile. 'It could prove to be quite entertaining.'

She gave him a flinty look. 'I can assure you that if you get sick again I will not be racing to your aid in the middle of the night. You can jolly well fend for yourself.'

'Suits me.'

She pressed her lips together for a moment. 'Nor

will I allow you to take advantage of me like you did this morning.'

'How did I take advantage of you?' he asked. 'You were in my bed.'

'Not because I wanted to be.'

His smile was arrogantly, *irritatingly* confident. 'No one forced you into it. You came of your own free will. And I have a feeling you'll be back before too long.'

Bella glared at him. 'Do you really think I'm that much of a pushover? I don't even like you. I hate you. I've always hated you.'

'I know, but that's why it will be such great sex,' he said. 'I can hardly wait to feel you come. I bet you'll go off like a bomb.'

Her cheeks fired with heat and she clenched her hands into fists. 'I am *not* going to have sex with you.'

He ran his eyes over her leisurely, heating her with the caress of his gaze as if he had physically touched her. She felt her breasts tingle, she felt her insides contract and shamelessly weep with want. 'It's going to happen,' he said. 'You can already feel it, can't you?'

'I feel nothing,' she bit out.

He took half a step to shrink the distance between their bodies. Bella had nowhere to move as the garden bed was behind her. She drew in a breath as he trailed a lazy finger across the sensitive skin stretched over her left clavicle. Her nerves leapt and danced and shimmied under his mesmerising touch. 'Can you feel that?' he asked, locking his gaze on hers.

She swallowed tightly as a host of sensations coursed

through her like a shivery tide. 'You have no right to touch me,' she said, although her voice wasn't as strong and determined as she had intended. It sounded breathless and husky.

'You give me the right every time you look at me like that,' he said, tracing a pathway down the neckline of her top.

She felt her breasts tighten in anticipation. Her breathing stalled. Her heart stuttered like an old diesel engine inside her chest. She scrunched her eyes closed, fighting for strength of will. 'I'm not even looking at you, see?' she said.

He leaned in closer. She *felt* him. She felt his thighs brush against hers, and a wave of heat went through her like a knife through soft butter. She felt the sexy breeze of his breath against the skin of her neck. She breathed in the warm, male scent of him: the sweat, the musk, the complex cologne with its intriguing layers of citrus, spice and wood. The hairs on the back of her neck lifted one by one as his lips moved against her skin in a caressing nibble that shot an arrow of need straight to her core.

Bella made a little whimpering sound in her throat, a mixture of frustration and acquiescence. 'I don't want you,' she said.

'I know you don't,' he said, brushing his lips against hers in a teasing touch and lift off caress.

'I hate you,' she said, but the words somehow lacked conviction.

'I know you do,' he said and sucked softly on her lower lip until her legs threatened to fold beneath her.

Bella grasped his head between her hands, seeking his mouth in blind passion. The hot press of his mouth on hers detonated her senses and sent them into a fiery tailspin. She pushed her body against his, hungry for him in a way she had never thought possible. She ached for his possession, an urgent pulsing ache that was centred at the feminine heart of her.

He gripped her hips and ground against her shamelessly as his mouth worked its masterful magic on hers. It was so raw and primal. She felt the hot, hard heat of him throbbing against her stomach. It awoke every earthy sense in her body.

His hands moved from her hips to tug at her clothes. Her senses shrieked in rapturous delight at the rough urgency. He had her sweater pulled up, her top out of her skirt and her bra undone before she could find the fastener on his jeans. The wintry air danced over her flesh, but before she could shiver, his calloused hands moved over her naked breasts, making every nerve twitch in response. Her nipples tightened as he rolled his thumb over them, her spine turning to liquid as he brought his mouth over each one in turn. She closed her eyes and gave herself up to the pleasure of feeling his rough, stubbly face moving over her soft skin.

His mouth came back to hers just as she undid his jeans. He grunted with approval as she finally freed him. The hot, silky length of him filled her hand. Her heart raced as she thought of him moving inside her. She had never been so lust-driven in her life. Every other sexual encounter paled to insignificance. No one had ever made her feel so alive and in tune with her senses. Her skin was super-sensitive to his touch, to the stroke and glide of his hands, to the hot, moist possession of his mouth.

He lifted up her skirt and ruthlessly ripped her knickers and tights down to her knees. Her mouth was still jammed on his, her tongue duelling with his in a battle that was not just about strength of wills but about mutual need.

He played her with his fingers, gently at first, exploring her in intimate detail, before upping the pace. She was swept up in the moment, unable to stop the sensations that ricocheted through her like a speeding bullet. She cried out as her body shuddered and shook against his fingers, her breath coming in startled gasps.

She sagged against him when it was over, shocked at how completely he had unravelled her.

Shocked and shamed.

She stiffened and pushed back from him, grabbing at her tights. 'Oh, dear God...'

His expression was inscrutable. 'We can finish this indoors,' he said, zipping up his jeans. 'I haven't got a condom in my tool belt.'

Bella felt anger shoot through her like a powerful, galvanising drug. This was all a game to him. He had no feelings for her. All he felt was lust. He had 'serviced' her to prove a point. He wanted to reduce her to a shameless hussy who was driven by physical desires instead of intellect and morality.

'You did that deliberately, didn't you?' she asked, shooting him a contemptuous glare as she tried to fix her disordered clothes. 'You seduced me like a common little trollop to prove a point.'

'I was right,' he said with a glinting look. 'You went off like a bomb.'

Bella swung her hand through the air and landed a stinging slap on his cheek. He barely flinched but her hand felt as if the bones had splintered. 'You...you *bastard*,' she said, cradling her hand to numb the jarring pain.

The silence pulsated with tension.

Bella suddenly wondered if he would hit her back. His face was a marble mask, his eyes soulless. Her gaze went to his hands; they were clenched tightly by his sides. Fear was like a cold, hard hand on the back of her neck. She stood rooted to the spot, staring at him with wide, uncertain eyes.

He slowly released a breath and unlocked his hands. 'Is that really the sort of man you think I am?' he asked.

She licked her paper-dry lips. 'I shouldn't have slapped you... I'm sorry...'

He picked up the ladder and tucked it under one arm. 'Apology accepted,' he said and strode away until he disappeared from sight.

CHAPTER SEVEN

EDOARDO sat behind the mahogany desk in the study and looked sightlessly at the figures in front of him on his computer screen. Work was usually the panacea for all ills but he couldn't get his brain to focus. All he could think about was the feel of Bella in his arms. His body still throbbed with desire. It was like a banked-down fire deep inside him. Just one spark of her gaze and he was alight again.

He had made her confront her desire for him but it had come at a price. The look on her face, the shadow of fear in her brown eyes as she had stood there, made his stomach churn. He had seen that look in his mother's eyes before his stepfather had raised his hand in one of his drunken rages. Even after all these years he could still hear the sound of that clenched fist landing on his mother's face or body.

He pushed back from the desk, stood up and wandered over to the window. The weather forecast had predicted a heavy fall of snow overnight. He could see the clouds gathering in brooding clusters on the horizon.

They reminded him of his mood.

Fergus got up from the rug with a tired sigh and made his way creakily to the door. Edoardo opened it for him just as Bella was walking past. She gave him a startled look and stepped backwards, one of her hands going to her milky throat. 'You scared me,' she said.

'That seems to be a habit of mine just lately,' he said.

Her eyes fell away from his. 'I know you're not like… that,' she said in a quiet voice.

'So you feel safe with me, do you, Bella?' he asked.

She slowly brought her toffee-brown eyes to his. 'Of course I do…'

'You don't sound very sure about that.'

Her teeth tugged at her lower lip for a moment. 'I know you would never physically hurt me,' she said.

'I sense a "but" lurking somewhere in that statement.'

She let out a wobbly little breath. 'This thing between us…it has to stop. It has to stop before it gets complicated.'

He slanted her a cynical smile. 'It's already complicated, Bella,' he said. 'Your father made it a hundred times more so by putting me in charge of your life.'

Her gaze appealed to his. 'You could always quit the guardianship. You'd be free of me and I'd be free of you. It's a win-win for both of us.'

'Not going to happen, princess,' he said. 'I made a promise to your father. He trusted me to keep you out of trouble. He worked damn hard to get where he got. I'm not going to stand by and see some gold-digging gigolo waltz into your life and take everything.'

'Why do you think I'm gullible enough to let something like that happen?' she asked with a frown.

'You're too trusting,' Edoardo said. 'You're so desperate for approval and acceptance you can't see the difference between genuine friendship and exploitation.'

She flashed him a glare. 'I have lots and lots of genuine friends. Not one of them exploits me.'

He cocked a brow. 'How much rent do you charge those four girls who share your house?'

She pressed her lips together without answering, her cheeks turning rosy red.

'Nothing, right?' he said. 'You're a fool, Bella. They're using you, and you can't or won't see it.'

'You know nothing about my friends,' she said. 'So I help them out with a place to stay—what of it? They help me in turn.'

'How?' he asked with a curl of his lip. 'Let me guess: they help you spend your allowance on useless fripperies each month.'

Her eyes gave an annoyed little roll. 'I don't have to explain my personal expenses to you.'

'For God's sake, Bella, you went through fifteen thousand pounds in the last couple of months,' he said. 'You can't keep spending like that. You have to take responsibility for yourself. I'm not going to be around to keep you on track for ever.'

She sent him a caustic look. 'I can keep myself on track. I don't need you.'

'You *do* need me,' he said. 'And you've got me for another year, so you'd better get used to it.'

'What's the point of stringing this crazy guardianship thing out for another year?' she asked. 'You want to be free of me just as much as I want to be free of you. Anyway, once I get married to Julian, you'll have to relinquish your hold over me.'

'You're not getting married until you're twenty-five,' he said. 'Not while I have anything to do with it.'

She clenched her hands by her sides, anger in every rigid line of her body. 'Is that why you've been busily trying to seduce me any chance you could?' she asked.

He returned her fiery look with cool ease. 'Are you going to tell your God-fearing boyfriend that you've slept with me?'

Her eyes turned to flint. 'I have *not* slept with you.'

'Are you going to tell him you had an orgasm with me, then?' he asked.

Her cheeks bloomed with colour again. 'I didn't have any such thing *with* you. You didn't…you know…' She whooshed out a little breath and shifted her eyes from his. 'We didn't go that far.'

'You probably won't have to tell him.'

Her eyes flew back to his. 'What do you mean?'

'He'll know as soon as he sees you,' Edoardo said. 'You won't be able to hide it, especially if he sees you interact with me.'

She clamped her lips together as if she was struggling to keep back a retort. She released them after a moment. 'I can't think of any situation or event where you and Julian would be present at the same time.'

'So you're not going to invite me to your wedding?' he asked.

She gave him a pointed look. 'Would you come if I did?'

Edoardo considered her question for a moment. Over the years his mind had occasionally drifted to the day when she would walk down the aisle to some man standing at the altar. He had no doubt she would make a beautiful bride. She would love being the centre of attention; it would be her chance to be a princess for the day.

But he hadn't planned on being there to see it.

'Weddings are not really my thing,' he said.

'Have you ever been to one?'

'Two, a few years ago,' he said. 'They're both divorced now.'

She folded her arms across her middle. 'Not all marriages end up on the rocks,' she said. 'Many couples spend a lifetime together.'

'Good for them.'

She frowned at him. 'You don't believe love can last that long?'

'I think people get love and lust confused,' he said. 'Lust is a transient thing. It burns itself out after a while. Love, on the other hand, is something that grows over time, given the right conditions.'

'I thought you didn't believe in love,' she said.

'Just because I haven't been in love myself doesn't mean it doesn't exist,' he said. 'I can see it works for some people.'

'But you don't think I'm in love, do you?'

'I think you want to *be* loved,' he said. 'It's understandable, given that your father's gone and your mother has always been too selfish to love you properly.'

Her teeth snagged her bottom lip again. 'You're making me out to sound tragic.'

Edoardo studied her for a moment. 'Don't throw your life away on someone who doesn't love you for the right reasons, Bella,' he said.

'Julian does love me for the right reasons,' she said. 'He's the first man I've met who hasn't pressured me to sleep with them. Doesn't that say something?'

'Is he gay?'

She gave him a look. 'Of course he's not gay. He has principles; standards. Self-control.'

'The man is a saint,' Edoardo said. 'I can't be in the same room as you without wanting to rip the clothes off your body and ravish you.'

Her eyes flitted away from his, her cheeks firing up yet again. 'You shouldn't say things like that,' she said.

'Why not?'

'You know why not.'

'You don't believe in speaking the truth?' he asked.

'Some things are better left unsaid.'

Edoardo came over to her and slowly lifted her chin with the end of his index finger. 'What are you so afraid of?' he asked.

She moistened her lips with a nervous dart of her tongue. 'I'm not afraid of anything.'

'You're afraid of being out of control,' he said. 'I make you feel out of control, don't I, Bella? I'm not like all those simpering boyfriends you surround yourself with. You can control them, but you can't control me. You can't even control yourself when you're with me. It scares you that I have so much power over you.'

She gave him a glittering glare. 'You don't have any power over me.'

He arched a brow as he trailed a finger over her bottom lip. 'Don't I?' he asked.

Her lip trembled under his touch before she wrenched herself out of his reach. 'You want to wreck my life, don't you?' she asked, eyes flashing. 'You want to cause trouble for me because you've always resented me for being born to wealth while you were born to nothing. You think by dragging me down to your level it will somehow even the score. Well, it won't. You will always be a reject who landed on his feet.'

Her taunting words rang in the silence.

'Feel better now you've got that off your chest?' Edoardo asked.

She put up her chin, her brown eyes still glittering with defiance. 'I'm leaving,' she said. 'I'm not staying another minute here with you.'

'Good luck with that,' he said. 'It's been snowing like a blizzard for the last hour. You won't get as far as the end of the driveway.'

'We'll see about that,' she said and flounced out.

'Damn it.' Bella slammed her hands on the steering wheel in frustration. She had been so determined to prove Edoardo wrong. And she had almost done it, too.

She *had* got further than the end of the driveway. She had made it to the road before her car had slipped sideways and become bogged up to the windows in a snowdrift. But now she was out of sight of the manor and, with the snow blocking the road for as far as she could see in either direction, she could be stuck here for hours. It was freezing cold in spite of the heater in her car. She knew she couldn't leave the engine running for too long without flattening the battery. She could call for roadside help, which might take hours to get here. Or she could call Edoardo.

She rummaged for her mobile in her bag on the seat beside her. She held it in her hand, looking at the screen for a long moment where she had pulled up Edoardo's number. As much as it pained her to admit defeat, she pressed the call button.

'Do you want me to come get you?' he asked without preamble.

Bella silently ground her teeth. 'If it's not too much trouble.'

'Stay in the car.'

She glanced at the wall of snow that had fallen against both of her doors. 'I can't get out even if I wanted to,' she said.

While she was waiting for Edoardo to come, her phone rang. Bella glanced at the caller ID and suppressed a groan. Her mother only ever called her when she wanted something, usually money. 'Mum,' she said. 'How are things?'

'Bella, I need to talk to you,' Claudia said. 'I'm in a bit of a fix financially. Have you got a moment to talk?'

Bella looked at the snow-covered landscape surrounding her little capsule of a car. 'All the time in the world,' she said with a jaded sigh. 'How much do you need?'

'Just a few thousand to tide me over,' Claudia said. 'I've decided to leave José. Things haven't been working out. I'm in London for a few days. I thought it'd be nice if we spent some time together—hang out a bit, you know? Go shopping, do girly things.'

'I'm not in London right now,' Bella said.

'Where are you?'

'I'm…um, out of town.'

'Where out of town?' Claudia asked.

Bella drew in a little breath and carefully released it. Would it hurt to tell her mother where she was? Maybe if she were a little more open with her, Claudia would start acting more like a mother towards her. She longed to have someone to talk to who would understand. She was tired of feeling so isolated and alone. 'I'm at Haverton Manor.'

'With…with *Edoardo*?'

'Yes… Well, not *with* him as such,' Bella said. 'I hardly see him. He does his thing. I do mine. He's—'

'I suppose he's told you a heap of lies about me, has he?' Claudia said. 'Your father was a sentimental fool to let him take control of your affairs. How do you know if he's ripping you off or not? He could be selling off your assets behind your back and you wouldn't know a thing about it.'

'He's not ripping me off,' Bella said. 'He's managing everything brilliantly.'

'How can you possibly trust him to do the right thing by you?' Claudia asked. 'Don't forget he would've gone to prison if it hadn't been for your father vouching for him. He's got bad blood.'

'I don't think you should judge someone on where or how they grew up,' Bella said. 'He had a difficult start in life. He was an orphan at the age of five. I think it's amazing how well he's done, given how hard things were for him.'

'Goodness me,' Claudia said. 'This is a turn up for the books, isn't it?'

Bella frowned. 'What do you mean?'

'You springing to Edoardo's defence,' Claudia said. 'You sound positively chummy with him. What's going on?'

'Nothing.' Bella could have kicked herself for answering so quickly. *Too quickly.*

She could almost see her mother's snide smile. 'You've slept with him, haven't you?'

'What on earth makes you think that?' Bella said, injecting her tone with as much disdain as she could. 'You know how much we've always hated each other.'

'Hate doesn't stop people having sex with each other,' Claudia said. 'Some of the best sex I've had was with men I positively loathed.'

Bella hadn't planned on telling Claudia about her

engagement until it was official, but she would do almost anything to avoid an account of her mother's lurid and colourful sex life. 'I'm getting engaged,' she said.

'Engaged?' Claudia gasped. 'Oh, dear God, not to Edoardo?'

Bella frowned as she tried to imagine Edoardo putting a ring on her finger—or any woman's finger, when it came to that. She couldn't quite see it. He would never be one to declare his feelings if he had any. He would never admit to needing someone.

He certainly would *never* admit to needing *her*.

He wanted her, but that was different. He didn't need her in an emotional sense. He didn't need anyone. He was like a wolf that had separated himself from the pack. No one would ever see what he felt on the inside. 'No, not to Edoardo,' she said. 'To Julian Bellamy.'

'Have I met him?'

'No, we've only been dating for three months.'

'Is he rich?'

'That has nothing to do with anything,' Bella said. 'I love him.'

'When did you *not* love a boyfriend?' Claudia asked. 'You fall in and out of love all the time. You've been doing it since you were thirteen. What if he's only after your money?'

Bella rolled her eyes. 'You sound just like Edoardo.'

'Yes, well, he might not be from the right side of the tracks but he's certainly street smart,' Claudia said. 'Your father wouldn't have a bad word said about him.

I think he secretly hoped you would make a match of it with him.'

'What?' Bella asked, her stomach doing a little free fall. 'With Edoardo?'

'Why else would he have written his will the way he did?' Claudia asked. 'I bet he put Edoardo in control so you would have to see him regularly. He was hoping you'd fall in love with each other over time.'

'I am *not* going to fall in love with Edoardo,' Bella said.

'You'd be the icing on the cake for a man like him,' Claudia continued. 'It would make his rags-to-riches tale complete, wouldn't it? The well-born trophy bride to produce some blue-blooded heirs to dilute the bad blood flowing in his veins.'

Bella felt a strange tingle deep in the pit of her belly when she thought of her body swelling with Edoardo's child. She put a shaky hand over her abdomen, trying to quell the sensation. 'Mum, I have to go,' she said. 'I'll send you some money as soon as I can. I'm…in the middle of something right now.'

'I suppose you'll have to ask Edoardo for permission,' Claudia said sourly. 'Don't let him come between us, Bella. I'm your mother. Don't ever forget that.'

'I won't,' Bella said, thinking of the day, all those years ago, when her mother had left with her lover without even bothering to wave goodbye.

Edoardo found Bella almost buried in a ditch fifty metres from the front gate to the manor. She wound down the window as he stepped off the tractor. 'If you're going to say I told you so, then please don't waste your breath,' she said.

'You don't do things by halves, do you?' he asked.

'Can you get me out?'

'Sure,' he said. 'Stay in the car and keep the wheels straight while I tow you out.'

She sat and glowered at him from behind the steering wheel as he hitched the towrope to the bumper bar. He towed the car out, and once it was out of the ditch, he got her to join him on the tractor for the journey back to the house. 'Are you warm enough?' he asked as he made room for her beside him on the seat. 'You can have my jacket.'

'I'm f-fine,' she said through chattering teeth.

He shrugged himself out of his jacket and wrapped it around her slim shoulders. 'You don't have to fight me just for the heck of it, Bella,' he said.

She bit her lip and looked away. 'It's a habit, I guess.'

'Habits can be broken.'

Edoardo drove the tractor with the car towed behind all the way back to the manor. The snow kept falling but even more heavily now. It cloaked everything as far as the eye could see in a thick white blanket.

The air was tight with cold.

Every breath he or Bella exhaled came out in a foggy mist in front of their faces. He glanced at her and saw her huddled inside his coat, her hands gripping the edges together across her chest. She looked small, defenceless and vulnerable. 'Hey,' he said gently, bumping her shoulder with his.

She blinked and looked at him. 'Sorry, did you say something?'

'Penny for them.'

'Pardon?'

'Your thoughts,' he said.

'Oh...'

'What's wrong?' he asked.

'Nothing.' She looked away again and huddled further into his jacket.

Edoardo brought the tractor to a stop and helped her down. She hesitated before she placed her hand in his. 'You're freezing,' he said, keeping her hand within the shelter of his.

'I forgot to bring my gloves,' she said.

He released her hand. 'Go inside,' he said. 'I'll sort your car out. Go get warm. I'll be in in a minute.'

'Edoardo?'

He straightened from where he was untying the towrope from the bumper bar and looked at her. 'Yes?'

She chewed at her lower lip for a moment. 'I need some extra money,' she said. 'Would you be able to transfer five thousand into my account?'

He frowned. 'You don't have a gambling problem, do you?'

Her eyes widened in affront. 'Of course not!'

'What do you want it for?'

Her expression became haughty. 'I don't see why I have to tell you what I spend *my* money on,' she said.

'You do while I'm still in control of it,' he said.

'My mother thinks you're skimming off the profits to fund your own nest egg,' she said with a hard little look.

'And what do you think, Bella?' he asked. 'Do you think I'd stoop so low as to betray the trust your father placed in me?'

She turned to go to the house. 'I need the money as soon as possible.'

'For your mother, I presume?'

Her back stiffened, and after a tiny pause she turned back around to face him. 'If it was your mother, what would you do?' she asked.

'You're not helping her by propping her up all the time,' he said. 'She's become dependent on you. You'll have to wean her off or she'll eventually drain you dry. It's one of the reasons your father orchestrated things the way he did. He knew you would be too soft and generous. At least I can say no when it needs to be said.'

'Did she ask you for money when she came the other day?'

'Amongst other things.'

Her brows moved together. 'What other things?'

'I'm not going to badmouth your mother to you,' he said. 'Suffice to say I'm not her favourite person in the world.'

She nibbled at her lower lip. 'I'm sorry if she offended you.'

'I've got a thick skin,' he said. 'Now, go inside before yours is frozen solid.'

She met his gaze again. 'I didn't mean what I said

earlier, you know. I think you're one of the most decent men I've ever met.'

'The cold has got to you, hasn't it?' Edoardo said with a teasing half-smile.

Her gaze fell away from his and he rolled up the tow-rope as he watched her walk towards the manor, her slim figure still encased in his jacket. It was so big on her it almost came to her knees. She looked like a child who had been playing in the dress-up box. He felt a funny tug inside his chest, as if a tiny stitch was being pulled against his heart.

Once the door had closed behind her, he let out a breath he hadn't realised he had been holding. 'Don't even go there,' he muttered under his breath and strode towards the barn.

CHAPTER EIGHT

EDOARDO came into the kitchen an hour later to find Bella poring over a cookbook that belonged to Mrs Baker. She had an apron on over her clothes and there was a swipe of flour across her left cheek. She looked up as he came in. 'I hope you don't mind, but I'm cooking dinner,' she said. 'I thought I should start to pull my weight around here since I can't leave right now.'

He hitched up one brow. 'Can you cook?'

She gave him a quelling look. 'I've been taking lessons from one of my flatmates,' she said. 'She's a sous chef in a restaurant in Soho.'

'The one your ex-boyfriend owned?'

She gave a little sigh as she looked at the ingredients in front of her. 'I only went out with him a couple of times,' she said. 'The press made it out to be much more than it was. They always do that.'

'I guess everyone wants to know what Britain's most eligible girl is up to,' he said.

'I sometimes wish I didn't come from such a wealthy background,' she said with a little frown.

Edoardo leaned against the counter. 'You don't mean

that, surely?' he said. 'You lap it up. You always have. You wouldn't know what to do with yourself if you didn't have loads of money.'

'My friends' mothers give *them* money or buy them stuff or take them shopping,' she said, still frowning. 'I'm tired of feeling responsible for my mother's bills.'

'You gave her the money?'

'Yes, and she hasn't even sent a text or called me to thank me.' She let out a dispirited sigh. 'She's probably spent it all by now.'

'I've been thinking about what I said earlier,' he said. 'It's really none of my business who you give your money to. She's your mother. I guess you can't turn your back on her.'

After a little silence she looked up at him with those big brown eyes of hers. 'I wish I could be sure people liked me for *me*. How can I know if they like me because of who I am as a person? I don't even know if my mother loves me or simply sees me as a meal ticket.'

He reached forwards to brush the flour off her cheek with the end of his index finger. 'Sorting out the friends from the hangers-on is always a challenge, even for a person without wealth. You just have to trust your gut feeling, I suppose.'

Her shoulders went down as she sighed again. 'I think what you said before was right: I want to be loved so much that it clouds my judgement.'

'It's not wrong to want to be loved,' he said. 'We wouldn't be human if we didn't.'

She looked up at him again, her eyes soft and luminous. 'Do you want to be loved?'

Edoardo gave an off-hand shrug. Loving was something he didn't do any more. He suspected he had forgotten how. He certainly wasn't booking in any time soon for a refresher course either. 'I can take it or leave it.'

A little frown creased her forehead. 'You can't really mean that,' she said. 'You just don't want to be let down again or abandoned.'

He curled his lip, threatened by how close to the truth she was. He refused to let anyone close to him. Godfrey had been an exception, but it had taken years, and even then he hadn't told him everything about his past. 'Got me all figured out, have you, Bella?'

'I think you push people away because you're frightened of becoming too attached,' she said. 'You like to be in total control of your life. If you had feelings for someone else, they could take advantage of you. They could leave you just like your parents did.'

Edoardo felt a ridge of steel ripple through his jaw until his teeth were locked so tightly together he wondered if he'd be left with nothing but powder.

He thought of the first home he had been sent to after the authorities had stepped in when he'd been ten years old. He had already had five years of his stepfather's capricious and cruel treatment. Five years of living in dread, quaking with fear night and day in case things turned nasty.

The hands that had fed and clothed him, and at times even been kind to him, could turn within a blink of an eye into vicious weapons. It didn't matter how well-behaved he was. Sometimes the anticipation of the brutality was so torturous he would deliberately play up just to get it over with. But even then he could never prepare himself. He'd had no way of knowing when his stepfather would strike. His body had run solely on adrenalin. The 'flight or fight' mode had been jammed on.

He hadn't stood a hope of settling in anywhere.

Looking back now, he could see the foster parents he had been sent to had done their best. Some had been better than others; they had tried to offer him shelter and support but he had sabotaged their every attempt to get close to him. Then Godfrey Haverton had taken him in and, in his quiet and unobtrusive way, shown him that it was up to him to make something of his life. Under Godfrey's steady but sure tutelage, he had learned how to become a man, a man with self-control and self-respect—a man who was the agent of his own destiny, not at the mercy of others.

But he wasn't going to parade his past to Bella, of all people. He had locked it away and it was staying there.

'You don't know what the hell you're talking about,' he said.

'I think I do,' she said in a quiet and assured voice that was far more threatening than if she had shouted the words at him. 'I think you want what everyone else wants. But deep down you feel you don't deserve it.'

He gave her a mocking look. 'Did you read that in a self-help book, or is it something you just made up on the spot?'

She drew in a breath and slowly released it. 'I didn't read it anywhere,' she said. 'I just sense it—the same way my father sensed it. I think he understood you from the word go. He didn't push you or force affection on you. He waited for you to come to him when you trusted him enough to do so.'

Edoardo gave a disparaging laugh but the sound grated even on his own ears. 'You're making me sound like an ill-treated dog,' he said.

Her eyes meshed with his, soft and yet all-seeing—*knowing*.

The silence stretched and stretched.

He felt every beat of it like a hammer blow inside his head.

'What happened to you, Edoardo?' she asked.

The memories tapped him on the shoulder with their long, craggy fingers: *Come here,* they taunted. *Remember the time he hit you with the belt until you were bleeding? Remember the icy-cold showers? Remember the gnawing hunger? Remember the raging thirst?*

He pushed them away but one more crept up behind him and caught him off-guard.

Remember the cigarettes?

'Stop it, Bella,' he said tightly. 'I have no interest in dredging up stuff I've forgotten long ago.'

'You haven't forgotten it, though, have you?' she asked.

He clenched and unclenched his fists, his stomach feeling as though a crosscut saw was working its way through it. He felt the pain in his back. It had happened so long ago but he could still remember the searing pain and the helplessness. Oh, dear Lord, how he had hated the helplessness. Sweat broke out on his upper lip. He could feel it beading between his shoulder blades as well. His head throbbed with the memories, all of them jostling for their starring moment centre-stage.

'Edoardo?' Bella's hand touched him on the arm. 'Are you all right?'

Edoardo looked down at her. She was standing so close he could smell her shampoo as well as her perfume. Her eyes were full of concern, her soft mouth slightly open. He could hear her breath going in and out in soft little gusts.

His mobile phone pinged with the sound of an incoming text, and the memories scuttled back to the shadows like sly, secretive rats running from the light of an opened door.

He let out a slowly measured breath. 'I know you mean well, Bella, but there are some things that are just best forgotten,' he said. 'My childhood is one of them.'

She stepped back from him, her hand falling back by her side. 'If ever you want to talk about it...'

'Thanks, but no,' he said and, briefly checking his phone, added, 'Look, I won't be in for dinner after all.'

Her expression clouded. 'You're going out in this weather?'

'Rebecca Gladstone needs a hand with something,' he said. 'I'm not sure how long I'll be.'

She screwed up her mouth, her eyes losing their softness to become glittery and diamond-hard. 'What does she need a hand with?' she asked. 'Turning back the sheets on her bed?'

'Green doesn't suit you, Bella.'

Her brows jammed together. 'I'm not jealous,' she said. 'I just think it's disgusting to lead someone on when you have no intention of taking their feelings seriously.'

'You're a fine one to talk,' he said.

'What's that supposed to mean?'

'While your intended fiancé is out of sight, you've been up to all sorts of mischief, haven't you?'

She coloured up and glowered at him at the same time. 'At least I'm not messing with your feelings,' she said. 'You don't have any, or at least certainly not for me.'

'Does that annoy you, Bella?' he asked. 'That I haven't prostrated myself before you like all your other suitors, declaring my undying love for you at every available opportunity?'

She gave him a flinty look. 'I wouldn't believe you if you did.'

Edoardo gave a little rumble of laughter. 'No, you wouldn't, would you? You know me too well for that. I might want you like the very devil, but I don't love you. That stings a bit, doesn't it?'

'It doesn't bother me one little bit,' she said with a pert hitch of her chin. 'I have no feelings for you either.'

'Other than lust.'

Her cheeks pooled with colour. 'At least that is something I can control,' she said.

'Can you?' he asked, taking her chin between his finger and thumb, holding her gaze steady. 'Can you really?'

Her throat rose and fell, and her eyes flickered. 'Why don't you try me and see?'

He was sorely tempted. He felt the urge rising in him like a flash flood. Blood pumped and poured. His need for her was a hungry beast inside him, rampaging through his body until he was almost shaking with it.

But instead he dropped his hand from her face and stepped away. 'Maybe some other time,' he said.

For a nanosecond he thought her expression showed disappointment, but she quickly masked it. 'There's not going to be another time,' she said. 'As soon as this snow melts, I'm out of here.'

'What if it doesn't melt for another week?' he asked as he shouldered open the door.

She set her mouth grimly. 'Then I'll go out there with a hair dryer and melt it myself.'

Bella slept fitfully until about two in the morning. She got up and looked out of the window. The snow was still falling but not as heavily now. It looked like a winter fairyland outside. It was a scene she was going to miss dreadfully when she left Haverton Manor for the final time. She tried to imagine how it would be once the guardianship period was over. There would be no reason to see Edoardo again. No more twice-yearly meetings. No more monthly phone calls, texts or emails. He would go his way and she would go hers.

They would never have to see or speak to each other ever again.

She turned from the window with a frown. She had to stop thinking about him. She had to stop wondering why he was the enigma he was. What had put that hard cynicism in his eyes? What had made him so self-sufficient that nothing or no one touched his heart?

She couldn't stop thinking of him as a little five-year-old orphan. Who had looked after him? Comforted him? Who had nurtured him? Who had loved him? Had anyone?

For all these years she had thought of him as a rebel who didn't fit in anywhere, who didn't *want* to fit in anywhere. But what if his childhood had made him that way? What would it take to unlock the guard he had on his heart?

Would he ever come to a point in his life where possessions and financial security were no longer enough? Would he crave the connection he had been pushing away for most of his life?

Bella went downstairs in search of a hot drink and was waiting for the milk to heat in the microwave when Edoardo came in. He was still dressed in the clothes he'd had on earlier and there were snowflakes in his hair.

'Waiting up for me, Bella?' he asked as he shrugged off his coat.

She gave him a scornful look. 'You must be joking.'

'Rebecca sends her regards,' he said and dusted the snow out of his hair with one hand.

Bella glared at him. 'You talked about me while you were…in *bed* together?'

'We weren't anywhere near a bed.'

'Please spare me the lurid details,' she said with a roll of her eyes.

'I was helping her with a horse that had injured itself on a neighbouring property,' he said. 'Do you remember the Atkinsons' place? The new owner has thoroughbreds. One of the brood mares cut her foreleg on some wire. Rebecca needed an extra pair of hands.'

'Oh…' She chewed at her lip for a moment.

'Rob Handley is the new owner,' he said. 'He's a bit shy but he's fine once you get to know him.'

Bella frowned at him. 'Why are you telling me this?'

He gave a shrug. 'Just thought you might like to let Rebecca know some time if you're talking to her. Rob got off to a bad start with her. She thinks he's arrogant. It's a shame, because he really likes her. They'd make a great couple.'

Bella cocked her head at him. 'Don't tell me you're a romantic at heart?'

'Not at all,' he said. 'A blind man could see those two belong together. They just need a little nudge in the right direction. You want to make me one of those?' He indicated the hot chocolate she had on the counter.

Bella made the drink and handed it to him. Her fingers touched his and a shockwave of heat ran up her arm. She quickly put her hand back down by her side. 'While we're on the subject of perfect couples, I'd like to firm up some plans for my wedding,' she said.

His eyes collided with hers. 'No.'

Her brows snapped together. 'Will you at least listen to me?'

'You're making a big mistake, Bella,' he said. 'Can't you see how foolish this is? Look at what's been going on between us. How can you think you'll be happy settling down with a man who you can go for weeks or months without making love to you?'

Bella glared at him. 'Not every man is a slave to his desires,' she said. 'Some men have self-control.'

'Yeah, well, let's see how much self-control he has after a year,' he said.

'I'm not waiting a year,' she said. 'I told you. I want to get married in June.'

'What is a year in terms of your whole life?' he said. 'Rushing into marriage can be disastrous for women, even in this enlightened day and age.'

'I'll sign a pre-nuptial agreement if that will ease your concern,' she said. 'I'm sure Julian won't mind. In fact he'll probably insist on it.'

'It's not just about the money,' he said. 'I don't believe you're in love with this guy. How can you be? Look at how you respond to me.'

Bella glared at him. 'That's *your* fault.'

'How is it my fault?'

'Because you've done nothing but try it on with me from the moment I arrived,' she said. 'You haven't touched me in years, not since that night when I was sixteen. Why now? Why now when I'm about to marry someone else?'

His jaw clenched tight as he put his mug down on the counter. 'You think I haven't wanted to touch you over the years?' he said. 'God damn it, Bella, are you blind? Of course I wanted to touch you. You were too young back then and you were half-tanked with alcohol. By the time I felt you were old enough, your father got sick. And then he died, and when he made me your guardian, that complicated things.' He raked a hand through his hair. 'If I'd known what your father had planned, I would've tried to talk him out of it.'

Bella frowned at him. 'I thought you cooked this up with him,' she said. 'Did you really know nothing about it?'

He sucked in a breath and released it audibly. 'I knew he was worried about how you would manage your wealth,' he said. 'He felt you would be easy pickings for someone who was after your money. He knew you had a soft heart.'

'I didn't show much of that soft heart when he needed it, did I?' she asked sadly.

He tipped up her chin and met her eyes. 'It wasn't all your fault, Bella,' he said. 'Your father could be very stubborn when he wanted to be. He pushed you away just as much as you pushed him away.'

'Like you do?'

He dropped his hand from her face. 'I'm nothing like your father.'

'Yes you are,' Bella said. 'That's why you got on so well. You were kindred spirits. He saw himself in you. I've never realised it until now. He had a rough start in life, too. His mother died when he was young; I think he was only about six or seven. He was sent to live with distant relatives because his father had to go away for work. He didn't like talking about it. It was like a wound he didn't want anyone else to see.'

'You've really missed your calling, haven't you?' he said with a sneer of a smile. 'Just think, if you hadn't made a career out of doing lunch and shopping, you could've have been a psychologist.'

'Go on,' Bella said, glaring at him in irritation. 'Mock me. Make fun of me. That's what *you've* made a career out of, isn't it?'

He came up close and grabbed her chin between his finger and thumb. 'Let's see how good your psychologist's skills are, shall we?' he said. 'Why do you think you're rushing off to marry a man you barely know?'

Bella stared him down. 'I love him, that's why.'

'You're panicking, that's why,' he said. 'You've only got a year until a truckload of money lands in your lap. You're not sure how you're going to handle it, are you? You're worried that it will be too much to deal with on your own so you've latched on to the first reliable, steady person you think will be able to help you.'

'That's not true,' she said. 'I want to settle down and have a family. I don't want to be on my own any more. I want to belong to someone.'

He pulled her up against him. 'You're frightened of the passion that's burning inside you,' he said. 'You're worried you're going to end up like your mother, flitting from shallow affair to shallow affair.'

Bella strained against his iron-strong hold. 'I'm nothing like my mother,' she protested. 'I'm not going to marry for lust. Lust doesn't come into it at all.'

'No, well, it can't, can it?' he said. 'Not when your lust is directed elsewhere.'

Bella felt the hot probe of his erection. She felt the need rising up in her like a giant, swamping wave. It overpowered her defences. How could she resist him when her body was programmed to respond to him and only him? 'I don't want to want you,' she said.

He fisted a hand in her hair, his mouth so close she could feel his breath on her lips. 'Do you think I want to want you?' he asked. 'I've fought it for as long as I can remember.'

It thrilled Bella to hear his gruff confession. For so long she had thought he felt nothing for her. His indifference had annoyed her so intensely, but all that time he had been fighting his attraction.

But what was the point in telling her now?

Why was he telling her now?

'Don't you think you've left it a bit late to tell me?' she said. 'I'm about to announce my engagement.'

He brushed his mouth against hers, once, twice. 'Is it too late?' he asked.

Bella wasn't sure what he was asking. She licked her dry lips and looked at his mouth, that sensual, wicked mouth that could make her feel things she had no right to be feeling. She wanted to feel that mouth on hers again. She wanted to feel that mouth on her body, on her breasts, on her inner thighs, on the very heart of her desire. 'You don't love me,' she said, running a fingertip over his bottom lip, her soft skin catching on his evening stubble.

'You don't love me either,' he said. 'If you did, you wouldn't be promising to marry someone else, now, would you?'

She sent her fingertip over the contour of his upper lip this time. 'Would you want me to love you?' she asked.

'No,' he said. 'That's not what I want at all.'

She stilled the movement of her finger and looked up into his eyes, her heart beating double time at the smouldering look in his blue-green gaze. 'Then what do you want?' she asked.

He cupped her bottom with his hands, bringing her in close to the heated trajectory of his erection. 'Do you really need to ask that?' he said.

Bella felt her breath hitch in her chest as his head came down in slow motion towards hers. She had the chance to step away. She had the chance to say no. She had more than enough time to tell him she had no intention of making love with him.

But she didn't.

CHAPTER NINE

BELLA closed her eyes just as his mouth touched down on hers. It was one of those brush-and-release kisses that made her senses sing with delight. His tongue flickered against hers, cajoling hers into erotic play. She responded with a shiver of reaction that felt like champagne bubbles flowing beneath her skin.

He increased the pressure of his lips on hers, the taste-and-tease action of his tongue changing to a more determined thrust and retreat. The primal intent was unmistakable. It made her body hum with longing to feel him inside her, stroking, thrusting. She could already feel the dew of need between her thighs and that little clenching pulse pulling on her inner muscles.

She gave a soft whimper as he cupped the back of her head as his tongue drove deep into her mouth, his pelvis rock-hard against hers. She was spinning with need, her hands flying all over him to find access to his skin. 'I want you,' she whispered breathlessly against his mouth. 'I know it's wrong, but I want you.'

'It's not wrong,' he said and ran his hands up under

her jumper in search of her breasts. 'It's inevitable. It always has been.'

Bella gasped as his calloused hands caressed her. She worked at his shirt buttons, not even caring that one of them popped off and pinged to the floor. She pressed hot kisses to his neck and down his sternum, her hands going on ahead and working on the belt and fastener on his jeans.

He growled in male pleasure as she finally uncovered him. He was so thick and strong in her hand, silky smooth and already moist at the tip. 'Bedroom,' he said against her lips and swept her up in his arms.

'I'm too heavy,' she protested. 'You'll do your back in.'

'Don't be ridiculous,' he said. 'What sort of men have you been dating? You weigh next to nothing.' He shouldered open the door and carried her upstairs, stopping every now and again to torture her mouth with the heat and fire of his.

Bella was almost out of her head with need by the time they got to his bedroom. He laid her on the bed and came down over her, his mouth clamping down on hers. She ran her hands up under his loosened shirt, discovering the planes and contours of his back and shoulders. He was so lean and yet so muscular, his skin warm and dry to her touch. She could smell the hint of man beneath the intricate layers of his aftershave. It called out to the primal woman in her, in a language as old as time itself.

He leaned his weight on one arm as he ripped off

his shirt and tossed it to the floor at the side of the bed. Bella shivered in anticipation as he started to remove her clothes. Her jumper went first, ending up on the floor. Her bra followed, but not before he had suckled each of her nipples through the lace. It was such an erotic thing to do, and the tickly barrier of the lace somehow made it all the more pleasurable.

He kissed his way down her stomach, dipping his tongue in the tiny pool of her belly button. She felt herself tensing as his fingers started to peel back the lace of her knickers.

'What's wrong?' he asked, stilling his hand. 'Am I going too fast?'

'No... It's just I haven't waxed recently.'

'Good,' he said. 'There's nothing I like more than a real woman.'

Bella held her breath as he gently tugged the lace down to uncover her. She saw the way his eyes darkened with desire. 'You're beautiful,' he said.

The sensation of his finger outlining her form was unbelievable. He explored her with his fingers, taking it gently, waiting for her to relax before he inserted a finger, then two. He withdrew his fingers and lowered his mouth to her, tasting her in a gentle sweep of his tongue. She breathed in sharply as the sensations took her by surprise. What if she made a fool of herself? It was too intimate. What if she didn't respond properly? She gasped and tried to pull away.

'Relax,' he soothed. 'Go with it. Don't tense up.'

'I'm not very good at this,' Bella said, biting down on her lower lip.

'This is about you, not me. It's your pleasure. You take all the time you need.'

She lay back as he continued stroking her softly, his fingers gentle and yet sure. He waited until she was totally at ease before he caressed her again with his tongue. He used slow, stroking movements, gauging her reaction, varying the pressure and speed until she felt the sensations ricocheting through her. They came in rolling waves that coursed through and over her, spinning her, tossing her, tumbling her, until she was gasping out loud. 'Oh, God,' she said in a rush. 'That was… unbelievable.'

He came back over her, brushing her hair back from her forehead with his hand, his eyes thoughtful as they studied hers. 'You're not very confident sexually, are you?' he said.

Bella lowered her gaze and stared at his Adam's apple. 'I'm not a virgin, if that's what you're asking. I've had sex heaps and heaps of times.'

His index finger tipped up her chin. 'How many partners have you had?'

She looked into his blue-green gaze. 'Five…'

He tilted his head. 'Five?'

She blew out a little breath. 'OK, six, if you count the first time, but I never do as it was a complete and utter disaster.'

'What happened?'

'It was that Christmas I stayed in town,' she said. 'I

was determined to prove I was mature enough to have sex, contrary to what you had said that night when we kissed. I hate to say it, but you were right; I wasn't mature enough. It was over before it began. I ended up in tears and the guy left the party with someone else.'

He smoothed her hair again, his eyes holding hers in a sensual lock that made her insides quiver with longing. 'I want you,' he said. 'I wanted you then and I want you now.'

Bella locked her arms around his neck, her pelvis on fire where it was being probed by the heat of his. 'Make love to me,' she whispered.

He bent his head to her mouth, kissing her with drugging sensuality. Her spine melted like honey in a heatwave. His erection throbbed with primal urgency against her and she instinctively went in search of it, shaping him with her fingers, delighting in the deep guttural groan he made against her lips.

His mouth moved to her breasts, subjecting each one to a hot swirl of his tongue before suckling on her. Then, even more pleasurably, he trailed his tongue to the sensitive underside of each breast, making the nerves beneath her skin go haywire.

Bella writhed beneath him, desperate for that final possession. Her body was slick with want. 'Please...' she said.

He reached for a condom and handed it to her. 'You want to put it on me?'

Bella tore the packet with her teeth, took the condom out and carefully pulled it over him, caressing him as she went. He sucked in a breath, pushed her back down and came over her, his weight supported on his arms. He parted her gently, waiting for her to accept him before going further. She became impatient and lifted her hips towards his. He groaned again and surged into her with a long, thick thrust that sent a shiver down her spine.

He started to move, slowly at first, but then the pace picked up. Bella felt each delicious movement, the friction sending her senses reeling. Every tiny muscle in her body tensed as the pressure built. She could feel her body climbing, straining, crying and screaming out for release that was frustratingly just out of her reach.

He slipped a hand beneath her bottom and lifted her higher against him, his thrusts even more determined. 'Don't hold back, Bella,' he said. 'Let yourself go.'

His other hand went in search of the heart of her need, the tiny, swollen pearl of her clitoris that was so sensitive she could not hold back a gasp as the storm in her body erupted. She gripped him tightly, her teeth sinking into his shoulder as the tumultuous waves picked her up and tossed her into the abyss. Around and around she went, a burst of sensations like a thousand explosions inside her body.

Bella held him as he worked towards his own release, the thrusting motion of his body sending aftershocks of pleasure through hers. She stroked his back and shoulders, feeling the tight clench of his muscles as he pitched forward into oblivion. He groaned deeply and shuddered, his breath coming out in a harsh gasp against her neck.

She listened to the sound of his breathing in the aftermath, holding his totally relaxed body against hers. She didn't want to move. Her body was in such a blissful state of lassitude, every muscle felt like it had been set free. She was floating in a sea of ecstasy, in tune with her body in a way she had never been before.

'I don't want to move just yet,' he said against the sensitive skin below her earlobe.

'Nor me,' she said as she slid her hands over the taut curve of his buttocks.

He positioned himself above her by leaning on one of his forearms, and the other hand he used to trace a feather-light pathway over each of her eyebrows, her nose, her cheeks, her top lip and then her lower one. 'You were amazing,' he said. 'Truly amazing.'

Feeling a little out of her depth, Bella focused her gaze on his collarbone, tracking her fingertip back and forth along its ridge. 'It's never been like that for me before,' she said. 'I've never…you know…'

A frown moved through his eyes. 'You've never orgasmed during sex?' he asked.

'No,' she said. 'It's my fault, I know. I over-think everything and worry about stuff. I get myself in a state. I'm always kind of relieved when it's over.'

He cupped her face, his thumb stroking along her cheek in a slow caress. 'What stuff do you worry about?'

Bella rolled her lips together. 'The usual: my thighs, my stomach, my breasts.'

His frown was incredulous. 'Bella, you're beautiful. You're perfect. How can you possibly worry about things like that?' he asked.

'I know, it sounds so…so shallow,' she said.

'Not shallow,' he said. 'Just insecure.'

'Yep,' Bella said with a self-deprecating twist of her mouth.

His thumb paused in its stroking action, his blue-green gaze steady on hers. 'You have no need to be. You really don't. You're one of the most beautiful women I've ever met.'

She gave him a tremulous smile. 'Thank you.'

He brushed the pad of his thumb over her bottom lip. 'This thing between us…' He paused for a moment. 'I want it to continue.'

Bella's heart gave a little stumble. 'For how long?'

He studied her expression for another beat or two. 'I'm not one for putting a timeline on relationships,' he said. 'Let's just see how it goes, shall we?'

Bella felt reality slap her in the face. She knew exactly how it would go: he would have his fun and move on. He wasn't promising her anything—no emotion, no love, no future—just sex. Right from the start, all he had wanted to do was to stop her marrying before she was twenty-five. What better way than to temporarily distract her with the delights of his love-making? But how long would an affair between them continue? Even if it did continue for a few weeks, or even months, he wasn't going to offer her the things she yearned for most. 'Aren't you forgetting something?' she asked.

His brows came together. 'You're surely not still determined to go ahead with that ridiculous engagement?'

'Why wouldn't I?' she asked.

He lifted himself away and got off the bed, one of his hands raking a pathway through his hair. 'I'm offering you a relationship.'

'You're offering me a fling,' Bella said.

His cheek moved in and out as he clenched his teeth. 'That's all I can offer you,' he said.

'It's not enough for me,' she said, swinging her legs over the bed to collect her clothes. 'I don't want to live like my mother, going from fling to fling. I want to settle down.'

'How can you sell yourself so short?' he asked, capturing her arm to stop her moving past. 'You're setting yourself up for a passionless life. Why can't you see it?'

Bella tried to shake off his hold but he held her fast. 'I want a normal life.'

'What's normal about marrying a man you don't love?' he asked.

'I *do* love him,' she said.

He gave a mocking grunt. 'And yet you just had sex with me.'

'It was just sex,' she said. 'It's just a physical thing. It means nothing.'

'Do you really believe that?' he asked.

Bella wanted to believe it. She *needed* to believe it. 'I should never have slept with you,' she said. 'It was a mistake. I wasn't thinking.'

'No, maybe not, but you were feeling,' he said, pulling her closer, right up against his naked body. 'Like you're doing now. Can you feel what you do to me, Bella? What we do to each other?'

Bella could and it sent a wave of hot, pulsing longing through her. His erection was pressed against her thigh. She felt her feminine core tingling in anticipation, the nerve-endings still sensitised from their passionate coupling earlier.

His mouth came down and covered hers and in a heartbeat she was lost. Her arms snaked around him, holding him as close as she possibly could. She wanted to crawl inside his skin, to melt into him so that her body didn't ache with this maddeningly feverish want.

Her hands delved into his hair, her fingers threading through the thick black strands. She breathed in the scent of him, that erotic mix of his maleness with the delicate overlay of her perfume and body musk.

His hands slid down to the curve of her back and pressed her hard against him. Bella felt the potent power of him like an electric current through her body. All of her senses were screaming for his possession—it was a raw hunger that could not be satiated any other way.

She took him in her hand, stroking him, relishing the satiny feel of his skin, delighting in the iron-strong length of him. She loved hearing those deep, unmistakably male noises he made in the back of his throat—guttural groans that had a distinctly primal quality to them. She loved the way his mouth moved with such heated fervour on hers, the way his stubble was so sexily raspy on the soft skin of her face.

He used his teeth in playful little bites against her lips, tugging and releasing, tantalising her with that little hint of danger in the caress. She bit back with little nips that she followed up with gentle sweeps and flicks of her tongue.

He walked her backwards, thigh against thigh until the backs of her knees felt the bed. She tumbled backward, all legs and arms and red-hot need. He quickly applied a fresh condom and came down over her, his weight pinning her down, his mouth still locked on hers as his body speared hers in one deliciously vigorous thrust that made the breath hitch in her throat and her bones melt.

He set a fast pace that made shivers course down her spine and the fine hairs on the back of her neck dance and twitch in response. She felt the contraction of her muscles, all the sensitive nerves twanging as he rocked against her with passionate, heart-stopping urgency.

'You drive me insane, do you know that?' he said against her kiss-swollen mouth.

'Ditto,' Bella said, taking another nip at his lower lip.

He worked his way down her neck. 'Am I going too fast for you?'

She angled her head so he could get better access. 'Can you go faster?'

'I don't want to hurt you,' he said, pulling back his pace a bit. 'You're so tiny compared to me. I feel like I'm crushing you.'

'You're not,' she said, urging him on with little hip movements. 'You feel just right.'

He kissed her mouth again, lingeringly and tantalisingly. Bella writhed beneath him, her body so wired she felt like she was going to implode. He read her movements as if he had direct access to her thoughts and feelings. He slipped a hand between their bodies and found the swollen nub of nerve-endings that were all shrieking and clamouring for release.

It was a cataclysmic explosion of feeling. Her whole body quaked with it as if she had been caught in the epicentre of an earthquake. She couldn't stop from crying out, her breath coming out in jerky little gasps as the aftershocks shuddered through her.

She was still gasping as he came. She felt every powerful thrust as he emptied himself. She skated her hands down his back, holding him against her, wanting to prolong the deep connection of their bodies. There was something profoundly moving about his total loss of control. Was she deluding herself to think that what they had experienced together was different from anything else he had encountered with previous partners? Was it crazy of her to want to be something to him other than yet another sexual conquest?

Edoardo eased himself up on his forearms to look at her. 'You're frowning,' he said as he brushed a flyaway strand of hair back off her face. 'I didn't hurt you, did I?'

'No, of course not,' Bella said, lowering her gaze.

He smoothed the little crease between her eyebrows with the pad of his finger. 'I know what you're thinking.'

She gave him a wry look. 'So you can read my mind as well as my body, can you?'

He searched her gaze for a moment. 'Don't beat yourself up for giving in to me,' he said. 'This was always going to happen—you and me in bed together.'

'Because you wanted to prove a point.'

'I'm not trying to prove anything,' he said, frowning a little. 'I just think you need to take a bit more time about your decision. You're panicking about your future; it's understandable. You're about to inherit a fortune. It's a lot of responsibility for someone so young. You're looking for someone to help share that responsibility—someone reliable. But I don't want you to make a mistake that you'll end up regretting for the rest of your life.'

'Would you approve of *anyone* I chose to marry?' she asked.

He held her gaze for a beat or two before he moved away to get off the bed. 'I'd better let Fergus out,' he said.

Bella frowned as she saw him reach for his trousers on the floor. 'What's that on your back?'

'It's nothing,' he said, shaking out the creases in his trousers and stepping into them. 'Just a couple of chicken-pox scars.'

She grabbed at the sheet and draped it around herself as she padded over to him. 'They look pretty big for chicken-pox scars,' she said, putting a hand on his arm to stall him. 'Let me see.'

'Leave it, Bella,' he said and shrugged off her hold.

Bella looked up into his inscrutable features.

'Why have you got those little white circles below

your tan line?' she asked. 'There must be eight or ten at least.'

It was an aeon before he spoke. A battle seemed to be playing out on his face. She could see the shadows flickering in his eyes as each second passed. The column of his throat looked tight, as if he was having trouble swallowing. His jaw was tightly clenched; she could see the in-and-out movement of a tiny muscle in the centre of his cheek. 'They're burns,' he said.

'Burns?' She frowned. 'What sort of burns?'

'Cigarette burns.'

Bella's eyes flared in shock. 'Cigarette burns? But how did you…? Oh, dear God.' She clapped her hands against her mouth, too horrified even to say the words out loud.

'Clever, wasn't it?' Edoardo said with bitterness in each and every word. 'He was careful to put them where no one would see. He couldn't get away with blackening my eyes or leaving me visibly bruised. He didn't want anyone asking tricky questions.'

Bella felt tears sprouting in her eyes. Her chest ached with the thought of him as a little boy being brutally burnt. What other horrors had he endured? Was that why he never spoke of his past? Was it just too horrible to recall? 'Your stepfather abused you?' she asked.

His mouth flattened to a thin line of bitterness. 'Only physically,' he said. 'He did worse to my mother.' A muscle twitched in his jaw. 'He was an absolute bastard to her. I couldn't do a thing to protect her. He wore her down until she finally gave up on life. She took an overdose. I found her.'

Bella swallowed as she thought of how awful it must have been for him. To find his mother dead, the one person he thought he could rely on gone for ever, leaving him under the care of a madman. How dreadful for a young child to be exposed to such violence. He must have been so terrified, so lost and alone once his mother had died. 'I'm so sorry...' she said, blinking back tears. 'It must have been dreadful for you. I can't bear to even think about it. How on earth did you survive it?'

'Save your tears,' he said with a brusqueness that was jarring. 'I don't need anyone's pity.'

Bella's stomach churned with anguish as the thoughts came crowding in: a small motherless child with no one but a violent stepfather to take care of him; no loving father to go to for protection; no grandparents or extended family.

No one.

No wonder he was so self-reliant. He'd had no one to rely on since he was a little boy. He trusted no one. He needed no one. He loved no one.

'How did you finally get away from him?' she asked.

'The authorities stepped in when I was ten,' he said. 'A teacher at school noticed I was unwell. I hadn't had food for a week. They sent a social worker around.'

Her bottom lip trembled as she struggled to control her emotions. 'I'm so sorry...'

'It's in the past,' he said. 'I want to leave it there.'

'But what about justice?' she asked. 'Did your stepfather get arrested for child abuse?'

'He fed the authorities the line that I was a difficult kid,' he said. 'He couldn't control me. I was a rebel—I had conduct disorder, or some such thing. The thing is, I didn't know how to behave. I *was* uncontrollable. At times I was like a wild animal. I had so much anger stored up inside, I caused trouble and mayhem wherever I went.'

'But it wasn't your fault,' Bella said. 'The odds were stacked against you. But my father saw through all that to who you are on the inside—to who you had the potential to be.'

'Your father saved my life,' he said. 'I was on the road to nowhere when he offered me a home.'

'I think you helped him just as much as he helped you,' Bella said. 'You took his mind off the divorce from my mother. Before that he was sliding into a deep depression. You gave him a new focus. He really did see you as a surrogate son.'

Edoardo let out a jagged sigh. 'I didn't tell him about my past,' he said. 'I know he would have liked me to. He was very patient. He never pressured me but I just didn't want to go there.'

'Did he ever see the scars on your back?' Bella asked.

'No, but other people have.'

'Other people, as in lovers?'

'Yes,' he said, placing his arms through his shirt. 'But you're the first who didn't buy the chicken-pox story.' He slowly did up the buttons, his eyes still trained on hers. 'I hope I don't have to tell you that I would rather this didn't go public. I've spent years of my life trying to forget.'

She frowned. 'How could you think I would even think to do such a thing?'

'It wouldn't be the first time a woman sought revenge when things didn't go her way,' he said.

'You have an appalling view of women,' she said.

He gave a whatever shrug. 'Just speaking as I find.'

Bella bit her lip and looked away. She was just one of many lovers he'd had. Tonight was nothing out of the ordinary. It had rocked her world completely but it was just another encounter for him.

'What's wrong?'

She wrapped her arms around her body. 'Nothing.'

He came over and placed his hands on the tops of her shoulders. Bella felt his warm hard body behind her. She ached to lean back and give herself up to the pleasure of being in his arms. But hadn't she already stepped too far over the boundaries? How was she going to get back to her neat, ordered life? Her body would always want him. It wasn't something she could turn off or on at will. She had made it a whole lot worse by experiencing the sensual delights of his love-making. How would she ever settle for anyone else after him?

'Contrary to what you might think, this was special tonight,' he said against her hair.

She turned in his arms and looked up into his blue-green eyes. 'Do you really mean that?' she asked.

He cupped her face in his hands, his thumbs moving

back and forth in a caressing motion across her cheeks as his eyes made love with hers. 'Do you have to go back to London straight away?' he asked.

Bella felt her heart do a crazy little somersault. 'What are you saying?'

He brushed his mouth against hers. 'Stay with me for a few days.'

Bella thought of the danger of staying with him. So many dangers—not just the danger of someone finding out about their affair, but the danger of her falling in love with him. Wasn't she more than halfway there already?

She linked her arms around his neck and said against his already descending mouth, 'I'll stay.'

CHAPTER TEN

THE snow had long melted but Bella kept putting off returning to London. She was aware of the clock ticking on her time with Edoardo. By tacit agreement neither of them mentioned her upcoming engagement. Bella felt as if the girl who was about to become engaged to Julian Bellamy was someone else entirely—nothing to do with her. It was like living a parallel existence. She had compartmentalised her life in such a way as to have it all, or at least to have what she could while she could.

And Edoardo was what she wanted.

Since the night he had revealed his past to her, she had started to see him for the sensitive and strong, resilient man he was underneath his cynical façade. He was an intensely private person. She had never met a more private person. He loathed gossip. He didn't have time for idle chit-chat. He was a man with a strong work ethic; he didn't believe in people being handed things for free.

He made Bella see her privileged background quite differently. She didn't like admitting it, but she *had* taken so much for granted. She hadn't thought much about the sacrifices her father had made in order to provide her with an inheritance that was beyond the dreams of most people. She felt incredibly guilty for resenting that her father hadn't focused all of his attention on her. But Edoardo made her see that her father had been working to provide for her, not for himself. Her father had been stung badly by the divorce from her mother and had spent the rest of his life rebuilding his empire so Bella could have a secure future. Her father had not said the words, but he had shown it in his actions.

As the week was drawing to a close, Bella went down to the village for supplies and was shocked to see a couple of journalists with cameras at the ready step out of a car as she came out of a shop. She put her head down and turned to go back the other way but within moments they were striding alongside her on the footpath.

'Tell us about your relationship with the reclusive Edoardo Silveri,' one journalist said as he followed her along the footpath. 'Is it true you are currently staying with him at Haverton Manor, the house that once was your family home?'

Bella put her head down and kept walking. She knew from experience it didn't matter what she said; they would twist it to make it sound like something else entirely.

'A local source told us Mr Silveri was a teenage rebel with a criminal past,' another journalist said as they came alongside. 'Would you like to comment on what it's like to be involved with a bad boy who made good?'

Bella swung her gaze to the pushy journalist. She

could not bear to have Edoardo painted in such a way. 'He's not a bad boy,' she said. 'He's never been bad. It's the people who let him down and hurt him who are bad. They're the ones who should be exposed and brought to justice.'

'Word has it Mr Silveri would never have made it without considerable help from your father,' the first journalist said.

Bella turned to face them. 'That's not true,' she said. 'Edoardo was always going to make it in spite of his background. That's just the sort of person he is. He's strong and determined. My father saw those qualities in him and nurtured them. He would be very proud of the man Edoardo has become. Now, please leave me alone. I have nothing more to say.'

Bella pretended to do more shopping until she was sure she wasn't being followed before she drove back to Haverton Manor. She wondered if she should tell Edoardo about the paparazzi in the village but then decided against it. She didn't want anything to spoil the rest of the time they had together. It would all too soon draw to a close. She couldn't stay down here for ever, even though she longed to. But she couldn't settle for anything less than total commitment. If Edoardo didn't love her enough to want to spend the rest of his life with her, then she would have to walk away, even though it would break her heart to leave him.

Bella had only been back at the manor half an hour when she got another call from her mother. She answered it while she was making the bed up with fresh linen in Edoardo's room. 'Mum,' she said tucking the phone between her cheek and her neck as she straightened the covers. 'I was wondering when you were going to call.'

'Yes, well, I've been busy sorting out the mess José left me with,' Claudia said. 'Speaking of bills, can you lend me a couple more thousand?'

'Lend?'

'Don't use that tone with me, young lady,' Claudia said. 'I'm still your mother, you know.'

'You're always leaning on me to sort out your finances. Dad gave you a massive settlement after the divorce. What have you done with it all?'

'Oh, well, now, listen to you,' Claudia said in a la-de-da tone. 'You're a fine one to criticise. You haven't had to work for anything in your life.'

'I know that,' Bella said. 'But I'm going to work now. As soon as I get my inheritance, I'm going to set up a trust fund for an orphanage. In the meantime, I'm going to look for work as a volunteer. I want to make a difference in a child's life, just like Dad did with Edoardo.'

'Your father's little experiment certainly backfired, didn't it?' Claudia said.

'I'm not even going to ask you what you mean by that,' Bella said.

'I called around at the house in Chelsea and the girls said you weren't home,' Claudia said. 'Don't tell me you're still holed up with Edoardo.'

'I'm coming back on Saturday,' Bella said. 'I'm meeting Julian at the airport.'

'What's he going to think when he hears you've spent the last week or so with another man?' Claudia asked.

Bella moved away from the bed as if that would put some distance between her and her conflicted feelings. 'Mum, I'm not going to go ahead with the engagement. I want to talk to Julian in person about it. I don't think it's fair to him to do it on the phone.'

Claudia gave a little scoffing noise. 'That thug has got under your skin, hasn't he?' she said. 'I knew he would. I told you what he's up to. He wants you for your pedigree. Nothing else.'

Bella's hand tightened on the phone. 'Edoardo is *not* a thug,' she said. 'He's a gentle and caring man. You don't know him. He's not what you think at all.'

'You've been sleeping with him, haven't you?' Claudia said.

'Mum, I don't want to have this conversation with you.'

'He only wants you for your money,' Claudia said. 'That's why he won't allow you to give me any. He wants it all to himself.'

'No, that's not true,' Bella said, springing to his defence with all the emotion she had tried for so long to keep under wraps. It came bubbling out of her like a drain that had finally been unblocked. 'He's not offering to marry me. He won't marry anyone. It's because of his past. He suffered terribly as a child. You have no idea of what he's been through. He's the most amazing person I've ever met. I won't have you or anyone say such horrible things about him.'

'You silly little fool,' Claudia said. 'I suppose you fancy yourself in love with him, do you?'

Bella looked out of the window to where Edoardo was coming back across the fields with Fergus. He looked up and smiled at her, raising his hand in a wave. She smiled and waved back, her heart feeling as if someone had pressed it between two book ends. 'I think I have always loved him,' she said, but her mother had already ended the call.

Edoardo was clearing the last of the snow from the driveway when Bella came out to him. She was dressed in a pom-pom hat and mittens and looked so adorably cute he felt as if someone had grabbed him inside his chest. She had a little frown on her face and he put the shovel to one side so he could gather her hands in his. 'Why the long face?' he asked.

She blew out a breath that misted in front of her face. 'Nothing…'

He pushed up her chin. 'Hey,' he said. 'You were smiling when I waved to you half an hour ago. What's happened?'

She chewed at her lower lip. 'I had a talk to my mother.'

'And?'

Her shoulders went down. 'I told her I'm not going to prop her up any more. She didn't like hearing it. She hung up on me.'

Edoardo gathered her close. 'You did the right thing,'

he said. 'For too long you've been the parent in that relationship.'

She looked up at him with those big brown eyes. 'I also told her I'm not going ahead with my engagement. I'm going back to London on Saturday to talk to Julian.'

He studied her features for a moment's silence. 'I see.'

The tip of her tongue slipped out to moisten her lips. 'I think you're right,' she said. 'I need more time to think about my future.' She paused for a moment, her eyes still meshed with his. 'You were right about something else.' Another little pause. 'I'm not in love with him. I don't think I was ever in love with him.'

'What made you finally realise that?' Edoardo asked.

There was something in her eyes as she held his gaze that tugged on his heart like a small child pulling at his mother's skirt. 'I guess I must have finally grown up,' she said. 'Took me long enough, didn't it?'

He put her from him and stepped a couple of strides away, shoving a hand through his hair. 'I don't want you to get the wrong idea, Bella,' he said. 'I told you what I was prepared to offer. We can continue our affair, but that's all it will ever be.'

She looked at him with such raw longing that the tug on his heart became almost painful. 'We could have such a great future together,' she said.

'Your father trusted me to keep you safe,' Edoardo said. 'He didn't want you to throw your life away on an impulse. What you're doing now is exactly what he was worried about. Ten days ago you were determined to marry this Bellamy fellow, now you think you've suddenly developed feelings for me. Who's it going to be next week, or next month?'

'I haven't suddenly developed feelings for you,' she said. 'These are not new feelings. I think they've been here all the time. I'm still getting my head around them. I need some time to think. These last few days have been amazing...but I'm not sure I can settle for an affair. I want the whole fairy tale.'

Edoardo let out a heavy sigh and brought her close again, resting his head on top of hers. 'I don't want to hurt you, Bella,' he said. 'But I just can't make those sorts of promises.' He breathed in the scent of her hair, felt her body melt against him like she was a part of him. He had never wanted anyone like he wanted her. He had thought his desire for her would have burned out by now but if anything it had become even more intense. He *ached* for her. But making a commitment to her, or to anyone, was beyond his capabilities. He could not envisage allowing someone—even someone as adorable and endearing as Bella—to have the power to abandon him.

He was the one who left when the time came.

He was the one who locked his feelings away so no one could exploit them.

He was the one who never loved.

Bella's infatuation with him would soon end. He was sure of it. She had fallen in and out of love ever since she'd hit her teens. Their little fling would run its course and she would go back to London and slot back into her high-society life.

At least this way she would never know how much he would miss her when she went.

Edoardo rose early the next morning. Not that he'd had a lot of sleep, but then neither had Bella, when it came to that. Making love with her during the night, knowing that she was leaving within the next twenty-four hours, had deeply unsettled him in spite of his resignation that things between them could go no further. He was used to distancing himself when relationships ran their course. He never suffered agonies of conscience or regret. He cut loose and moved on. Why, then, should it be any different this time? But something about the way Bella had curled up in his arms with her head resting against his chest had made something work loose inside his chest. Every time he took a breath, he felt it catch.

During the long hours before dawn, he had found himself dreaming of a future with her, of them living together at Haverton Manor as husband and wife. Of her happy laughter filling the empty rooms and halls of the house. He even thought of other laughter—the laughter of children, *their children*, running through the house, turning it into the home it was meant to be.

He tried to blink away the thoughts but they came back like moths circling around a light.

He could have it all.

He could have Bella *and* Haverton Manor.

They could build a family together, a solid, happy future.

She could leave him just like her mother had left Godfrey: devastated, alone, miserable.

The old panic seized him. How long before Bella wanted the bright lights of the city instead of his company? How long before her interest in him waned—a week? A month? A year? How could he live on that knife-edge? Every day would be an agony of wondering if it was going to be the last. He was used to disappointment. He had taught himself to always be prepared for it. It was easier to have nothing than to have everything and then lose it.

But then an even more disturbing thought joined the others. What if she didn't care for him at all? What if her little fling with him had been nothing more than payback all along? She had been vocal right from the start about her fury at him inheriting her childhood home. What better way to get back at him than pretend to be in love with him only to walk away so the press could pity or pillory him in equal measure?

He turned to his computer in an effort to distract himself, but as he pulled up the newspapers online, his eyes started to narrow in anger. It seemed he didn't have to wait in agonised anticipation for Bella's betrayal.

It was already there for everyone to see.

Bella came downstairs after sleeping in until ten in the morning. Edoardo had kept her awake for hours making passionate love with her. She could still feel the movement of his body in hers with each step she took. She wondered if he was feeling the wrench as she was about leaving for London the following day. Was that why there had been that edge of desperation in his lovemaking last night? He had held her for hours, his arms wrapped around her as if he never wanted to let her go. She had longed for him to say the words she most longed to hear, but he had said nothing. She was hoping her trip back to London would show him how much she had come to mean to him. Surely he would soon see how empty the days and nights were without her?

He was proud and private. It would take him a while to see what he was throwing away; it would take him even longer to admit to it. But after last night she felt a little glow of confidence burning inside her. It had *felt* like he loved her last night. He hadn't said the words out loud but his body had said them for him. All he needed was some time to come to terms with his feelings. He was used to locking them away. He was used to denying them. But how long could he deny the powerful connection they had forged? It wasn't just great sex. It was a connection that went far deeper than that. She felt close to him in a way she had never felt with anyone before. He had let her in to the most private part of his being. She *knew* him now. She knew his values, his strengths and weaknesses, his true self.

Bella pushed open the study door and found him standing stiffly in front of the window. 'Edoardo?' she said.

He turned and raked her from head to foot with his

gaze. It wasn't one of his smouldering 'I want to make love with you' looks. It was much more menacing than that. 'I've spoken with the lawyer,' he said in a cold, hard voice that was nothing like the deep, sexy rumble she had heard during the night and early hours of the morning.

'Pardon?'

He shoved a sheaf of papers towards her on the desk. 'You're on your own,' he said. 'I'm no longer your financial guardian.'

Bella swallowed and took an uncertain step towards the desk. 'What are you talking about? What do you mean? I don't understand...'

His eyes were like blue-green chips of ice. 'I want you out of here within the hour,' he said. 'Don't bother packing. I'll get Mrs Baker to do it when she comes back, plus everything else of yours left in the nursery. I want nothing of yours left in this house.'

'Edoardo... What are you say—?'

'It was a good plan.' His hands were tight fists by his rigid sides. 'Very convincing, too. Not many people manage to pull the wool over my eyes but I have to hand it to you—you came pretty damn close.'

Bella felt a chill freeze her spine. 'What plan? I'm not following you. You're not making sense. Why are you being so beastly all of a sudden?'

He swung the computer screen around so she could see it. 'That's what you've done,' he said. 'You planned it from the start, didn't you? It was the perfect revenge. I can't believe how well you set me up.'

Bella looked at the computer screen where he had pulled up a selection of online newspapers. The headlines made her heart screech to a stop:

Self-Made Tycoon's Tragic Past Revealed
Former Bad Boy Victim of Child Abuse
Affair with Heiress Heals Wounded Heartthrob

There was a photograph of Edoardo kissing her in front of Haverton Manor. It had been taken only a couple of days ago—obviously through a telephoto lens, as Bella couldn't recall seeing anyone about. But then she remembered the journalists she had run into in the village. Had they been spying on them? Had they dug a little deeper in to his past? She looked up at him in bewilderment. 'You think *I* set this up?' she asked.

'Don't give me that doe-eyed, innocent look,' he said through tight lips. 'Get the hell out of here before I throw you out.'

'I didn't do this,' Bella said. 'How can you *think* I would do something like this? Don't you know me at all?'

His eyes flashed pure hatred at her. 'You were the *only* person who could have done it,' he said. 'I've told no one about my past. Not a damn soul. Now the whole bloody world knows about it, thanks to you. I knew I shouldn't have trusted you. You've always been a little two-faced cow. You wanted to get me back for not agreeing to your engagement. Well, you can marry whomever you like. I don't give a damn.'

Bella was reeling with shock, hurt and disbelief. 'I can't believe you think I would do this to you on purpose,' she said. 'There were journalists in the village when I went down for milk yesterday. I didn't tell you because—'

'Because you lured them down here with a tell-all exclusive, didn't you?' he said with a snarl. 'What did you think that last headline was going to do—force me to get down on bended knee and ask you to marry me?'

Bella glanced at the *Affair with Heiress Heals Wounded Heartthrob* headline. She swallowed tightly and looked at him again. 'I didn't say anything to them about...' She flushed and dropped her gaze. 'I might have mentioned something to my mother...'

He let out an expletive. 'So the two of you cooked this up, did you?' he said. 'I should've guessed. That's why she came down a couple of days ahead of you, to scope out the scene.'

'No,' Bella said, her heart sinking in despair. 'That's not what happened at all. I didn't do it on purpose. I just mentioned you'd had a terrible childhood. She was saying mean things about you and I thought—'

'You thought you'd have a cosy little gossip and destroy everything I've worked so hard for,' he said bitterly.

'Why does people knowing about your past destroy anything?' Bella asked. 'You've got nothing to be ashamed of. People will admire you for being so resilient. I know they will.'

His eyes glittered with contempt. 'I don't expect you

to understand,' he bit out. 'You love all the attention. You're never out of the damn papers. You couldn't have picked a better way to get back at me. I value my privacy about everything. You *knew* that.' He curled his lip. 'All that talk of love and wanting the fairy tale—what a load of rubbish. You don't love anyone but yourself. You never have.'

Bella was struggling not to break down. Only her pride kept her from having an emotional meltdown. She was so hurt, so devastated that he believed her to be capable of such loathsome behaviour. But it wasn't just his lack of trust that hurt her the most. He was pushing her away, locking her out, *rejecting* her. It was so crushing to be dismissed as if she had meant nothing to him other than a temporary diversion—a pretty toy that hadn't turned out to be all it had promised to be. If he cared even an iota for her, wouldn't he be doing everything to try to understand how this had come about? Wouldn't he understand that her openness was not wrong, just different from his need for privacy? 'I guess that's it, then,' she said, straightening her shoulders. 'I'll get on my way.'

'I never want to see you again,' he said as he glowered at her broodingly. 'Do you understand? Never.'

'Don't worry,' she said with a toss of her head as she swung away to the door. 'You won't.'

CHAPTER ELEVEN

IT WAS weeks before the furore in the press died down. Just about every person who had ever had anything to do with Edoardo during his childhood came out of the woodwork to give an exclusive. The worst of it was that even though his stepfather was now dead, his new wife and family sprang to his defence as if he had been a plaster saint. No doubt having been assured that no one could prosecute a dead man, they made him out to be the victim of a smear campaign.

It totally disgusted Bella. She felt sick every time she saw another article. She felt to blame, even though all she had tried to do was make her mother understand how difficult his childhood had been for Edoardo.

Her mother was unrepentant, however. Bella had hoped Claudia might contact Edoardo and apologise, but her mother seemed to relish the fact that his tragic past was being talked about by every man and woman on the street.

Bella had thought about contacting him herself and explaining that it had been her mother who had given the tell-all interview to the press, but she knew he wouldn't believe her. He didn't trust her. He didn't trust anyone.

The lawyer had contacted Bella and she now had full control of her finances. But it was a bittersweet victory. She had more money than she knew what to do with.

But she felt terribly, achingly lonely.

The nights were the worst. Her friends would try to get her to go out with them to party or for dinner but she preferred to stay at home, curl up on the sofa and mindlessly watch whatever was on television. Sometimes she didn't even have the energy to switch it on; instead she would sit staring blankly into space, wondering how someone with so much wealth could be so miserably, desperately unhappy.

Julian had been gracious about her breaking off their relationship, which more or less confirmed that her decision to end it had been the right one. He had seemed more concerned that she would still donate a large sum to his mission. If he had truly loved her, wouldn't he have fought just a little bit for her?

Which brought her thoughts right back to Edoardo. He hadn't fought for her either. He hadn't even given her the benefit of the doubt. He had evicted her from his life as if she meant nothing to him.

Bella blew out a breath and tossed the sofa cushion to the floor. There was no point thinking about Edoardo. She was going to be on the other side of the world this time next week. She had organised a trip to Thailand to visit the orphanage she was now the proud patron of. So far she had managed to keep *that* out of the press. She couldn't wait to get away and put this whole dreadful episode behind her.

Edoardo was brooding over some plans for a big development he was working on in a nearby county when Mrs Baker came in with his coffee. He had a migraine starting at the backs of his eyes, the third one he'd had this week. It felt like dress-making pins were being drilled into each eyeball. 'Thanks,' he said, briefly glancing at her.

Mrs Baker stood with her arms folded across her ample chest, her lips pressed firmly together.

'Is there a problem?' he asked.

'Have you seen today's papers?'

He kept his gaze trained on the plans in front of him. 'I haven't looked at the paper in weeks,' he said. 'There's nothing of interest to me in them.'

Mrs Baker took a folded up paper out of her apron pocket and handed it to him. 'I think you need to see this,' she said. 'It's about our Bella.'

Edoardo looked at the folded newspaper without touching it. 'Take it away,' he said and returned to his plans. 'I have no interest in what she's up to. It has nothing to do with me any more.'

Mrs Baker unfolded the paper and started to read. '"Society heiress Arabella Haverton has been named as the much-speculated about, anonymous patron for an orphanage in Thailand. Miss Haverton has reputedly already spent hundreds of thousands of pounds on food, clothing and toys for the children. She refused to confirm or deny the rumour when she boarded a flight to Bangkok yesterday."' She lowered the paper and gave Edoardo a beady look. 'Well, what do you think?'

He leaned back in his chair, rolling a pen between his finger and thumb. 'Good for her,' he said.

Mrs Baker frowned. 'Is that all you can say?'

He tossed the pen to the desk. 'What do you want me to say?' he asked. 'I don't care what she spends her money on. I told you—it's nothing to do with me any more.'

The housekeeper puffed herself up like a broody hen. 'What if something happens to her over there?' she asked. 'What if she gets some horrible tropical disease?'

He gave her a bored look before turning back to his papers. 'They do have doctors over there, you know.'

Mrs Baker's voice choked up. 'What if she decides to stay there?' she asked. 'What if she *never* comes back?'

Edoardo drew in a short breath and glowered at her. 'Why should that be of any concern to me?' he asked. 'I'm glad to see the back of her.' *Liar,* he thought. *You miss her so much, you're almost sick with it.*

'You're not,' Mrs Baker said, speaking his thoughts out loud. 'You're miserable. You're like a bear with a sore head. You're not the same man since she was down here with you. Even Fergus is off his food.'

Edoardo picked up his pen again and started clicking it for something to do with his hands. He wasn't sure he liked being *that* transparent. Next thing, he would be made a fool of in the press for being heartbroken over his failed relationship with Bella. That would be the last straw. He was not going to be painted as a lovesick fool, not if he could help it. 'That's because Fergus is old,' he said.

'Yes, well, one day you'll be old too,' Mrs Baker said. 'And what will you have to show for your life? A fancy house and more money than you can poke a stick at, but no one to mop your brow when you have one of your headaches, no one to smile at you and tell you they love you more than life itself. A blind man could see Bella isn't capable of spilling her guts to the press. She's open with people, but that's what's so loveable about her. She wears her heart on her sleeve. No, that leak to the press was the work of her mother.' She slapped the paper on his desk. 'You can read all about Claudia Alvarez's exclusive interview on her daughter's charity efforts on page twenty.'

Edoardo frowned as he looked at the paper lying on his desk. He had already considered the possibility that Bella wasn't responsible for that leak to the press. He knew what journalists were like. And, yes, Mrs Baker was right; Bella was like an open book when it came to her feelings.

But it didn't change a thing.

He didn't want to expose himself to the pain of loving someone, especially someone like Bella. She was flighty and impulsive. How long would it be before she fell in love with someone else? He would feel abandoned all over again. He couldn't bear to feel that wretched feeling of having no one—no one at all.

He was fine on his own. He was used to it.
He would get used to it again.

Sure, it had been miserably lonely around here without her. The house seemed too big for him now; the empty rooms mocked him as he wandered past. His bedroom was the worst. He could barely stand to be in there with the lingering trace of Bella's perfume haunting him. The long, wide corridors echoed with his solitary footsteps. It even felt colder in spite of him cranking up the heating. Even Fergus kept looking up at him with a hangdog look on his face, reminding him that all the colour and joy had gone out of his life. *He* had sent it out of his life. He had sent Bella away when the one thing he wanted was to have her close.

He raised his gaze back to the housekeeper's. 'Don't you have work to do?' he asked.

Mrs Baker pursed her lips. 'That girl loves you,' she said. 'And you love her but you're too darned stubborn to tell her. You're even too stubborn to admit it to yourself.'

'Will that be all?' he asked with an arched brow.

'She's probably crying herself to sleep every night,' she said. 'Her father would be spinning in his grave; I'm sure of it. He thought you would do the right thing by her. But you've abandoned her when she needed you the most.'

He pushed back his chair and got to his feet. 'I don't want to listen to this.' *I know I've been a stupid fool. I don't need my housekeeper to tell me. I need time to think how I'm going to dig my way out of this and win*

Bella back. Is there a way to win her back? Isn't it already too late?

Mrs Baker's eyes watered up. 'This is her home,' she said. 'She belongs here.'

'I know,' he said as he expelled a long, uneven breath. 'That's why I'm sending her the deeds. The lawyers are sorting it out as we speak.'

Mrs Baker's eyes rounded. 'You're not going to live here any more?'

'No.' Giving up Haverton Manor was the easy bit. Losing Bella was the thing that gutted him the most. What had he been thinking? *Had* he been thinking? What would the rest of his life be like if she went off and married someone else? What if she had *their* children instead of his? How could he bear it? He wanted her. He *loved* her. He adored her. She was his world, his future, his *heart*. But it was too late. He had hurt her terribly. She would never forgive him now. He didn't dare hope she would. He was already preparing himself for the disappointment. It was best if he took himself out of the picture and let her get on with her life. He had never belonged in it in the first place.

'But what about Fergus?' Mrs Baker asked.

'Bella can look after him,' he said. 'He's her father's dog, after all.'

'But that old dog loves you,' she said. 'How can you just walk away?'

He gave her a grim look. 'It's for the best.'

Bella spent the first few days at the orphanage in a state of deep culture-shock. She barely ate or slept. It wasn't that the children weren't being cared for properly, more that she couldn't quite get her head or her heart around the fact that the little babies and children she played with daily had nobody in their lives other than the orphanage workers. She spent most nights sobbing herself to sleep at their heartbreaking plight. Each day from dawn till late at night she gathered them close and tried to give them all the love and joy they had missed out on. She showered them with affection and praise. She played with them and read to them; she even sang to them with the few nursery rhymes she remembered from her own early childhood before her mother had left.

'You will exhaust yourself if you don't take a proper break now and again,' Tasanee, one of the senior workers, said during Bella's second week.

Bella kissed the top of an eight-week-old baby girl's downy head as she cradled her close against her chest. 'I don't want to put Lawan down until she goes to sleep,' she said. 'She cries unless someone is holding her. She must be missing her mother. She must sense she's never coming back.' *And I know what it's like to feel so alone and abandoned.*

'It is sad that her mother and father died,' Tasanee said as she touched the baby's cheek with her finger. 'But we have a couple lined up to adopt her. The paperwork is being processed. She will have a good life. It is easier for the babies; they don't remember their real parents. It's the older ones who have the most trouble adjusting.'

Bella looked across to where a group of children were

playing. There was a little boy of about five who was standing on the outside of the group. He didn't join in the noisy game. He didn't interact with anyone. He just stood there watching everything with a serious look on his face. He reminded her of Edoardo. How frightening it must have been for him to feel so alone, to face daily the horrible abuse from a vindictive stepfather. Bella ached for the little boy he had once been. She ached for the future she so desperately wanted with him but now could never have. She determined she would do all she could for each and every one of these children so that they would not suffer what he had suffered.

'Miss Haverton?' Sumalee, another one of the orphanage helpers, came across to Bella once she had put Lawan down for her nap. 'This came for you in the post.'

Bella took the A4 envelope. 'Thanks.' She peeled it open and took out the document inside. Her eyes nearly popped out of her head when she saw what it was. 'I think there's been a mistake...'

'What's wrong?' Sumalee asked.

Bella gnawed at her lip as she shuffled through the other papers that had come with the deeds to Haverton Manor. 'I think I might have to go back to Britain to sort this out...'

'Will you come back soon?' Sumalee said.

Bella tucked the document back inside the envelope and gave the young girl a quick, reassuring smile. 'Don't worry. I'll be back as soon as I can,' she said. 'I have to see a man about a dog.'

* * *

Edoardo was loading the last of his things in his car when he saw a sports car come speeding up the driveway. Fergus got up from the front step and started wagging his tail, a soft whine sounding from his throat. 'For God's sake, don't gush,' Edoardo said out of the side of his mouth. 'She's probably only back to argue over some of the fine print.'

Bella got out of the car and came towards him, bringing the scent of spring flowers with her. 'What the hell is going on?' she asked, waving a sheet of paper at him.

'It's yours,' Edoardo said. 'The manor is yours, and so is Fergus.'

Her brows jammed together over her nose. 'Are you without *any* feeling at all?' she asked. 'That dog loves you. How can you just—' she waved her hands about theatrically '—just hand him over like a parcel you don't want?'

'I can't take him with me.'

'Why not?' she asked. 'Where are you going?'

'Away.'

'Away where?'

He slammed the boot. 'I don't belong here. It's your home, not mine.'

She shoved the papers at him. 'I don't want it.'

He shoved the papers back. 'I don't want it either,' he said.

She glowered at him. 'Why are you doing this?'

'Your father was wrong to give me your home,' he said. 'This is your last connection with him. I don't feel right about taking it from you.'

'It's your last connection with him too,' she said.

He gave a shrug. 'Yes, well, I have plenty of memories that will make up for that.'

'You can't just walk away,' Bella said. 'What about Fergus? I thought you loved him.'

Edoardo bent down and ruffled the old dog's ears. 'I do love him,' he said. 'He's been an amazing friend.' He straightened. 'But it's time I moved on.'

'So you're just going to leave?' she asked.

'It's for the best, Bella,' he said.

'The best for whom?' she asked. 'Fergus is going to pine for you; you know he will. And what about Mrs Baker? She's devoted her life to looking after you. Are you just going to walk away from everyone who loves you?'

He opened the driver's door of his car. 'Goodbye, Bella.'

Bella put her hands on her hips. 'You're not going to say it, are you?' she said. 'You're too proud or too stubborn or both to admit that you care for someone. That you *need* someone, that you actually *love* someone.'

His eyes met hers. 'Will telling you I love you erase the horrible things I said to you?' he asked.

She gave a huffy lift of one shoulder, her expression still cross. 'I don't know... It wouldn't hurt to try.'

Edoardo felt a corner of his mouth lift up. How cute was she, with that haughty look on her face? She was trying to be angry but he could see the love shining through the cracks of her armour. It gave him hope. It eased the painful ache of impending disappointment he always carried with him. 'Will telling you I love you make you forgive me for sending you away like that?' he asked.

She gave another little shrug, but this time a tiny sparkle came into her eyes. 'I don't mind a bit of grovelling when it's warranted,' she said.

Edoardo looked into her toffee-brown eyes and felt a giant wave of emotion roll through him. How could he not love her? Hadn't he *always* loved her? When had he *not* loved her? 'I guess I'd better get started, then,' he said. 'This could take a while. You're not in a hurry, are you?'

Her eyes glinted some more. 'I'll make the time,' she said. 'I wouldn't want to miss this for the world.'

He took a breath as he captured both of her hands in his. 'I'm sorry for what I said, for how I treated you, for how I pushed you away.' He pulled her into his chest, burying his head against the side of her neck. 'I'm not the right person for you. I don't know how to love someone without holding back.'

'Yes, you do,' she said, pulling back to look up at him with adoring eyes. 'You do know how to love. I've seen it in so many ways. You're exactly like my father. You don't say it with words. You say it in actions.'

He stroked her face as if he couldn't quite believe she was here in person. 'I've missed you so much,' he said. 'I can't believe I sent you away like that. It was cruel and heartless. But if it's any consolation, I hurt myself just as much. Maybe that's why I did it. On some deeply subconscious level, I didn't feel I deserved to be loved by you.'

'I didn't betray you to the press,' she said with a solemn look. 'Not intentionally, at least. I just didn't like the way everyone was making you out to be the one at fault. It made me so angry. I wanted to put them straight.'

'I know you didn't do it on purpose,' he said. 'I think I knew that from the start. I was just looking for an excuse to send you away. You got too close. I wasn't able to handle it. I've spent most of my life pushing people away—even people who cared about me.'

Bella nestled closer. 'I love you,' she said. 'I love everything about you. I think I probably always have.'

He put her from him so he could meet her gaze. 'I think your father knew that,' he said. 'He was so afraid you would rush off and marry the first man who asked you. He made me promise to keep you from marrying anyone before you were twenty-five. But it looks like I'm going to have to break my promise to him after all.'

She looked at him quizzically. 'What do you mean?'

'Will you marry me?' he asked.

Bella gaped at him. 'But I thought you never wanted to…?'

'That was before,' he said. 'I've seen the error of my ways. Besides, what am I going to say to Mrs Baker? She's going to have my guts for garters if I don't do the right thing by you.'

Bella looped her arms around his neck and smiled at him. 'We can't have Mrs Baker upset, now, can we?'

He grinned at her. 'So, is that a yes?'

Her eyes were brimming with happy tears as she looked up at him. 'When have I ever been able to say no to you?'

He cupped her face in his hands and locked his gaze on hers. 'I love you. I've never said that to anyone before, but I plan to say it every day for the rest of our lives.'

She smiled up at him radiantly. 'I love you too.'

'I want to have a baby with you,' he said, rubbing his nose against hers. 'Maybe even two babies. And then maybe we can adopt a couple of children.'

'I want that too,' she said, letting out a little sigh of bliss. 'I want it so much.'

'Then we'd better get started, don't you think?' he said.

'What?' she said, pretending to be shocked. 'Right now?'

'Right now,' he said and scooped her up in his arms and carried her towards the house.

* * * * *

IF YOU CAN'T STAND THE HEAT...

JOSS WOOD

For their love and support, I have so many friends to thank. Old friends, new friends, coffee friends and crying friends. Friends who know me inside out and friends I've just met. But, because we share a friendship based on raucous laughter, craziness, sarcasm, loyalty and love, this book is especially dedicated to Tracy, Linda and Kerry.

Joss Wood wrote her first book at the age of eight and has never really stopped. Her passion for putting letters on a blank screen is matched only by her love of books and travelling—especially to the wild places of Southern Africa—and possibly by her hatred of ironing and making school lunches.

Fuelled by coffee, when she's not writing or being a hands-on mum, Joss, with her background in business and marketing, works for a non-profit organisation to promote the local economic development and collective business interests of the area where she resides. Happily and chaotically surrounded by books, family and friends, she lives in KwaZulu-Natal, South Africa, with her husband, children and their many pets.

CHAPTER ONE

'ELLIE, YOUR PHONE is ringing! Ellie, answer it now!'

Ellie Evans grinned at her best friend Merri's voice emanating from her mobile in her personalised ring tone, then eagerly scooped up the phone and slapped it against her ear.

'El?'

'Hey, you—how's the Princess?' Ellie asked, sorting through the invoices on her desk, which essentially meant that she just moved them from one pile to another.

'The Princess' was her goddaughter, Molly Blue, a six-month-old diva who had them all wrapped around her chubby pinkie finger. Merri launched into a far too descriptive monologue about teething and nappies, interrupted sleep and baby food. Ellie—who was still having a hard time reconciling her party-lovin', heel-kickin', free-spirited friend with motherhood—*mmm*-ed in all the right places and tuned out.

'Okay, I get the hint. I'm boring,' Merri stated, yanking Ellie's attention back. 'But you normally make an effort to at least pretend to listen. So what's up?'

Her friend since they were teenagers, Merri knew her inside out. And as she was her employee as well as her best friend she had to tell her the earth-shattering news. Sitting in her tiny office on the second floor of her bakery and delicatessen, Ellie bit her lip and stared at her messy desk. Panic, bitter and insistent, crept up her throat.

She pulled in a deep breath. 'The Khans have sold the building.'

'Which building?'

'This building, Merri. We have six months before we have to move out.'

Ellie heard Merri's swift intake of breath.

'But why would they sell?' she wailed.

'They are in their seventies, and I would guess they're tired of the hassle. They probably got a fortune for the property. We all know that it's the best retail space for miles.'

'Just because it sits on the corner of the two main roads into town and is directly opposite the most famous beach in False Bay it doesn't mean it's the best...'

'That's exactly what it means.'

Ellie looked out of the sash window to the beach and the lazy ocean beyond it. It had been a day since she'd been slapped with the news and she no longer had butterflies about Pari's, the bakery that had been in her family for over forty years. They had all been eaten by the bats on some psycho-drug currently swarming in her stomach.

'Why can't we just rent from the new owners?'

'I asked. They are going to do major renovations to attract corporate shops and intend on hiking the rents accordingly. We couldn't afford it. And, more scarily, Lucy—'

'The estate agent?'

'Mmm. Well, she told me that retail space is at a premium in St James, and there are "few, if any" properties suitable for a bakery-slash-coffee-shop-slash-delicatessen for sale or to rent.'

After four decades of being a St James and False Bay institution Pari's future was uncertain, and as the partner-in-residence Ellie had to deal with this life-changing situation.

She had no idea what they—she—was going to do.

'Have you told your mum?' Merri asked quietly.

'I can't get hold of her. She hasn't made contact for ten days.

I think she's booked into an ashram…or sunning herself in Goa,' Ellie replied, her voice weary. Where she *wasn't* was in the bakery, with her partner/daughter, helping her sort out the mess they were in.

Your idea, Ellie reminded herself. *You said she could go. You suggested that she take the year off, have some fun, follow her dream...* What *had* she been thinking? In all honesty it had been a mostly symbolic offer; nobody had been more shocked—horrified!—than her when Ashnee had immediately run off to pack her bags and book her air ticket. She'd never thought Ashnee would leave the bakery, leave *her*…

'El, I know that this isn't a good time, especially in light of what you've just told me, but I can't put it off any longer. I need to ask you a huge favour.'

Ellie frowned when she picked up the serious note in Merri's voice.

'Anything, provided that you are still coming back to work on Monday,' Ellie quipped. Merri was a phenomenal baker and Ellie had desperately missed her talent in the bakery while she took her maternity leave.

The silence following her statement slapped her around the head. Oh, no…no, no, *no*! 'Merri, I need you,' she pleaded.

'My baby needs me too, El.' Merri sounded miserable. 'And I'm not ready to come back to work just yet. I will be, but not just yet. Maybe in another month. She's so little and I need to be with her…please? Tell me you understand, Ellie.'

I understand that I haven't filled your position because I was holding it open for you—because you asked me to. I understand that I'm running myself ragged, that the clients miss you…

'Another month?' Merri coaxed. 'Pretty please?'

Ellie rubbed her forehead. What could she say? Merri didn't need to work, thanks to her very generous father, so if she forced her to choose between the bakery and Molly Blue the bakery would lose. *She* would lose...

Ellie swallowed, told herself that if she pushed Merri to come back and she didn't then it was her decision...but she felt the flames of panic lick her throat. They were big girls, and their friendship was more than the job they shared—it would survive her leaving the bakery—but she didn't want to take the chance. Her head knew that she was overreacting but her heart didn't care.

She had too much at stake as it was. She couldn't risk losing her in any way. She'd coped for over six months; she'd manage another month. Somehow.

Ellie bit her top lip. 'Sure, Merri.'

'You're the best—but I've got to dash. The Princess is bellowing.' Now Ellie could hear Molly's insistent wail. 'I'll try to get to the bakery later this week and we can talk about what we're going to do. Byeee! Love you.'

'Love you...' Ellie heard the beep-beep that told her the call had been dropped and tossed her mobile on the desk in front of her.

'El, there's someone to see you out front.'

Ellie glanced from the merry face of Samantha, one of her servers, peeking around her door to the old-fashioned clock above her head, and frowned. The bakery and coffee shop had closed ten minutes ago, so who could it be?

'Who is it?'

Samantha shrugged. 'Dunno. He just said to tell you that your father sent him. He's alone out front...we're all heading home.'

'Thanks, Sammy.' Ellie frowned and swivelled around to look at the screens on the desk behind her. There were cameras in the front of the shop, in the bakery and in the storeroom, and they fed live footage into the monitors.

Ellie's brows rose as she spotted him, standing off to the

side of a long display of glass-fronted fridges, a rucksack hanging off his very broad shoulders. Week-long stubble covered his jaw and his auburn hair was tousled from finger raking.

Jack Chapman. Okay, she was officially surprised. Any woman who watched any one of the premier news channels would recognise that strong face under the shaggy hair. Ellie wasn't sure whether he was more famous for his superlative and insightful war reporting or for being the definition of eye candy.

Grubby low-slung jeans and even grubbier boots. A dark untucked T-shirt. He ran a hand through his hair and, seeing a clasp undone on the side pocket of his rucksack, bent down to fix it. Ellie watched the long muscles bunching under his thin shirt, the curve of a very nice butt, the strength of his brown neck.

Oh, *yum*—oh, stop it now! Get a grip! The important questions were: why was he here, what did he want and what on earth was her father thinking?

Ellie lifted her head as Samantha tapped on the doorframe again and stood there, shuffling on her feet and biting her lip. She recognised that look. 'What's up, Sammy?'

Samantha looked at her with big brown eyes. 'I know that I promised to work for you tomorrow night to help with the *petits fours* for that fashion show—'

'But?'

'But I've been offered a ticket to see Linkin Park and they are my favourite band...it's a free ticket and you know how much I love them.'

Ellie considered giving her a lecture on responsibility and keeping your word, on how promises shouldn't be broken, but the kid was nineteen and it *was* Linkin Park. She remembered being that age and the thrill of a kick-ass concert.

And Samantha, battling to put herself through university, couldn't afford to pay for a ticket herself. She'd remember it for for ever…so what if it meant that Ellie had to work a couple of hours longer? It wasn't as if she had a life or anything.

'Okay, I'll let you off the hook.' Ellie winced at Samantha's high-pitched squeal. 'This time. Now, get out of here.'

Ellie grinned as she heard her whooping down the stairs, but the grin faded when she glanced at the monitor again. Scowling, she reached for her mobile, hastily scrolling through her address book before pushing the green button.

'Ellie—hello.' Her father's deep voice crooned across the miles.

'Dad, why is Jack Chapman in my bakery?'

Ellie heard her father's sharp intake of breath. 'He's there already? Good. I was worried.'

Of course you were, Ellie silently agreed. For the past ten years, since her eighteenth birthday, she'd listened to her father rumble on and on about Jack Chapman—the son he'd always wanted and never got. 'He's the poster-boy for a new generation of war correspondents,' he'd said. 'Unbiased, tough. Willing to dive into a story without thinking about his safety, looking for the story behind the story, yet able to push aside emotion to look for the truth…' Yada, yada, yada…

'So, again, why is he here?' Ellie asked.

And, by the way, why do you only call when you want something from me? Oh, wait, you didn't call. I did! You just sent your boy along, expecting me to accommodate your every whim.

Some things never changed.

'He was doing an interview with a Somalian warlord who flipped. He was stripped of his cash and credit cards, delivered at gunpoint to a United Nations aid plane leaving for Cape Town and bundled onto it,' Mitchell Evans said in a clipped voice. 'I need you to give him a bed.'

Jeez, Dad, do I have a B&B sign tattooed on my forehead?

Ellie, desperate to move beyond her default habit of trying

to please her father, tried to say no, but a totally different set of words came out of her mouth. 'For how long?'

God, she was such a wimp.

'Well, here's the thing, sugar-pie...'

Oh, good grief. Her father had a *thing*. A lifetime with her father had taught her that a thing *never* worked out in her favour. 'Jack is helping me write a book on the intimate lives of war reporters—mine included.'

Interesting—but she had no idea what any of this had to do with *her*. But Mitchell didn't like being interrupted, so Ellie waited for him to finish.

'He needs to talk to my family members. I thought he could stay a little while, talk to you about life with me...'

Sorry...life with him? What life with him? During her parents' on-off marriage their home had been a place for her mum to do his laundry rather than to live. He'd lived his life in all the countries people were trying to get out of: Iraq, Gaza, Bosnia. Home was a place he'd dropped in and out of. Work had always been his passion, his muse, his lifelong love affair.

Resentment nibbled at the wall of her stomach. Depending on what story had been consuming him at the time, Mitchell had missed every single important event of her childhood. Christmas concerts and ballet recitals, swimming galas and father-daughter days. How could he be expected to be involved in his daughter's life when there were bigger issues in the world to write about, analyse, study?

What he'd never realised was that he was her biggest issue...the creator of her angst, the source of her abandonment issues, the spring that fed the fountain of her self-doubt.

Ellie winced at her melodramatic thoughts. Her childhood with Mitchell had been fraught with drama but it was over. However, in situations like these, old resentments bubbled up and over.

Her father had been yakking on for a while and Ellie refocused on what he was saying.

'The editors and I want Jack to include his story—he *is* the brightest of today's bunch—but getting Jack to talk about himself is like trying to find water in the Gobi Desert. He's not interested. He's as much an enigma to me as he was when we first met. So will you talk to him?' Mitchell asked. 'About me?'

Oh, good grief. Did she have to? Really?

'Maybe.' Which they both knew meant that she would. 'But, Dad, seriously? You can't just dump your waifs and strays on me.' He could—of course he could. He was Mitchell Evans and she was a push-over.

'Waif and stray? Jack is anything but!'

Ellie rubbed her temple. Could this day throw anything else at her head? The bottom line was that another of Mitchell's colleagues was on her doorstep and she could either take him in or turn him away. Which she wouldn't do…because then her father wouldn't be pleased and he'd sulk, and in twenty years' time he'd remind her that she'd let him down. Really, it was just easier to give the guy a bed for the night and bask in Mitchell's approval for twenty seconds. If that.

If only they were *normal* people, Ellie thought. The last colleague of her father's she'd had to stay—again at Mitchell's request—had got hammered on her wine and tried to paw her before passing out on her Persian carpet. And every cameraman, producer and correspondent she'd ever met—including her father—was crazy, weird, strange or odd. She figured that it was a necessary requirement if you wanted to chase down and report on human conflicts and disasters.

Mitchell's voice, now that he'd got his own way, sounded jaunty again. 'Jack's a good man. He's probably not slept for days, hasn't eaten properly for more than a week. A bed, a meal, a bath. It's not that much to ask because you're a good person, my sweet, sweet girl.'

My sweet, sweet girl? Tuh!

Sweet, sweet sucker, more like.

Ellie sneaked another look at Mr-Hot-Enough-to-Melt-Heavy-Metal. He did have a body to die for, she thought.

'Have you met Jack before?' Mitchell asked.

'Briefly. At your wedding to Steph.' Wife number three, who'd stuck around for six months. Ellie had been eighteen, chronically shy, and Jack had barely noticed her.

'Oh, yeah—Steph. I liked her...I still don't know why she left,' Mitchell said, sounding plausibly bemused.

Gee, Dad, here's a clue. Maybe, like me, she hated the idea of the man she adored being away for five of those six months, plunging into the situation in Afghanistan and only popping up occasionally on TV. Hated not knowing whether you were alive or dead. It's no picnic loving someone who doesn't love you a fraction as much as you love your job.

She, her mother and Mitchell's two subsequent wives had come second-best time after time...decade after decade. And she'd repeated the whole stupid cycle by getting engaged to Darryl.

She'd vowed she'd never fall in love with a journalist and she hadn't. But life had bust a gut laughing when she'd become engaged to a man she'd thought was the exact opposite of her father, only to realise that he spent even less time at home than her father had. That was quite an accomplishment, since he'd never, as far as she knew, left London itself.

She'd been such a sucker, Ellie thought. Still was...

Maybe one of these days she'd find her spine.

Ellie looked down at her mobile, realised that her father hadn't said goodbye before disconnecting and shrugged. Situation normal. She glanced at the monitor again and saw the impatience on Jack's face, caught his tapping foot. The muscles in his arms bulged as he folded them across his chest. Although the feed was in black and white she knew that his eyes were hazel…sometimes brown, sometimes green, gold, always compelling. Right now they were blazing with a combination of frustration, exhaustion and a very healthy dose of annoyance.

He was different from the twenty-four-year-old she'd met a decade ago. Older, harder, a bit damaged. Ellie felt an unfamiliar buzz in her womb and cocked her head as attraction skittered through her veins and caused her heartbeat to fuzz…

She tossed her mobile onto her desk and pushed her chair back as she stood up and blew out a breath.

It didn't matter that he was tall, built and had a sexy face that could stop traffic, she lectured herself. Crazy came in all packages.

'Jack?'

Jack Chapman, standing in the front section of the bakery—aqua stripes on the walls, black checked floors, white cabinets, a sunshine-yellow surfboard—whirled around at the low, melodious voice and blinked. Then blinked again. He knew he was tired, but this was ridiculous…

He'd been expecting the awkward, overweight, shy girl from Mitch's wedding not this…*babe*! This tropical, colourful, radiant, riveting, dazzling babe. With a capital B. In bold and italics.

Waist-length black hair streaked with purple and green stripes, milk-saturated coffee skin, vivid blue eyes and her father's pugnacious chin.

And slim, curvy legs that went up to her ears.

'Hi, I'm Ellie. Mitchell has asked me to put you up for the night.'

His pulse kicked up as he struggled to find his words. He eventually managed to spit a couple out. 'I'm grateful. Thank you.'

Whoa! Jack dropped his pack to the floor and resisted the

impulse to put his hand on his heart to check if it was okay. With his history…

You are not having a heart attack, you moron! Major overreaction here, dude, cool your jets!

So she wasn't who he'd been expecting? In his line of work little was as expected, so why was his heart jumping and his mouth dry?

Jack rocked on his heels, looked around and tried not to act like a gauche teenager. 'This is a really nice place. Do you own it?'

Ellie looked around and the corners of her mouth tipped up. 'Yep. My mum and I are partners.'

'Ah…' He looked at the empty display fridges. 'Where's the food? Shouldn't there be food?'

Her smile was a fist to his sternum.

'Most of the baked goods are sold out and we put the deli meats away every night.' She fiddled with the strap of her huge leather tote bag. 'So, how was your flight?' she asked politely.

Sitting on the floor of a cargo plane in turbulence, with bruised ribs and a pounding headache? Just peachy. 'Fine, thanks.'

The reality was that he was exhausted, achingly stiff and sore, and his side felt as if he had a red-hot poker lodged inside it. He wanted a shower and to sleep for a week. His glance slid to a fridge filled with soft drinks. And he'd kill someone for a Coke.

Ellie caught his look and waved to the fridge. 'Help yourself.'

Jack grimaced. 'I can't pay for it.'

'Pari's can afford to give you a can on the house,' Ellie said wryly.

The words were barely out of her mouth and he was opening the fridge, yanking out a red can and popping the tab. The tart, sugary liquid slid down his throat and he sighed, knowing the sugar and caffeine would give him another hour or two of energy. Maybe...

He swore under his breath as once again he realised that he was stuck halfway across the world. He couldn't even pay for a damn soft drink. He silently cursed again. He needed to borrow cash and a bed from Ellie until his replacement bank cards were delivered. He grimaced at the sour taste now in his mouth. Having to ask for help made him feel...out of control, helpless. Powerless.

He hated to feel beholden, but he reminded himself it would only be for a night—two, maximum.

Jack finished his drink and looked around for a bin.

Ellie took the can from him, walked behind the counter and tossed it away. 'Help yourself to another, if you like.'

'I'm okay. Thanks.'

Ellie's eyebrows lifted and their eyes caught and held. Jack thought that she was an amazing combination of east and west: skin from her Goan-born grandparents, and blue eyes and that chin from her Irish father. Her body was all her own and should come with a 'Danger' warning. Long legs, tiny waist, incredible breasts...

Because he was very, very good at reading body language, he saw wariness in her face, a lot of shyness and a hint of resignation. Could he blame her? He was a stranger, about to move into her house.

'Funky décor,' he said, trying to put her at ease. Hanging off the wall next to the front door was a fire-red canoe; its seating area sprouting gushing bunches of multi-coloured daisy-like flowers. 'I don't think I've ever seen surfboards and canoes used to decorate before. Or filled with flowers.'

Ellie laughed. 'I know; they are completely over the top, but such fun!'

'Those daisy things look real,' Jack commented.

'Gerbera daisies—and I don't think there's a point to flower arrangements if they aren't real,' Ellie replied.

He'd never thought about flowers that way. Actually, he'd never thought about flowers at all. 'What's with the signatures on the canoe?'

Ellie shrugged. 'I have no idea. I bought it like that.'

Jack shoved his hand into the pocket of his jeans and winced when the taxi driver leaned on his horn. Dammit, he'd forgotten about *him*. He felt humiliation tighten his throat. Now came the hard part, he thought, cursing under his breath. A soft drink was one thing...

'Look, I'm really sorry, but I've got myself into a bit of a sticky situation... Is there any chance you could pay the taxi fare for me? I'm good for it, I promise.'

'Sure.' Ellie reached into her bag, pulled out her purse and handed him a couple of bills.

Jack felt the tips of his fingers brush hers and winced at the familiar flame that licked its way up his arm. His body had decided that it was seriously attracted to her and there was nothing he could do about it.

Damn, Jack thought, as he stomped out through the door to pay his taxi fare. He really didn't feel comfortable being attracted to a woman he was beholden to, who was his mentor's beloved daughter and with whom he'd spend only two days before blowing out of her life.

Just ignore it, Jack told himself. *You're a grown man, firmly in control of your libido.*

He blew air into his cheeks as he handed the money over to the taxi driver and rubbed his hand over his face. The door behind him opened and he turned away from the road to see Ellie lugging his heavy rucksack through the door. Ignoring his burning side, he broke into a jog, quickly reached her and took his pack from her. The gangster bastards had taken his iPad, his satellite and mobile phones, his cash and credit cards, but had left him his dirty, disgusting clothes.

He would've left them too...

'Here—let me take that.' Jack took his rucksack from her.

'I just need to lock up and we can go,' Ellie said, before disappearing back inside the building.

Jack waited in the late-afternoon sun on the corner, his rucksack resting against an aqua pot planted with hot-pink flowers. He was beginning to suspect—from her multi-coloured hair and her bright bakery with its pink and purple exterior—that Ellie liked colour. Lots of it.

Mitchell had mentioned that Ellie was a baker and he'd expected her to be frumpy and housewifey, rotund and rosy—not slim, sexy and arty. Even her jewellery was creative: multi-length strands of beads in different shades of blue. He could say something about lucky beads to be against that chest, but decided that even the thought was pathetic...

He heard the door open behind him and she reappeared. She pulled the wooden and glass door shut, then yanked down the security grate and bolted and locked it.

Jack looked from the old-style bakery to the wide beach across the road and felt a smile form. It was nearly half-past six, a warm evening in summer, and the beach and boardwalk hummed with people.

'What time does the sun set?' he asked.

'Late. Eight-thirty-ish,' Ellie answered. She gestured to the road behind them. 'I live so close to work that I don't drive... um...my house is up that hill.'

Jack looked up the steep road to the mountain behind it and sighed. That was all he needed—a hike up a hill with a heavy pack. What else was this day going to throw at him?

He sighed again. 'Lead on.'

Ellie pulled a pair of over-large sunglasses from her bag and put them on, and they started to walk. They passed an antique store, a bookstore and an old-fashioned-looking pharmacy—he needed to stock up on some supplies there, but that would raise some awkward questions. He waited for Ellie to initiate the conversation. She did, moments later, good manners overcoming her increasingly obvious shyness.

'So, what happened to you?'

'Didn't your father tell you?'

'Only that you got jumped by a couple of thugs and were kicked out of Somalia. You need a place to stay because you're broke.'

'Temporarily broke,' Jack corrected her. Mitchell hadn't given her the whole story, thankfully. It was simple enough. He'd asked a question about the hijackings of passing ships which had pushed the warlord's 'detonate' button. He'd gone psycho and ordered his henchman to beat the crap out of him. He'd tried to resist, but six against one...bad odds.

Very bad odds. Jack shook off a shudder.

'So, is there anything else I can do for you apart from giving you a bed?'

Her question jerked him back to the present and his instinctive answer was, *A night with you in bed would be great*.

Seriously? *That* was what he was thinking?

Jack shook his head and ordered himself to get with the programme. 'Um...I just need to spend a night, maybe two. Borrow a mobile phone, a computer to send some e-mails, have an address to have my replacement bank cards delivered to...' Jack replied.

'I have a spare mobile, and you can use my old laptop. I'll write my address down for you. Are you on a deadline?'

'Not too bad. This is a print story for a political magazine.'

Ellie lifted her eyebrows. 'I thought you only did TV work?'

'I get the occasional assignment from newspapers and magazines. I freelance, so I write articles in between reporting for the news channels,' Jack replied.

Ellie shoved her sunglasses up into her hair and rubbed her eyes. 'So how are you going to write these articles? I presume your notes were taken.'

'I backed up my notes and documents onto a flash drive just before the interview. I slipped it into my shoe.' It was one of the many precautionary measures he took when operating in Third World countries.

'They let you keep your passport?'

Jack shrugged. 'They wanted me to leave and not having a passport would have hindered that.'

Ellie shook her head. 'You have a crazy job.'

He did, and he loved it. Jack shrugged. 'I operate best in a war zone, under pressure.' He loved having a rucksack on his back, dodging bullets and bombs to get the stories few other journalists found.

'Mitchell always said that it's a powerful experience to be holed up in a hotel in Mogadishu or Sarajevo with no water, electricity or food, playing poker with local contacts to the background music of bombs and automatic gunfire. I never understood that.'

Jack frowned at the note of bitterness in her voice and, quickly realising that there was a subtext beneath her words that he didn't understand, chose his next words carefully. 'Most people would consider it their worst nightmare—and to the people living and working in that war zone it is—but it *is* exciting, and documenting history is important.'

And the possibility of imminent death didn't frighten him at all. After all, he'd faced death before...

No, what would kill him would be being into a nine-to-five job, living in one city, doing the same thing day in and day out. He'd cheated death and received a second swipe at life... and the promise he'd made so long ago, to live life hard and fast and big, still fuelled him on a daily basis.

Jack felt a hard knot in his throat and tried to swallow it down. He was alive because someone else hadn't received the same second swipe...

'We're here.'

Ellie's statement interrupted his spiralling thoughts and Jack hid his sigh of relief as she turned up a driveway and approached a wrought-iron gate. Thank God. He wasn't sure if he could go much further.

Ellie looked at the remote in her hand, took a breath and briefly closed her eyes. He saw the tension in her shoulders and the rigid muscle in her jaw. She wasn't comfortable... Jack cursed. If he had been operating on more than twelve hours' sleep in four days he would have picked up that the shyness was actually tension a lot earlier. And it had increased the closer they came to her home.

'Look, you're obviously not happy about having me here,' Jack said, dropping his pack to the ground. 'Sorry. I didn't realise. I'll head back to the bakery—hitch a lift to the airport.'

Ellie jammed her hands into the pockets of her cut-offs. 'No—really, Jack...I told my father I'd help you.'

'I don't need your charity,' Jack said, pushing the words out between his clenched teeth.

'It's not charity.' Ellie lifted up a hand and rubbed her eyes with her thumb and index finger. 'It's just been a long day and I'm tired.'

That wasn't it. She was strung tighter than a guitar string. His voice softened. 'Ellie, I don't want you to feel uncomfortable in your own home. I told Mitch that I was happy to wait at the airport. It's not a big deal.'

Ellie straightened and looked him in the eye. 'I'm sorry. I'm the one who is making this difficult. Your arrival just pulled up some old memories. The last time I took in one of my father's workmates I was chased around my house by a drunken, horny cameraman.'

He sent her his I'm-a-good-guy grin. 'Typical. Those damn cameramen—you can't send them anywhere.'

Ellie smiled, as he'd intended her to. He could see some of her tension dissolve at his stab at humour.

'Sorry, I know I sound ridiculous. And I'm not crazy about talking about my relationship with Mitchell for this book you're helping him write—'

'I'm *helping* him write? Is that what he said?' Jack shook his head. Mitchell was living in Never-Never Land. It was *his* book, and *he* was writing the damn thing. Yes, Mitchell Evans's and Ken Baines's names would be on the cover, but there would be no doubt about who was the author. The sizeable advance in his bank account was a freaking big clue.

'Your father...I like him...but, jeez, he can be a pain in the ass,' Jack said.

'So does that mean you don't want to talk to me about him?' Ellie asked, sounding hopeful and a great deal less nervous.

Jack half smiled as he shook his head. 'Sorry...I do need to talk to you about him.'

He raked his hair off his face, thinking about the book. Ken's fascinating story was all but finished; Mitch's was progressing. Thank God he'd resisted all the collective pressure to get him to write his. Frankly, it would be like having his chest cracked open without anaesthetic.

He was such a hypocrite. He had no problems digging around other people's psyches but was more than happy to leave his own alone.

Jack looked at Ellie, saw her still uncertain expression and was reminded that she was wary of having a strange man in her house. He couldn't blame her.

'And as for chasing you around your house? Apart from the

fact that I am so whipped I couldn't make a move on a corpse, it really isn't my style.'

Ellie looked at him for a long moment and then her smile blossomed. It was the nicest punch to the heart he'd ever received.

CHAPTER TWO

JACK LOOKED UP a lavender-lined driveway to the house beyond it. It was a modest two-storey with Old World charm, wooden bay windows and a deep veranda, nestled in a wild garden surrounded by a high brick wall. The driveway led up to a two-door garage. He didn't do charming houses—hell, he didn't do *houses*. He had a flat that he barely saw, boxes that were still unpacked, a fridge that was never stocked. In many ways his flat was just another hotel room: as impersonal, as bland. He wasn't attached to any of his material possessions and he liked it that way.

Attachment was not an emotion he felt he needed to become better acquainted with...either to possessions or partners.

'Nice place,' Jack said as he walked up the stairs onto a covered veranda. Ellie took a set of keys from the back pocket of those tight shorts. It *was* nice—not for him, but nice—a charming house with loads of character.

'The house was my grandmother's. I inherited it from her.'

Jack glanced idly over his shoulder and his breath caught in his throat. *God, what a view!*

'Oh, that is just amazing,' he said, curling his fingers around the wooden beam that supported the veranda's roof. Looking out over the houses below, he could see a sweeping stretch of endless beach that showed the curve of the bay and the sleepy blue and green ocean.

'Where are we, exactly?' he asked.

Ellie moved to stand next to him. 'On the False Bay coast. We're about twenty minutes from the CBD of Cape Town, to the south. That bay is False Bay and you can see about thirty kilometres of beach from here. Kalk Bay is that way—' she pointed '—and Muizenberg is up the coast.'

'What are those brightly coloured boxes on the beach?'

'Changing booths. Aren't they fun? The beach is hugely popular, and if you look just north of the booths, at the tables and chairs under the black and white striped awning, that's where we were—at Pari's.'

'It's incredible.'

'Your room looks out onto the beach and the bathroom has a view of the Muizenberg Mountain behind us. There are some great walks and biking trails in the nature reserve behind us.'

Ellie nudged one of two almost identical blond Labradors aside in an attempt to get close enough to the front door and shove her key in the lock. Pushing open the wooden door with its stained glass window insert, she gestured for Jack to come into the hall as she automatically hung her bag onto a decorative hook.

'The bedrooms are upstairs. I presume that you'd like a shower? Something to eat? Drink?'

He probably reeked like an abandoned rubbish dump. 'I'd kill for a shower.'

Jack had an impression of more bright colours and eclectic art as he followed Ellie up the wooden staircase. There was a short passage and then she opened the door to a guest bedroom: white and lavender linen on a double bed, pale walls and a ginger cat curled up on the royal purple throw.

'Meet Chaos. The *en-suite* bathroom is through that door.'

Ellie picked up Chaos and cradled the cat like a baby. Jack scratched the cat behind its ears and Chaos blinked sleepily.

Jack thankfully dropped his backpack onto the wooden

floor and sat down on the purple throw at the end of the bed while he waited for the dots behind his eyes to recede. Ellie walked to the window, pulled the curtain back and lifted the wooden sash to let some fresh air into the room.

He dimly heard Ellie ask again if he wanted something to drink and struggled to respond normally. He was enormously grateful when she left the room and he could shove his head between his knees and pull himself back from the brink of fainting.

Because obviously he'd prefer not to take the concept of falling at Ellie's feet too literally.

Ellie skipped down the stairs, belted into the kitchen and yanked her mobile from her pocket.

Merri answered on the first ring. 'I know that you're upset with me about extending my maternity leave...'

'Shut up! This is more important!' Ellie hissed, keeping her voice low. 'Mitchell sent me a man!'

Merri waited a beat before responding. 'Your father is procuring men for you now? Are you *that* desperate? Oh, wait... yes, you are!'

'You are so funny...not.' Ellie shook her head. 'No, you twit, I'm acting as a Cape Town B&B for his stray colleagues again, but this time he sent me Jack Chapman!'

'The hottie war reporter?' Merri replied, after taking a moment to make the connection. She sounded awed and—gratifyingly—a smidgeon jealous. 'Well?'

'Well, what?'

'What's he like?' Merri demanded.

'He's reluctantly, cynically charming. Fascinating. And he has the envious ability to put people at ease. No wonder he's an ace reporter.' When low-key charm and fascination came wrapped up in such a pretty package it was doubly, mind-alteringly disarming.

'Well, well, well...' Merri drawled. 'It sounds like he has made *quite* an impression! You sound...breathy.'

Breathy? No, she did not!

But why did she feel excited, shy, nervous and—dammit—scared all at the same time? Oh, she wasn't scared of *him*—she knew instinctively, absolutely, that Jack was a gentleman down to his toes—but she was on a scalpel-edge because he was the first man in ages who had her nerve-endings humming and her sexual radar beeping. And if she told Merri *that*...

'You're attracted to him,' Merri stated.

She hated it when Merri read her mind. 'I'm not...it's just a surprise. And even if I was...'

'You are.'

'He's too sexy, too charming, has a crazy job that I loathe, and he'll be gone in a day or two.'

'Mmm, but he's seriously hot. Check him out on the internet.'

'Is that what you're doing? Stop it and concentrate!' She gave Merri—and herself—a mental slap. 'I have more than enough to deal with without adding the complication of even *thinking* about attraction and sex and a good-looking face topping a sexy body! Besides, I'm not good at relationships and men.'

'Because you're still scared to risk giving your heart away and having to take it back, battered and bruised, when they ride off into the sunset?'

Merri tossed her own words back at her and Ellie grimaced.

'Exactly! And a pretty face won't change anything. My father and my ex put me through an emotional grinder and Jack Chapman has the potential to do the same...'

'Well, that's jumping the gun, since you've just met him, but I'll bite. Why?'

'Purely because I'm attracted to him!' Ellie responded in

a heated voice. 'It's an unwritten rule of my life that the men I find fascinating have an ability to wreak havoc in my life!'

They dropped in, kicked her heart around, ultimately decided that she wasn't worth sticking around for and left.

Merri remained silent and after a while Ellie spoke again. 'You agree with me, don't you?'

'No, don't take my silence for agreement; I'm just in awe of your crazy.' Merri sighed. 'So, to sum up your rant: you are such a bum magnet when it comes to men that your rule of thumb is that if you find one attractive then you should run like hell? Avoid at all costs?'

'You've nailed it,' Ellie said glumly.

'I want to see how you manage to do this when the man in question has moved his very hot self into your rather small house.'

Ellie disconnected her mobile on Merri's hooting laughter. Really, with friends like her...

Returning to the spare bedroom with towels for his bathroom and a cold beer in her hands, Ellie heard a low groan and peeked through the crack in the door to look at Jack, still sitting on the edge of the bed, his hands gripping the bottom of his shirt, pale and sweating.

Hurrying into the room, she dumped the towels on the bed, handed him the beer and frowned. 'Are you all right?'

Jack took a long, long drink from the bottle and rested the cold glass against his cheek. 'Sure. Why?'

'I noticed that you winced when you picked up your backpack. You took your time walking up the stairs, and now you're as white as a sheet and your hands are shaking!'

Jack rubbed the back of his neck. 'I'm a bit dinged up,' he eventually admitted.

'Uh-huh? How dinged up?'

'Just a bit. I'll survive.' Jack put the almost empty beer bottle on the floor and gripped the edge of his shirt again.

Ellie watched him struggle to pull it up and shook her head at his white-rimmed mouth.

'Can I help?' she asked eventually.

'I'll get there,' Jack muttered.

He couldn't, and with a slight shake of her head she stepped closer to the bed, grabbed the edges of his T-shirt and helped him pull it over his head. A beautiful body was there—somewhere underneath the blue-black plate-sized bruises that looked like angry thunderclouds. He had a wicked vertical scar bisecting his chest that suggested a major operation at one time, and Ellie bit her lip when she walked around his knees to look at his back. She couldn't stifle her horrified gasp. The damage on his back was even worse, and on his tanned skin she could see clear imprints of a heel here and the toe of a boot there.

'What does the other guy look like?' she asked, trying to be casual.

'Guys. Not as bad as me, unfortunately.' Jack balled his T-shirt in his hand and tossed it towards his rucksack. 'The Somalians decided to give me something to remember them by.'

Jack sat on the edge of the bed, bent over and, using one hand and taking short breaths, undid the laces of his scuffed trainers. When they were loose enough, he toed them off.

Jack sent her a crooked grin that didn't fool her for a second. 'As you can see, all in working order.'

'Anything broken?'

Jack shook his head. 'I think they bruised a rib or two. I'll live. I've had worse.'

Ellie shook her head. 'Worse than this?'

'A bullet does more damage,' Jack said, standing up and slowly walking to the *en-suite* bathroom.

Ellie gasped. 'You've been *shot*?'

'Twice. Hurts like a bitch.'

Hearing water running in the basin, Ellie abruptly sat down. She was instantly catapulted back in time to when she'd spent a holiday with Mitchell and his mother—her grandmother Ginger—in London when she was fourteen. He'd run to Bosnia to do a 'quick report' and come back in an ambulance plane, shot in the thigh. He'd lost a lot of blood and spent a couple of days in the ICU.

It wasn't her favourite holiday memory.

Jack didn't seem to be particularly fazed about his injuries; like Mitchell he probably fed on danger and adrenalin… it made no sense to her.

'You do realise that you could've died?' Ellie said, wondering why she even bothered.

Jack walked back into the room, dried his face on a towel he'd picked up from the bed and shrugged. 'Nah. They were lousy shots.'

Ellie sighed. She couldn't understand why getting hurt, shot or putting yourself in danger wasn't a bigger deterrent. She knew that Jack, like her father, preferred to work solo, shunning the protection of the army or the police, wanting to get the mood on the streets, the story from the locals. Such independence ratcheted up the danger quotient to the nth degree.

There was a reason why war reporting was rated as one of the most dangerous jobs in the world. Were they dedicated to the job or just plain stupid? Right now, seeing those bruises, she couldn't help but choose *stupid*.

'So, before I go…do you want something to eat?'

Jack shook his head. 'The pilot stood me a couple of burgers at the airport. Thanks, though.'

'Okay, well, I'll be downstairs if you need anything…' Ellie couldn't resist dropping her eyes to sneak a peek at his stomach. As she'd suspected, he had a gorgeous six-pack—but her attention was immediately diverted by a mucky, bloody sanitary pad held in place by the waistband of his jeans.

She pursed her lips. 'And that?'

Jack glanced down and winced. With an enviable lack of modesty he flipped open the top two buttons of his jeans, pulled down the side of his boxer shorts and pulled off the pad. Ellie winced at the seeping, bloody, six-inch slash that bisected the artistic knife and broken heart tattoo on his hip.

'Not too bad,' Jack said, after prodding the wound with a blunt-edged finger.

'What is that? A knife wound?'

'Mmm. Psycho bastards.'

'You sound so calm,' Ellie said, her eyes wide.

'I *am* calm. I'm always calm.'

Too calm, she thought. 'Jack, it needs stitches.'

'This is minor, Ellie.' Jack looked mutinous. 'I'm going to give it a good scrub, slather it in the antiseptic I always carry with me and slap another pad on it.'

'Who uses sanitary pads for *this*?'

'It's an army thing and it serves the purpose. I'm an old hand at doctoring myself.'

Ellie sighed when Jack turned away to rummage in his rucksack. He pulled out another sanitary pad, stripped the plastic away and slapped the clean pad onto his still bleeding wound. She saw his stubborn look and knew that he'd made up his mind. If she couldn't get Jack to a hospital—he was six-two and built; how could she force him?—she'd have to trust him when he said that he was an old hand at patching himself up.

'When my bank cards arrive I'll go down to the pharmacy and get some proper supplies,' Jack told her.

Ellie sucked in a frustrated sigh. 'Give me a list of what you need and I'll run down and get it. I'll be back before you're finished showering.' She held up her hand. 'And, yes, you can pay me back.'

Jack looked hesitant and Ellie resisted the impulse to smack the back of his head. 'Jack, you need some decent medical supplies.'

Jack glared at the floor. She saw his broad shoulders dip in defeat before hearing his reluctant agreement. Within a minute he'd located a notebook from the side pocket of his rucksack and a pen, and he wrote in a strong, clear hand exactly what he wanted. He handed her the list and Ellie knew, by his miserable eyes, that he was embarrassed that he had to ask for her help. *Again.*

Men. Really...

The mobile in her pocket jangled and Ellie pulled it out, frowning at the unfamiliar number. Answering, she heard a low, distinctively feminine voice asking for Jack. Ellie's brows pulled together... How on earth could anyone know that Jack was with her? She had hardly completed that thought before realising that the jungle drums must be working well in the war journalists' world. Her father was spreading the news...

Ellie handed her mobile to Jack and couldn't help wondering who the owner of the low, subtly sexy voice was. Lover? Colleague? Friend?

'Hi, Ma.'

Or his mother. Horribly uncomfortable with the level of relief she felt on hearing that he was talking to his mother, Ellie scuttled from the room.

Jack lifted the mobile to his ear on an internal groan. He just wanted to go and lie down on that bed and sleep. Was that too much to ask? Really?

'I haven't been able to reach you for a week!' said his mother Rae in a semi-hysterical voice.

'Mum, we had an agreement. You only get to worry about me after you haven't spoken to me for three weeks.' Jack rubbed his forehead, actively trying to be patient. He understood her worry—after all that he'd put her and his father through how could he not?—but her over-protectiveness got very old, very quickly.

'Are you hurt?' his mother demanded curtly.

He wished he'd learnt to lie to her. 'Let me talk to Dad, Mum.'

'That means you're hurt. Derek! Jack's hurt!'

Jack heard her sob and she dropped the phone. His father's voice—an oasis of calm—crossed the miles.

'*Are* you hurt?'

'Mmm.'

'Where?'

Everywhere. There was no point whining about it. 'Couple of dents. Nothing major. Tell Mum to calm down to a mild panic.' Jack heard his mum gabbling in the background, listened through his father's reassurances and waited until his father spoke again.

'You mother says to please remind you to visit Dr Jance. Does she need to make an appointment for you?'

He'd forgotten that a check-up was due and he felt his insides contract. He did his best to forget what he'd gone through as a teenager, and these bi-yearly check-ups were reminders of those dreadful four years he'd spent as a slave to his failing heart. He tipped his head back in frustration when he heard Rae demand to talk to him again.

'Jack, the Sandersons contacted us last week,' she said in a rush.

Jack felt his heart contract and tasted guilt in the back of his throat. Abruptly he sat down on the edge of the bed. Brent Sanderson. He was alive because Brent had died. How could he *not* feel guilty? It was a constant—along with the feeling that he owed it to Brent to live life to the full, that living that way was the only way he could honour his brief life, the gift he'd been given...

'In six weeks it will be seventeen years since the op, and

Brent was seventeen when he died,' Rae said with a quaver in her voice.

She didn't need to tell him that. He knew *exactly* how long it had been. They'd both been seventeen when they'd swapped hearts.

'They want to hold a memorial service for him and have invited us…and you. We've said we'll go and I said that I'd talk to you.'

Jack stretched out, tucked a pillow behind his head and blew out a long stream of air. He tried not to dwell on Brent and his past—he preferred the *it happened; let's move on* approach—and he really, really didn't want to go. 'It's a gracious invitation but I'm pretty sure that they'd be happy if I didn't pitch up.'

'How can you say that?'

'Because it would be supremely difficult for them to see me walking around, fit and healthy, knowing that their son is six feet under, Mum!'

They'd given him the gift of their son's heart. He'd do anything to spare them further pain. And that included keeping his distance…

'They aren't like that and they want to meet you. You've avoided meeting them for years!'

'I haven't avoided them. It just never worked out.'

'I'll pretend to believe that lie if you consider coming to Brent's service,' Rae retorted.

His mother wasn't a fool. 'Mum, I'll see. I've got to go. I'll visit when I'm back in the UK.'

'You're not in the UK? Where are you?' Rae squawked.

Jack gritted his teeth. 'You're mollycoddling me, and you know it drives me nuts!'

'Well, your career drives *me* nuts! How can you, after fighting so hard for life, routinely put yourself in danger? It's—'

'Crazy and disrespectful to take such risks when I've been given another chance at life. I'm playing Russian Roulette with my life and you wish I'd settle down and meet a nice girl and give you grandchildren. Have I left anything out?'

'No,' Rae muttered. 'But I put it more eloquently.'

'Eloquent nagging is still nagging. But I do love you, you old bat. Sometimes.'

'Revolting child.'

'Bye, Ma,' Jack said, and disconnected the call.

He banged the mobile against his forehead. His parents thought that guilt and fear fuelled his daredevil lifestyle. It did—of course it did—but did that have to be a bad thing? They didn't understand—probably because he could never explain it—but playing it safe, sitting behind a desk in a humdrum job was, for him, a slow way to die. At fourteen he'd gone from being a healthy, rambunctious, sporty kid to a waif and a ghost, his time spent either in hospital rooms or at his childhood home. He'd just *existed* for more years than he cared to remember, and he'd vowed that when he had the chance of an active life he'd live it. Hard and fast. He wanted to do it all and see it all—to chase the thrills. For himself and for Brent. Being confined to one house, person or city would be his version of hell. His parents wanted him to settle down, but they didn't understand that he wouldn't settle down for anything or anyone. He had to keep moving—and working to feel alive.

Jack switched off the bedside light and stared up at the shadows on the ceiling, actively trying not to think about his past. As per normal, his job had thrown him a curveball and he'd landed up in a strange bed in a strange town. But, he thought as his eyes closed, he was very good at curveballs and strange situations, and meeting Mitch's dazzling daughter again was very much worth the detour.

On his second night in Ellie's spare room, Jack put aside the magazine he'd been reading, rolled onto his back and stared at the ceiling above his bed. The air-conditioning unit hummed softly and he could hear the croaky song of frogs in the garden, the occasional whistle of a cricket. It wasn't that late and his side throbbed.

Knowing that he wouldn't be able to sleep yet, he flipped back the sheet and stood up. After yanking on a pair of jeans he quietly opened the door and walked to the stairs. Navigating his way through the dark house, he walked into the front lounge, with its two big bay windows, leaned against the side wall and looked through the darkness towards the sea. Through the open windows he could hear the thud of waves hitting the beach and smell the brine-tinged air.

Ellie's distinctively feminine voice drifted through the bay window, so he pulled back the curtain. He looked out and watched her walk up the stairs to the veranda, mobile to her ear and one arm full of papers and files. She looked exhausted and he could see flour streaks on her open navy chef's jacket. Jack glanced at the luminous dial of his watch...ten-thirty at night was a hell of a time to be coming home from work.

'Ginger, my life is a horror movie at the moment.'

Ginger? Wasn't that Mitchell's mother? Ellie's Irish grandmother?

'Essentially I need Mum to come back but it's not fair to ask her. I'm chasing my tail on a daily basis, it's nearly month-end, I have payroll and I need to pay VAT this month. And I need to move the bakery but there's nowhere to move it to! And, to top it all, your wretched son has sent me a house guest!'

So she wasn't as sanguine about having him as a guest as she pretended to be. Jack watched as she balanced the stack of papers and two files on the arm of the Morris chair.

'No, he's okay,' Ellie continued. 'I've had worse.'

Only okay? He was going to have to work on that.

Ellie used her free hand to dig into her bag for her house keys and half turned, knocking the unstable pile with her hip.

The files tipped and the papers caught in the mild evening wind and drifted away.

'Dammit! Ginger—sorry, I have to go. I've just knocked something over.'

Ellie threw her mobile onto the seat of the Morris chair, then started to curse in Arabic. His mouth fell open. His eyes widened as the curses became quite creative, muddled and downright vulgar.

Jack thought that she could do with some help so he stepped over the sill of the low window directly onto the veranda and started to collect the bits of paper that were scattered all over the floor.

'Do you actually know what you're saying?' he demanded, when she stopped for ten seconds to take a breath.

Ellie sent him a puzzled look. 'Daughter of a donkey, son of a donkey, your mother is ugly, et cetera.'

Uh, no. Not even close. 'Do me a favour? Don't ever repeat any of those anywhere near an Arab, okay?'

Ellie slowly stood up and narrowed her eyes. 'They are rude, aren't they?'

He didn't need to respond because she'd already connected the dots.

'Mitchell! He taught me those when I was a kid.' It was so typical of Mitch's twisted sense of humour to teach his innocent daughter foul curse words in Arabic. 'I'm going to kill him! I take it you speak Arabic?'

'Mmm.' He'd discovered that he had a gift for languages while he was a teenager, when he'd been unable to do anything more energetic than read.

Ellie sent him a direct look. 'So, do you speak any other languages?'

Jack shrugged. 'Enough Mandarin to make myself understood. Some Japanese. I'm learning Russian. And Dari…'

'What's that?'

'Also known as Farsi, or Afghan Persian. Helpful, obviously, in Afghanistan.'

Ellie stared at him, seemingly impressed. 'That's incredible.'

Jack shrugged, uncomfortable with her praise. 'Lots of people speak second or third languages.'

'But not Farsi, Russian or Mandarin,' Ellie countered. 'I'm useless. I can barely spell in English.'

'I don't believe that.'

'You can ask Mitchell if you like. Nothing made him angrier than seeing my spelling test results,' Ellie quipped. 'Besides, English is a stupid language...their and there, which and witch, write, right, rite.'

'And another wright,' Jack added.

'You're just making that up,' she grumbled.

'I'm not. It's one of the few four-word homophones.' Jack's grin flashed. 'W.R.I.G.H.T. Someone who constructs or repairs things—as in a millwright.'

'Homophones? Huh.' Ellie heaved an exaggerated, forlorn sigh. 'Good grief, I'm sharing my house with a swot. What did I do to deserve that?'

Jack laughed, delighted. 'Life does throw challenges at one.'

After they'd finished collecting the papers Ellie sat down on the couch, rolling her head on her shoulders.

Jack sat on the low stone wall in front of her. 'Tough day?' he asked, conversationally.

Ellie slumped in the chair. 'Very. How can you tell?'

Jack lifted his hands. 'I heard you talking to your grandmother.'

'And how much did you hear?'

'You're pissed, you're stressed, something about having to move the bakery. You've had worse house guests than me.'

Even in the dim light he could see Ellie flush. 'Sorry.

Mitchell tends to use me as his own personal B&B... I didn't mean to make you feel unwelcome.'

'Am I?'

Ellie threw her hands up and sent him a miserable look. 'You're not. I'm more frustrated at Mitchell's high-handedness than at the actual reality of a house guest, if that makes sense.'

Jack nodded, hearing the truth in her statement, and relaxed. 'Mitch does have a very nebulous concept of the word *no*,' he stated calmly.

'And he's had twenty-eight years to perfect the art of manipulating me,' Ellie muttered. 'Again, that's not directed at you personally.'

Jack laughed. 'I get it, Ellie. Relax. Talking about relaxing...' Jack walked back into the house, found a wine rack and remembered that he'd seen a corkscrew in the middle drawer when he was looking for a bread knife earlier. He took the wine and two glasses back to the veranda. 'If I ever saw a girl in need of the stress-relieving qualities of alcohol, it's you.'

'If I have any of that I'll fall over,' Ellie told him, covering a yawn with her hand.

'A glass or two won't hurt.' Jack yanked the cork out, poured the Merlot and handed her a glass.

Ellie took the glass from him and took the first delicious sip. 'Yum. I could drink this all night.'

'Then it would definitely hurt when you wake up.' After a moment's silence, he succumbed to his curiosity. 'Tell me what that conversation was about.'

Ellie cradled the glass in her hand and eyed Jack across the rim. Shirtless, and with bare feet, he was a delectable sight for sore eyes at the end of a hectic day. 'You're very nosy.'

'I'm a journalist. It's a job requirement. Talk.'

She wanted to object, to tell him he was bossy—which he was—but she didn't. Couldn't. She needed someone to offload on and maybe it would be easier to talk to a stranger who was leaving... When *was* he leaving? She asked him.

Jack grinned. 'Not sure yet. Is it a problem if I stay for another night or two? I like your house,' he added, and Ellie's glass stopped halfway to her mouth.

'You want to stay because you like my house? Uh...why?'

'Well, apart from the fact that we haven't yet talked about Mitch, it's...restful.' Jack lifted a bare muscled shoulder. 'It shouldn't be with such bright colours but it is. I like hearing the sea, the wind coming off the mountain. I like it.'

'Thanks.' Ellie took a sip of wine. It would be nice to know if he liked her as much as he liked her house, but since she'd only spent a couple of hours with him what could she expect? Ellie couldn't believe she was even thinking about him like that. It was so high school—and she had bigger problems than thinking about boys and their nice bodies and whether they liked her back.

Jack topped up her wine glass and then his. He squinted at the label on the bottle. 'This is a nice wine. Maybe I should go on a wine-tasting tour of the vineyards.'

'That's a St Sylve Merlot. My friend Luke owns the winery and his fiancée Jess does the advertising for the bakery.'

'And we're back full circle to your bakery. Talk.' Jack boosted himself up so that he sat cross-legged on the stone wall, his back to a wooden beam.

His eyes rested on her face and they encouraged her to trust him, to let it out, to *talk* to him...

Damn, he was good at this.

Ellie's smile was small and held a hint of pride. 'Pari's Perfect Cakes—'

'Who was Pari, by the way?' Jack interrupted her.

'My grandmother. It was her bakery originally. It means "fairy" in India.' Pain flashed in her eyes. 'As you saw, Pari's is a retail bakery and delicatessen, with a small coffee shop.'

'It doesn't look like a small operation. How do you manage it all?'

'Well, that's one of my problems. We have two shifts of bakers who make the bread and the high turnover items, and Merri, my best friend, used to do the specialised pastries. I do special function cakes. My mum did the books, stock and payroll and chivvied us along. It all worked brilliantly until recently.'

Jack held up his hand. 'Wait—back up. Special function cakes? Like wedding cakes?'

'Sure—but any type of cakes.' Ellie picked up her mobile and quickly pressed some buttons. 'Look.'

Jack put his glass of wine next to him on the wall and leaned forward to take the device. He flipped through the screens, looking at her designs.

'These are amazing, Ellie.'

'Thank you.'

He looked down at her mobile again. 'I can't believe that you made a cake that looks exactly like a crocodile leather shoe.'

'Not any shoe—a Christian Louboutin shoe.'

Jack looked puzzled. 'A what?'

'Great designer of shoes?' Ellie shook her head.

'Sorry, I'm more of a trainers and boots kind of guy.' Jack handed the mobile back to her. 'So, what went wrong at the bakery?'

'Not wrong, exactly. Merri had a baby and started her maternity leave. She told me yesterday that she's extending it.'

'She *told* you?'

Ellie heard the disbelief in Jack's voice and quickly responded, 'She asked…suggested…kind of.'

Jack frowned. 'And you said yes?'

'I didn't have much of a choice. She doesn't need to work and I didn't want to push her into a corner and…'

'And you couldn't say no,' Jack stated with a slight shake of his head.

'And I suppose you've never said yes when you wanted to say no?' Ellie demanded.

'I can't say that I've never done that. I generally say what I mean and I never let anyone push me around...'

'She didn't...' Ellie started to protest but fell silent when she saw the challenging expression on Jack's face. This wasn't an argument she would win because—well, she *did* get pushed around. Sometimes. Would he understand if she told him that, as grown-up and confident as she now was, she still had intense periods of self-doubt? Would he think her an absolute drip because her habit reaction was to make sure everyone around her was happy? And if they were they would love her more?

'What else?' Jack asked, after taking a sip of wine.

Ellie swirled the wine in her glass. 'My mother has taken a year's sabbatical. She always had this dream to travel, so for her fiftieth birthday I gave her a year off. A grand gesture that I am deeply regretting now. But she's in seventh heaven. She's got a tattoo, has had at least one affair and has put dreadlocks in her hair.'

'You sound more upset about the dreadlocks than the affair.'

Ellie shrugged. 'I just want her home—back in the bakery. She managed the place, did the paperwork and the accounts, the payroll and just made the place run smoothly.'

And while I say that I want everyone to be happy I frequently resent the fact that she left, that Merri left—okay, temporarily—and I have to carry on, pick up the pieces. When do I get to step away?

'So, you're stressed out and doing the work of two other people?'

'And none of it well,' Ellie added, her tone sulky.

Jack smiled. 'Now, tell me about having to move.'

Ellie gave him the rundown and cradled her glass of wine in her hands. She felt lighter for telling him, grateful to hand over the problem just for a minute. She didn't expect him to solve the problem, but just being able to verbalise her emotions was liberating.

And, amazingly, Jack just listened—without offering a solution, a way to fix it. If he wasn't ripped and didn't have a stubble-covered jaw and a very masculine package she could almost pretend he was a girlfriend. He listened like one. *Keep dreaming*, she thought. Not in a million years could she pretend that Jack was anything but a hard-ass—literally and metaphorically—one hundred per cent male.

Ellie yawned, curled her legs up and felt her eyes closing. She felt Jack take the glass from her hand and forced her eyes open.

'Come on. You're dead on your feet.' Jack took her hands and hauled her up.

He'd either overestimated her weight or underestimated his strength because she flew into his chest and her hands found themselves splayed across his pecs, warm and hard and...*oooooh*... Her nose was pressed against his sternum. She sucked him in along with the breath she took...man-soap, man-smell...*Jack*.

She felt tiny next to his muscled frame as his hands loosely held her hips, fingers on the top of her bottom. A lazy thumb stroked her hipbone through the chef's jacket and Ellie felt lust skitter along her skin. She slowly lifted her head and looked at him from beneath her eyelashes. There was half a smile on his face, yet his eyes were dark and serious...

He lifted his hand and gently rested his fingers on her lips. She knew what he was thinking...that he wanted to kiss her. Intended to kiss her.

Ellie just looked up at him with big eyes. She felt like a deer frozen in the headlights, knowing that she should pull away, unable to do so. She could feel his hard body against hers, his rising chest beneath her palms. His arms were strong, his shoulders broad. She felt feminine and dainty and...judging by the amount of action in his pants...desired.

He stepped back at the same time as she pushed him away. She shoved her hands into her hair, squinting at him in the moonlight. This was crazy... She was adult enough to recognise passion that could be perilous—wild, erratic and swamping. But lust, as she'd learnt, clouded her thinking and stripped away her practicality. Lust, teamed with the brief emotional connection she'd felt earlier, when she'd opened up a little to him, had her running scared.

Bum magnet.

Jack cocked his head. 'So, not a good idea, huh?'

Ellie bit her lip. 'Really not.'

Jack lifted a shoulder and sent her a rueful smile. 'Okay. But you're a very tempting sight in the moonlight so maybe we should go in before I try to change your mind.'

When she didn't move, Jack reached out and ran a thumb over her bottom lip.

'You can't just stand there looking up at me with those incredible eyes, Ellie. Go now, before I forget that I am, actually, a good guy. Because we both know that I could persuade you to stay.'

Ellie erred on the side of caution and fled inside.

CHAPTER THREE

EVERY TIME HIS foot slapped the pavement a hot flash of pain radiated from his cut and caused every atom in his body to ache. It was the morning after almost kissing Ellie, and he was dripping with perspiration and panting like a dog.

He placed his hand against his side and winced. He shouldn't be running, he knew that, but running was his escape, his sanity, his meditation. And, thinking about things he shouldn't be doing, kissing Ellie was top of the list. Why was he so tempted by his blue-eyed hostess? Especially since he'd quickly realised that she wasn't into simple fun and games, wasn't someone he could play with and leave, wasn't a superficial type of girl. And he didn't do anything *but* superficial.

But there was something about her that tweaked his interest and that scared the hell out of him.

He started to climb the hill back home and—dammit! He *hurt*. Everywhere. *Suck it up and stop being a pansy*, he told himself. *You've had a heart transplant—a cut and a beating is nothing compared to that!*

Jack pushed his wet hair off his forehead and looked around. Good Lord, it was beautiful here...the sea was aqua and hunter-green, cerulean-blue in places. White-yellow sand. Eclectic, interesting buildings. He was lucky to be here, to see this stunning part of the world...

Brent never would.

Brent never would. The phrase that was always at the back of his mind. Intellectually he knew it came from survivor's guilt—the fact that he was alive because Brent was dead. In the first few months and years after the op he'd been excited to be able to do whatever he wanted, but he knew that over the past couple of years the burden of guilt he felt had increased.

Why? Why wasn't he coming to terms with what had happened? Why wasn't it getting easier? The burden of the responsibility of living life for someone else had become heavier with each passing year.

The mobile he'd borrowed from Ellie jangled in his pocket and he came to an abrupt stop. Thankfully he was back at Ellie's place. He didn't think he could go any further.

'So, what do you think of Ellie?' Mitchell said when Jack pushed the green button on the mobile and held it up to a sweaty ear.

'Uh...she's fine. Nice.'

She was...in the best sense of the word. A little highly strung, occasionally shy. Sensitive, overwhelmed and struggling to hide it. Sexy as hell.

'So, have you talked to her about me yet?'

Jack lifted his eyebrows at Mitchell's blatant narcissism and felt insulted on Ellie's behalf.

'Ellie's well, but over-worked. Her bakery is fabulous; she's running it on her own as her mum is overseas,' he said, his tone coolly pointed as he answered the questions Mitch should have thought to ask.

'Yeah, yeah... But how far have you got with the book? Did you get my e-mail? I sent it just now.'

His verbal pricks hadn't dented Mitchell's self-absorbed hide. Jack wished he could reach into the phone and slap Mitchell around the head. Had he always been so self-involved? Why hadn't he noticed before? Jack sighed and looked at his watch. It wasn't quite seven yet. Far too early to deal with Mitchell.

'Firstly, my laptop is still in Somalia, and, contrary to what you think, I don't hover over my laptop waiting for your e-mails,' Jack said as he made his way into the house, up the steps and into his room. Jack heard Mitchell splutter with annoyance but continued anyway. 'And, by the way, why did you teach Ellie such crude Arabic insults when she was a little girl? They are, admittedly, funny as hell, because she gets them all mixed up, but really...'

'She still remembers those, huh?'

Jack pulled his T-shirt over his head, walked into the bathroom and dropped it into the laundry basket. Yanking a bottle of pills out of his toiletry bag, he shook the required daily dosage into his hand, tossed them into his mouth and used his hand as a cup to get water into his mouth.

Those pills were his constant companions, his best friends. He loved them and loathed them in equal measure.

'And why did you tell Ellie that I'm *helping* you write this book?'

As per normal, Mitch ignored the questions he didn't want to answer. 'So, have you spoken to Ellie yet about *me*?'

'No. The woman works like a demon. I haven't managed to pin her down yet.' Jack frowned. 'And she's not exactly jumping for joy at the prospect.'

Mitchell didn't answer for a minute. 'Ellie and I have had our ups and downs...'

Ups and downs? Jack suspected that they'd had a lot more than that.

'She didn't like me being away so much,' Mitchell continued.

Jack rolled his eyes at that understatement. As he walked over to the window his eye was caught by two frames lying against the wall, behind the desk in the corner. Pulling them out, he saw that they were two photographs of a younger Ellie and a short blond man in front of the exclusive art gallery

Grigson's in London. Jack asked Mitch who the man in the photograph was.

'Someone she was briefly engaged to—five, six years ago.' Jack heard Mitchell light a cigarette. 'She wanted to get married. He didn't.'

Jack felt a spurt of sympathy for the guy. He'd had two potential-to-become-serious relationships in the past ten years and they'd both ended in tears on his partner's face and frustration on his. They'd wanted him to settle down. He equated that to being locked in a cage. He'd liked them, enjoyed them, but not enough to curtail his time or freedom for them.

'Jack? You still there?' Mitchell asked in his ear.

'Sure.'

'I spoke to most of our commissioning editors today and told them that you've been injured. They will leave you alone for three weeks. Unless something diabolical happens—then all bets are off,' Mitchell stated.

That was enough to yank his attention back, and fast. Jack felt his molars grinding. 'You do know I get very annoyed when you interfere in my life, Mitchell?'

Mitchell, never intimidated, just laughed. 'Oh, get over yourself! You haven't taken any time off in two years and we all know that leads to burnout. You've been flirting with it for a while, boyo.'

'Crap.'

'If you don't believe me, check your last couple of stories. You've always been super-fair and unemotional, but there's a fine line between being unemotional and robotic, Jack. You are drifting over that line. Losing every bit of empathy is every bit as problematic as having too much.'

'Again...crap,' Jack muttered, but wondered if Mitchell had a point. He remembered being in Egypt six weeks ago and watching a paramedic work on a badly beaten protester.

He'd been trying to recall if he'd paid his gas bill. Maybe he was taking the role of observer a bit too far.

'I'm going to courier you my notebooks, my diaries,' Mitchell told him. 'Get some sun, drink some wine. But if you don't get cracking on my book…'

Mitch repeated the most gruesome of Ellie's Arabic curses from the night before and Jack winced.

Jack tossed the mobile onto the bed, slapped his hands on his hips and stared at the photographs he'd replaced against the wall. Ellie… Maybe he should think about leaving, and soon. Almost kissing her last night had been a mistake…

Sure, he was attracted to her—she was stunning; what man wouldn't be? If she was a different type of girl then he could have her, enjoy her and then leave. Unfortunately he wasn't just physically attracted, and he *knew* that mental attraction was a sticky quagmire best avoided. And, practically, while Mitch wouldn't win any Father of the Year awards he might not approve of them hooking up, and he didn't want to cause friction between him and his subject, mentor and colleague.

Ellie, with her cosy house and settled lifestyle—the absolute opposite of what he liked and needed—was also far more fascinating than he generally liked his casual partners to be. Because fascination always made leaving so much harder than it needed to be.

'Morning.'

Ellie jumped as he entered the kitchen, looking tough and rugged and a whole lot of sexy. She could see that his hair had deep red highlights in the chocolate-brown strands. He'd scraped off his beard and the violet stripes under his eyes were almost gone. He did, however, still have that glint in his eyes—the one that said he wanted to tear up the bedcovers with her.

Ellie cursed when she felt heat rising up her neck.

'Can I get some coffee?'

Jack's question yanked her out of her reverie and she nodded, reaching for a mug above the coffee machine to give her hands something to do.

'You're up early,' she said when she'd found her voice.

Jack took the cup she handed him and leaned against the counter, crossing his legs at the ankles. 'Mmm. Good coffee. I went for a run this morning along the beachfront. It was... absolutely amazing. It's such a beautiful part of the world.'

'It is, but should you be exercising yet?'

'I'm fine.'

Yeah, she didn't think so—but it was his body, his choice, his pain. Ellie shook her head, picked up her own cup and sipped. She echoed his stance and leaned against the counter. Tension swirled between them and Ellie thought she could almost see the purple elephant sitting in the room, eyebrow cocked and smirking.

Maybe it would be better just to get it out there and in the open. But she couldn't get the words out... How she wished she could be one of those upfront, ballsy girls who just said what they felt and lived with the consequences.

She was still—especially when it came to men—the shy, awkward girl she'd been as a teenager.

Jack's eyebrows pulled together. 'The wariness is back in your eyes. Why?'

'Uh...last night. Um—' Oh, great. Now her tongue was on strike.

Jack, no slouch mentally, immediately picked up on what she was trying to say. 'The kiss that never happened?'

Ellie blushed. 'Mmm.'

'Yeah—sorry. I said I wouldn't hit on you and I did.' His tone didn't hold a hint of discomfort or embarrassment.

Ellie bit the inside of her lip. That wasn't what she'd expected him to say. Actually, she had no idea *what* she'd thought he'd say. The purple elephant grinned. 'I just... It's just that...'

Jack scratched the underside of his jaw and looked at her with his gold-flecked eyes. 'Relax, Ellie,' he said. 'It won't happen again…'

Ellie lifted her eyes to meet his and swallowed. In his she could read desire and lust and a healthy dose of amusement… as if he could read her thoughts, understand her confusion.

'Well…' he drawled as his finger gently pushed back a strand of hair that had fallen over her left eye. 'Maybe I should clarify that. I'll try not to let it happen again. You're very, very kissable, Ellie Evans.'

Ellie's eyes narrowed. She might not be the most assertive person in the world but that didn't mean he could look at her with those hot eyes and that smirky expression. Or presume that whatever happened between them would be solely *his* decision. Ellie narrowed her eyes, gripped the finger that had come to rest on her cheek and bent it backwards.

Hating personal confrontation, but knowing she needed to do this for the sake of her self-respect, she took a deep breath and forced the words out. 'There's only one person who will decide what happens between us and that will be me—not you.'

Jack grimaced and yanked his index finger out of her grip. He shook his finger out and sent her a surprised look. But, gratifyingly, there was an admiration in those hazel eyes that hadn't been there before and she liked seeing it there.

Jack sent her an approving smile. 'Good for you. I was wondering if you could stand up for yourself.'

Ellie narrowed her eyes. 'When I need to. No casual kissing.'

'Can we do *non*-casual kiss…?' Jack held up his hands at her fulsome glare. 'Joke! Peace!'

'Ha-ha.' Ellie rolled her shoulders. 'Would you like to go to work for me today?' she asked, blatantly changing the subject. 'I could do with a day off.'

'Okay—except my sugar icing and sculpting skills are sadly lacking. I can, however, make a mean red velvet cake.'

Ellie lowered her cup in surprise. 'You can bake?'

Ellie thought she saw pain flicker in his eyes. When he spoke his voice was gruff.

'Yes, I can bake. Normal stuff. Not pastries and croissants and fancy crap.'

Fancy crap? Well, that was one way to describe her business.

'Who taught you?' Ellie asked, openly curious.

'My mother.'

Ellie lifted her eyebrows. 'Sorry, I can't quite picture you baking as a kid. On bikes, on a sports field, camping—yes. Baking…no.'

Jack placed his cup on the counter and turned his face away from her. 'Well, it wasn't from choice.'

He sipped his coffee and when he looked at her again his face and eyes were devoid of whatever emotion she'd seen. Fear? Anger? Pain? A combination of all three?

This time it was Jack's turn to change the subject. 'So—breakfast. What are we having?'

Ellie looked at her watch and shook her head. 'No time. I need to go. I was supposed to be at work an hour ago.'

Jack shook his head. 'You should eat.'

'I'll grab something at the bakery.'

Well, she'd try to, but she frequently forgot. There just wasn't time most days. Ellie sighed. One of these days she'd have to start eating properly and sleeping more, but it wouldn't be any time soon. Maybe when Merri came back she could ease off a bit…but she probably wouldn't.

After all, she had a business to save.

Ellie looked at Jack, who was pulling eggs and bacon out of her fridge. Her mouth started to water. She'd kill for a proper fry-up…

Ellie pulled her thoughts away from food. 'So, I've given you keys to the house and I've just paid the deposit for you to hire a car. It should be delivered by eight so you won't be confined to the house any more.'

'The receipt for the deposit?' Jack sent her a level look.

Ellie rolled her eyes. He was insistent that she kept receipts for everything she spent so that he could repay her. 'In the hollow back of the wooden elephant on the hall table. With all the others.'

The annoying man wouldn't even allow her to buy milk or bread without asking for a receipt.

'Thanks.'

Jack slit open the pack of bacon and Ellie whimpered. She really, really didn't have time. She picked up her keys and bag, holding her chef's jacket in one hand.

'Pop down to the bakery later. I'll show you around. If you want to,' she added hastily.

Jack's smile had her melting like the gooey middle of her luscious chocolate brownies.

'I'll do that. See you later, then.'

Ellie bravely resisted the arc of sexual awareness that shimmered between them and sighed as she walked out of the kitchen.

In your dreams, Ellie. Because that was the only place making love to Jack was going to happen.

And even there her heart wasn't welcome to come to the party. Her heart, she'd decided a long time ago, wasn't allowed to party with *anyone* any more.

Later, dressed in denim shorts, flip-flops and an easy navy tee, Jack slipped through the front door of Pari's and looked over Ellie's business.

There were café-style tables outside, giving patrons the most marvellous view of the beach while they sipped their coffee and ate their muffins, and more wrought-iron tables inside, strategically placed between tables piled with preserves and organic wines, ten different types of olive oil and lots of other jars and tins of exotic foods with names he barely recognised. The décor was bohemian chic—he'd noticed that before—and all effortlessly elegant. Huge glass display fridges held a wide variety of pastries and cakes, and in another layer thick pink hams, haunches of rare roast beef and dark sausages.

It looked inviting and happy, and there was a line of people three deep at the wide counter, waiting to be served. The place was rocking, obviously extremely popular, and Jack suddenly realised what effort would be needed to move the bakery. If Ellie could find a place to move it to...

'Jack!'

Jack whipped his head up and saw Ellie approaching a table in the back corner of the room, a bottle of water in her hand. A good-looking couple sat at the table and Ellie motioned him over. Jack threaded his way through tables and people and ended up at the table, where a fourth chair was unoccupied.

'Paula and Will—meet my friend Jack. Take a seat, Jack,' Ellie said.

After shaking hands with Will, Jack pulled out the chair and sat down.

'I'm just about to chat to them about their wedding cake, but before we start does anyone want coffee?' Ellie continued.

Jack wasn't sure why he was sitting in on a client consultation, but since he didn't have anything better to do decided to go with the flow. He ordered a double espresso and noticed that Will was frowning at him.

'Do I know you?' Will asked, puzzled.

This was one of the things he most liked about Cape Town—the fact that people hardly recognised him. While he wasn't famous enough to attract paparazzi attention in the UK, his face was recognisable enough to attract some attention.

'I have one of those faces,' he lied.

Ellie sent him a grin. 'I'm just going to run through some ideas with Will and Paula, then I'll show you around.'

She placed her notebook on the table and switched into work mode, outwardly confident. Jack listened as the couple explained why they now wanted a Pari's cake—their cake designer had let them down at the last moment—and watched, amazed, as Ellie took their rather vague ideas and transformed them into a quickly sketched but brilliantly drawn concept cake. He sampled various types of cake along with the couple, and when they asked for his opinion confirmed that he liked the Death by Chocolate best. Though the carrot ran a close second. Or maybe the fudge...

If he hung around the bakery more often Jack decided he'd have to add another couple of miles to his daily run to combat the calories and the cholesterol.

Ellie watched her clients go as she gathered her papers and shoved a pencil into the messy knot of hair behind her head.

'Today is Monday. Their wedding is on Saturday. I'm going to have to do some serious juggling to get it done for them.' Ellie rubbed her hand over her eyes.

'So why are you doing it, then?' Jack asked, curious.

'They are a sweet couple, and a wedding cake is important,' Ellie replied.

'Sweet? No. But they sure are slick.'

Ellie looked puzzled. 'What do you mean?'

She might be confident about her work but she was seriously naïve when it came to reading people, instinctively choosing to believe that people put their best foot forward.

Jack leaned his forearms on the table and shook his head. 'El, they were playing you.'

'What are you talking about?'

'They decided to come to you for their wedding cake—but it wasn't because their cake designer let them down. They knew there was no chance you'd make their cake at such late notice if they didn't have a rock-solid reason and they appealed to the romantic in you.'

'But why would you think that? I thought they were perfectly nice and above-board.'

'She doesn't blink—at all—when she lies, and his eyes slide to the right. Trust me, they were playing you.'

'Huh...' Ellie wrinkled her nose. 'Are you sure?'

Of course he was. He'd interviewed ten-year-olds with a better ability to lie. 'So, what are you going to do?'

Ellie stood up and shrugged. 'Make them their cake, of course. Let's go.'

Of course she was. Jack sighed as he followed her to the back of the bakery. She was going to produce a stunning, complicated cake in five days and their guests would be impressed, not knowing how she'd juggled her schedule to fit it in.

'I'm beginning to suspect you're a glutton for punishment,' Jack told Ellie as she pushed through the stable door leading to the back of the bakery. And a sucker too. But he kept that thought to himself.

She threw a look at him above her shoulder. 'Maybe—but did you notice that they didn't ask for a price?'

He hadn't, actually.

'And that order form they signed—at the bottom it states that there is a twenty-five per cent surcharge for rush jobs. Pure profit, Jack.'

Well, maybe not so much of a sucker.

Ellie walked over to a stainless steel table and tossed her sketchpad onto it. She scowled at the design they'd decided on. 'There's a standard surcharge for rush jobs,' she admitted. 'But I really don't need the extra profit.'

'And now you're angry because they played you?' Jack commented.

'I was totally sucked in by Paula's big blue eyes, the panic I saw on her face. Will played his part perfectly as well, trying to reassure her while looking at me with those *help me* eyes!'

'They were good. Not great, but good.'

'*Arrgh!* I need the added pressure of making a wedding cake in five days like I need a hole in my head!'

'So call them up and tell them you can't do it,' Jack suggested.

That would mean going back on her word, and she couldn't do that. 'I can't. And, really, couldn't you have given me a heads-up *before* I agreed to make their damn cake?'

Jack cocked his head. 'How?'

'I don't know! You're the one who is supposed to be so street-wise and dialed-in... Couldn't you have whispered in my ear? Kicked my foot? Written me a damn note?'

Jack's lips quirked. 'My handwriting is shocking.'

'It is not. I've seen your writing!' Ellie shoved her hands into her hair. Her shoulders slumped. 'Useless man.'

'So I've been told.' He reached out and laid a hand on her shoulder, his expression suddenly serious. 'Sorry. It never occurred to me to interfere.'

She looked at him, leaning back against the wall, seemingly relaxed. But his eyes never stopped moving... He hadn't said anything to her because he was an observer. He didn't get involved in a situation; he just commentated on it after the fact. She couldn't blame him. It was what he did. What journalists did.

She would have appreciated a heads-up, though. *Dammit.*

Ellie heard a high-pitched whistle and snapped her head up, immediately looking at the back section of the bakery, where the production area flowed into another room. Elias, one of her head bakers, stood at the wide entrance and jerked his head. Something in his body language had Ellie moving forward, and she reached her elderly staff member at the same time Jack did.

'What's wrong, Elias?' Ellie asked when she reached him.

Ellie felt Jack's hand on her lower back and was glad it was there.

Elias spoke in broken English and Ellie listened carefully. Before she had time to take in his words, never mind the implications, Jack was also demanding to know what the problem was.

'One of the industrial mixers is only working at one speed and the other one has stopped altogether,' she explained.

'That's not good,' Jack said.

'It's a disaster! We have orders coming out of our ears and we need cake. *Dammit!* Nothing happens in the bakery without the mixers... Elias, how did this happen?'

Elias shifted on his feet and stared at a point behind her head. 'I did tell you, Miss Ellie...the mixers...they need service. Did tell you...bad noise.'

Ellie scrubbed her face with her hands. He was right. He *had* told her—numerous times—but she'd been so busy, feeling so overwhelmed, and the mixers had been working. It had been on her list of things to do but it had kept getting shoved to the bottom when, really, it should have been at the top.

Ellie placed her hands over her face again and shook her head. What was she going to do?

When she eventually dropped her hands she saw that Elias was walking out of earshot. Jack had obviously signalled that they needed some privacy. He placed his hands on the mixer and lifted his eyebrows at Ellie.

'Dropped the ball on this one, didn't you?' he remarked.

Ellie glared at him, her blue eyes laser-bright. 'In between juggling the orders and paying the staff and placing orders for supplies, I somehow forgot to schedule a service for the mixers! Stupid me.' She folded her arms across her chest as she paced the small area between them.

'It was, actually, since this is the heartbeat of your business.'

Did he think she didn't know that? 'I messed up. I get it... It's something I'm doing a lot of lately.'

'Stop feeling sorry for yourself and start thinking about how you're going to fix the problem,' Jack snapped.

She felt the instinctive urge to slap him...slap *something*.

'You can indulge in self-pity later, but right now your entire production has stopped and you're wasting daylight.'

His words shocked some sense into her, but she reserved the right to indulge in some hysterics later. 'I need to get someone here to fix these mixers...' Ellie saw him shake his head and she threw up her hands. 'What have I said wrong now?'

'Priorities, Ellie. What are you going to do about your orders?'

'You mean the mixers,' Ellie corrected him.

Jack shook his head and reached for the paper slips that were stuck on a wooden beam to the right of the mixers. 'No, I mean the orders. Prioritise the orders and get...what was his name...Elias...to start hand-mixing the batter for the cakes that are most urgent.'

That made sense, Ellie thought, reluctantly impressed.

Ellie took the slips he held out and a pen and quickly prioritised the orders. 'Okay, that's done. I'll get him working on these.'

Jack nodded and looked at the mixers. 'Are these under guarantee or anything?'

'No. Why?'

'Got a toolbox?'

'A toolbox? Why? What for?'

'While Elias starts the hand-mixing I'll take a look at these mixers. I know my way around machines and motors. It's probably just a broken drive belt or a stripped gear.'

'Where on earth would you have learnt about machines and motors?' Ellie demanded, bemused.

'Ellie, I spend a good portion of my life in Third World

countries, on Third World roads, using Third World transportation. I've broken down more times in more crappy cars than you've made wedding cakes. Since I'm not the type to hang about waiting for someone else to get things working, I get stuck in. I can now, thanks to the tutelage of some amazing bush mechanics, fix most things.'

Ellie shut her flapping mouth and swallowed. 'Okay, well…uh…there's a basic toolbox in the storeroom and a hardware store down the road if you need anything else.'

Jack put his hands on his hips. 'And get on that phone and get someone here to service those mixers. I might be able to get them running but they'll still need a service.'

Ellie looked at him, baffled at this take-charge Jack. 'Jack—thank you.'

'Get one of the staff to bring me that toolbox, will you?' Jack crouched on his haunches at the back of one of the machines and started to work off the cover that covered the mixer's motor. 'Hell, look at this motor! It's leaking oil…it's clogged up…when was this damn thing last serviced?'

Ellie, who thought that Jack wouldn't appreciate hearing that she hadn't the faintest clue, decided to scarper while she could and left Jack cursing to himself.

CHAPTER FOUR

ELIAS LAUGHED WHEN Jack messed up the traditional African handshake—again—and slapped him on the shoulder. 'We'll teach you yet, *mlungu*.'

'Ma-lun-goo?' Jack tested the word out on his tongue.

'"White man" in Xhosa,' said the old Xhosa baker.

'Ah.' Jack stared at Elias and a slow grin crossed his face. 'I heard you talking Xhosa earlier. I love the clicking sound you make. If I were staying I would want to learn Xhosa.'

'If you stay…' Elias grinned '…I teach you.'

'There's a deal,' Jack said, before bidding him goodnight and turning back to the rear entrance of the bakery.

Ellie looked up as he walked towards her and ran the back of her hand over her forehead. 'Bet you're regretting ambling down the hill this morning,' she said with a grateful smile.

'It's been an…interesting day,' Jack said, conscious of a dull headache behind his eyes. 'A baptism by grease, flour, sugar and baking powder…'

'I never expected you to help with either the fixing or the mixing, but thank you.'

He'd resurrected one of the mixers, and when a part arrived for the other mixer in the morning he'd have that up and running within an hour. While he'd been working on the mixers he'd watched Elias and his assistant falling further and further behind on the orders, and had instantly become their best friend when he'd got the one mixer working.

'Elias really battled physically to do that hand-mixing.'

Ellie cocked her head. 'So that's why you stepped in to help him?'

He shrugged. 'I thought he was going to have a heart attack,' Jack admitted.

He'd mixed the batter for more than a hundred and twenty cupcakes and, under Elias's beady eye, also mixed the ingredients for two Pari's Paradise Chocolate cakes and more than a few vanilla sponge cakes. His shoulders ached and his biceps were crying out for mercy...

'He's stronger than he looks. He should've retired years ago, but he doesn't want to and I can't make him.' Ellie sighed. 'He's worked here since the day the bakery opened. It's his second home, and as long as he wants to work I'll let him. But maybe I should try to sneak in another assistant.'

'Sneak in?'

'It took me six months to get him to accept Gideon in his space.' Ellie grinned. 'He's a wonderful old gent but he has the pride of Lucifer. I'm surprised he let you do anything.'

'Yeah, but I *did* get his beloved mixer working.'

'That you did,' Ellie agreed. 'And I'm so grateful. You worked like a dog today.'

Which raised the question...*why* had he bust his gut to help this woman he barely knew? He was an observer, not a participator, and her bakery wouldn't have gone into bankruptcy if they'd waited for a mechanic to fix the mixers. But he'd felt compelled to step up and get stuck in, to help her, to...

Aargh! He must have taken a blow to the head along with the stabbing and the beating, because this wasn't how he normally rolled.

Jack, frustrated at not recognising himself, thought that he'd kill for a beer or two. He stood next to Ellie's table and leaned his shoulder against a wall, watching her work. She'd been in the bakery for nearly twelve hours and she was still working on another cake. The nightshift of two more bakers were starting their shift and Ellie would probably be there to see them off in the morning.

She might tend to panic when she hit a snag but he admired her work ethic.

And her legs... Who would've thought that a chef's jacket over shorts and long tanned legs could look so sexy? Jack swallowed, uneasy at the realisation that he wanted...no, *craved* her.

He'd never had this reaction to any woman before. Generally it was easy come, easy go. Nothing about Ellie so far had been easy, and he suspected that nothing would be. Jack shifted on his feet as desire flared. It would be easy to seduce her, but that would make leaving in a couple of days that much more complicated. Because somehow he instinctively knew that he couldn't treat her as a casual encounter. There was something about Ellie that tugged at him—some button that she pushed that made him suspect that this was a woman worth getting to know...

And that was more terrifying than being caught in the crossfire in any hot zone anywhere in the world. They had yet to make flak jackets to protect against emotional bullets.

Ellie looked up from the bare cake in front of her, which had been cut into the vague shape of a train and was covered in rough white icing. She sent him a tired smile. 'I'm wondering what I can give you for supper.'

Jack pried himself off the wall and walked away from the table she was working at. 'Something simple...let's order pizza.'

Ellie sighed and Jack saw relief flicker on her face.

'Okay. I just need to finish this and we can go home. Or you can go home and I'll follow in a bit.'

Jack hooked a stool with his foot and rolled it towards him, sinking down onto it with a groan. 'I'll wait for you.'

Ellie pulled out a ball of fire-engine-red dough from a container and started to knead it with competent hands.

Jack stretched out his legs. 'What are you making with that red dough?'

'It's not dough. It's fondant icing. It's for a train cake,' Ellie explained. She gestured to what looked like a big pasta roller on the table next to hers. 'It goes in there to flatten it out, then I'll drape it over the cake.'

'Does it have to be done tonight?'

'It should be. Luckily, I can make this in my sleep.' Ellie slapped her hand into the fondant and caught his look. 'What? Why are you looking at me like that?'

'I was just thinking about your business, what you do here.' He hadn't been, but he suspected that she wasn't ready to hear what he'd really been thinking...which involved her being naked and sliding all over him.

Oh, Lordy-be, there was that smile that made her womb vibrate. It was a combination of schoolboy naughtiness and sex-on-a-stick, and Ellie thought that stronger women than her would have trouble resisting it. She opened her mouth to ask what he was smiling about and practically bit her tongue in half to keep the words from escaping.

The hell of it was that while she'd initially thought that Jack might be all flash, today he had proved that he was more than just a hot body with a reasonably sharp brain. How many men of her acquaintance would have jumped in to help, tinkering with a motor and getting splattered with grease and then patiently mixing endless batches of batter—a thankless, back-breaking, horrible job to do by hand—without a word of complaint?

Ellie smoothed icing over the front of the train. The ability to give without asking for something in return, to jump into a situation and offer help when it was most needed, was a rare quality and unfortunately deeply attractive. Even more so than his hot body and masculine face.

Ellie's hand stilled on the cake as a panicked thought jumped into her head. She wanted him to go—now—tonight. She wanted him to go before she started imagining him in her bakery, in her life…before she started dreaming of a clear mind to keep her focused, a steady hand to prod her along, a hard body to touch and taste, then to curl up against at night.

Ellie fisted her hand and had to stop herself from punching the cake. She was suddenly ridiculously, outrageously angry at herself. Why was she even letting thoughts like those into her head? Considering what-ifs and maybes? Yes, he was a good-looking guy who gave her a buzz, a man nice enough to help her out, but there was no call to start thinking that he was anything more than a transient visitor. He was nothing but her father's friend, a brief acquaintance, and realistically she wasn't his type.

Oh, she was attractive enough for a brief fling, but she wasn't stupid enough to believe that she could ever be more than that. *Nobody will give up their freedom and time for monogamy with you…*

Jack had got up, rested his hand on her clenched fist and forced her fingers open.

Ellie twisted her lips and blew out a breath, but kept her eyes fixed on the cake.

'I think that's enough for now. We need pizza and beer and to chill,' he said.

Ellie pulled her hand out from beneath his and brushed her hair off her forehead with the tips of her fingers, leaving a trail of red icing on her forehead. 'This cake…'

'Will still be here tomorrow.' Jack took her hand again and pulled her away from the table. He leaned forward and his voice was low, seductive and sexy in her ear. 'Beer. Pizza.'

Ellie looked at the half-white, half-red train. Beer, pizza and conversation with an interesting man versus a stupid train cake…? No contest.

The woman amazed him, Jack thought. Twenty minutes ago Ellie had looked as if she was about to collapse, but now, sitting across from him at a table on the deck of an admittedly fake, slightly scruffy Italian restaurant, she looked sensational. She'd pulled her hair back into a sleek ponytail which highlighted her amazing cheekbones and painted her lips a glossy soft pink. She'd sorted out the smudged make-up around her eyes and she looked and smelled as if she'd just stepped out of a shower.

He, on the other hand, felt as if he'd spent the day hauling hay and cleaning out stables. He took a long sip of his beer and sighed as the bittersweet liquid slid down his throat. The night was warm, the surf was pounding, he had a beer in his hand and a pretty girl across the table from him.

The only scenario that sounded better was if he'd had pizza in his belly and the girl was naked beneath him.

'There's that smile again,' Ellie murmured.

'Huh? What smile?'

Ellie rested her chin in the palm of her hand. 'You get this secretive, naughty, sexy smile…'

'Sexy?' The light on the deck was muted but Jack grinned as he saw her blush.

'Yeah, well…anyway. So, I'm starving.' Ellie looked around, not trying to hide the fact that she was looking to change the subject. 'Where's that pizza?'

Jack decided to let her off the hook—mostly because flirting caused his pants to wake up and start doing its happy dance.

He looked around and narrowed his eyes. 'Have you had any more thoughts about the bakery?'

Ellie wrinkled her nose. She took a sip from her glass of wine and glanced at the ocean. 'Moving it, you mean?'

'Mmm.'

'I have an idea that I'm working on,' Ellie said mysteriously.

His curiosity was instantly aroused. 'You can't leave me hanging!' Jack protested when she didn't elaborate.

Ellie smiled. 'There might be a property that could work.'

'You don't have much time,' Jack pointed out.

'I know. Six months.'

Under the table Jack felt Ellie crossing her legs and he heard her sigh.

'I want to hyperventilate every time I think about it.'

'Call your mother and tell her to come home. It's her business too, El. You don't have to carry this load alone. Tell her about having to move. Tell her that you need help.'

'I can't, Jack. She's been working in that bakery for ever, never taking time off. Now she's living her dream and having such a blast. I can't ask her to give that up. Not just yet. And…and I feel that if I do I'm admitting failure. That I need my mummy to hold my hand.'

Jack shook his head. 'So you'd rather work yourself to a standstill, knocking yourself out, instead of asking your friend to come back to work and your mother to come back and help you?'

'Making sure that the people I love are happy is very important to me, Jack.'

'Not if it comes at too high a price to *you*.'

She'd inherited Mitchell's irritable, don't-mess-with-me stare.

'You're really sexy when you're irritated,' he commented idly, unfazed.

'I suspect that you can be annoying…' she paused for a beat and bared her teeth at him '…all the time.'

Jack grinned at her attempt to intimidate him. She looked as scary as a Siamese cat with an attitude disorder.

Ellie rubbed her temple with her fingertips. 'Can we not talk about the bakery tonight? I'd like to pretend it's not there for five minutes.'

Jack agreed and sighed in relief when he saw a waiter heading their way with pizzas. It wasn't a moment too soon. He thought his stomach was about to eat itself.

'So, why war reporting?' Ellie asked, when they'd both satisfied their immediate hunger.

Ellie wound a piece of stray cheese around her finger and popped it into her mouth. Jack nearly choked on the bite of pizza he'd just taken. *Hell*... He quickly swallowed and pulled his mind out of the bedroom. She was getting harder and harder to resist. And he *had* to resist her...mostly because she *was* so damn hard to resist.

Ellie repeating her question wiped the idea of sex—only temporarily, he was sure—from his brain.

'When I was about fifteen I watched a lot of news, and Mitch and other war reporters were reporting from Iraq. I was fascinated. They seemed larger than life.'

'He was. Is.'

'Then he was interviewed and he spoke about the travelling and the adrenalin and I thought it was a kick-ass career.'

Jack bit, swallowed and grinned. 'I still think it is.'

Ellie's eyes were a deep blue in the candlelight and Jack felt as if she could see into his soul.

'How do you deal with the bad stuff you've seen? The violence, the suffering, the madness, the cruelty? How do you process all of that?'

Jack carefully placed his slice of pizza back down on his plate. He took a while to answer, and when he did he was surprised to hear the emotion in his voice. 'It took some time but I've programmed myself to just report on the facts. My job is to tell the story—hopefully in a way that will facilitate change. I observe and I don't judge, because judgement requires an emotional involvement.'

'And you don't get emotionally involved,' Ellie said thoughtfully. 'Does that carry over into other areas of your life?'

Jack stiffened, wondering where she was going with that question. 'You mean like relationships and crap like that?'

'Yeah—crap like that.' Ellie's response was bone-dry.

He had to set her straight. Right now. Just in case she had any ideas...

'Like your father, my life doesn't lend itself to having a long-term relationship. Women tend to get annoyed when you don't spend time with them.'

'Yep, I know what that feels like. Any woman who gets involved with a war reporter is asking to put her emotions through a meat-grinder,' Ellie replied. 'God knows that's exactly what Mitchell did to me.'

She didn't give him time to respond and was frustrated when she changed the subject.

'So, how is the book coming along?'

Ellie pushed her plate away and Jack frowned. She'd barely managed to eat half her medium pizza and he had almost finished his large. 'Well, apart from the fact that I can't get a certain reporter's daughter to sit down and answer my questions, fine.'

He saw guilt flash across her face. 'Oh, Jack, I'm so sorry! You probably want to leave, head home, and I'm holding you up—'

Jack shook his head. Where did this need to blame herself for everything come from? She was so together and confident in some ways—such a train wreck when it came to her need to please.

'Ellie, stop it!' Ellie's mouth snapped shut and Jack thought that was progress. 'Firstly, if I wanted to leave I would've made a plan to go already. Secondly, as I said, I like your house, I like this area, and when I start feeling pressurised for time I'll tell you and we'll get down to it. As long as you do not want me out of your house we're good. *Do* you want me to leave?'

'No, you're reasonably well house-trained,' Ellie muttered. Jack grinned.

'So, why aren't you prepared to write your story? Mitchell said that you were asked to.' Ellie picked up the thread of their conversation again.

Because my story isn't just my story and it's a lot more complicated than people think. Jack swallowed those words and just shrugged.

Ellie picked an olive off her pizza and popped it into her mouth. They sat in a comfortable silence for a while, until Ellie spoke again. 'I think I know why you are reluctant to tell your story.'

This should be good. A little armchair analysis. 'Really? Why?'

'In light of what you said earlier, digging into your own story, analysing your life choices, would require emotional involvement. You can't stand back and just observe your own life. You can't be objective about yourself. Then again, who can?'

It was Jack's turn to stare at her, to feel the impact of her insightful words. He couldn't even begin to start formulating an argument. There wasn't one, because her observation was pure truth.

Jack drained the last inch of beer in his bottle and threw his serviette onto the table. 'You ready to go?'

Ellie nodded, pushed her chair back and pulled her purse out of her bag. He ground his teeth as she placed cash under the heavy salt cellar. Where the hell were his new bank cards? He was sick of not having access to funds.

He stopped at the cashier on the way out and asked for a

receipt, and he knew without looking at Ellie that she was rolling her eyes at him.

'Jack, you worked in the bakery. I'll pay for dinner.'

'No.' Jack took the printed bill from the manager and shoved it into his pocket.

'Stop being anal.'

Jack gripped her ponytail and tugged gently. 'Stop nagging. I thought we agreed that if I'm living in your house then I'll pick up the tab?'

She tossed her head. 'We never agreed on anything!'

Jack's grin flashed. 'It's easier if you just do it my way.'

'In your dreams.'

It was shortly after six the following evening when Jack returned from a trip to Robben Island, the off-coast prison that had housed Nelson Mandela for twenty-four years, and his mind was still on the beloved South African icon when he walked into Ellie's kitchen.

He kicked off his shoes, dumped the take-away Chinese he'd picked up on the way on the kitchen table and tossed his brand-new wallet containing his brand-new bank cards onto the table. Inside was enough cash to reimburse Ellie for everything she'd paid for so far. Thinking about Ellie, he wondered where she was.

Jack walked back into the hall and stood at the bottom of the stairs, calling her name. Her bag was on its customary hook and her mobile sat on the hall table. Jack walked back to the kitchen, onto the back deck, and finally found her, sprawled out on a lounger in the shade of one of the two umbrellas that stood next to her pool.

She was asleep, with an open sketchbook on her bare, flat stomach and a piece of charcoal on the grass below her hand. She was dressed in a tiny black and blue bikini and he spent many minutes examining her nearly-but-not-quite naked body.

Her long damp hair streamed over her shoulders and across the triangles that covered her full breasts. She had a flat, almost concave stomach, slim hips and long, smooth legs with fine muscles. The tips of her elegant feet were painted a vivid pink that reminded him of Grecian sunsets.

Very alluring, very sexy, Jack thought, sinking to the grass next to her chair. In order to stop himself from undoing those flimsy ties keeping those tiny triangles in place, he picked up the sketchpad and flipped through the pages.

The sketches were rough, jerky, but powerful, full of movement. She'd sketched her house, capturing its fat lines and bay windows, and there was a sketch of her dog, head on paws, his eyes soulful. There was a rather bleak landscape of cliffs and shadows which oozed sadness and regret.

Jack gasped at his likeness, grinning up at him from another white page. She'd captured his laugh and, worse, the attraction to her he'd thought he was hiding so well.

'Snoop.'

Jack snapped the book closed and looked up into her face. Her eyes were still closed and her eyelashes were ink-black on her face.

'I thought you were still asleep. I was trying to be quiet.'

'I'm a really light sleeper,' Ellie said, and held out her hand for her sketchpad.

Jack reluctantly handed it over. 'These are good—'

'It's something I do to pass the time.' Ellie tossed the pad on top of a box of charcoal sticks and sat up, covering her mouth as she yawned. 'Talking of which, what *is* the time?'

Jack looked at his watch. 'Half-six.'

Ellie looked horrified. 'I went for a swim around five and thought I'd take fifteen minutes to chill... I must've dozed off.'

Jack drew his thumb across the purple shadow under her eye. 'It looks like you needed it. What time did you finish last night? I saw your light was still on after midnight.'

'One? Half-one? I finished the VAT return and paid some creditors.' Ellie swung her legs off the sunchair, her feet brushing Jack's thighs. 'I've got a couple of hours' work tonight and then I'll be caught up. I shouldn't have fallen asleep...I meant to work after my swim.'

Jack clenched his fists in an effort not to reach for her. She looked so tired, so young, so...*weary* that all he wanted to do was take her in his arms and ease her stress. He shoved his hand into his hair. *She tries to hide it,* he thought, *but she's wiped out in every way she can be by the responsibilities of her business.* He wished there was something he could do for her. Dammit, was he starting to feel protective over her? He didn't know how to handle her, deal with her. He was used to resilient, emotionally tougher women, and Ellie had him wanting to shield her, shelter her.

'I need to think about what to make for supper,' Ellie said as she stood up, unfurling that long, slender body.

Her voice was saturated with exhaustion and he felt irritation jump up into his throat. 'Ellie, I am *not* another one of your responsibilities!' he snapped.

Ellie blinked at him. 'You don't want me to make supper?'

'No. For a number of reasons. The first being that I bought supper—Chinese. My replacement bank cards arrived,' he explained when she looked at him enquiringly. 'Also, I really think you need to learn that the world will not stop turning if you stop for five minutes and relax. You never stop moving, and when you do you're so exhausted that you can't keep your eyes open.'

Ellie picked up a sarong and wound it around her hips. 'Jack, please. I really don't want to argue with you.'

Jack nodded. 'Okay, I won't argue. I'll just tell you what to do. You're going to change into something that doesn't stop traffic and then we're going for a walk. On the way we'll stop and have a beer at one of the pubs on the beachfront. Then we'll come home, eat Chinese, of which you will have a reasonable portion, and then you're going to bed. Early.'

'Jack, it's hot. I don't feel like a walk and I can't take the time—'

'Yeah, you can,' Jack told her. 'And I know you're hot. You're standing there in a couple of triangles cooking my blood pressure. So this should help both of us cool off.'

Jack scooped her up, ignored her squeal and stepped, still dressed, into the deep end of her gloriously cold, sparkling blue pool.

CHAPTER FIVE

'IT'S SUCH A stunning evening. Would you like to take the long route to the beachfront?' Ellie asked him as they stepped onto the road outside her house. 'It's a ten-minute walk instead of a five-minute walk but I'll show you a bit of the neighbourhood.'

'Sure,' Jack agreed, and they turned left instead of right.

He walked next to Ellie, his hands loose in the pockets of his shorts. The sea in front of them was pancake-flat and a patchwork quilt of greens and blues. It was make-your-soul-bump beautiful. The temperature had dropped and she was cool from the swim and the light, short sundress she was wearing.

She was really looking forward to an icy margarita and Jack's stimulating, slightly acerbic company.

A little way away from the house Jack broke their comfortable silence. 'By the way, I was contacted today by the Press Club. They've heard that I'm in town and have invited me to their annual dinner. I'd like you to go with me, but I know how busy you are. Any chance?'

Ellie's heart hiccupped. A date! A real date! *Whoop!* She did an internal happy dance. 'When is it?'

'Tomorrow. Tomorrow *is* Friday, right? It's black tie, I'm afraid.'

A date where she could seriously glam up? Double *whoop!*

'So, do you think you can leave work early for a change?' Jack enquired. 'It's a hassle going to these functions on my own.'

In a strange city where he knew no one of course it would be. And the world wouldn't stop turning if she left work a little earlier than normal. Besides, Merri would come in for an hour or two.

'Sure. That sounds like fun.'

'Great.' Jack moved between her and a large dog that was walking along the verge of a house with its gates left open.

Ellie appreciated his innate protectiveness but she knew Islay. He was as friendly as he was old.

Jack cleared his throat. 'Ellie, I was only supposed to spend one, maybe two nights in your house...'

'And tonight will be your fourth night,' Ellie replied quietly. 'Do you want to leave?'

Jack shook his head. 'Just the opposite, actually. Mitch, being Mitch, has put the word out to the network editors that I'm hurt and need some time off.'

Ellie flicked a glance at his hip. 'You *are* hurt.'

'Superficially.' Compared to what he'd gone through, his stab wound was minimal. 'Anyway, I'm off for a few weeks unless—'

She knew the drill. Journalists were only 'off' until the next story came along. 'Unless some huge story breaks.'

Jack nodded his agreement. 'So, I thought I'd stay in Cape Town for a bit longer.'

'In my house?' Ellie heard the squeak in her voice and winced. She sounded like a demented mouse.

'Well, I could move into a hotel, but I spend enough time in hotels as it is and I'd rather pay you.'

Ellie stopped in her tracks and turned to look at him. 'You'd pay to live with me?'

What exactly did he mean by that? What would be included in that deal? Not that she believed for one minute that he'd make her an offer that was below-board, but she just wanted to make sure… And really, how upset would she be if he suggested sleeping together? Since she was constantly thinking about sex with him…not very.

His grin suggested he knew exactly what she was thinking. 'It's a simple transaction, Ellie. Someone has to get paid to put my butt into a bed and I'd prefer it to be you and not some nameless, faceless corporation.' Jack stepped forward and his thumb drifted over her chin. 'A bed, food, coffee. No expectations, no pressure.' Damn.

'Oh.' Ellie dropped her head and thought she was an idiot for feeling disappointed. *You don't want to get involved, on any level, with any man—remember, Ellie?* Especially a man like Jack. Too good-looking, too successful, too much. Rough, tough, unemotional and—the big reason—never around.

But she wanted him. She really did.

Jack dropped his hand and Ellie was glad, because she didn't know for how much longer she could stop herself reaching up and kissing him, tasting those firm lips, feeling the rasp of his stubble under her lips, her fingers. She watched him walk away and after two steps he turned and looked back at her.

He must have seen something on her face, because his steps lengthened and then his hands were on her hips, yanking her into him. His mouth finally touched hers sweetly, gently, before he allowed his passion to explode. His quick tongue slipped between her lips, scraped her teeth and tangled with her own in a long, deep kiss that had no end or beginning.

One hand held her head in place and the other explored her back, her hip, the curves of her bottom, the tops of her thighs. Ellie slid her hand up his back, under his loose T-shirt, and acquainted herself with his bare flesh, the muscles in his back, that strip of flesh above his shorts and the soft leather belt. He was heat and lust and passion in its purist, most concentrated form; causing her nipples and her thighs to press together to subdue the deep, insistent throbbing between them.

He kissed her some more.

Ellie wasn't sure how much time had passed when he finally lifted his head and rested his forehead against hers. 'I'm burning up, on fire from wanting you. That's why I haven't kissed you before this.'

'Why did you kiss me now?' Ellie whispered back, her hands gripping his sides.

'Because you looked like you wanted me to—really wanted me to.'

She really had. And she wouldn't object to more.

Jack stepped back, linked his hands behind his head. The muscles in his arms bulged. 'I can't take you to bed… I mean of course I *can*. I want to. Desperately. But it would be the worst idea in the world.'

It didn't matter that she agreed with him. She wanted to know why he thought so. 'Why?'

Jack's mouth twisted. 'I'm not good for you. I'm hard and cynical, frequently bitter. I have seen so many bad things. You're arty and creative and…innocent. Untainted.'

'No, I'm not.' Ellie pursed her lips. He made her sound like a nun. 'You're not a bad man, Jack.'

'But I'd be bad for *you*.' Jack dropped his arms and stared out to sea. 'I am not a noble man, Ellie, but I'm trying to do the right thing here. Help me out, okay?'

Ellie lifted her hands in puzzlement. 'How am I supposed to do that?'

Jack glared at her. 'Well, for starters you could stop looking at me as if you want to slurp me up through a straw. Sexy little dresses like that don't help—and you're *very* lucky that you kept possession of that thing you call a bikini this afternoon. Short shorts and tight tops are out too…'

'Would you like me to walk around in a tent?' Ellie asked

sarcastically, but secretly she was enjoying the fact that she could turn him on so quickly. It was a power she'd never experienced before, a heady sensation knowing that this delicious man thought that she was equally tasty.

'That might work,' Jack replied.

Ellie pulled in a breath as he stepped forward and took her much smaller hand in his. His expression turned sober.

'El, I like you, but I think you have enough going on in your life without the added pressure of an affair with me. I need to write your father's life story and I don't know how objective I'm going to be if I am sleeping with his daughter.'

Ellie kept her eyes on his and gestured him to continue. Everything he'd said so far had made sense, but she could still feel his lips on hers, his big hands on her skin. Taste him on her lips.

'It's been a long time since I just liked a woman, enjoyed her company. Can we keep this simple? Try to just be friends? That way, when I leave, there won't be any…stupid feelings between us.' Jack stared down at her fingers. 'You know it's the smart thing to do.'

Ellie sighed and wished she could be half as erudite as he was. Sure, words were the tools of his trade, but he made her feel as thick as a peanut butter sandwich when it came to expressing herself. Only two words came to mind, and neither were worthy of this conversation.

'Yeah, okay,' she muttered.

Jack smiled and ran his thumb over her knuckles before dropping her hand. 'So, will you go to the camping store for a tent or shall I?'

'Make sure it's a pink one.' Ellie looked around and her expression softened. 'Oh, we're here!'

'Where?' Jack asked as she grabbed the edge of his shirt and tugged him across the road.

Ellie walked up to some wrought-iron gates and wrapped

her fingers around the bars, looking at the dilapidated double-storey building.

Jack tugged on the chain that held the gates together. 'What *is* this place?'

'It was a library at the turn of the century, then it was turned into a house, but it's been empty a couple of years. I've heard a rumour that old Mrs Hutchinson is finally considering selling it. Restored, this building would be utter perfection. Two storeys of whimsy, with balconies and bay windows galore. Its irregular shape reminds me of a blowsy matron in a voluminous skirt and a peculiar hat. Romantic, eccentric and very over the top.'

Jack immediately picked up where she was going with this. 'You're thinking of this place for the bakery?'

'It's just around the corner from the present location, with ample parking space. I took a box of cupcakes to the Town Planning office and...well, bribed them into letting me take a look at the building plans. There is a lot of space, but not too much...enough to hold the bakery, the delicatessen and a proper breakfast and lunch restaurant.'

Jack put his hands on his hips. 'It's difficult to comment without seeing the place. Let's go in.'

Ellie pointed at the sign on the fence. '"No Trespassers".'

'If I obeyed those signs I'd never get a story,' Jack said, and pulled at a rusty iron post on the fence. It moved, and he gestured Ellie through the gap he'd created. 'You're slim enough to climb through here.'

'And you?'

Jack grabbed the top of the fence with his hands, yanked himself up and held his body weight while he swung his legs onto the railing. Within seconds he was on the other side and his breathing hadn't changed.

Ellie shook her head as she slipped through the fence. 'If

you've split open your cut you're going to the emergency room,' she told him.

'Yes, Mum.' Jack grinned and led her up to the huge front door. He pursed his lips at the lock. 'No breaking in through *this* door.'

'We're not breaking in through any door!' Ellie stated as he pulled her away from the front door and around the house. 'Seriously, Jack, that's a crime!'

Jack peered through a window. 'Relax, there's nothing to steal, so if we get caught we can plead curiosity. I'm good at talking my way out of trouble.'

'Jack!'

Jack stopped at a side door. 'Good. Yale lock. Pass me a hairpin, El.'

'You are not going to… Hey!' Ellie slapped her hand against her head where Jack had yanked the pin from her hair. 'That hurt!'

'Sorry.' Jack opened the pin, inserted it into the lock and jiggled the handle. Within a minute the door swung open to his touch. 'Bingo.'

'I cannot believe that you picked that lock! Who taught you that?'

'You really don't want to know.'

Ellie looked curious. 'No, tell me. Who?'

'Your father, actually.'

Ellie rolled her eyes and Jack just grinned as he placed a hand on her lower back and pushed her inside.

'I *so* didn't need to know that!' she muttered.

'Relax.' Jack placed his hands on his hips and looked into the room to his right. 'Kitchen through here—an enormous one, but it needs to be gutted. God, Ellie, the ceiling is falling down!'

'I never said it didn't need work. Look at these floors, Jack. Solid yellow-wood.'

Jack looked at the patch of direct sunlight on the warped wood and at the hundreds of holes in it. 'White ants, Ellie, white ants. I bet the house is infested with them.'

'Are you always this pessimistic?' Ellie asked as she opened doors on either side of the passage.

'I just think you should slow down to a gallop. I can see the look in your eye. If you could you'd slap the deposit down,' Jack said. He picked at a piece of wallpaper and a strip came off in his hand. 'Before you even consider doing that I suggest you get an architect to look at the place, and a civil engineer to check that it's not going to fall down.'

It was sensible, unemotional advice—but sensible was for later. Right now she wanted to feel, sense, imagine.

Jack ducked his head into another room and Ellie heard what she swore was a screech. 'Did you squeal?' she called.

Jack hurried out of the room. 'Girls squeal. Men...don't. A rat nearly ran over my shoe! I hate rats!'

'Well, you squeal like a girl, and I'd rather have rats than white ants,' Ellie replied as they stepped into a massive hallway which was dominated by a two-storey-high ceiling and a thoroughly imposing staircase. Coloured sunshine from the stained glass inserts next to that imposing front door threw happy patterns onto the wooden floor.

'Okay, this is amazing,' Jack admitted.

'It's unbelievable,' Ellie said, falling hard.

Nothing had prepared her for the immediate visceral connection she felt to this property. She walked to the bay window behind the staircase and looked out onto the wilderness beyond, with its overgrown shrubs and trees. She could easily imagine the rambling, once stunning gardens that surrounded the house, like carefully chosen accessories on a red-carpet dress. Ellie walked the area downstairs and quickly established that the place could, without a huge amount of construction, be adapted to house the bakery.

It just took imagination—and she had lots of that.

'Why hasn't someone converted it into a restaurant? A bed and breakfast? An art gallery?' Jack asked when she rejoined him in the hall.

'Many have tried. Many have failed. Mrs Hutchinson hasn't ever been prepared to sell. She doesn't need the money and this building was her childhood home.' She shrugged at Jack's enquiring face. 'Basically, she's bats. The town fruitcake. She's refused offers—huge offers—for stupid reasons. Perceived lack of manners, not polishing your shoes. One man wore too much jewellery.'

'She sounds bonkers,' Jack said.

'That's one way of putting it,' Ellie said briskly, and tipped her head to look up at him. 'Let's finish with the breaking and entering. I could murder a drink.'

Jack followed her down the passage back to the side door, which he yanked open for her. 'Technically, it was only entering. We didn't break anything.'

'Semantics,' Ellie said as he pulled the door shut behind him and they headed back down the winding driveway to the road.

'You really are a bit of a pansy, aren't you?' Jack leapt over the fence and jammed his hands in his pockets as he waited for her to climb back through the gate.

She was just straightening up when she heard a car approaching and slowing down. Ellie looked up and straight into the eyes of the driver, who was looking at her curiously.

'Oh, *dammit.*'

Jack looked from her to the disappearing Toyota. 'Problem?'

Ellie slapped the palm of her hand against her forehead. 'That was Mrs Khumalo, the busiest of St James's busybodies. Soon it will be all over town either that I am having secret trysts with a married man, or that I am buying the property, or that I'm joining a cult and this is going to be its headquarters.'

Jack laughed as she stomped down the road. 'Cool. As the great Oscar Wilde said, "There's only one thing in the world worse than being talked about, and that is *not* being talked about".'

'Grrr.'

They fell into an easy silence on their walk home from the pub, and Ellie enjoyed the fact that they could be quiet together, that neither of them felt the need to fill the space with empty words.

Jack took the keys from her hand and opened the front door for her, nudging the dogs out of the way with a gentle knee so that she could walk in first. In the hallway Ellie dropped her bag on the side table and placed her hands on her back, stretching while Jack examined the life-size nude painting of a blonde on a scarlet velvet couch on the opposite wall. She wore only her long hair and a waist-length string of pearls... and a very come-hither grin.

'I can't stop looking at this painting.'

Since it was a nude painting of a gorgeous woman, Ellie wasn't surprised. Most men had the same reaction.

'Who *is* that?'

'My best friend Merri.'

Jack stepped up to the portrait and lightly touched the canvas with the back of his knuckle. 'I meant the artist. The way he's captured the blue veins in her pale skin, her inner glow... God, he's amazing!'

Ellie felt a spurt of pure, unadulterated pleasure. 'Thanks.'

Jack's mouth fell open. '*You* painted this?'

'Mmm. I studied Fine Art at uni and lived in London for a while, but I couldn't support myself by selling my art so I came home and started work at the bakery.'

'It's brilliant. But you left out quite a bit between uni and coming back to Cape Town.' He touched the frame with his fingertips. 'And this is more than something you pass time with.'

Ellie felt the familiar stab, the longing to immerse herself in a big painting that sucked her into a different dimension. 'It used to be my passion. It isn't any more.'

'Why not?'

'I painted that just before I went to the UK. I'd finished uni and was going to conquer the world. I was so in love with art, painting, creating. I was...*infused* by art.'

Jack sat on the bottom stair and patted the space next to him. Ellie sat down and rested her arms on her knees, looking at Merri's naughty smile.

'Were you always arty?'

Ellie shrugged. 'I think I started when I was about six. I remember the first time I fell into a drawing.'

'Tell me.'

Ellie felt her voice catch. 'Mitchell was home. He'd just come back from somewhere in Africa. He was working in his study—nothing strange there—and the door was open. He was reading aloud an article he'd written...he did that. He read all his articles aloud.'

'He still does.'

'It was a report on the genocide happening in Rwanda—Burundi—somewhere like that. The report was graphic, horrific...' Ellie shuddered and felt Jack's strong arm around her waist, his hand on her hip. This time there was nothing sexual about his touch. It was pure comfort. 'Mitchell called it like he saw it: women, old people, children. Severed heads, limbs...'

'I know, sweetheart. Skip that part. Tell me about the art.' Jack rested his chin on her hair, shaken by the idea of a little girl hearing that. Damn Mitch and his stupidity. The man was a talented journalist, but as a father...useless.

'I couldn't get the pictures his words conjured out of my brain and the only thing I could think of to do was draw.

Happy things—butterflies, princesses. I had nightmares for a while, and I'd wake up and hit my desk to paint or colour.' Ellie sighed. 'Mitchell could never censor himself. He had no conception of sensibility—that young kids didn't need to know that sixteen Afghan rebels had been executed and their decapitated heads paraded through the streets as a warning and that he'd witnessed it. It drove my mother mad that he couldn't keep his mouth shut in front of me.'

'But you had your art?'

'I did. He reported on brutality and war, violence, and I tried—still try—to counter that by producing beauty. It used to be through oils. Now it's through cake and icing.' Ellie shrugged and managed a smile.

Jack saw her staring at Merri's portrait and caught the pain and sadness in her eyes. There was more to this story or he wasn't a journalist. 'Why did you give it up?'

'Can we skip this part?' Ellie asked with a wobble in her voice.

'I'd really like to know.' Jack lowered his voice, made it persuasive.

'You ask me all these questions but you won't talk about yourself,' Ellie complained.

True. 'I know. I'm sorry. But tell me anyway.'

'Short story. He was the owner of an exclusive art gallery in Soho.' Grigson's, Jack remembered. The short blond from that photo in his room. 'He offered me an exhibition, told me I was the next big thing. I fell deeply, chronically in love with him. I found out later that was his *modus operandi*. I wasn't the first young artist he'd seduced into bed with that promise.'

Jack winced.

'I was swept away by him. He dealt in beauty and objects of art. He was a social butterfly—had invitations to something every night of the week. But he never took me along to anything. Like my father, he dropped in and out of my life. I kept asking him about the exhibition, spending time with me, taking me along, but he kept fobbing me off.'

'Bastard,' Jack growled.

'I told him that I wanted to break it off and he responded by proposing. I thought that meant that he'd change, but nothing did. I saw less of him than ever.'

'So what precipitated the break-up?' Jack briefly wondered why he was so interested in her past, why he felt the need to find the jerk and put him into a coma.

'I told him that I was done with waiting around for him. He responded by telling me that I was a mediocre artist who'd never amount to anything. That he'd just wanted to sleep with me occasionally but I wasn't worth the hassle…that it was, essentially, not worth my being around, him trying to keep me happy.'

Forget the coma. He now had the urge to put the guy six feet under. When Mitch had mentioned him he'd initially felt sorry for him, because he'd thought that she must have been pushing him into marriage, but he was the one who'd messed *her* around, messed her up. No wonder she tried so hard to be indispensable to the people she loved; she thought she had to try harder to be loved.

The two men she'd loved the most had hurt her, damaged her the most. God, the ways that love could mess up people. Just another reason why he wanted nothing to do with it…

'Anybody since then?' Jack asked, although he knew there hadn't been.

'No.'

Needing to move, to work off his anger, Jack jumped up and jogged up the stairs to inspect another painting. He placed his hands on his hips and looked around at the art covering the walls.

'Good grief, Ellie, some of these paintings are utterly fantastic. I'm trying to work out which ones are yours, because not all of them are.'

'Some are by fellow art students; others I've picked up along the way,' Ellie said, pride streaking through her voice. 'You like art?'

'I love art. Sculpture. Architecture,' Jack confirmed, quickly moving up the stairs to examine a seascape.

He placed a hand on his hip and winced at the movement. Ellie watched his body tense. His face was illuminated by the spotlight above his head. The violet shadows beneath his eyes were back and his face was pale beneath his slight tan.

Jack Chapman, she decided, had no concept of how to pace himself. He'd recently suffered a horrendous beating, had a nasty knife wound, and yet he'd spent the day sightseeing. She could see that he was exhausted and in pain, and she knew that he was one of those men who would carry on until he fell down.

He came across as easygoing and charming but there was a solid streak beneath the charm, a strength of character that people probably never saw beneath the good looks and air of success. His thought-processes were clear-headed and practical. While he'd challenged her decisions and her actions she didn't feel as if he was judging *her*.

He'd coaxed her past out of her and he was a fabulous listener. He listened intently and knew when to back away from the subject to give the guts-spiller some time to compose themselves.

Ellie caught his slight wince as he walked back down the stairs and she shook her head at him. 'For goodness' sake—will you sit down before you fall down?'

Jack's strong eyebrows pulled together. 'I'm fine.'

'Jack, you're not fine. You're exhausted and your body is protesting. Take a seat in the lounge, watch some TV. Do you want something to drink?'

Jack raked his hand through his hair. 'Nothing, thanks. Mind if I veg out on the veranda for a while?'

'Knock yourself out,' Ellie said. 'I'll plate up the Chinese.'

'Hey, El?' Jack called.

Ellie poked her head around the kitchen door. 'Yes?'

Jack rattled off an Arabic curse and Ellie wrinkled her nose. 'Something...something donkey. Sorry...what?'

'I just called your ex a bleeping-bleeping horse's bleeping ass.'

Ellie laughed. *Nice, Jack.*

After supper they headed back to the veranda and watched as dusk fell over the long coastline. Lights winked on as they sipped their red wine, sharing the couch with their bare feet up on the stone wall. Jack placed his arm along the back of the couch and Ellie felt his fingers in her hair. She turned to look at him but Jack was watching her hair slide between his fingers.

'It's so straight, so thick.'

Ellie felt his hands tug the band from her hair and felt the heavy drop as her hair cascaded down her back, could imagine it flowing over Jack's broad hand. She heard his swift intake of breath, felt his fingers combing her hair.

'I love the coloured streaks. They remind me of the flash of colour in a starling's wing.'

There was that creative flair again—this time with words. And there was that sexual buzz again. Ellie licked her lips. 'They're not my real hair.'

'Still pretty.' Jack lifted a strand of her hair and because it was so long easily brought it to his nose. 'Mmm...apple, lemon...flour.'

Ellie could not believe that she was so turned on by a man sniffing her hair. 'Jack...'

His eyes deepened, flooded with gold. He drifted the ends

of her hair over his lips before dropping it and sliding his big hand around her neck. 'Yeah?'

Ellie dropped her eyes. 'We weren't going to do this, remember?'

'Shh, nothing is going to happen,' Jack said.

He dropped his arm behind her back, wrapped it around her waist and pulled her so that she was plastered against his hard body. Ellie swung around and rested her head against his chest, deeply conscious of his warm arm under her breasts.

'Did you submit your piece on that Somalian pirate-slash-warlord?' Ellie asked, to take her mind off the fact that she wanted to move his hands to more deserving areas of her body. Her breasts, the backs of her knees, between her legs.

'Yes. I didn't get as much information from him as I wanted to, but it was okay.'

'Have you worked out what you said that set him off?'

She felt Jack shake his head. 'Nah. I think he was high... and psychotic.'

'That might be it.' Ellie rested her hands on his arm, feeling the veins under his skin. 'Tell me about yourself. Mother? Father? Siblings?'

'Like you, I was an only child. I'm not sure why,' Jack replied.

Ellie half smiled. 'Tell me what you were like as a kid.'

She felt him stiffen at her question. 'At what age?'

Strange question. 'I don't know...ten?'

Jack's laugh rumbled through his chest. 'Hell on wheels. Maybe that's why my folks didn't have another kid. They probably despaired in case they'd have another boy.'

Ellie laughed. 'You couldn't have been *that* bad.'

'I was worse. Before I was eight I'd broken a leg, had three lots of stitches and lost most of my teeth.'

Ellie's mouth fell open. 'How on earth did you manage to do that?'

'The broken leg came from ramping with my BMX. The ramp I'd built myself collapsed. The teeth incident was from a fight with Juliet Grafton. I called her ugly—which she was. She was also built like a brick outhouse and her father was a boxing champion. Her mean right hook connected with my mouth. Stitches—where do I start? Falling off bikes, roofs, rocks...'

Ellie raised an eyebrow.

'But I was cute. That counted for a lot.'

She wanted to tell him he was still cute, but she suspected he already knew that, so instead she just watched night fall over the sea.

CHAPTER SIX

ELLIE WALKED INTO the ballroom on Jack's arm and looked around the packed space, filled with black-suited men and elegant women. His appearance caused a buzz and Ellie felt the tension in Jack's arm as people turned to watch their progress into the room. To them he was a celebrity, and well respected, and a smattering of applause broke out.

Jack half lifted his hand in acknowledgement. When he spoke, he pitched his voice so that only she could hear him. 'Those are the most ridiculous shoes, Ellie.'

Ellie grinned at the teasing note in his voice. He'd already told her that he liked her shimmery silver and pink froth of a cocktail dress, and she knew that her moon-high silver sandals made her calves look fantastic. She *felt* fantastic; she was sure it had a lot to do with the approval in Jack's expressive eyes.

'And, as I said, that is a sexy dress. Very you. Bright, colourful, playful.'

Ellie looked around and half winced. 'Most women are wearing basic black.'

'You're not a basic type of girl. And colour suits you.' He touched the hair she'd worked into a bohemian roll, with curls falling down her back. 'Gorgeous hair...make-me-crazy scent...'

'So I'll do?'

Jack took her hand and his words were rueful. 'Very much so.'

Ellie smiled with pleasure, then lifted her eyebrows as a tall blonde with an equine face stalked up to Jack, took his hand and kissed his cheek. Jack lifted his own eyebrows at her familiarity as she introduced herself as the Chairperson of the Press Club. Ellie forgot her name as soon as she said it.

'I have people who'd like to meet you,' she stated in a commanding voice.

'I'd like to get my date a drink first,' Jack said, untangling himself from her octopus grip.

'Ellie?'

Ellie turned at the deep voice and looked up into laughing green eyes in a very good-looking face. 'Luke? What are *you* doing here?'

'St Sylve is one of the club's sponsors,' he told Ellie, after kissing her on the cheek. He held out his hand to Jack. 'Luke Savage.'

'You drink Luke's wine all the time at home, Jack,' Ellie told him after they'd been introduced. 'Where's Jess, Luke?'

Luke looked around for his fiancée and shrugged. 'Probably charming someone for business.'

'Jack, I really *must* take you to meet some people.'

The blonde tugged on Jack's sleeve and Ellie caught the irritation that flickered in his eyes.

Jack looked at Ellie and then at Luke. 'Will you be okay?'

Ellie smiled at him. 'Sure. I'll hang with Luke and Jess and see you at dinner.'

Jack nodded and turned away.

Ellie looked up at Luke and pulled a face. 'We're going to be placed at some awfully boring table, I can tell, with Horse Lady neighing at Jack all night.'

Luke grinned. 'Well, we're sitting with Cale and Maddie—'

Ellie squealed with excitement. 'They're here too?'

'Cale *is* a sports presenter and journalist, El.'

'I *so* want to sit with you guys!' Ellie fluttered her eyelashes up at him.

Luke winked at her. 'We'll just have to see if we can make that happen.'

Ellie felt a feminine arm encircle her waist and turned to look into her friend's laughing deep brown eyes.

'Are you flirting with my husband-to-be, Ellie Evans?'

Ellie laughed and kissed Jess's cheek. ''Fraid so.'

'Can't blame you. I flirt with him all the time. Now, tell me—why and how are you here with the very yummy Jack Chapman?'

Luke had somehow organised that they were all at the same table, and Jack felt himself relaxing with Ellie's charming group of friends. They were warm and down-to-earth and Jack was enjoying himself.

He leaned closer to Ellie and lowered his voice. 'How do you know all these people?'

Ellie sent him a side-glance out of those fabulous eyes. 'Maddie and I went to uni together. I met Luke through her, and Cale—he and Cale are old schoolfriends. But I've known Jess for years and years—before she and Luke met. Her company does Pari's advertising.'

'So, El,' Luke said as he picked up a bottle of wine from the ice bucket on the table and topped up their glasses with a fruity Sauvignon, 'what's this I hear about you having to move your bakery?'

Ellie wiped her hands on a serviette and pulled a face. 'I have to find new premises in less than six months.'

'And have you found anything?' Cale asked.

'Maybe. There's an old building close to the bakery that might work. It's supposed to be on the market, but I need to find an architect—someone who can look at the house and tell me if it's solid and if I can do the alterations I'm thinking of—before I put in an offer.'

Luke looked at Cale and they both nodded. 'James.'

'Another friend from uni?' Jack asked with a smile on his face.

Luke and Cale laughed, but didn't disagree with him. Luke told Ellie that he'd send her his contact details and the rest of the table moved onto another subject.

'Are you seriously considering that building for the bakery?' Jack asked Ellie, resting his cheek on his fist.

'Maybe. Possibly.' Ellie fiddled with her serviette. 'I'll speak to James and see what he says. Then I'll have to run it by my mum.'

'Understandable, since Pari's will be paying for it.' Jack saw something flash across her face and frowned. '*You're* paying for it? How would you...? Sorry—that has nothing to do with me.'

'How would I pay for it? It's fine. I don't mind you asking. Ginger—my grandmother—set up a trust for me when I was little and she's pretty wealthy. Pari's would pay me rent. That's if I actually decide to buy and renovate the building.'

There it was again—that lack of confidence in her eyes. 'Why do you doubt yourself?'

'It's a lot of money, Jack.' Ellie twisted the serviette through her fingers. 'What if it's a disaster? What if I end up disappointing my mother, Merri, my grandmother Pari's memory...? God, my *customers*?'

'That's a lot of disappointing, El. And a lot of what-ifs.' Jack placed his hand on hers and held them still. 'You love that building. Yours eyes light up when you talk about it. When are you going to start trusting yourself a little more?'

Ellie bit that sexy bottom lip—the one he wanted so badly to taste again.

'Merri says that I'm too much of a people-pleaser. That I have this insane need to make the world right for everyone.'

He didn't think Merri was wrong. 'You need to start listening to yourself more and to underestimate yourself less.'

Ellie twisted her lips. 'And not to think that I'm indispensable and the world will stop turning if I say no... I'm a basket case, Jack.'

Jack sent her an easy grin. 'We're all basket cases in our own way. You're just a bit more...vulnerable. Softer than most.'

'I need to grow a bit more of a spine.'

'I think you're pretty much perfect just as you are.'

Jack sighed as the Master of Ceremonies started to talk. He'd much rather talk to Ellie than listen to boring speeches. He heard the MC introducing him and grimaced. His was probably going to be the most boring speech of all. He felt Ellie's hand grasp his knee and a bolt of sexual attraction fizzed straight through him.

'You didn't tell me that you were making a speech!' she hissed.

He stood up, buttoned his jacket and looked down at her. 'Yeah, well, for some reason they find me interesting.'

'Weird. I simply can't understand why,' Ellie teased.

Jack swallowed his laughter before moving away from her and heading for the podium, thinking that he could think of a couple of things he'd rather be doing than giving a speech. Top of the list was doing Ellie. In the pool, in the kitchen, in the shower...

Jack reached the podium, looked at the expectant faces and let his eyes drift over to his table. Luke raised his glass at him. Maddie rested her arms on the table and sent him a friendly smile. Ellie, being Ellie, pulled a quick tongue at him and he swallowed a grin.

There wasn't much wrong with the world if Ellie was in it, making him laugh.

***

It had been heaven to be in Jack's arms, even if it was just for a couple of slow dances around the edge of the dance floor. In her heels she'd been able to tuck her face into his neck, feel his warm breath in her hair, on her temple. There had been nothing demure about their dancing. They'd been up close and personal and neither of them had been able to hide their desire. Her nipples had dug into his chest and her stomach brushed his hard erection. Their breaths mingled, lips a hair's breadth apart. She was certain that someone would soon notice the smoke and call the fire brigade.

The music had changed now, from slow to fast, and Jack's broad hand on her lower back steered her back to their empty table. He pulled out a chair for her and looked from her to a hovering waiter.

'What can I get you to drink? G&T? A cocktail? Or do you feel like sharing a bottle of red wine?'

'That sounds good.'

Ellie crossed her legs as Jack took the chair next to her and flipped open the wine list he'd been handed. He held it so that Ellie could scan the selection with him.

Ellie tapped the list with her finger. 'I don't really care as long as it has alcohol and is wet. Any of Luke's wines are good. St Sylve's.'

She sounded nervous, Jack thought. So she should, even if she had only a vague idea of how close she'd come to being ravished on the dance floor.

Jack rubbed his forehead. *Ravished.* Only Ellie could make him think of such an old-fashioned word. Pulling himself together, he ordered the wine, then slipped off his suit jacket before loosening the collar on his white dress shirt and yanking down his tie in an effort to get more air into his lungs. Now, if only he could sort his tented pants out.

'That's better.'

Ellie touched her hair and smiled wryly. 'I wish I could do that to my hair.'

He wished *he* could do that to her hair. He'd spent many hours thinking about that hair brushing his stomach, about wrapping it around his hands as he settled himself over her... Jack shifted in his chair. What was *with* this woman and her ability to short-circuit his brain? He dropped his eyes to her chest, where the fabric of her dress flirted with her cleavage and showed just a hint of a lacy pink bra.

Kill me now, Jack thought.

Ellie draped a leg over a knee and looked across the room. He could see her rapidly beating pulse at the base of her neck and knew that she was just as hot for him as he was for her. Not that he needed any confirmation. The little brush of her stomach across his body on the dance floor had been a freaking big clue.

Their wine was delivered and their conversation dried up. Jack didn't care. He just wanted to drink her in, lap her up... He gulped his wine, thoroughly rattled at how sexy he found her. Deep blue eyes, that sensual mouth, the scent of her sweetly sexy perfume. She had such beautiful skin, every inch of which he wanted to explore, taste, caress...

Sitting there, looking at her, he became conscious of something settling inside of him... To hell with being sensible and playing it safe. He knew what he wanted and he was damn well going to ask for it.

He reached over and lightly rested the tips of his fingers on the inside of her wrist, smiling wryly when he felt her pulse skitter. He lifted his hand, pushed a strand of hair that had fallen over her eyes behind her ear.

He leaned over and spoke in her ear. 'I can't do this any more. I've tried everything I can to resist you but enough is enough. Let's go home. Let me take you to bed.'

He saw the answer in her eyes and didn't wait for her nod

before taking her hand and leading her—wine, function and friends forgotten—out of the room.

Jack waited while she locked the front door and then backed her up against it, his body easily covering hers. He'd removed his jacket and she could feel the heat from his body beneath his shirt. His chest flattened her breasts and her breath hitched in response. This was so big, she thought, so overpowering...

His hands were large and competent, stroking her waist and skimming her ribcage in a sensual promise of what was to come. His hands skirted over her bottom and he lifted her up and into him, forcing her to wrap her legs around his waist. His hands held her thighs, steaming hot under the frothy skirt of her favourite dress. One heel dropped to the floor and it took a slight shake of her other foot for her remaining shoe to drop as well. Jack's mouth finally brushed hers and his tongue dipped into her mouth in a long, slow slide.

Jack walked with her to the stairs and at the first step allowed her to slip down him. He cradled her head in his hands and rested his forehead on hers.

'Upstairs?' he whispered, and Ellie felt the word and his breath drift over her face.

She nodded, ordered her legs to move and lightly ran up the stairs. She turned into her darkened bedroom and realised that Jack was a second behind her. He yanked her to him and walked her backwards to her big double bed. She felt the mattress dip under her weight, and dip some more as she was pushed on her back and Jack crawled over her.

She felt one of the straps of her dress fall down a shoulder and Jack's lips on her smooth skin. He was everything she'd ever wanted, she thought: strong, sexy, amazingly adept at making heat and lust pool in her womb. She'd never felt so intimately invested in a kiss, an embrace...so desperate to have his mouth on her, his fingers on her, to touch him, explore him, know him.

This could mean something, Ellie thought. This could mean something...huge.

Jack sat back on his haunches and pulled her up, kissing her as his hands looked for the zip at the back of her dress. Cool air touched her fevered skin as his hands wandered and soothed, danced over her skin, while his tongue did an erotic tango with hers.

Then her dress fell to her waist and she half sat, half lay in her strapless bra, her torso open to his hot gaze.

It had been so long. She'd half forgotten what to do. Should she undo the buttons of his shirt, pull it over his head? Let him do it himself? Could she do that? Should she do that? Ellie brushed her hand over his hip and felt the padding of his dressing. Another thought dropped into her scrambled head. Should he even be doing this? What if he pulled the skin apart and he started bleeding again?

'Your cut...' Ellie murmured, sitting up in an effort to escape those searing eyes.

'Is fine,' Jack replied, stroking her from shoulder to hand.

Ellie rested her forehead on his collarbone and sighed. She wanted this, wanted to immerse herself in this experience with him, but suddenly her mind was jumping around like a cricket on speed, playing with thoughts that were not conducive to inspiring or maintaining passion. Thoughts like, What did this mean to him? To her? With all her previous lovers—okay, all two of them—she'd felt and given love and thought that that love was reciprocated to a degree. There was nothing like that with Jack. They had nothing more between them than a burgeoning friendship and a searing, burning passion.

It had been so long since Darryl, and she was so out of practice. Would she be enough for him? She had enough pride to want to get this right. Was she knowledgeable enough, sexy enough, passionate enough to make this something that he'd remember?

Jack pulled her dress over her head and ran his index finger above the edge of her bra, his finger tanned against her creamy skin. Ellie looked down at his finger and closed her eyes, confused and bemused. She wanted him, but she wasn't wholly convinced that she was ready...

She should say no. She needed to say no...

Jack looked down at her breasts spilling over her frothy bra and thought that he'd never seen anything as beautiful in his life. Her skin had a luminosity that he'd never seen before—the palest blush on a creamy rose. Her ribcage was narrow, her arms slim, and her fingers were still on his hip. He could feel the heat in them through his pants, as tangible as her very sudden, very obvious mental retreat.

Going, going...oh, crap...*gone*.

Jack knew that he could kiss her, could stoke those fires again, but if she wasn't as fully in the moment with this as he was—had been—then it wasn't fair to her or—*dammit*—to him. He wanted her engaged, body, mind and soul. He could have physical sex with other women. He wanted, *expected* more from Ellie. Why and how much more he wasn't sure, but still...

Jack ran his hand over her head and sat back, his knees on either side of her legs. Ellie looked at him with big, wide eyes the colour of blue moonlight and ran her tongue over her top lip. He really wished she wouldn't do that...it made him think of the plans he'd had for that tongue. Hot, wicked, sexy plans.

Dammit... He sighed.

There were a bunch of reasons why he shouldn't be doing this, he thought. All of them valid. He was here for a limited time and she wasn't the type of girl who indulged in brief affairs. They were already living in the same house, so if they slept together they'd step over from friendship into sex-coloured friendship which was the gateway for affection, which led to attachment and a myriad of complications.

And what if that happened and he found himself liking living with her and not wanting to leave? How could he reconcile that with the promise he'd made to himself and to others that he'd live life to its fullest? His hard, fast, take-no-prisoners lifestyle—a life spent on planes, trains and hotel rooms—was not conducive to a full-time lover and invariably led to disappointment and sometimes to disaster.

'Jack?'

Jack blinked and lifted his eyebrows. 'Mmm?'

'You're a bit...heavy,' Ellie said in a small voice.

Jack immediately moved off her legs and sat on the edge of the bed. 'Sorry,' he muttered.

'No, it's okay. Just...um...need to get my blood circulating,' Ellie said in a jerky voice.

Jack sat sideways on the bed and thought that Ellie looked breathtaking in the low light that spilled into the room from the passage. Her mouth was soft and inviting and her hair was mostly out of its elaborate style, falling in waves over her shoulders.

Jack, all concerns forgotten, started to lean forward, intent on kissing the life out of her, but he made the mistake of looking into her eyes. They were round and slightly scared—and utterly, comprehensively miserable. He wondered how long it would take for her to call it quits, how far she'd take him down the road before she realised that she wasn't mentally ready to sleep with him.

It turned out not to be long at all...

'I'm sorry.' Ellie's voice was jerky and full of remorse. 'I really can't do this.'

So, she did have guts. Good to know, Jack thought. And at least she was honest.

'Okay.'

Jack saw Ellie cross her arms over her chest so he stood up and walked over to her bedroom door, unhooked her dressing gown. He passed it to her and moved on to stand at her open window, looking out at the dark night. When he turned around again Ellie's gorgeous body was covered, chest to knee, in a silky wrap that was almost as heart-attack-inducing as the dress she'd worn earlier.

He had to get out of her room before he did something he would regret. Like haul her back into his arms.

So he walked over to her and dropped a kiss on her temple. 'It's late. Maybe we should get some sleep.'

He thought it was a tragedy when Ellie didn't try to stop him when he walked out of the room.

Ellie woke, dressed and stumbled down the stairs half asleep. The noise of the television from the lounge jerked her fully awake and immediately caused memories of the previous night to rush back with the power of a sumo wrestler. She groaned. Jeez, she'd had all the sophistication of a pot plant. It had been so long, and she'd been so nervous, so self-conscious and hadn't been able to stop the weird thoughts buzzing around her head. She'd been worried about him seeing her naked and she'd stressed about whether he would stay the night with her, how much foreplay he expected and whether he was enjoying himself.

She'd been unable to let go, and if she was so attracted to him shouldn't she be able to lose herself in him? Wasn't that what lust-filled lovers did?

Ellie stood in the doorway to the lounge and stared at her wooden floor.

'Morning,' Jack said from the corner of the room, where he sat in a violet chair, leaning forward, his hands loose between his knees.

Elle lifted her head and squinted at him. 'Morning. How long have you been up?'

'Not too long.'

Ellie rested her hand on the doorframe. 'I'll go and make coffee.'

Jack nodded to a steaming cup of coffee that stood on the coffee table. 'I heard you moving around as I came down the stairs so I made you a cup.'

'Thanks.' Ellie walked across the room to pick up her cup and wrapped her hands around it. The purple elephant was back and was laughing like a maniac. But she wasn't going to consider raising the subject. It was embarrassing enough thinking about it. Talking to him about it would be absolutely impossible!

And that was even before she realised how preoccupied and distant Jack looked.

'I thought I'd get caught up with what's happening in the world. Do you mind?' he said.

'No.'

He gestured to the TV. 'Your dad is in Kenya, reporting on the riots.'

Okay, she'd go with world politics if that was all he had.

'They are having elections soon,' he added.

She *so* didn't care. She wanted to know what he was going to do now, how she was supposed to act. Ellie bit her lip, walked further into the room and looked at her father's familiar face on the screen.

'He's looking tired.' Ellie sat down on the couch and tucked her legs up under her as Mitchell answered questions from the anchor in New York.

'He texted me earlier. He thinks there's big trouble brewing.'

Jack turned up the volume on the TV set and she listened with half an ear as Mitchell spoke about the situation in Kenya.

He's nearly sixty, Ellie thought, wondering whether he had any thoughts about retiring. Because that wasn't something he'd ever discuss with *her*.

'I'm going there.'

Ellie took a moment to assimilate his statement. 'Going where?'

'To Kenya. A massive bomb was found and defused and the country is on a knife edge. I have contacts there,' Jack explained. He lifted his cup. 'I'm going to head out as soon as I've finished my coffee.'

'Ah...'

'I'm the closest reporter, and if I can get on a flight now I'll be with Mitch within a couple of hours. He's going to need help covering this.'

'Why?'

Jack frowned. 'It's news, Ellie, and news is my job. I know Nairobi. I want to be there.'

Ellie's heart sank. Of course he did. It didn't matter that he was beaten up, hurt and tired, or that he'd kissed her senseless, there was a story and he needed to follow it. It was the nature of the beast.

The fact that she was acting like a nervous, awkwardly shy Victorian nerd was also a very good excuse for him to run from her—fast and hard. Could she blame him?

Ellie refocused as Jack answered his ringing mobile. 'Hey, Andrew. No, I managed to get a seat on the next flight out to Nairobi. I'll be at the airport in—' he looked at his watch '—an hour. In the air in three.'

It took forty-five minutes to get to the airport, which left fifteen minutes for him to pack up and walk out of her life, Ellie thought. Last night she'd been lost in this man's arms and this morning he was making plans to walk out through the door without giving her a second thought.

And that just summed up all her experiences with war reporters. Nothing was more important than the story...ever.
Ever.

Jack leaned forward in his seat. He really didn't want to be on this plane, was unenthusiastic about going to Kenya, but all through the night, unable to sleep, he'd known that he couldn't stay with Ellie, that he needed to get some distance. From her...from the feelings she pulled to the surface.

Last night, for the first time in years, he'd allowed himself to become mentally engaged with a woman, and in doing so he'd caught a glimpse of all that he was missing by not allowing that intimate connection. The warmth of her smile, the richness of her laughter, her enjoyment of being with him all added another layer to the constant sexual buzz that took it from thrilling to frightening.

They'd been emotionally and physically in sync and he'd loved every second of the previous evening—even if she had called a halt to it. Hell, he'd loved every minute of the past few days. He could, if he let himself, imagine a lifetime of evenings drinking wine on the veranda, taking evening walks with her, making love to her.

Brent had never got to experience anything like this....

The thought chilled him to the bone. *Brent.* And, dear God, he needed to make a decision about going to that memorial service, to face his family...to face his demons, the never-ending guilt of being alive because that teenage boy was dead.

Jack rubbed his face. If he hadn't had a heart transplant, if he'd grown up normal, what would his life be like? Where would he be? What would he be? Would he be married yet? Have kids?

How much of his reluctance to get involved was his own reticent nature and how much was driven by guilt? Was he avoiding love and permanence not only because he felt that his job didn't allow it but also because he felt he didn't deserve it? That if Brent couldn't have it why should he?

He already had his heart—was he entitled to happiness with it as well? Jack let out a semi-audible groan.

The elderly lady next to him, with espresso eyes and cocoa skin, laid an elegant hand on his arm.

'Are you all right, my dear?'

Jack dredged up a smile. 'Fine, thanks.' He saw doubt cross her face and shrugged. 'Just trying to work through some stuff.'

She rattled off a phrase in an African language he didn't recognise.

'Sorry, I don't understand.'

'African proverb. Peace is costly but it is worth the expense.'

Indeed.

CHAPTER SEVEN

ELLIE SNAPPED AT one of her staff and, after apologising, realised that she desperately needed a break from the bakery. Taking a bottle of water from the fridge, she walked out through the front door into the strong afternoon sunlight. Checking for cars, she walked across the street and sat on the concrete wall that separated the beach from the promenade and stretched out her bare legs. She flipped open the buttons of her chef's tunic and shrugged it off, allowing the sea breeze to flow over her bare shoulders in her sleeveless fuchsia top.

It had been four hellish days since Jack's abrupt departure. She had the concentration span of a flea and her thoughts were a galaxy away from her business and her craft.

His memory should have faded but she could still remember, in high definition, her time spent with Jack. The way his eyes crinkled when he smiled, the flash of white teeth, those wizard-like eyes that made you want to spill your soul.

She missed him—really missed him. Missed his manly way of looking at a situation, his clear-headed thought-processes, and she missed bouncing ideas about Pari's off him. She missed her friend.

But more than missing him she was also now seriously irritated. Furious, in fact. Partly at Jack, for whirling out of her house like a dervish, but mostly at herself. How stupid was she to think that she could rely on him, that he wouldn't drop her like a hot brick for a story, for a situation?

The men she was attracted to always ran out on her, so why had she thought it would be different with Jack? He'd been in her life for under a week and she was livid that, subconsciously at least, she'd come to rely on him in such a short time. For advice, for a smile, for conversation and company at the end of a long day. How could she have forgotten, even for one minute, that war reporters always, *always* left, usually at a critical time in her life?

She couldn't help the memory rolling back—was powerless against the familiar resentment. She'd been fourteen and she'd entered a drawing of a lion into a competition in a well-known wildlife magazine. Out of thousands of entries throughout the country she'd won the 'Young Teenager' category. She'd been due to receive her prize at a prestigious televised awards ceremony. She'd spent weeks in a panic because Mitchell was on assignment, and the relief she'd felt when he'd arrived back home three days before the ceremony had been overwhelming.

Everything had been super-okay with her world. The thought of going up onto that stage in front of all those people had made her feel sick, but her handsome dad would be in the audience so she'd do it. She would move mountains for him.

Then someone had got assassinated and he'd flown out two hours before the event…which she'd been too distraught to attend.

Ellie straightened her shoulders. She was no longer that broken, defeated, sad teenager who'd flung her arms around her father and begged him not to go.

She sipped her water and narrowed her eyes. She'd looked up the political situation in Kenya, and while it was tense it wasn't exploding. Jack hadn't needed to high-tail it out of her house. He was running from her—probably looking for an excuse to get away from her hot and cold behaviour, her lack of confidence in that sort of situation and her disastrous bedroom skills. If Jack had bailed just because of that, if she never saw him again—and who knew if she would, since *she hadn't heard from him since he'd left*—then good riddance, because then he was an idiot. As angry and...she searched for the word...*disappointed* as she felt, she knew that she was worth far more than just to be some transient woman who provided him a bed and some fun in it.

Ellie heard a long wolf whistle and looked up to see Merri leaving Pari's, two bottles of water in her hand. She'd obviously left Molly Blue with someone in the bakery—probably Mama Thandi—and was sauntering across the road as if she owned it.

Merri handed her another bottle of water and sat next to her, stretching her long body. A car passing them drifted as the driver gaped at her sensational-looking friend. Merri, as per normal, didn't notice. Ellie was quite certain that the majority of motor car accidents in Muizenberg were somehow related to Merri and the effect she had on men's driving.

'Now, tell me, why are you looking all grumpy and sorry for yourself?'

Ellie cracked open the second bottle of water and took a long swallow. How did she explain Jack to Merri?

The best way was just to blurt it all out. 'I nearly slept with Jack.'

'Good for you!' Merri gaped at her. 'Wait...did you say *nearly*? What is wrong with you, woman?'

There was no judgement in Merri's voice, and Ellie knew that her 'almost sleeping with Jack' story wouldn't even create a blip on her shock radar. Merri was pretty much unshockable.

Unlike her, Merri was a thoroughly modern woman. Not a drip.

'Do you want to talk about it?' Merri asked.

Ellie shook her head. 'Yes. No. Maybe. Still processing. Very confused.'

'So it wasn't just sex, then?'

'We didn't get that far. I said that I wasn't ready and he backed off.'

'Nicely?'

'What do you mean?'

'Was he nice about it? No tantrums, accusations, saying you led him on?'

Ellie shook her head. 'Of course not. He just passed me my dressing gown and said goodnight.'

'Huh. I *really* have to start dating nicer guys,' Merri stated thoughtfully. 'So why couldn't you go through with it?'

Ellie looked out to sea and wondered if she could escape this conversation. As if sensing her thoughts, Merri hooked her arm in hers and kept her in place.

'It was fine—great. I was totally in the moment and then—' Ellie snapped her fingers '—like that, my brain started providing a running commentary.'

'Oh, I hate it when it does that,' Merri agreed. 'I remember being so caught up in the intensity of being with this one guy, and then he took off his shirt and he had a pelt of chest hair. And back hair. It was like he was wearing a coat...*ugh*. My brain started making jokes at his expense. Does Jack have back hair?'

'Uh...no.'

'Did he make animal sounds?'

'No.'

'Talk dirty?'

'No.'

'Have a really small—?'

'Merri!' Ellie interjected, cutting her off. 'He's fine—gorgeous, in fact! He didn't do anything wrong!'

'Then what was the problem?' Merri asked, puzzled. 'He's

gorgeous, nice, and you were into him.' She looked Ellie in her eyes and twisted her lips. 'Ah, *dammit*, Ellie!'

'What?' Ellie demanded.

'When you told me that Jack was staying with you we talked about you getting emotionally entangled with him.' Merri shook her head in despair. 'And you have, haven't you?'

'I'm not entangled with him. Or at the very least I'm trying not to get emotionally attached to him. When we were getting it on I had this thought that he could become a big thing if I let him.'

'And how is that *not* getting emotionally involved with him?' Merri demanded.

'The key phrase is *if I let him*,' Ellie protested.

Merri was silent for a while, and her voice was full of hope when she spoke again. 'Are you not just getting lust and feelings mixed up? Sometimes sex is just sex and it doesn't always have to be more.'

'I know that…and I tried to think that. Unfortunately I can't just think of him as a random slab of meat.'

'Try harder.' Merri sighed forlornly. 'Have I taught you nothing?' She narrowed her eyes in thought. 'Maybe you need to practise the concept of casual sex a bit more? I have a friend who is always up to…helping the cause.'

Ellie hiccuped a laugh at Merri's outrageous suggestion. 'Thanks, but no. Really.'

They both heard Merri's name being called, and across the street Mama Thandi stood with Molly in her arms, her face wet with tears. 'I'm coming!' Merri called back as she stood up.

She bent and kissed Ellie goodbye and a nearby jogger nearly ran straight into a lightpole.

Merri was right. She had to wrap her head around the concept of casual sex. And if—big if!—Jack came back, then she'd have to decide whether she could separate sex and emotion, because becoming emotionally attached to Jack would be a disaster of mega proportions.

They were fire and water, heaven and hell, victory and defeat. Maybe there *was* something fast and hot between them sexually, but fast and hot weren't enough to sustain a relationship. Relationships needed time and input, and at the very least for the participants within said relationship to be on the same continent for more than a nano-second.

Like Mitchell, Jack was the ultimate free spirit: an adventurer of heart and soul who needed his freedom as he needed air to breathe.

Apart from the fact that she didn't want to—was too damn scared to—become emotionally involved with a man who was just like her father, Ellie knew that she wasn't exciting enough, long term, for someone as charismatic as Jack. Darryl had put her childhood fears and suspicions into words five minutes before he'd left her life for good.

'You need to face facts, Ellie. You're not enough—not sexy enough, smart enough, interesting enough—for a man to make sacrifices for. Nobody will give up their freedom and time for monogamy with you. Nobody interesting, at least.'

It was something she'd suspected all her life, and having someone—him—verbalise it had actually been a relief. Even if it had hurt like hell.

Ellie watched the afternoon crowds walk down the promenade, smiling at the earnest joggers, the chattering groups of women walking off their extra pounds. Kids on bicycles weaved through the crowds and skateboarders followed in their wake. It was a typical scene for a hot day in the summer.

Ellie saw a taxi pull up across the road just down the street from the bakery before she half turned to look at the sea. A number of cargo ships hovered on the horizon and a sailboat zipped by closer to shore. Reaching for her bottle of water, she looked back at the bakery and saw a man climb out of the taxi, his hand briefly touching his side. His broad shoulders and long legs reminded her of Jack...but this man had short hair, wore smart chinos, a long-sleeved white shirt with the cuffs rolled back and dark, sleek sunglasses. Then the sun picked up the reddish glints in his hair...

Jack?

Ellie yelped and dropped her water bottle as he paid the driver and pulled that familiar black rucksack from the boot of the taxi.

Jack... Jack was back.

Oh, good God... Jack. Was. Back.

As if he sensed her eyes on him Jack straightened and looked across the road. Ellie folded her arms and bit her lip. There was no way that she was going to run across the road like a demented schoolgirl and hurl herself into his arms...as much as she wanted to.

Ellie gnawed on her bottom lip as he lifted his rucksack with one hand, dropped it over his shoulder and slowly walked across the road. When he reached her he dropped the rucksack at her feet and sent her a small grin.

'Hi, El.'

Ellie's stomach plummeted and twisted as her name rolled off his tongue. She tucked her hands into the back pockets of her jeans and rocked on her heels.

'You're back. And you cut your hair...' Ellie stuttered and her heart copied her voice.

The corner of Jack's mouth lifted as he brushed his hand over his short back and sides. 'Seems like it.'

'I thought you would've headed home...' Ellie said, wishing she could hug him and also that she could finish a sentence. What *was* it about this man who had her words freezing on her tongue?

His eyes didn't leave hers. 'I have a flat in London but it certainly isn't home.' His mouth lifted in that teasing way that she'd missed so much. 'Besides, I paid you for three weeks' board and lodging and I'd like to get my money's worth.'

Ellie grinned. 'That sounds fair.' She could smell him from where she stood: sandalwood and citrus, clean soap and sexy male. Ellie breathed him in and again wished she were in his arms.

She looked up into his face and sighed at the stress in his eyes, the deeper brackets around his mouth. 'Rough trip?'

He shrugged. 'I've had worse.' He took her hand and raised her knuckles to place a gentle kiss on them. 'I'm sorry I didn't call...I wasn't sure what to say.'

Ellie's eyes narrowed as she remembered that she was supposed to be cross with him. 'I have to say that when it's required you can vacate a house at speed.'

Jack pushed his hair off his forehead. 'Yeah, sorry. I'm not used to explaining my actions... I've been on my own for too long and I'm not good at stopping to play nice.'

Ellie pulled her hand out of his and tapped her finger against her chin. 'How's my dad?'

'He's fine.' Jack went on to explain what he'd done in Kenya, the outcome of the contact he'd made with his numerous sources. His words were brief and succinct but Ellie could hear the tension in his voice, saw pain flicker in and out of his eyes and wondered what he wasn't telling her.

'Something else happened. Something that rocked you.'

Shock rippled across Jack's face. Then those shutters fell over his eyes and he dropped his gaze from hers, looking down at the pavement. When he lifted his head again his expression was rueful. 'The sun is shining; it's a stunning afternoon. I want to go home, climb into my board shorts and hit the surf. I just want to forget about work for a while.'

Ellie wished she could join him but gestured to the bakery. 'I still have a couple of hours' work to do.'

'Of course you do. I'll meet you back here at closing time.'

Jack picked up his rucksack and slung it over one shoulder. 'It's good to be back, El.'

Ellie watched him cross the street and turn the corner for home. Jack was back and the world suddenly seemed brighter and lighter and shinier.

That couldn't, in *any* galaxy, be good.

'So, he hasn't made a move on you again?'

'No, not even close. Then again, he's barely spoken to me,' Ellie answered Merri, who was in for the afternoon, helping her make Sacher Torte for an order to be picked up that evening.

Princess Molly Blue, as beautiful as her mother, was fast asleep on Mama Thandi's back, held in place by a light cotton shawl wrapped around her back and Mama's chest. Ellie looked at Mama, who was quickly plaiting strips of dough for braided bread; it really was a very efficient way to carry on working and let your baby be close to you. Ellie hoped Merri was taking notes.

'What do you mean?'

'He's been back for two days and I've barely seen him.' Ellie shrugged. 'We eat supper together and then he disappears to his room to work.' She tightened the ties of her apron and frowned. 'There are friends, lovers and acquaintances. Jack left as a friend, was briefly—sort of—a lover, and he's come back as the last.'

Merri split a vanilla pod and scraped out its insides with a knife. 'What changed? Do you think it was because you said no?'

Ellie separated the whites and yolks of eggs as she considered the question. 'I don't know. Maybe.'

'If that's the reason then he's a jerk of magnificent proportions,' Merri stated, adding the vanilla to butter and sugar and switching on the beater.

'He might as well be a guest in my B&B, except that he packs the dishwasher, makes dinner if I'm working late and even, very kindly, did a load of my laundry with his own. I just want my friend back,' Ellie added.

'No, you don't. You want to sleep with him,' Merri said in a cheerful voice.

'No! Well, yes. But I can't. Won't.'

'Uh…why?'

'Because, as you said, I can't seem to separate the emotion and the deed,' Ellie admitted reluctantly. 'If I sleep with him I risk—'

'Caring for him, falling in love with him. Why would that be the worst thing that could happen to you?'

Ellie viciously tipped the egg whites into another mixing bowl and reached for a hand-beater. 'I don't want to talk about this any more.'

'Tough.'

Ellie shut off the hand-beater and checked on the chocolate that was melting in a *bain-marie*. 'We don't have enough time for me to list the reasons…'

'Yes, we do. Spill.'

'He has a job I hate. He's never around. I don't have time for a relationship—'

Merri pointed a wooden spoon at her. 'Quit lying to yourself, El. The biggest reason you are so scared is because he doesn't need you, and we all know that you live to be needed.'

Ellie looked at her, shocked. 'That's so unfair.'

'Ellie, you take pride in being indispensable. You *need* people to need you. You need to love more than you need love, and you recognise that Jack doesn't need your love to survive, to function. You're terrified of being rejected…'

'Aren't we all?' Ellie demanded.

'No. Some of us realise that you can't force someone to love you just because you want him to.'

'Bully for you,' Ellie muttered mutinously.

Merri stared at her, her eyes uncharacteristically sombre. 'I don't think I ever realised until this moment how much your father's lack of attention and Darryl's scumbag antics scarred you.'

Ellie wanted to protest that she wasn't scarred, that she was just being careful, but she knew it wasn't true. She'd suspected for a long time that she was emotionally damaged, and Merri's words just confirmed what she'd always thought.

So maybe it was better that she and Jack kept their distance, kept the status quo.

'Can we talk about something else? Molly Blue? Is she teething yet?'

Merri grinned at her. 'No, I don't want to talk about my baby.'

She'd been talking about Molly for six months straight and she didn't want to talk about her now? How unfair, Ellie thought.

'I still want to talk about you. Let's talk about your inability to say no...'

Ellie, past the point of patience, threw an egg at her.

Ellie rolled over and looked, wide-eyed, at the luminous hands of her bedside clock. It was twelve-seventeen and she wasn't even close to sleep. Throwing off her sheet, she cocked her head as she heard footsteps going down the stairs.

It seemed she wasn't the only person who was awake.

Ellie pulled a thigh-length T-shirt over her skimpy tank. It skimmed the hem of her sleeping shorts. Deciding against shoes, she flipped her thick plait over her shoulder, left the room and walked down the darkened stairs. She knew where he'd be: standing on the front veranda, looking out to the moonlit sea.

He wasn't. He was sitting on one of the chairs, dressed in

running shorts and pulling on his trainers. Ellie hesitated at the front door and took a moment to watch him, looking hard and tough, as he quickly tied the laces in his shoes. It was after midnight—why was he going for a run? It made no sense...

'What are you doing?' she asked, stepping through the open door.

Jack snapped his head up to look at her and she caught the tension in his eyes. 'Can't sleep.'

'So you're going for a run?'

Jack shrugged. 'It's better than lying awake looking at the ceiling.'

Ellie folded her arms and looked at the top of his head. For the past four days he'd been quiet, and tonight at dinner he'd said little, after which he'd excused himself as usual to do some work. Despite hoping that he'd come back downstairs, she hadn't seen him since he'd left the table.

Jack stood up and started to stretch, and Ellie wondered if this was Jack's way of expelling stress and tension. She might indulge in a good crying jag but he went running. Maybe, just maybe, she could get him to try talking for a change.

She crossed her arms as she stepped outside, then walked up to him and nudged him with her shoulder.

'Why don't you talk to me instead of hitting the streets?'

'Uh—'

'C'mon.' Ellie boosted herself up on the stone wall so that she faced Jack, her back to the sea. 'What's going on, Jack? Has something happened?'

Jack placed his arm behind his head to stretch out his arms and Ellie noticed his chest muscles rippling, his six-pack contracting, that nasty scar lifting. She forced herself to take her mind off his body and concentrate on his words.

'Nothing's happened...'

Dammit, he simply wasn't going to open up. Ellie felt a spurt of hurt and disappointment and hopped off the wall.

'Okay, Jack, don't talk to me. But don't treat me like an idiot by telling me that nothing happened!'

Ellie headed for the front door and was stopped by Jack's strong arm around her stomach.

'Geez, Ellie. Cool your jets, would you?'

Ellie whirled around, put her hands on his chest and shoved. Her efforts had no impact on him at all. 'Dammit, I just want you to talk to me!'

'If you gave me two seconds to finish my sentence then you'd realise that I am trying to talk to you!' Jack dropped his arms and pointed to the Morris chair. 'Sit.'

Ellie sat and pulled her feet up to tuck them under her, her expression mutinous. She'd give him one more chance, but if he tried to fob her off with 'nothing happened' again she'd shove him off the wall.

Jack sat on the edge of the wall. 'Kenya was a fairly routine trip in that nothing *unusual* happened. I hit the streets, found my contacts, got some intel, reported. I worked, hung out with the rest of the press corps.'

Ellie pulled a face. 'Sorry.'

Jack placed his hand behind his ear. 'What was that?'

Ellie glared at him. 'You heard me. So if the trip was fairly routine, then what's bugging you?'

'Exactly that...the fact that the trip felt so routine. Unexciting, flat.'

Ellie scratched her forehead. 'I'm sorry, I don't understand.'

'I'm not sure if I understand either. There are certain reasons I do what I do. Why I do it. I need the adrenalin. I need to feel like I'm living life at full throttle.' Jack must have seen the question on her face because he shook his head. 'Maybe some day I'll tell you why but not now. Not tonight.'

Not ready yet. She could respect that. 'Okay, so you need the thrill, the buzz of danger...'

'Not necessarily danger—okay, I like the danger factor

too—but in places or situations like that there's always a buzz, an energy that is so tangible you can almost reach out and taste it. I feed on that energy.'

'And there wasn't any this time?'

Jack closed his eyes. 'Oh, there was—apparently. Everyone I spoke to said that there was something in the air, a sense that the place was on a knife edge, that violence was a hair's breadth away. The journalists were buzzing on the atmosphere and I didn't pick up a damn thing. I couldn't feel it. I felt like I was just going through the motions.'

'Oh.'

'There are different types of war correspondent. There are the idealists—the ones who want to make a difference. There are the ones who, sadly, feed off the violence, the brutality. There are others who use it to hide from life.' Jack scrubbed his hands over his face. 'I report. Full-stop. Right from the beginning I knew that it wasn't my job to save the world. That my job was to relay the facts, not to get involved with the emotion. I have always been super-objective. I don't particularly like making judgement calls, mostly because I can always see both sides of the story. Nobody is ever one hundred per cent right. But I always—*always!*—have been the first to pick up the mood on the street, the energy in the air.'

'Do you ever take a stand? Get off the fence?' Ellie asked him after a short silence. 'Make a judgement call?'

Jack thought about her question for a moment. 'Personally or professionally?'

'Either. Both.'

'When it comes to political ideologies I am for neutrality. Personally, I've experienced some stuff...gone through a lot... so when bad things happen I measure it up against what I went through and frequently realise that it's not worth getting upset about. So I don't get worked up easily, and because of that I probably don't get involved on either side of anything either.'

Whoa! Super-complicated man. 'Okay, so getting back to Kenya...'

'I made an offhand comment to Mitch about feeling like this and that led to a discussion about me. He said that I've become too distant, too unemotional, too hard. He used the word "robotic". *Am* I robotic, El?'

Ellie stood up, sat on the wall next to him and dropped her head onto his shoulder. 'I don't think you are, but to be fair I haven't seen you in that situation or seen you report for a long time—six months at least.'

'He also said that I'm desensitised to violence, that I don't see other people's pain. That I'm becoming heartless.'

That was rich, coming from her father, Ellie thought, the King of Self-Involvement. Except her father was very good at what he did, so he might have a point. But Ellie didn't believe that Jack was as callous as he or her father made him out to be. It was more likely that he used his emotional distance as a shield.

'Is not caring just a way to protect yourself from everything bad you've seen?'

Jack shrugged. 'I have no idea. Mitch said that I'm burnt out, that it's affecting my reporting, that I'm coming across as hard. He said that I need to get my head in the game, take some time off to fill the well. We had a rip roaring argument...'

'He sent you home?'

Jack looked rebellious. 'As much as he likes to think he does, Mitchell doesn't *send* me anywhere. I left because there wasn't much more to report on except for rehashing the same story.' Jack stared at his feet.

'Is he right? *Are* you burnt out?' Ellie asked quietly, keeping her temple on his shoulder.

'I don't know.'

'I think you need to give yourself a break. You were beaten up in Somalia, stabbed, kicked out of the country. You've just come back from a less than cheerful city. When did you last take a proper holiday, relax…counter all the gruesome stuff you've witnessed with happy stuff?'

'Happy stuff?'

'Lying on a beach, surfing, drinking wine in the afternoon sun. Napping. Reading a book for pleasure and not for research. Um…sleeping late. In other words, a holiday?'

'Not for a while. Not for a very long time,' Jack admitted, placing his broad hand on her knee.

'Thought so. Maybe you should actually do that?'

'I don't know how to relax, to take it easy. It's not in my nature. I like moving, working, exploring. I need to keep moving to feel alive.'

'Maybe that's what you've conditioned yourself to feel… but it's not healthy.' Ellie yawned and reluctantly lifted her head off his arm.

Jack stood up and ran a gentle hand over her hair. 'Get some sleep, El. There's no point in us both being exhausted.'

Ellie didn't think about it. She just stood up, wrapped her arms around his waist and laid her cheek on his bare chest. 'Don't beat yourself up, Jack. Mitchell might think he's always right, but he's not.'

'I kind of think he might be this time.'

'Well, I hope you didn't tell him that. You'll never hear the end of it.' Ellie placed her forehead on his chest and kept one hand on his waist.

Jack stood ramrod-straight and for the longest minute Ellie held her breath, certain that he would push her away. Eventually his arms locked around her back and he buried his face in her hair. Ellie rubbed her hands over his back, met his miserable eyes and ran her hand across his forehead, down his cheek to his chest. Her hands dropped, brushed the waistband of his shorts, and she felt tension—suddenly sexual—skitter through his body. She moved her hands to put them on his hips and felt his swift intake of air.

'I missed you,' he said, his voice gruff.

'I missed you too.'

Jack closed his eyes and his arms tightened and his lower body jumped in reaction to her words. She could feel his heat and response through her light cotton shirt and sleeping shorts and she wanted him...

She didn't want to want him. She couldn't afford to want him.

She forced herself to say the words. 'I need to go to bed, Jack.'

Jack immediately released her and she suddenly felt colder without his heat.

'Go on up. I'm going for a run.'

Ellie nodded. 'Thanks, by the way.'

One eyebrow rose. 'For...?'

'Talking to me. I thought you were mad at me, so it was a bit of a relief. Sorry I jumped to the wrong conclusion in the beginning.'

Jack sent her a small grin. 'Next time you jump to conclusions I won't give you a second chance.'

Ellie patted his chest. 'Yes, you will.'

'I'm afraid you're probably right,' Jack said softly, and jogged down the stairs.

The night was warm and the streets were deserted, and the sea was his only companion as he ran along the promenade, his feet slapping against the pavement. Sweat ran down his temples and down his spine into the waistband of his shorts. His body felt fluid but his mind was a mess.

God, it felt good to run. Apart from the fact that it kept his heart working properly, it was easier to think when he was running.

He hadn't lied to Ellie—he *hadn't* connected with the story or the atmosphere in Kenya and that worried him—but he certainly hadn't told her the whole truth. How could he? How could he explain to her that he'd spent his days in Kenya missing her, thinking about her? He'd never allowed anyone to distract him from the job at hand, yet she had. He'd be walking the streets, seeing an old man whittling away at a piece of wood, and he'd think Ellie would crouch down next to him and demand to know what he was creating. He'd drink his morning coffee at the hotel and wish he was standing on her veranda, watching the endless blues and greens of the sea.

His nights were a combination of fantasy and frustration, thinking about what he wanted to do to and with her amazing body.

When he'd seen her on the wall that afternoon he'd come back his thumping heart had settled, sighed. And he'd known he had the potential to fall deeper and deeper in trouble. Emotional trouble.

He'd known her for only days and she'd stirred up all these weird feelings inside him. Why? What was it about her that made him feel as if he'd stepped outside of himself? He could talk to her. He wanted to talk to her. Take this evening, for example. He would never have spoken to any of his previous girlfriends like that…hell, he'd barely *spoken* to them. He'd just flown in from wherever, climbed into bed, kept said girlfriend in bed until he needed to leave and then left. He didn't know how to act as part of a couple on an on-going basis, and before he'd landed in Cape Town he'd never come close to being tied down by anyone or anything. He excelled in saying goodbye and never looking back. He'd had a second chance at life and he'd made a promise to live it hard, because he'd always believed it would be an injustice to live a small life… to confine himself to a humdrum job…to be shackled by a house or a lover.

His beliefs, so firmly held for so long, were starting to waver.

And that was why he'd scuttled out of Ellie's house last week. He hadn't needed to go to Kenya but it had been a damn good excuse to put some distance between them.

Jack stopped and, breathing heavily, placed his hands on his hips. In the low light of the sodium streetlights he stared out to the breaking waves as clouds scuttled across the moon. Little in life made sense any more... He could easily have gone back to London after Kenya but he'd headed south instead. What was happening to him?

He'd been shot, beaten up and stabbed. He'd sneaked behind enemy lines, walked into the compounds of drug cartels, through whorehouses filled with the dregs of humanity who'd slit his throat just for the fun of it—just to get a story. He'd seen the worst of what people could do to each other and yet he'd never felt fear like this before...

He was terrified he was becoming emotionally involved with her—would do practically anything to stop that happening. Ellie had hit the nail squarely in one of their many conversations; he was an observer, not a participator. Involvement with her would require a decision, taking a stand for her, sticking around, partaking in a life together.

He didn't want to do that—wasn't ready to do that. Wouldn't do that. He needed to find some perspective, reconnect with his beliefs, reaffirm his values. Jack nodded at the sea. He had to make sure that he kept some emotional distance, guarded against any deepening of their relationship. It was the sensible decision—hell, it was the only decision.

And while he was making major decisions he really needed to decide what he was going to do about Brent's memorial service. Go or not? He was starting to feel that he needed to, that he needed to honour Brent, to say thank you for the gift of his life. But would seeing him make the Sandersons' day worse? Would being there deepen the guilt he felt?

Maybe he shouldn't go.

Jack swore as he resumed running. This was why it was better not to examine his thoughts and emotions too closely. It just confused him. And, talking about being confused, what had Ellie meant when she'd said she had thought that he was angry with her? Why would she think that?

Jack intended to find out.

CHAPTER EIGHT

JACK POUNDED UP the steps and flung open her bedroom door. He knew she wouldn't be asleep and she wasn't. She was sitting up in bed, working on her computer. Didn't she ever give work a rest?

'Why are you working?' he demanded crossly.

'I'm not. I'm catching up with friends.'

'At one in the morning?'

'Excuse me, at least *I'm* not the one running after midnight!' Ellie closed the lid of her computer and tapped her finger against it. 'Did you just burst in here to give me a hard time generally or was there a specific reason?'

Jack walked into the room and stood at the end of her bed. 'You said that you thought I was mad at you. Why, Ellie?'

Ellie plucked the sheet with her fingers and felt her face flaming in the dim light of her lamp. 'It's not important.'

Jack sat on the edge of the bed and placed his hand on her knee. 'I think it might be. Talk to me, El.'

Ellie shook her head and placed her computer on her bedside table. 'Jack, it really doesn't matter since you haven't made any...since we're not...'

'Sleeping together?' Jack sounded puzzled. 'Are you upset that I'm *not* sleeping with you?'

'Yes...no. I don't know. I thought you'd changed your mind about...me.'

Jack's expression was pure confusion. 'Let me try and decode that from girl-speak. Firstly, I couldn't run out of your house, not call you, then come back and expect to jump into bed with you. I thought we needed some time, and I've been dealing with all this other crap, so...' Jack rubbed the back of his neck. 'I changed my mind...? Hold on a sec—did you think that I didn't want to sleep with you? Why on earth wouldn't I want to sleep with you?'

'Good grief, Jack, you can't expect me to verbalise it!' Ellie cried.

'Well, if you want me to understand what's going on in that crazy head of yours, *yes*! Because I am lost!'

'I wasn't any good and it couldn't have been much fun for you,' Ellie mumbled. 'And I backed off midway.'

There was a long silence and Ellie felt Jack staring at her head. When he eventually spoke Ellie could hear the regret in his voice.

'Have you been worried about that since I left?'

'Mmm.'

Jack swore. 'And I left here with a rocket on my tail, not even thinking... Dammit!'

Ellie looked up at him. 'So you weren't mad that I said no?'

'Disappointed? Yes. Cross? Absolutely not.'

'Oh.'

Jack played with her fingers. 'Why *did* you stop, by the way? What happened?'

'My brain started a running commentary as soon as we got to my bedroom. I started to second-guess what we were doing—what I was doing. And whether I was getting it right.'

Jack cradled her cheek with his hand. 'Making love is not a test to be graded, sweetheart. Come on—cough it up. What else were you worrying about?'

'Whether I was enough for you. Whether I was practiced

enough. Cellulite...other crazy girl stuff.' Ellie stared at a point beyond his shoulder.

'You don't have a centimetre of cellulite, and if you do I *so* don't care. And if we're trading thoughts about that night then I should tell you that I'm sorry if I went too fast for you. I'd thought about having you so many times, in so many ways... and I guess I was nervous too.'

'Why were you nervous? You've had lots of sex before.'

'Yes, but I've never had sex with *you*!' Jack exclaimed. 'What? I'm not allowed to be nervous? I finally get the girl I've been fantasising about in bed and suddenly I'm a stud? It doesn't work like that, Ellie. The first time you make love to someone it's *always* the first time. I'm also worried about pleasing you. It never works out perfectly. We don't know each other's bodies, what the other person likes and/or doesn't like. It falls into place with time.'

Ellie continued to stare at her bedclothes.

'Sweetheart, I really need you to talk to me, to tell me what you're thinking,' Jack said quietly, his voice persuasive.

Ellie lifted her head and looked at him with sad eyes. 'Thank you for that—for saying all of that. And you're probably right. We just need time.'

'Exactly.'

Ellie held his gaze. 'But we have a problem. By my calculations, and from everything you've told me, you're staying another week at the most. Then you'll leave...probably around about the time we can start making mountains move. So my two questions are: how fair would that be to either of us? And, really, what would be the point?'

'It doesn't have to be love, Ellie. It doesn't have to be for ever. It can just be two people who are attracted to each other giving each other pleasure and company. The point can be...' Jack encircled her neck with his hand and smoothed his thumb over the tendons in her neck '...this.'

He touched the corner of her mouth with his.

'So sweet. Spicy.' He stroked her jaw and placed his lips on the spot between her jaw and her ear. 'Soft. The point can be that I think you have the most beautiful skin.'

Jack moved and dropped his other hand onto her bottom. In a movement that was as smooth as it was sexy, he pulled her onto his lap so that she straddled his thighs.

As sparks bolted down her inner thighs Ellie dimly remembered that she had to be pressing on his knife wound and tried to scramble off him. Jack's hand on her thighs kept her firmly in place.

'Nuh-uh—where are you going? I like you here,' he said.

'Your cut,' Ellie protested, her head dropping so that their noses were practically touching.

'I'm fine and you feel great,' Jack informed her, lifting his head to nibble on her mouth. 'I love your mouth...' he murmured. 'Love your eyes...fantastic skin...'

He lifted his hands from her thighs and placed them on her chest, holding the weight of her breasts in his hands. Ellie moaned as he thumbed her nipples into gloriously sensitive peaks.

'As for these...these are simply a point of their own.'

Ellie couldn't find any words, was drenched in the wet heat of his voice. She arched her back and rolled her neck as she pushed into his hands seeking more.

'You are so beautiful...' Jack dropped his hands down to her waist.

She shook her hair out and it spilled down her chest, over her brief tank top. Jack leaned back and just looked at her, his caress as bold as his eyes.

'Take it off,' he said, his voice hoarse. 'Let me look at you.'

Somewhere in some place deep inside her Ellie knew that she should probably say no, that she should climb off his lap and be sensible, but instead she arched her back, pulled her shirt over her head and held the garment in place against her chest. She hadn't thought it was possible for Jack's eyes to darken with passion, but they did and she saw his jaw clench.

She felt feminine and powerful and wondrously, wickedly wanton.

'You're killing me here, woman,' Jack growled and he lifted his hand to yank the shirt away. His nostrils flared as he took in her creamy skin now flushed with arousal. He held her face in his hands. 'Trust me, El. I'm going to show you exactly what the point of this is...'

Ellie walked into the bedroom from the bathroom, wrapped in a towel from waist to mid-thigh and towel-drying her hair. She looked from the clock to Jack, who was lying crossways across the bed, spread out on his stomach. 'We've wasted a good portion of the morning.'

'Hush your mouth, wench. A morning in bed is never wasted,' Jack said as he stood up and stretched. He was totally self-confident about his body and he had a right to be, Ellie thought. Apart from the nasty scar on his chest, he was perfect.

'How did you get that scar?' Ellie asked.

Jack lifted his hand up to his chest and immediately turned away. 'Operation.'

Ellie rubbed the ends of her hair between the folds of the towel. 'What operation?'

Jack walked past her and swatted her backside. 'The one I had in hospital.'

He stepped into the *en-suite* bathroom and Ellie heard water hitting the shower door. Well, that had gone well. *Not.* Obviously his scar-causing operation was not up for discussion. Ellie wondered why not. It couldn't be that big a deal, surely?

Jack raised his voice. 'This is such a waste of water...you should've let me shower with you.'

Ellie smiled at herself in the dressing table mirror. 'I couldn't trust you not to have your wicked way with me again.'

She'd thought about yanking him into the shower with her but she didn't think she could stand another bout of that sweet, sweet torture. Or maybe she could—in an hour or two, when all her nerve-endings had subsided slightly.

'You like my wicked ways.' Jack's voice was chock-full of self-satisfaction.

'I do? How can you tell?'

'Well, I think your begging was a huge hint,' Jack said dryly, before she heard the shower door open and close.

Ellie pulled fresh underwear out of her dresser drawer and quickly slipped into a matching aqua-green set. White shorts and a pretty floral top were perfect for a day to be spent at home…she had to stock up on cleaning products and dog food, spend some time on the internet paying personal bills, and she needed to finalise the arrangements for Jess's bachelorette party.

Maybe after that she could persuade Jack back into bed…

Jess! Jess and Luke! Oh, *man*! She'd forgotten that she was having lunch with them. She picked up her watch from the dresser and cursed again. She had barely ten minutes before they were due to pick her up. This was Jack's fault and his ability to make her forget everything when his clever hands were anywhere near her body.

Ellie stomped over to the bathroom and looked into the steam to the stunning body beyond. Tight buns, broad chest, a nice package…. A very nice package that knew exactly what it was doing…. *Concentrate, Ellie!*

'Jack?'

Jack, his head full of shampoo, turned around and lifted one eyebrow. 'Changed your mind? C'mon in. I'll wash your back.'

Ellie gestured to her clothes and tipped her head. 'No—no time. Listen, I just suddenly remembered that I made plans for today.'

She saw the disappointment on Jack's face before he rearranged his features into a blank mask. 'Okay. Have fun.'

Ellie tried not to roll her eyes and failed. 'I'm having lunch with Luke and Jess—I forgot. Want to join us?'

Pleasure, hot and quick, flashed in his eyes. 'Sure.'

Ellie thought she'd push her luck and try to satisfy her curiosity. 'So why won't you tell me about your scar?'

Jack tipped his head back under the stream of water. 'Because it's not important.'

'If it wasn't important then you'd talk about it,' Ellie told him, and sighed when she saw the shutters come down in his eyes. She was beginning to recognise that look. It meant that the subject was no longer up for discussion. Ellie blew out her breath. She'd made sweet love to him all night but that didn't mean she could go crawling around in his head. 'Okay, then, be all mysterious. But hurry up, because they'll be here any moment.'

Jack rinsed out the last of the shampoo, switched off the water and grabbed a towel that hung on the railing. He wrapped the towel around his waist and shoved his hair back from his face. Catching Ellie watching him, he placed his hand on her shoulder and leaned forward to drop a kiss on the corner of her mouth.

'You okay?'

'Fine.'

'Not too sore?' Jack placed his forehead against hers and his hands on her waist.

She was a little *burny* in places that shouldn't burn. 'A little.'

'Sorry.' Jack kissed her forehead and stepped back. 'I'm going to find something to wear. Jeans and open-collar shirt?'

'No, shorts and a T-shirt,' Ellie said, following him out of the bathroom. 'We'll probably end up on the rickety deck of some about-to-fall-down shack...'

Jack pulled a face. 'And that's where we'll eat?' he said, doubt lacing his voice.

'That's where you'll eat the most amazing seafood in the world. Luke knows all the best places to eat up and down the coast,' Ellie replied, and sighed when she heard the insistent pealing of her gate bell. 'That's them—early as usual. I'll see you downstairs.'

'Ellie?'

Ellie turned at Jack's serious voice. Oh, God, what was he going to say?

Jack's smile was slow and powerful. 'Thank you for an amazing night.'

Ellie floated down the steps. Ellie Evans, she mused, sex goddess. Yeah, she could get behind that title.

In the late afternoon Jess and Luke, seeing the old lighthouse a kilometre down the beach, decided that they should take a closer look at the old iron structure. Ellie and Jack, who were operating on a lot less sleep, shook their heads at their departing backs, took a bottle of wine and glasses to the beach, found an old log for a backrest and sat in the sand.

'How are you doing?' Jack asked, pouring wine into a glass and then handing it to her.

Ellie squinted at him. 'I'm utterly exhausted. I think we got about two hours' sleep.'

Jack covered his mouth as he yawned. 'I'm tired too. So, did you have fun?'

Ellie blushed. 'Yes, thanks. You?'

Jack laughed. 'I think the fact that I couldn't get enough of you answers that question better than I could with words.' He watched her face flush again and internally shook his head. Her confidence had really taken a battering at some point and never quite recovered.

'Tell me about your ex.'

Ellie looked as if he'd asked her to swallow a spider. 'Good grief—why?'

'Because I think that he messed up your head—badly. Dented your confidence.' Jack dug his toes into the sand as he looked at her. 'Did he?'

Ellie picked up a handful of sand and let it drift through her fingers. 'S'pose so. Not that I had much to start with.'

'And why would that be?'

Ellie tipped her head at him. 'Jack, you saw me. I was plump and very shy, and standing firmly in the shadow of my famous father—who was everything I wasn't. Good-looking, charming, erudite, confident. Then I went to art school.'

He loved that secret smile—the one that lit her up from the inside out. 'And...?'

'And I flourished. I found something I loved and excelled in. I was happy and the weight fell off me. Boys were asking me out on dates, and although I never went I *was* being asked.'

'Why didn't you go?'

'As I said, I was shy. They asked and I said no and I got the reputation of being hard to get. And, boys being boys, they thought that was cool, so I became more popular, which made me more confident and I finally started dating.'

'Where does the grim gallery owner fit in?' Jack asked, draping a possessive leg over hers.

'He was a friend of one of our final-year lecturers and he came to give a talk to the graduating class. On a whim he said that he'd look at our work in progress. He asked to see my portfolio, said that I had talent and told me look him up if I ever got to London, saying that he might offer me an exhibition.' Ellie watched a crab crawl out of a hole and scuttle towards the waves. 'A couple of months later I did meet up with him in London. We started a relationship and he slowly eroded every bit of confidence I'd worked so hard to acquire.'

'How?'

'My art wasn't up to standard.' Ellie shrugged as thunderclouds built in her eyes.

'Why did you stay with him?'

Ellie bit her bottom lip. 'Because he told me he loved me and said that he'd never leave. The two sentences I'd waited to hear all my life.'

Jack rubbed his eyes. 'Oh, sweetheart.'

'Then, during the little time he spent with me, he started on everything else. Clothes and hair. Weight. My cooking, my friends, my skill in the bedroom.'

Jack felt his mouth drop open with surprise, which was closely followed by the burn of fury. 'He said you were a bad lover?'

'No, he said that I was a damned awful lover and a blow-up doll would be more fun.'

If that...Jack swallowed the names he wanted to call Ellie's waste-of-skin ex. No wonder she'd frozen the other night. No wonder she seemed constantly to second-guess herself.

Ellie dug her bare feet into the sand. 'Merri thinks that he and my father scarred me emotionally.'

Well, yeah. 'What do you think?'

Ellie sipped her wine and dropped back so that her elbows were in the sand. 'Of course they did. I'm scared to get close to people because I don't want to run the risk of getting hurt and I know that they'll leave me. I tend to keep myself emotionally isolated. It's safer that way.'

'Safer isn't necessarily better,' Jack pointed out.

Ellie slanted him a look. 'You do the same thing, Jack Chapman, and don't think you don't.'

'What do you mean?' Jack asked, bewildered by her suddenly turning the tables on him.

'You observe, watch, report and walk away. You don't get involved, so you're as much as an emotional coward as me.'

Jack sighed as her well-made point hit him dead centre. He took a minute to allow his surprise to settle before placing his hand on her knee. 'Maybe I am, El.'

Jeez, he wished he could get the words out. It was a perfect time to tell her that they had no future, that she shouldn't expect anything from him, that he couldn't consider settling down with her—with anyone. That he couldn't afford to take this any deeper, to allow her to creep behind the doors and walls of his self-sufficiency.

Ellie's teasing voice snapped him out of his reverie. 'You awake behind those shades, Chapman?'

'Yep.' Jack hooked his arm around her neck, pulled her to him and dropped a hard kiss on her mouth. 'Just thinking.'

'Careful, you might hurt yourself,' Ellie teased, and yelped when his fingers connected with her ribcage. Her wine glass wobbled in her hand and she dropped it when his other hand tickled her under her arms.

'Jack! You wretch! Stop...please, Jack!' Ellie whimpered, and then her breath hitched.

He realised he was lying on her, her mouth just below his. Tickling turned to passion and laughter turned to need as he plundered her mouth.

Jack felt his heart sink into his stomach as he placed his head in the crook of her neck.

Dammit, Ellie, how am I ever going to find the strength to walk away from you?

'I hate hangovers,' Jack thought he heard Ellie mutter.

She was showered, teeth brushed and dressed, but she still looked headachey and miserable, huddled into the corner of the couch, tousle-haired and exceptionally grumpy. But, amazingly, still so sexy.

'Why did I drink so much last night?' she wailed.

Jack crouched down in front of her and smiled as he handed her a couple of aspirin and some water. 'Hey, in reply to every drunken text you sent at various times throughout the evening I suggested that you stop. You told me that you could handle it.'

'Well, I can't,' Ellie sulked.

'Tough it out, sunshine.'

It had been Jess's hen's party last night and Ellie had hosted the pre-clubbing ritual of cupcakes and champagne. When he'd run down the stairs at eight Ellie had been sitting on the edge of the couch and his eyes had rolled back in his head when he'd seen what she was—almost—wearing: a piece of sparkly scrap material covering her breasts, held in place by strings criss-crossing her back, tight jeans and screw-me heels. She'd pulled back her hair into a severe tail, and with dramatic make-up she'd looked dangerous and sexy.

She'd had 'trouble' written all over her face. He'd decided to leave the house before he carried her upstairs, made her change and lectured her on exactly what the men in the club would think, seeing her in that outfit.

When he'd heard her stumble in—with Jess, Clem Copeland and Maddie—it had been after two. The dogs had wandered upstairs at three, and at three-thirty he'd heard the shouted suggestion of skinny-dipping in the pool. He really deserved credit for not looking.

He'd known he must be getting old when he'd chosen to roll over and go back to sleep rather than spy on hot naked women cavorting in the moonlight.

He grinned as he placed his cup on the coffee table in front of them. Oh, he was enjoying this, he thought as he took the opposite corner of the couch and settled in, his laptop between his crossed knees.

Ellie held her head. 'What's with the computer?' she demanded. 'Oooh, I think there are a hundred ADD gnomes tap-dancing in my head.'

'You and I are going to talk about Mitchell,' Jack said pleasantly.

Ellie groaned. 'No, we're not.'

'Mmm, yes, we are.' Jack looked from his screen to her. His eyes were alert with intelligence, his fingers steady on the keyboard. He was after a story and she was part of it.

'Jack, please...'

'It's just a couple of questions about your father.'

'Questions I don't want to answer,' Ellie said stubbornly.

'Why not?'

'Because it doesn't change anything!' Ellie shouted, and watched as her head fell off her shoulders and rolled across the room. 'He wasn't there for me, *ever*! He was a drop-in dad, and I loved him far more than he loved me.'

Jack shook his head. 'How old were you when your parents got divorced?'

'Fifteen,' Ellie snapped.

'And how did your mother take it?'

'How do you think? She was devastated.' Ellie leaned forward to make her point, groaned and sank back. 'Do you know she never fell in love again after him? He was her one love. And he brushed us both off like we were nothing...'

Ellie felt a sob rise and ruthlessly forced it down. She'd shed enough tears over her father, her ex, men in general. Hangover or no, she wasn't going to shed any more. But she wanted to. She wanted to tell Jack how much it hurt, how much she wanted to be loved, cherished, protected. She didn't *need* to be—not as she had when she was a little girl—but she still had a faint wish to be able to step into a strong pair of arms and rest awhile.

Like now, when her head felt separated from her body and her stomach was staging its own hostile rebellion.

'So you ran from an emotionally and physically absent father to an emotionally and physically absent fiancé. Why?'

'That's not a question about Mitchell,' Ellie retorted.

'Why, El?'

'Because it's what I deserved! Because my love was never enough to keep someone with me! Because I choose badly!'

Jack sighed. 'Oh, El, that is off-the-charts crap. You had

a father who was useless and you had a bad relationship. It doesn't mean that *you* are useless!'

'Feels like it,' Ellie muttered. 'And might I point out that you dig around in my head, throwing questions at me, but you won't answer any of mine?' It wasn't fair that he wanted to delve into her life and emotions and he wouldn't allow her into his.

Jack's hands stilled on the keyboard and he sent her a shuttered look. His sigh covered his obvious irritation. 'What do you want to know?'

'You *know* what,' Ellie muttered. She gestured to his chest. 'Tell me about that scar. How did you get it?'

'Heart transplant,' Jack said, his voice devoid of inflection.

'Excuse me?'

'You heard what I said.'

Ellie sat up, her headache all but forgotten under this enormous news. 'But you look fine.'

'That's because I *am* fine! I've been fine for seventeen years!'

Ooooh, touchy subject. Even more touchy than her father issues. 'Hey, I'm still processing this—just give me a second, okay? How would you like me to react?'

'Well, for starters, I'd like you to take that look of pity off your face!' Jack picked his computer up and banged it down onto the coffee table. 'That's why I don't tell people—because they instantly go all sympathetic and gooey!'

Oh, wait... His sharp, snappy voice was pulling her headache right back.

'Stop putting words into my mouth! I never said that.' Ellie pulled her legs up and rested her chin on her knees, her eyes on his suddenly miserable face. His expression practically begged her to leave the subject alone, but he'd opened the door and she was going to walk on in. 'Why did you need a heart transplant?'

'I caught viral pneumonia when I was thirteen. It damaged my heart.'

'And how old were you when you had the transplant?'

'Seventeen.'

'Geez, Jack.' Ellie wanted to crawl into his lap to comfort him, but knew that any affection right now would be misconstrued, deeply unwelcome.

'Nobody outside of my family knows,' Jack warned her. 'It's not something that I want to become public knowledge.'

'Why not?'

'Because it doesn't define me!' Jack's eyes flashed with irritation.

'If it didn't define you to a certain point then you wouldn't keep it so secret,' Ellie pointed out. 'What's the big deal? So you were sick when you were a kid, and you got a new heart—?' Ellie sat up, curiosity on her face. 'Do you know whose heart you got?'

'Yes. It was another teenager. Killed in a car crash,' Jack said curtly. He nodded to his computer and glared at Ellie. 'Can we get back to the subject on hand?'

'No.' Ellie shook her head. 'I'm still trying to wrap my head around this. So you got viral pneumonia, which damaged your heart, and you were sick for a long time. Then you got a new heart and now you're fine?'

'I take anti-rejection pills every day and make a point of keeping myself healthy. Apart from that, and the scar, I'm as normal as anyone else.'

Physically, maybe, but Ellie suspected that there was a whole bunch of psychological stuff still whirling around in his head. She needed to understand how it had moulded the man in front of her. Because she had no doubt that it had. How could it not have? It was too big, too life-changing—in every sense of the word. 'Tell me about those years between falling sick and having the operation.'

'You're not going to let this go, are you?'

Jack rested his forearms on his knees in a pose she was coming to realise was characteristic of him and linked his hands.

'I became housebound, lacking energy, lacking breath. I got sick frequently. Sport, school, partying, girls were all out of the question...it was an effort just to stay alive. At the end stages just before the op, my heart was so damaged that I could hardly walk. I...*existed.*'

She could hardly imagine it—this vibrant, energetic, amazing man, who should have been an active, lively teen, restricted by his failing heart and deteriorating health. 'Frustration' and 'resentment' were words far too weak to describe some of the emotions he must have experienced at the time.

'And that time defined the rest of your life?'

'Yes.'

'How?'

'I hate being told what I can or can't do, that I have to stay in one place, that I can't pick up and leave. I lived a life of very few choices. I vowed to never limit myself again. For the best part of my teenage life I was so...*confined* that I promised myself I would never be again. And I promised Brent—'

'Who?'

'My donor. I promised him, and myself, that I would *live* life, not exist. Not try to protect myself. That I'd do everything he never had the chance to.'

Phew. Well, she'd asked.

Jack stood up abruptly. 'I need more coffee. Do you want another cup?'

The door slammed shut. Ellie shook her head and wished she hadn't. *Ow, my head!* How was she supposed to take in and think about Jack's monumental disclosure when her head was splitting apart?

No fair.

CHAPTER NINE

JACK LEFT THE room and Ellie stared at the spot he'd vacated and forced herself to concentrate. A heart transplant? Was he being serious? Of course he was, she'd seen his scar, but... *holy mackerel*. She'd expected to hear about a big operation, but a heart transplant was a very big deal. How could it not be?

Ellie heard Jack's footsteps behind her and sent him a wary look as he sat down beside her, another cup of coffee in his hand.

'You still want to talk about it, don't you?' Jack asked, his expression stating that he'd rather have his legs waxed.

Ellie leaned back and put her feet up on the coffee table. 'It's just another part of your history—like stitches or breaking a leg...though on a much mightier scale.'

'You laughed when you heard about those incidents. I can handle humour. I can't stand pity.' Jack glared at her.

'Sorry, I'm a bit short on heart transplant jokes,' Ellie shot back. 'And stop glaring at me! I didn't torture you to tell me.'

'You'd be surprised,' Jack retorted, looking miserable. 'I look into your eyes and I want to tell you...*stuff*.'

Ellie batted her lashes and Jack laughed. Reluctantly, but he laughed. 'You appear to be sweet but you are actually a brat, do you know that?'

'Sweet? *Ugh*.' Ellie wrinkled her nose. 'What a description. I prefer "amazing sex goddess".'

Jack's laugh was a lot easier this time. 'You are that too. But you'll have to keep proving it to retain the title.'

Ellie slapped his groping hands away and captured the hand closest to hers. 'I will, but I need to say something to you first.' His expression became guarded at her serious tone, but she decided to carry on anyway. She took a deep breath and spoke. 'I'm sorry for what you lived through but, although you probably won't believe me, I don't feel pity. If anything I'm in awe of what you've achieved, how you've refused to allow your past to limit you.'

Jack shoved a hand into his hair, squirmed, but Ellie ploughed on.

'You could've chosen to protect yourself, to hide out, to nurture yourself, and everyone would've understood. But because you're you you probably said to your heart, *Right, dude, we've both got a second chance. Hang on—we're going for a ride.* Am I right?'

'Yeah...I suppose.'

'I respect the hell out of you. You're also...well...not ugly... which doesn't hurt.'

Jack's laugh whizzed over her head as he reached for her and pulled her across his lap. Ellie looked up at him and swallowed. When she teamed her respect for him with his sharp intellect, his dry sense of humour and the fact that he was a very decent guy, her heart started doing somersaults in her ribcage.

Add their physical chemistry to the mix and she had a soupy mess that could blow up in her face.

Since they'd started sleeping together she'd refused to think of him as anything other than a brief affair. Whenever she found herself thinking about him in terms of more, she reminded herself that she only had tomorrow or the next day or the next and closed the door on those fantasies. She wouldn't think of him in any other context other than that of a short-term, big-fun, no-strings affair, because it would be so easy to allow him to slip inside her heart and her head and that way madness lay. He would leave—he'd told her he would—and she would be left holding her bruised and battered heart.

Jack's thumb brushed over her lips and he just looked down at her with a soft, vulnerable expression on his face that she'd never seen before. It was encounters like this that dragged her deeper into an emotional quagmire. He was so enticing, on both an emotional and physical level, that it was difficult to not slip over the edge into deeper involvement. She was teetering on the edge. But she had to step back...because thinking of anything else was, frankly, stupid.

There were a couple of things she was sure of: she could love him, really love him, but he didn't want or need her love. And he'd never need her, love her, as she needed him to.

Life was tough enough without having to compete with his job for his attention and his time. History had taught her that she'd end up either disappointing him or being disappointed. Both sucked equally, so why risk either? No, falling all the way in love with him was *not* an option, she thought as his mouth drifted across hers.

But it might be easier said than done.

It was the start of a new week and Jack, after spending hours at his computer, chipping away at Mitch's story, felt as if he needed a break. It was the middle of the afternoon so he walked down to the bakery and ducked behind the counter. Sliding behind Samantha, he shoved a mug under the spout and shot a double espresso into a cup. Yanking a twenty out of his pocket, he dropped it in the pocket of her apron and snagged a chocolate muffin before walking through the stable door into the bakery.

As was his habit, he spent a moment admiring Ellie's legs beneath the scarlet chef's jacket before walking over to her table and pulling at the ponytail that fell out of her baseball cap.

Ellie lifted her fondant-full hands, smiled at him and eyed his muffin. 'I'm starving—can I have some?'

Jack held the muffin to her mouth and sighed when Ellie took an enormous bite. 'Piglet.'

'I didn't have lunch,' Ellie explained. 'I got involved in this cake.'

Jack ran his hand down Ellie's back and popped the rest of the muffin into his mouth.

'You have people who slap together sandwiches for your customers not twelve feet from you—order something,' Jack suggested.

'Crazy day,' Ellie told him, and resumed working on a delicate cream rosebud that looked almost real.

He peered over her shoulder at the sugar-rose-scattered wedding cake. 'That's really pretty.'

'Thanks,' Ellie responded, her brow furrowed in concentration as she resumed work rolling a tiny petal.

Jack sat on a stool next to her table and watched her work. Her laptop stood open on the table in front of her and he gestured to it with his coffee cup. 'What's with the laptop?'

Ellie spared it a brief glance. 'I've been trying to talk to my mother about the having-to-move-the-bakery situation and she promised to find a place she could Skype from. I'm waiting for her call.'

Progress of a type, Jack thought, but he doubted that Ellie would share the full responsibility of Pari's with her mother. He could see the tension in the cords of her neck, in her raised shoulders. She didn't want to burden her mum and would find any excuse not to. And if he knew her—and he thought he did—she would downplay the situation she was in.

Sometimes Jack wanted to shake her. She had about five months to purchase the property, do the renovations and move the bakery if she didn't want to lose any trade. She was wasting daylight in so many ways…trying to charm the owner of the building into selling when she should be threatening to walk away…chatting to her mum via Skype when she should have demanded that she return home weeks ago… Jack sighed. He tried to negotiate, rather than confront people, but he could kick ass when he needed to. Ellie's confrontation style was that she didn't essentially *have* one.

Although she *did* have a way of making him emotionally vomit all over his shoes, Jack thought, thinking about their discussion yesterday. He couldn't believe that he'd told her about his operation, his life before he'd started living again. He'd never told anybody—never discussed his past. God, if it wasn't for his mother nagging him about his check-ups he wouldn't discuss it at all.

That would be the perfect scenario. How he wished he could erase the scar, the memories, the feeling that someone had him by the throat every time he thought about it. Ellie didn't understand how difficult talking about it had been for him. He'd felt as if he'd been giving birth while he was sitting on that couch, forcing the words through his constricted throat. He'd been catapulted back seventeen years to a place he'd never wanted to revisit. He'd always been reticent, self-contained, and being so sick had isolated him from his peers and made him more so. He didn't allow people into his mind or his heart easily.

Yet Ellie kept creeping in. Did that mean that they'd moved from being a casual relationship to something that mattered? If so, he sure hadn't planned on that happening…how had that happened? And when?

A day ago…a week ago…the first time he saw her in the bakery?

He'd thought that he'd be able to live with Ellie, sleep with Ellie and remain unaffected…*hah!* And some said he was a smart guy! He shoved his hands into his hair and tugged. Being in Cape Town was becoming a bit too complicated. He felt far too at home here in Ellie's house, among her things. He'd never meant it to be a place where he could see himself living...

Yet a part of him could. Maybe it was Ellie...okay, most of it *was* Ellie, but it didn't help that she lived in possibly one of the most beautiful places he'd ever seen. Mountains and sea, sunny days, aqua and cobalt water, a pretty town. She had nice friends, people he could see himself spending time with, an interesting job, a relaxed, comfortable house.

It was miles—geographically and mentally—away from his soulless, stuffy flat in London, with its beige walls and furniture...although he *did* miss his kick-ass plasma TV. If he ever moved here that would be the only household appliance he'd pay to ship out here...

Jack gripped the edge of the stool. He was allowing the romance of the setting, his sexual attraction to Ellie and the prettiness of this area cloud his practicality. He was going soft—and possibly crazy.

He needed to go back to work. Needed a distraction from his increasingly sentimental and syrupy thoughts. There was nothing quite like a conflict, a war or a disaster, to slap your feet back to the ground.

Jack's reflections were interrupted by a Skype call coming in on Ellie's computer. At her request, Jack hit the 'answer' button with his non-sticky finger and Ellie's brown-eyed mother appeared on screen. They could be sisters, Jack thought. A couple less laughter lines, long hair instead of short, blue eyes, not deep brown.

'*Namaste*, angel face,' said Ashnee, blowing her a kiss before wrapping her bare arms around her knees and grinning into the camera.

Ellie leaned on her elbows and stared at the screen. 'Mum, I miss you so much. You look fabulous!'

Ashnee fluffed her short hair. 'I feel fabulous. I see that I'm in the bakery. Busy?'

'Hugely,' Ellie said. 'And that's what I need to talk to you about.'

Jack listened as Ellie explained the situation to her mum, and from beside the computer watched the emotions cross Ashnee's face. There was sadness, regret and then resignation.

'And we definitely can't afford the new rent?'

Ellie shook her head. 'Nope.'

Ashnee looked down at her hands, beautifully decorated with henna designs. 'So we have to move? To the old Hutchinson place?'

'Mmm, if only I can get Mrs H to sell.'

Ellie looked up as the stable door opened and lifted her hand to greet Merri who, as per usual, had Molly Blue on her slim hip. She indicated that she was on a call and Merri nodded and wandered over to the table where she usually worked, where two less experienced bakers were making macaroons.

Ellie listened with half an ear as her mum repeated her words back to her. She knew it was Ashnee's way of thinking the problem through, so she half listened and watched the conversation between Merri and the other bakers. Merri looked cross and the bakers frustrated, and when Merri picked up a batch of baked macaroons and tossed them into the dustbin behind them Ellie felt her temper heat.

Merri had no right to do quality control when she wasn't even working on the premises. Right—she needed to sort this out before she ended up with no macaroons and no bakers.

'Mum...' Ellie reached out her hand, grabbed Jack's hard arm and pulled him into the camera's view '...meet Jack. Jack—Ashnee. Jack and I are kind of seeing each other... have a chat while I sort something out.'

'Uh...'

Jack looked from her to the screen but Ellie ignored his panicked face. Good grief, anyone would think she'd asked him to meet the Queen! Ellie rolled her eyes and walked across the bakery. One pair of annoyed and two pairs of mutinous eyes looked back at her.

'What are you doing, Merri?' she asked, keeping her voice low and even.

'The macaroons were lumpy,' Merri stated, allowing Mama Thandi to take Molly from her. Merri placed her hands on her hips. 'That means the mixture was under-mixed.'

Ellie walked over to the dustbin, opened it and grabbed one of the discarded macaroons. It wasn't Merri-perfect but they could have sold the product. And, dammit, Merri had wasted time and energy, electricity and ingredients, when she wasn't even supposed to be at work.

Ellie dropped the pastry back into the bin, closed her eyes and hauled in a deep breath. She felt like an old dishrag, with every bit of energy and enthusiasm wrung out of her. And the two people who'd always been her backstop, her support structure—the other two pillars of the bakery—were wafting in and out or, in her mum's case, wafting around the Indian sub-continent, while she buckled under the responsibility of keeping the bakery afloat.

It was her fault. She'd allowed them their freedom. But enough was enough. She was done, and if they didn't step up she'd collapse under the weight and Pari's would come crashing down.

She would *not* let that happen.

Ellie opened her eyes and as she did so took a step towards Merri, grabbed her wrist and pulled her across the bakery to her table.

'What is *wrong* with you?' Merri demanded when they reached Jack, rubbing at her wrist in irritation.

'You! *You* are what is wrong with me!' Ellie snapped back,

and then she pointed her finger to her mum, on the other side of the world. 'And you! Both of you are going to listen to me!'

Jack cocked his head and stepped back. *Clever man*, Ellie thought. Get out of the area about to be firebombed.

'You first.' Ellie looked at Merri. 'You either work here or you don't. You aren't allowed to walk into my bakery if you don't and do quality control.'

'I was just...' Merri's words trailed off.

Huh...Ellie thought. *My scary face is actually scary!* She steeled herself to say what she needed to. 'I love you, Merri, and I desperately want you to come back to work. Next week is the beginning of a new month. Either get your ass back to work on that day or get fired. Have I made myself clear?'

'Ellie, let's talk about this,' Merri replied, in her most persuasive voice.

'We're not talking about anything! That's the way it is. Be here or don't bother coming back.' Ellie held her stare until Merri turned away and flounced off.

Round Two, Ellie thought, and looked down at her mum. This next conversation would be just as hard, if not harder. She bit her lip and looked for the words. 'Mum, I know that I told you to take this time to travel, to live your dream, but I'm yanking you back. I need you here. I cannot do this alone.'

Ashnee looked at her for a long time and Ellie held her breath. What if she said no? Refused to give up her travelling? What would she do then? Ellie felt panic rise up in her throat at her mum's long silence. Just when she didn't think she could stand it any more Ashnee's huge smile filled the screen.

'Oh, thank God!'

Ellie blinked once, shook her head and blinked again. What was she so excited about?

'I didn't think I could stand another minute!' Ashnee cried. 'I've been desperate to come home! I'm sick of the heat and the crowds.'

'But... But...' Ellie looked at Jack, who was quietly laughing, obviously enjoying every minute of this drama. 'I don't understand.'

'Me neither!' Ashnee said cheerfully, dropping her bare feet to the floor. 'All I know is that I'm catching the first plane I can. Which might take a couple of days, since I'm somewhere near nowhere.'

Ellie sat down on her chair and looked bemused. 'Okay. Good. This is a bit overwhelming.'

'Love you, baby girl!' Ashnee blew her a kiss. 'I'll e-mail you as soon as I have some flight deets.'

And with a wink and a grin her mum was gone.

Ellie stared at the screen for a moment longer before looking up and around. Her mum was gone and Merri was nowhere to be seen. She rubbed her hands over her face, feeling slightly sick at her actions and her words. The impulse to go after Merri was overwhelming...what if she didn't come back? Ellie half stood and felt Jack's strong hand pushing her back into the chair.

'Don't you *dare* go running after her.'

Ellie looked up into Jack's laughing eyes and hauled in a deep breath. 'What have I done?' she whispered.

'Something you should've done ages ago,' Jack replied. He hooked a friendly arm around her neck and chuckled. 'And I have to say...when you finally decide to kick ass you don't take any prisoners.'

A few evenings later Jack wandered into the kitchen as Ellie took a plastic container from the fridge and placed it on the counter. After kissing her hello and getting a lukewarm response he sent her a keen look, trying to work out what was wrong—or more wrong than usual. He knew that she was super-stressed at work, and he suspected that their undefined relationship added another layer of tension to her.

They were reaching a tipping point, he realised. Soon one of them would have to fish or cut bait.

Leaning his forearms on the counter, he peered through the clear lid at tuna steaks covered in a sticky-looking marinade. In the past couple of weeks he'd had more home-cooked meals than he'd eaten since he left home, and fresh fish, properly done, was a treat he never tired of.

Ellie rolled her head and he knew that the knots in her neck were super-tight. 'Spit it out, El. What's wrong?'

'Apart from the normal?' Ellie tipped her head back and looked at the ceiling. 'Horrible day.'

'What happened?'

Ellie placed a strange vegetable on the wooden board and removed a sharp knife from the block of knives close by. He didn't recognise the vegetable and wrinkled his nose.

'Bok choy cabbage. It's good for you,' Ellie stated.

'If you say so. Your day?'

Ellie tossed the cabbage into a frying pan. 'Psycho bride, late deliveries, flood in the upstairs toilet. Samantha wrenched her ankle. Elias is sick.' Ellie took a huge sip of the wine he handed her and sighed with pleasure. 'I need this.'

Ellie pushed a tendril of hair back from her face as she heated another pan for the tuna. Working quickly and competently, she took the tuna steaks to the stove and tossed them into the hot pan. 'Will you get some spring onions out of the fridge, please?'

The steaks sizzled and the room was filled with the fragrant aromas of soy sauce, ginger and garlic. Grabbing his own knife, Jack sliced up the spring onions and asked her where she wanted them.

'In the pan with the bok choy,' Ellie replied. 'Can you get plates?'

Jack handed her the plates as directed. 'Did you manage to get to chat to your mum about the new premises at all?'

Ellie rubbed her eye with her wrist. 'I took her to see the place and showed her the plans that James the architect drew up. She likes it—likes the building, the plans. I'm not quite sure if it's the travelling or the jet lag or her spiritual journey, but she shrugged off the issue of me not having enough money in my trust fund to buy the building at Mrs H's price and do the renovations, insisting that it'll all work out.'

Ashnee had smiled, hugged her and told her that she just had to have faith—a commodity Ellie had run out of a long time ago.

She was also on the brink of losing her mind, and her life was a pie chart of confusion. The segment labelled 'Jack' was particularly large. Ellie looked at him, sitting at the kitchen table, savouring his wine, his long legs stretched out and his bare foot tickling a dog's neck. She knew that she had only days, maybe hours left with him, and every time she tried to envisage life without Jack in it, her breath hitched in her throat.

She'd never felt fear like this before... What she felt for him terrified her... This was true fear, being confronted with a life without Jack in it. He was only ever supposed to be a fling... when had he turned into someone so damn important? Someone she thought she was in love with?

Thought? Bah! Someone she was horribly, unconditionally, categorically in love with. Dammit...he had her heart in his hands and she knew that when he left he'd drop-kick it over a cliff. It was going to hurt like hell.

Ellie shoved her fist into her sternum and hoped like hell that she was confusing what she was feeling with indigestion. Well, she could always hope...

Ellie quickly plated the tuna steaks and sprinkled sesame seeds over the bok choy before putting them onto the plates.

She gestured to his plate. 'Eat. It's getting cold.'

Jack, looking thoroughly healthy and relaxed, eagerly took her advice and concentrated on his supper, which he ploughed through. He caught her look of amazement at his empty plate. She was barely halfway through hers.

'Hungry?'

'For food like that? Always.' Jack stood up and helped himself to the last piece of tuna steak and the other half of the bok choy cabbage.

'By the way, your mum phoned the bakery today, looking for you.'

Jack lifted his head and frowned. 'What? Why?' He picked up his mobile and shook his head. 'My mobile has a signal. What did she want?'

Ellie smiled. 'That's the odd thing...nothing, really. We had a perfectly pleasant chat about the bakery and what I do and...'

'And she was sussing you out. I told her I was staying with you.' Jack leaned back in his chair and sighed, frustrated. 'Sorry—only child, doubly over-protective mother because I was so sick for so long. She nursed me through it all and can't quite cut the apron strings.'

'I enjoyed chatting to her. Luckily I can talk and ice at the same time, because it was a long call. She said to remind you about Brent's memorial service. He's the donor of your heart, isn't he?'

'Mmm. He died when he was seventeen. It's been seventeen years...'

'Your mum said to let his family know if you can go. She said that they'd understand if you were on assignment.'

'That's code for *we'd rather not have you there*,' Jack sighed. 'It's a gracious invite, but I suspect that seeing me would be incredibly difficult for them. I imagine they'd feel guilty for wishing he was alive and not me. *I* feel guilty for being alive...'

'Oh, Jack.' Ellie rested her chin on her fist. 'Survivor's guilt?'

'Yeah. Are you going to say something pithy about me not needing to feel that?'

'I wouldn't dare. How could I, not having walked in your shoes?' Ellie toyed with her fork. 'So, are you going to go?'

Jack's eyes flickered with pain. 'I really don't know. But I do know that I have to be back at work some time next week.'

'Ah.' Ellie felt a knife-point deep in her heart. So he'd be gone within the week? Her heart stuttered and faltered and felt as if it would crumble. She had only days more with him. Days to make enough memories to last her a lifetime.

'El, don't look at me like that.'

'Like what?'

'Like you wouldn't say no if I took you right now,' Jack replied.

Ellie cocked her head, pretending to think as heat spread into her womb. She had such limited time to make memories that would have to last her a lifetime so she figured she might as well start immediately. 'I wouldn't say no.'

Jack's eyes widened and Ellie laughed at his shocked face.

'You're joking,' he said, his voice laced with disappointment.

Ellie fiddled with the edge of her top and sent him a slow smile. 'What if I'm not?'

Jack's fork clattered to his plate. 'I think my heart just stopped.'

He lifted his hand, leaned across the table and, as per usual, pushed back a strand of hair behind her ear. Ellie shivered as his finger rubbed the sensitive spot there and trailed down her neck.

'No going back, Ellie. Right here, right now,' Jack muttered, his eyes on her mouth.

Ellie leaned back in her chair and grinned at him as she pulled her tank top over her head to reveal a white, semi-transparent lacy bra.

Jack clutched his chest. 'Heart attack imminent.'

She stood up and walked around the table, standing in front of him while she undid the button that held her soft wrap-around skirt together.

'Well, I will slap you later for joking about that—right after I've had my way with you.'

Jack's eyes dropped as the skirt fell to a frothy puddle on the floor, showing her amazing long legs and the smallest scrap of white lace. Placing his hands on her hips, he turned her around. His finger traced the line of her underwear.

'Good God, I'm a goner,' he muttered, placing his mouth on the sensitive dip where her spine met her bottom.

'No, but you will be,' Ellie promised as she turned back. She gave him an impish look. 'Are you game to see how much this table can actually take?'

'Next week' was here. Despite her not wanting it to, it had crept stealthily and inexorably closer and had finally arrived. Despite her every effort Ellie had not been able to hold back time, and Jack was booked on a flight to London later that morning.

It was time to face reality, pay the piper, face the music, bite the bullet…to stop using stupid idioms.

Jack's clothes were on her bed, his toiletries were in a bag and not on her bathroom shelves, and he was preparing to walk out of her life. Ellie sat on the edge of her bed, sipping a cup of coffee she couldn't taste and wondering what to say, how to act.

It was D-day and she knew that she would have to break through the uneasy silence or else choke on the words that she needed to verbalise. Because if she didn't she was certain she'd regret her silence for ever.

He was too important, too crucial to her happiness for her to let him waltz away without discussing what he meant to her, what she thought they had. Courage, she reminded herself, was not an absence of fear but acting despite that fear.

She had to do this—no matter how scary it was, how confrontational it could become, he was worth it. She was worth it. *They* were worth it.

Too bad that her knees were knocking together and her teeth were chattering. She'd practised this, she reminded herself—had spent the past few nights lying awake, holding him, while the words she wanted to say ran through her head.

All she could remember of those carefully practised phrases was: *I'm in love with you* and *Please don't leave me.*

Ellie put her coffee cup down on the floor next to her feet and crossed her legs. She sat on her hands so that he wouldn't see how much she was shaking.

'Jack…'

Jack looked at her and she sighed at his guarded expression. 'Mmm?'

'Where to from here?' Ellie asked. She winced, hearing the way that the words ran into each other as she launched them out of her mouth.

She saw him tense, caught his jaw hardening. He picked up a pile of shirts and shoved them into his rucksack. 'Between you and I? Ellie, I'm coming back. I mean, I'd like to come back between assignments. To you.'

Well, that was better than him saying goodbye for ever, but it wasn't quite enough. Ellie sucked in her bottom lip. 'Why?'

Jack's eyes flashed in irritation. She could see that he'd been hoping to avoid this conversation. *Tough luck, Chapman.*

'What kind of question is that?'

'A very reasonable one,' Ellie replied. 'Why do you want to come back?'

'Because there's something cooking between us!'

Ellie stood up and walked over to the window, staring out at the sunlight-drenched garden. '"Something cooking between us"? Is that *all* you can say?' Ellie demanded.

'I don't know what you want me to say!' Jack was quiet for a long time before he spoke again. 'Okay...I've never felt as much for anyone as I do for you.'

Ellie shook her head and her ponytail bounced. Seriously? That was all he could come up with? Where had her erudite reporter gone—the one who relied on words for his living? Where had he run away to?

Well, if he wasn't going to open up she would have to. *Courage, Ellie.*

'Jack, this has been one of the best times of my life. I've loved having you here, with me. I don't want it to end but I am also not prepared to put my life on hold, waiting for you to drop back in.' She pulled in a breath and looked for words, hoping to make him understand her point of view. 'I can't spend my life wondering if you're alive or dead, worrying about you constantly. I don't want to deal with crappy signals and brief telephone calls and even briefer visits home. Living a half-life with you, missing birthdays and anniversaries and special days!' Ellie stated. 'I've lived that life. I hated that life.'

'That was your father, not me! Stop judging me by what he did and said. We are nothing alike!' His expression was pure frustration. 'I am not your father and I don't make promises I can't keep! When I say I'll do something, I'll *do* it. And might I point out that technology has made it a lot easier to stay connected.'

Ellie sent him an enquiring look.

'We have mobiles with great coverage, and when I can't get a signal on my mobile I'll have a satellite phone. I could be on Mars and still be able to call you. There is internet access everywhere, and we could talk every day—hell, every hour, if that's what you needed. And I couldn't survive only seeing you every six weeks. A week, two at the most, and I'd be home.'

'But you can't *guarantee* that!' Ellie shouted.

'Nobody can, Ellie! But I'll do my damnedest!'

Ellie swallowed. She wanted to believe him. She really did. And she believed that he believed it—right now. But without a solid commitment, a declaration of love and trust, it couldn't last. Long-distance relationships, especially those tinged with danger, had a finite lifespan. If he couldn't make a commitment then she had to let him go now, while she could. Now—before she completely succumbed to the temptation of heaven and hell that loving him would be.

Heaven when he came back; hell when he was away.

No, that grey space in between the two, purgatory, was the safest place for her to be. It was the only place where she could function as a semi-normal person.

Ellie shook her head. 'I'm sorry, a mostly long-distance relationship is not an option. I…can't.'

Jack threw up his hands. 'I don't understand why not.'

'Because all you've told me so far is that I am somewhat important and that you'll come back when you can. How can you ask me to wait for you when that's all you can give me?'

Jack pushed both his hands into his hair and linked his hands around the back of his head, his eyes devastated.

'Ellie, I'm doing the best I can. There's never been anyone who has come as close to capturing my heart as you. Ever. But I won't tell you something you want to hear just because you want to hear it. I'm giving you as much as I am able to. Can't you understand that?'

Oh, God, how was she supposed to resist such a naked, emotion-saturated statement? But she had to. There was too much at stake.

'It's not enough for me, Jack. It really isn't.'

'Ellie—'

Ellie held up her hand. 'Wait, let me get this out.' When she spoke again her voice was rich with emotion. 'Over the past couple of weeks I've come to realise—*you* taught me!—that I'm worth making sacrifices for. I think *you* are worth making sacrifices for. But the reality is that you're the one who would always be leaving. I can't force you to change that, I can't force you to need me, and I certainly can't force you to love me. All I can be is a person who can be loved, and I am. I know that now. I want it all, Jack. Dammit, I *deserve* it all!'

'You're asking me to give up my career—'

'I've never asked you to do that. I'm asking you to look at your life, to adjust it so that there is space for me in it. I'm asking you to make me a priority. I'm asking for some sort of commitment.'

Jack's voice was low and sad when he spoke again. 'I need to be able to move, Ellie, breathe. I can't live a humdrum life. I can't be confined—even by you.'

'It's not good enough, Jack. Not any more.' Ellie felt her heart rip out of her chest. 'I can't be with someone who thinks life with me would be humdrum, tedious, boring.'

'I didn't mean—'

'Yes, you did!' Ellie shouted, suddenly pushed beyond her limits. 'You want to think that a life with me would be unexciting and dull because anything else would mean that you would have to get emotionally involved, take a stand, make a choice that could lead to pain. Don't you think you're taking this protecting-your-heart thing a bit too far? You've stopped *living*, Jack.'

'Of course I'm living! What the hell do you think I've been doing for the past seventeen years?' Jack roared, his eyes light with fury.

'That's not living—it's reporting! Living is taking emotional chances, laughing, loving.' Ellie shoved her hands into her hair. 'I'm in love with you and I'm pretty sure that you're the man I can see myself living the rest of my life with. Would you consider loving me, living with me, creating a family with me?'

He stared at his feet, his arms tightly crossed. His body language didn't inspire confidence.

'This is emotional blackmail,' Jack muttered eventually, and Ellie closed her eyes as his words kicked her in the heart. And here came the pain, roaring towards her with the force of a Sherman tank.

'I'm sorry that you consider someone telling you that they adore you blackmail. Goodbye, Jack.' Ellie turned away and folded her arms across her torso, gripping hard. 'Lock the front door behind you, will you?'

'Ellie—'

Ellie whirled around, fury, misery and anger emanating from every pore. 'What? What else is there to say, Jack? I love you, but you're so damn scared of feeling anything that you won't step out of that self-protecting cocoon you've wedged yourself into! Of the two of us, *you* are the bigger pansy-assed coward and I am done with this conversation. Just leave, Jack. Please. You've played basketball with my heart for long enough.'

She heard him pick up his pack, jog down the stairs. From behind the curtain of the bay window Ellie watched him storm to his car, his broad shoulders tight and halfway up to his ears, his arms ending in clenched fists.

I love you, she wanted to say. *I love you so much it scares me. I wish you knew how to take a real chance, how to risk your very precious heart.*

But two sentences kept tumbling over and over in her head. *Please don't leave me. Please come back.*

But he didn't stop, didn't turn around. When she saw his car back down her driveway and watched the tail-lights disappear down the road and out of sight, Ellie sank to the floor and buried her face in her hands.

It was over and she was alone. Again.

CHAPTER TEN

FIVE DAYS AFTER he'd left Cape Town Jack and his cameraman were standing next to a pile of rubble that had once been a primary school on the outskirts of Concepción, Chile. What had originally been a black car was buried under a pile of rocks. A massive earthquake had hit the region and Jack had been asked if he'd like to report on it. He hadn't even left transit at Heathrow. He'd just caught the first flight he could to Chile.

Behind them were mounds of bricks and twisted iron and the half-walls of the decimated school. Since the quake had struck early in the morning most of the children hadn't arrived yet for lessons, but Jack knew from talking to the family members who stalked the site that there had been an early-morning staff meeting and there were still a few teachers unaccounted for. Their relatives were still digging through the rubble, slowly moving piles of bricks to find the bodies of their loved ones. Few held out any hope for their survival. The devastation was too widespread, too intense, for hope to survive for long.

Jack rubbed his hands over his face as he prepared to link live to New York. He didn't want to be here, he thought. He wanted to go home to that bright house with its eclectic art and two rambunctious dogs. He wanted to run with the dogs on the beach, stretch out on the leather couch, listen to the sea at night and the wind in the morning.

He wanted Ellie.

But Ellie would mean giving this up, Jack reminded himself. He couldn't…this was what he did, what he was. He needed to work…. Jack blew out his breath. But was that just years of habit talking? He couldn't avoid the truth…he *needed* her. As much as his work. More.

Jack leaned back against a dusty car and lifted his head to the sunlight. He'd been seventy degrees of dim that last night in St James. He'd thought he was so strong, so in control. While she'd launched those emotional arrows at his soul he'd kept telling himself that it wouldn't hurt, that he'd be fine. Now, five days and too much horror later, he felt as if he'd taken a series of punches to his stomach and heart. He was doubled over in pain.

He was generally level-headed and unemotional, and in truth he'd never been a crier. He could count on one hand the amount of times he'd wept since he was a child. Even the bleakest times of his illness, the fear he'd felt when he'd had the transplant and the relief of being normal again had never reduced him to tears, but the fact that he'd lost Ellie had had him choking down grief more than once or twice. The early hours of the morning were the worst; that was when he felt as if his heart was being physically yanked from his chest.

What was he going to do? Sacrifice his job for her? Sacrifice her for the job? Be bored with a normal life with Ellie in it or miserable with an action-packed existence without her?

He didn't know—couldn't make a decision. All he was certain of was that he missed her, that his world had gone from bright colours to monochrome, that he was plodding through each day feeling adrift without his connection to her. He was fine physically. Mentally and emotionally he was a train wreck. He felt as if he'd been stripped of all his internal organs—heart included—that he was just a shell of a man, marking time.

Ted, his cameraman, told him he was about to go live so Jack stood up straight and waited for the signal. He greeted the anchorwoman and launched into his report. Death, destruction, the cost of rebuilding people's lives...

Jack was midway through when a commotion from the decimated building behind him caught his attention. He knew that noise—it was an indication that someone had been found. Still live to New York, he bounded with Ted over the rubble to where a lone man, his face ravaged with grief, was furiously tossing bricks and stones off a pile. Jack recognised his look of terrible excitement, of despair-ravaged hope. He'd found someone he loved...

Jack, forgetting that he was live on international TV, picked up his pace and scuttled across the rubble to where the man was sinking into a hole he'd dug. Jack saw a strand of long black hair flowing around a half-sheared brick and his heart stopped. He swallowed. It was exactly the shade of Ellie's hair...

The young man was sobbing as he yanked debris away from her. *'Mi esposa, mi esposa,'* he muttered frantically, tears streaming down his face.

His wife. All he could see was his wife's hair...

Jack swallowed and jumped into the small hole with him, started to throw bricks, planks and stones away from where he imagined her head and body was. The problem was that her hair was so long—she could be lying in any direction.

Minutes felt like hours and his back muscles and biceps were screaming in pain. His shirt was soaked onto his body but Jack refused to quit. There was no sound coming from the victim but Jack knew that didn't mean she was dead. He refused to believe she was dead...

What if this was Ellie? How would he be feeling? The thought kept hurtling through his brain. Desperate, out of control, terrified. He wouldn't be able to live without her...

Jack lifted a board up and away and there she lay, her beautiful face unmarked by the falling building. Her eyes were open, glassy, but Jack didn't need to check her pulse to see that she was still alive. The hand lifting up towards the young man was a solid enough hint.

Jack yelled at Ted to call for the medics and was surprised to see that Ted was still filming. Why wasn't he helping them? Surely the woman was more important than the story? He felt sickened by Ted's callousness, the fact that he could just observe and not participate, to report but not become involved.

Then again, he couldn't blame him either. Wasn't that what *he* did, story after story, situation after situation?

Jack caught the bottle of water someone threw down, cracked the seal and gently poured a tiny bit of water into the woman's mouth. He didn't want to lift her neck, he had no idea what injuries she had, and her legs were still pinned beneath the debris. Her husband had his face buried in his hands, sobbing uncontrollably.

Jack gently dripped water from the bottle into her mouth and they waited. The young man was now talking to his wife, and Jack felt the lump in his throat grow as he watched them interact, listened to their conversation. It was blindingly obvious that they loved each other so much, that they were ecstatic to be given a second chance.

All his life he'd avoided love, thinking that it equalled confinement. That he'd lose his freedom. That a love affair would hamper his individuality and compromise his independence. He now realised that, compared to losing Ellie, none of it meant a damn thing. His feelings for her scared him, but he knew he was a better man for loving her and that she was worth any emotional risk. He'd been so careful to control every aspect of his life and it was a revelation to discover that being out of control was the best feeling in the world. Being in love felt marvellous. He loved the way it made him feel...

With her he'd found the place he most wanted to be—the home he'd thought he didn't need. She was the one person, the one place, where he could be truly intimate and feel safe. Secure. Looked after. Loved. She had given him the gift of balance and stability and his throat swelled with emotion. He needed to get back to her...

Jack wet the corner of his T-shirt and wiped the victim's face. He saw relief and gratitude in her eyes.

'Muchas gracias,' she whispered between dry and swollen lips.

Jack swallowed, nodded and ran his hand over his head as he heard the rescue workers and medics approaching. He sent her a quick smile and backed away, lifting himself out of the small area to allow for medical assistance.

It was only as he walked away from them and Ted that he realised that his face and cheeks were wet with tears.

Across the world Ellie worked in her bakery, waiting for her staff to come in to work. Her heart was haemorrhaging, she decided, as a lone tear dripped off her chin and landed on the pale pink wedding cake beneath her. It had been nearly a week since Jack had left and she missed him with an intensity that astonished her. The memory of the night he'd left was on constant replay in her head, and she relived the moment of her heart ripping apart on a daily, hourly basis, causing pain to shoot through her system. There was no relief from the memories. Every room in the house made her think of Jack, and she hadn't been able to eat at her kitchen table since he'd left.

She wasn't eating, wasn't sleeping, wasn't thinking. Her hands shook. She felt constantly cold. Ellie looked at the tiny tearstain on the cake and felt grateful she could cover it with a sugar rose. Idly she wondered if she should be making wedding cakes with a scorched heart. Wedding cakes should be made with love and hope, not with sadness and regret.

Ellie looked up to see Merri in front of her, dressed in a bright pink apron. 'Reporting for duty, ma'am.'

Ellie just managed to smile. She'd totally forgotten her threat to fire her if she didn't arrive for work, and now a part of her wished Merri *hadn't* come back, so that she would be so busy she'd never have to think, feel, again.

'It's about time,' Ellie muttered, and held out her arms for a hug.

She stepped into her friend's arms and hung on. After a while she stepped back, felt Merri's hand between her shoulderblades and turned her head to look into her deeply concerned face.

'You okay?' Merri asked.

'Jack left.' Ellie shook her head and wiped her eyes with the corner of her apron. 'I can't seem to stop hurting. I think I'm okay, then it sneaks up on me and *wham*! Dammit—I'm dripping again.'

'God, El, how long have you been like this? Why didn't you call me?'

Ellie winced, feeling the headache pounding between her eyes. 'I couldn't—can't—talk about him.' She bit her lip. 'I feel like I've been eviscerated with a butter knife.'

'Oh, sweetie. You're fathoms deep in love with him.'

Ellie nodded.

Merri sat down on the chair next to Ellie's table and sent her a sympathetic look. 'I'm sorry you couldn't make it work, but sometimes love just isn't enough.'

'It's supposed to be,' Ellie whispered.

Merri's voice was laced with regret and loss. 'In books and movies. In real life…? Not so much.'

Ellie stared past Merri's head. 'I'm worried about him. My imagination is in overdrive.'

'Jack knows how to look after himself.' Merri put her arms

on the table. Her face was uncharacteristically serious. 'Ellie, I've never seen you so unhinged. I'm worried about *you*.'

'So is my mum.' Ellie stared at her flour-dusted shoes. 'She keeps telling me that I can't live like this, that I have to do something about him...but what can I do? Nothing! He's gone and he isn't coming back.'

'You need to try and relax. Get a decent night's sleep and find a way to work through this.'

'I'm trying—'

'Try harder. If you carry on like this you'll be on antidepressants in a month, in a loony bin in three months.'

'I know that I'm a mess.' Ellie gripped the bridge of her nose with her thumb and forefinger. 'I feel like I am marinating in pain.' She flipped Merri a tiny smile. 'Does that sound desperately melodramatic?'

'Yes, but you're entitled.'

Merri draped an arm across her shoulder and they both looked down at the wedding cake. Merri tipped her head so that it touched Ellie's. 'Sweetie, I'll be here to hold your hand every step of the way, to talk to you and to cry with you. But this cake...?'

'What's wrong with it?'

Merri picked up a swatch of fabric off the table and held it against the cake. 'Wrong shade of pink, honey.'

Jack shoved his hands into his coat pockets as he left the church where Brent's memorial service had just ended. It was over, and yet he didn't feel the relief he'd expected to. He'd delayed his return to Cape Town to be here but he wondered if he'd ever manage not to feel guilty for being alive. He needed to get to Ellie. She'd understand, help him work through this.

Now he needed to avoid the Sandersons if he could. What could he say to them? He was sorry? He was...but it sounded stupid, seeing that he lived because Brent had died. There they all were—Mrs Sanderson hugging his mother by the gate, Mr Sanderson, his eyes pink from cold and tears, talking to his dad.

He should say something. Anything… But he really just wanted to walk away. They couldn't—wouldn't—want to talk to him.

Jack had made it halfway to his car when he heard his name being called.

'Jack!'

He felt the hand on his arm, turned and looked down into Brent's mother's elegant face. He winced internally.

'Where are you rushing off to?' she asked.

Jack, guilt holding his heart in a vice grip, looked around for a means of escape. 'Uh…'

'I'm so glad you came. *We're* so glad you came.'

Oh, Lord, now Mr Sanderson had joined them. Any moment his parents would join the party and he'd be toast. Jack forced himself to put his hand out and shake Mr Sanderson's hand. 'Sir. It was a nice service.'

'We're very happy you made it, Jack. And call me David.'

'I'm June.'

Oh, this was getting to be fun. *Not*. Jack jammed his freezing hands back into his coat pockets and reluctantly nodded when David asked him if he'd take a short walk with them through the cemetery. Jack sent his mother a miserable look over his shoulder and followed Brent's parents to Brent's headstone. June dusted some snow off the face of the stone and rested her gloved hand on top.

'We've wanted to talk to you for a while. We've been following your career,' David said. 'You've made quite a name for yourself.'

'Thank you.'

'You didn't want to come today,' June said. 'You didn't want to see us. Why not?'

Jack looked at a point beyond her face. 'I thought it would hurt you too much.'

'And? Come on—spit it out,' June coaxed.

Her eyes encouraged him to be honest, and for a moment he felt as if he was seventeen again and terrified.

'And it kills me to know that Brent had to lose his life so that I could have mine,' Jack said in a rush, scared that if he didn't get the words out he never would.

June's eyes filled with tears and her face softened. 'Sweetheart, his death had nothing to do with you. It was his time to go...'

'But—'

'But nothing. I'm just grateful that you had a second chance at life. Grateful that you haven't wasted his gift...' June took his hand between hers. 'Yet your mother tells us you have no home, no family, no partner. It worries her. It worries *us*. Why not?'

'Uh—'

'When we gave you our son's heart we expected you not to waste your second chance. We also expected you to make the most of your second chance,' David stated, his voice firm but gentle. 'But we never wanted you to feel guilty—only thankful.'

His mother must have had more than a few discussions with them about him for them to be having this conversation, Jack realised. He wasn't sure whether to be grateful or to wring her neck for interfering. He smiled inside. He'd go for grateful.

'So you think it would be okay if I fell in love? Had a family? Even knowing that Brent never had that chance and I do, with *his* heart?' he asked, holding his breath.

David placed his hand on his shoulder and squeezed. 'Not only do we think it's okay, we think it's important. It's another chance—another opportunity for you to be fulfilled—and that's all we ever wanted. For you to make the most of his gift, to wring out as much happiness as you can from life. Brent had a generous spirit and that would be his wish.'

'And it's ours...' June added.

Jack swallowed the tears he felt at the back of his throat as their words picked up the last of his guilt and flew away with it. He managed what he suspected was a watery grin. 'Well, there is this girl, and she's been giving our heart a run for its money...'

June grinned and put her hand into the crook of his elbow. 'Ooh, a feisty one. I like her already.'

Three days later Ellie sat cross-legged in the middle of the driveway and gazed at what she was privately calling Ellie's Folly. Fascinated, she rested her elbow on her knee and her chin in her hand and just looked. The house preened in the spotty sunlight that appeared now and again from between low black clouds, like an elderly showgirl remembering her former life.

Rolled up and sticking out of the back pocket of her shorts was the agreement of sale that Mrs H had finally signed an hour before.

'Enough is enough,' she'd told Mrs H, after carefully explaining what she intended doing with the property. 'Either accept my offer or I'm walking away.'

'But—'

'Permanently. Pari's will close down, jobs will be lost and St James will lose a landmark institution. I'm tired of your vacillations and games. I'm dealing with enough drama as it is and I don't need any more. The ball is in your court.'

Getting tough had paid dividends and the old lady had signed at a price that allowed her enough cash to do the renovations. She was now the owner of a gorgeous old building that needed lots of love and attention. Thank goodness—because she seriously needed the distraction of hard work.

It had been a good day. If she ignored the fact that she was still miserable and heartbroken and so, so sad.

Ellie felt something cold nudge her shoulder and looked sideways to see a large frappe in one of Pari's takeaway glasses. She'd told her mum that she'd be here and wasn't surprised by her presence.

'Isn't she stunning?' Ellie breathed, unable to take her eyes off the building.

'She is—but you are even more so.'

Ellie scrambled to her feet as that deep voice caressed her. She looked at him, wide-eyed with astonishment.

Jack was back and he was standing in front of her, looking fit and fantastic.

Ellie took a step back, feeling totally disorientated and more than a little scared. Why was he back? Oh, her battered heart had lifted at the sight of his wonderful face, but how it would hurt when he left again. How would she survive this? Would she ever get used to him dropping in and out of her life?

Yet…she didn't care. After the past days of hell on earth it didn't matter. None of it mattered. Because, as sobering and shocking as the concept was, there was nothing she wouldn't do for him. The reality was that she'd never loved anyone or anything as much as she loved Jack…she would give up Pari's for him, move to the ends of the earth for him…she'd even live through having her insides scraped out with a teaspoon every time he went on a dangerous assignment if it meant having him smile at her, laugh with her, hold her after making love to her.

He was back, she loved him and she'd do anything to be with him.

Ellie dropped her iced coffee to the driveway and only just stopped herself from flinging herself against his chest and weeping like a fool. Instead she put the heels of her hands to her temples and shrugged her shoulders. 'Okay, I surrender.'

'You surrender what?' Jack asked conversationally, his finger tapping his still full cup of coffee.

'Do you want me to leave Pari's? I can make cakes in London. I'll take Rescue Remedy and yoga and meditation classes every time you go on assignments to hellholes. I'll get through it.' Ellie stumbled to the low wall that ran parallel to the driveway, sat down and dropped her head into her hands. 'What do you need me to do?'

'Now, *why* would you do all that, El?' Jack asked.

She felt him sit down next to her. 'Because I love you and I can't live without you,' Ellie muttered to the concrete. She felt his big hand on the back of her neck as tears dripped onto the paving below.

Jack pulled her head to his shoulder and held it there as he continued to sip his coffee. 'That's a hell of an offer, El.'

Ellie looped her arms around his waist, still staring at their shoes. She sniffed, the reality of what she'd offered slowly sinking in. She'd miss Merri and her staff, her customers and this new building that she'd never have the chance to turn into something special. And her house—she really loved her house—but she'd take her pets. That wasn't negotiable.

She'd miss the beach and the city but she'd have Jack… Her racing heart settled. She'd have Jack sometimes and it would be all right. Anything was better than nothing.

She felt Jack's kiss in her hair before he let her go. Ellie wiped her eyes with the back of her wrist and sniffed.

'I have a counter-offer,' Jack said, his voice vibrating with emotion.

'You do?'

'As it happens, I love you too.' The corners of his mouth kicked up when her mouth fell open. He put his finger under her chin and pushed it up so that her teeth clicked together. 'I can't—won't—ask you to uproot your wonderful life. But I *can* ask you if I can share it.'

There went her jaw again. 'Sorry?'

Jack pulled his feet up, bent his legs and rested his arms on his knees. His cup was on the wall next to his feet. The late-summer breeze blew his hair off his forehead. 'I want to stay here, live in your house with you. On an on-going and permanent basis.'

'Uh—'

Jack managed to grin. 'Work with me here, darling. I'm trying, very badly, to propose.'

'Propose what?' Ellie said blankly, still stuck three sentences behind, on the 'I love you too' comment.

'I can't imagine my life in any form without you in it so... will you marry me?' Jack asked.

'Uh—what?'

'You? Me? Married?'

'You want to *marry* me?' Ellie squawked.

'That's what I keep saying. But the question is, do you want to marry *me*?'

Jack bit his lip, anxiety written all over his face. Ellie couldn't believe that her tough warrior—a man who'd faced untold danger, who'd lived through and overcome so much in his life—was scared of rejection, scared that her answer might be no.

Gathering her last two wits together, she leaned forward and placed her hands on his knees.

'Yes. Absolutely.'

Jack dropped his forehead to his chest in relief and Ellie rubbed her thumbs over the bare skin on the inside of his knees. He was warm and strong and vital and her world suddenly made sense again.

'I *do* love you, El,' Jack muttered, his voice hoarse as he looked at her with blazing eyes.

Her heart constricted and fluttered and, lifting her hands, she gently held his face. 'I love you too. Welcome home.'

***

Ellie sat sideways between Jack's legs, his arms loosely around her waist and his chin on her head. They'd been quiet for a while after his proposal, both happy to savour the moment.

She didn't want to break the spell, but Ellie knew that they still had a couple of issues to work through. 'What about kids, Jack? Do you want any?'

He looked down at her and half shrugged. 'Sure. When?'

Ellie blinked. 'Excuse me?'

Jack squeezed her waist. 'I don't think you really heard me before, or took in what I said, but I want it all. But it starts with you. If you want kids now, later, whenever… I just want to make you happy.'

Ellie blinked, swallowing as emotion—love—grabbed her heart. 'Oh, you slay me.' She pushed her hair back. 'I'd like your baby, Jack—hell, I'd *love* your baby. But not right now. I'd like us to take a little time for ourselves. Just to *be*, to get used to our new life together, before we throw another person into the mix.'

'We can do that.' Jack pulled up her T-shirt and put his warm hand on her bare skin.

Ellie shivered at his touch and hoped that she never stopped responding like this.

She tipped her head back and sideways to look up at him. 'You said that you just want me to be happy but I want *you* to be happy—how are we both going to be happy?'

Jack let out a joyful laugh. 'You really didn't hear me earlier, did you?'

Ellie blushed. 'I kind of tuned out after you told me you loved me. Tuned back in when you proposed. In between it's a bit blurry.'

Jack scooted backwards so that he could look down into her face. He was hers—a warrior soldier with a scarred body, warm smile and vulnerability in his eyes.

'Okay, are you concentrating?'

Ellie laughed. 'Jack!'

'El, I love it here—love your dogs, your city, your friends. I'm happier here than anywhere else.' He ran the edge of his thumb over her trembling bottom lip. 'I've been a fighter all my life but I'll fight hard for you—fight to share your sunshine-filled life.'

'But your career—'

Jack shrugged. 'I still want to do parts of it—with your support. But I can pick and choose my stories a bit better. I don't always need to go into hot areas, chase the conflicts. I can do human drama stories, crime, special reports. I might have to go away now and again, but I meant what I said. There are ways for us to communicate every day and I wouldn't want to be away from you for long.'

Ellie swallowed. How long was long? 'A month? Two?'

Jack laughed. 'Are you mad? I couldn't survive that long without you! A week—maybe ten days at the most. And that would be pushing it.'

Ellie grinned. Jack was not going to be an absent husband, a forgetful lover. He was right. He was nothing like her father.

She tapped his knee in warning. 'Do *not* get hurt again.'

She felt his lips smile against hers. 'Deal.'

Ellie toyed with his fingers. 'But, Jack, if you need to go into a situation that's dangerous, I meant what I said. I'll find a way to deal with it. I don't want you to miss it or feel cheated.' She needed him to understand. 'You were right. You are nothing like my dad or my ex. And I am nothing like that shy, plump insecure little girl. I can cope with you being away for short periods as long as we keep communicating...'

'Don't think this is only from your side. I need to connect with you as well, sweetheart. I missed you so much when I was in Chile. I felt...*bereft*.'

Ellie draped her thighs over his and scooted closer, so that she could link her hands at the back of his neck. 'Was it bad?'

'Yeah. It was.' Jack nodded.

'I saw the footage of you rescuing that woman,' Ellie said quietly. 'Merri caught it on the news and I downloaded the clip from the internet.'

'I guess they aren't calling me unemotional any more, since I was caught crying on camera.' Jack rubbed his forehead with the tips of his fingers. 'She looked like you. Long black hair, creamy skin. Gorgeous. Her husband was a train wreck and I kept thinking: how would I feel if this was you? Gutted, shell-shocked, scared witless.' Jack frowned. 'I've been scared in my life, El, but nothing compares to how terrified I was when I considered what it would feel like to lose you permanently.' Jack shuddered before he spoke again. 'I went to Brent's service—spoke to his parents.'

'That must have been hard. How was it?'

Jack smiled. 'It was...healing. For all of us. Me especially.'

'I'm so glad.' Ellie's breath hitched. 'I know that you're not into these mushy moments, but I just want to keep telling you how much I love you...'

'I don't mind hearing that.' Jack's mouth kicked up as his hand cradled the side of her head. 'And ditto for me. There's so much I still want to say...'

'Like?'

'Like my world has colour again now that you are back in it.' His eyes turned serious. 'El, I love my work, but I love you more. I'll never cheat on you. I promise to be faithful. And I promise, as far as I'm humanly able, to be here when you need me. I promise to be with you on the important dates, and if and when we have kids I'll look at my career and see what I can change to be an active, involved dad.'

Ellie opened her mouth to speak but Jack shook his head.

'You're my life. You're what makes me happy. I want to

wake up next to you, wander down to the bakery for breakfast, be with you at night. Unfortunately I have to earn money, and I do enjoy what I do. But if I have to choose between the two I'll choose you.'

'You don't have to choose.' Ellie gulped as Jack lifted his thumbs to wipe away her tears. His mouth lifted at the corners and his eyes darkened with emotion, and Ellie caught a glimpse of his soul, overflowing with love for her.

He took her hand and placed it on the left side of his chest. 'I've protected my heart in every way I can. Physically, emotionally, spiritually. It's on loan to me and now I'm giving it to you…this heart that saved my life—it's yours.'

Ellie gulped a sob and the stream of tears that she'd been holding back slid down her face. Leaning into him, she placed her cheek against his, and when she thought she could talk sensibly again she took his hand and echoed his action by putting it on her chest. 'Then take mine. Keep it safe.'

'I promise I will.'

And they both knew, in a way only lovers could understand, that their hearts were joined—married—on that low stone wall outside a decrepit house in the late-afternoon summer sun.

EPILOGUE

Six months later

ELLIE FELT HER mum's arm around her waist as she stood at the edge of the crowd, waiting to be called by the Master of Ceremonies to make her speech. Merri stood on her other side, with Molly Blue in her pushchair, sucking a doughnut.

It was the day of Pari's grand re-opening and the new building was restored to its formal splendour. The gardens might need a year or two to mature, but spring was almost upon them and she could see tiny shoots of new growth on the rescued rose bushes, on the trees and bushes.

The bakery had been operating for a week and there had been problems—but nothing insurmountable. Business was booming in the bakery, in the new restaurant, in the tiny art studio/gift shop she'd set up to display her artwork and some works by other artists from the area.

She only had one little issue... Her fiancé—the man she was due to marry in a month—was not yet home. He was nowhere to be seen. She had no idea why he was delayed because every time she called him his mobile went straight to voicemail, and he'd left his satellite phone at home. She could feel her mum and Merri's rising annoyance—this was her big day and he wasn't here. Ellie knew that her mum was trying to keep back all the 'I told you so' and 'war reporters—consistently unreliable' phrases that she desperately wanted to utter.

Ellie resisted looking at her watch. Jack would get here, and if he didn't he would have a damn good excuse for not being able to make it. Over the past six months he'd done everything he'd said he would and he loved her absolutely, intensely, ferociously. He'd never deliberately hurt her and sometimes things happened. *Life* happened.

'Relax, guys,' Ellie told them, sending them both a great big smile. 'I am.'

'Has he forgotten how to use a phone?' Ashnee demanded. 'I'm really quite annoyed with him—'

'You can read me the Riot Act later, Ash,' Jack said from behind them, and Ellie squealed in delight as she whipped around. 'Right now, I'd like to kiss my girl.'

Then his big hands were cradling her face, his lips were on hers and the tectonic plates deep in the earth shifted and settled. When he finally lifted his head he smiled down at her. 'Sorry—battery on my mobile died. And I got a speeding fine on the way here.'

'I *knew* you would get here on time.' Ellie smiled. 'Missed you.'

'Missed you too,' Jack replied.

Ellie pulled her bottom lip between her teeth. 'How did it go with the cardiologist?'

His heart transplant wasn't a secret any more. It wasn't something he discussed, but it was out in the open. 'Fine—situation normal. He says that you're looking after my heart beautifully.'

Her lips twitched. 'Good.'

'I'm sorry that I had to delay my return. I really wanted to be home sooner. But I decided to wait for your present.'

Ellie held his hand between both of hers. 'My present? What is it?'

Jack's eyes flashed with mischief. 'It's a few things, actually. Two of them are my parents, who insisted on being here for Pari's re-opening.'

Ellie and Ashnee, who'd instantly bonded with Jack's mother Rae, danced on the spot. 'That's fabulous news. I'm so happy they're here. Where are they?' Ellie demanded, looking around at the sizeable crowd.

'Over there. With your other present—Mitch. He flew back from New York with me.'

Jack gestured to the crowd to the right of them and Ellie's heart hitched when Mitchell raised his hand and waved it in her direction. Her dad was here...finally...at one of the most important occasions of her life. Ellie felt her heart stumble. This was Jack's doing, she knew. She *so* appreciated the fact that he'd gone to the effort of getting him here, that he thought that Mitch being here would make her happy. And it did—sort of. She'd invited Mitch but never expected him to come. It was such a relief to know that she didn't need her dad's approval any more; she'd finally accepted that her father wasn't father material and his lack in that department had nothing to do with her.

He was—had been—a shocking father, but she could forgive him anything since he'd sent Jack into her life.

'Thank you.' Ellie rose up on her toes to kiss Jack's mouth.

'Pleasure.' Jack ran a hand over her hair as the Master of Ceremonies began his speech. Jack bent his head to whisper in her ear. 'I love you. I'm proud of what you've done, and it's fabulous. But...'

'But?'

'But keep the speeches short, sweetheart, so that I can pull you into a pantry and kiss the hell out of you.'

'That's all you want to do?' Ellie looked at him and shook her head, eyes dancing. 'Damn, I must be getting boring! Got to watch that...'

Ellie grinned as Jack's shout of laughter followed her all the way to the podium.

True happiness, she decided, really was laughing and living and loving well. She tossed Jack a grin as she launched into her very, very, *very* short speech.

After all, she had her man to kiss...

* * * * *

SIZZLE

KATHERINE GARBERA

It's funny how you can know someone her entire life and still be surprised by how much you still enjoy hanging out with her years later. This book is dedicated to my sister Donna. Love you, DD.

Special thanks to Kathryn Lye for insight in the early stages when I was going down a wrong path.

USA TODAY bestselling author **Katherine Garbera** is a two-time MAGGIE® Award winner who has written more than seventy books. A Florida native who grew up to travel the globe, Katherine now makes her home in the Midlands of the UK with her husband, two children and a very spoiled miniature dachshund. Visit Katherine on the web at katherinegarbera.com, or catch up with her on Facebook and Twitter.

1

STACI ROWLAND RAN THE LAST block and a half to the Hamilton Ramsfeld kitchen and studios. She was late, more than late she was on the verge of blowing the chance of a lifetime—the chance to be on *Premier Chef*. And the chance to win half a million dollars and have her own television cooking show. The chance to get back into a Michelin starred kitchen and prove that all the raw young talent she'd had hadn't been wasted.

She was running late because she was a little short of money this week, which was her own fault because she'd blown every cent of her disposable income on a new set of knives for this competition. Gas prices were high and she hadn't been able to afford a tank of gas from San Diego to Santa Monica so instead she'd had to bus it.

Now sweat was dripping down her back, she was overheated and the knives she carried in her left hand were starting to feel as if they weighed a ton. She ran through the front doors of the building, air-conditioning immediately starting to cool her damp back. She glanced at the empty reception desk.

"Damn," she said, under her breath, rushing to the desk to find a clipboard with a list of names, including hers and instructions to take the elevator to the fourteenth floor. She pushed the elevator button and opened her purse to search for the letter she'd received from the Premier Chef producers, hoping it had an exact room number on it. The bell pinged and she stepped into the elevator car, catching the toe of her shoe on the lip of the gap, which sent her sprawling forward.

Staci cursed as she tumbled through the air expecting to hit the floor and instead hit a warm solid person. She heard his curse as a stream of cool liquid washed over both of them. She glanced up, an apology on her lips, and froze as she stared into a pair of Caribbean blue eyes. She tried to push herself free but her hand slipped on his arm and he gripped her waist to keep her upright.

"Oh fudge," she said. "I'm just not having a good day."

He was tall and, she could tell from the way he was holding her, well built with a muscled chest and strong shoulders. His jaw was square with an almost bullish set to it and when he looked down at her with those brilliant blue eyes of his, they were frosty. Not frosty enough to dry the sweat dripping down her back but she felt a definite chill. Great, she thought, it was as if the universe was conspiring to ruin her day.

"I'm sorry," she said.

"It's cool," he said, his southern drawl washed over her senses and she did a double take. He had casually ruffled dark black hair that curled over his forehead. His body was lean and muscular not typical of every chef she'd met. And she had no doubt that he was a chef. "Maybe next time you should look where you are going?"

"Thanks, I hadn't thought of that," she shot back. Not in a mood to be sweet and cheery since she was overheated and as the liquid dried on her skin it felt sticky. "What were you drinking?"

"Sweet tea," he said.

Of course he was since his voice was all Southern plantations and magnolia trees she wasn't surprised. She brushed her hands over her clothes and shook her head. "Someone up there really hates me."

"Up there?" he asked, reaching around her to push the button for the fourteenth floor.

"The universe or heaven or whatever you like to call the fickle fates," she said, tucking a strand of her short hair behind her ear.

"Why are you blaming an unseen power when you are clearly running late?" he asked. "If you'd been here on time none of this would have happened."

"Touché," she said.

Silence grew between them and Staci tried to just let it be, but she hated quiet...always had.

"Are you here for the competition?" she asked. It was an educated guess, but one she suspected would be confirmed since he held a bag of chef knives in one hand.

"Yes," he said. "I hope you are better in the kitchen than you are in the elevator."

"Oh, you haven't seen me at my best in the elevator," she said with a wink. Then holding out her hand to him, she introduced herself. "I'm Staci Rowland."

"Remy...Stephens," he said. His handgrip was firm and his hand was warm in hers. His hands showed signs that he'd been a chef for a while with burn marks and nicks that had long since scarred over. If his hands were any indication the man could cook.

She stared at his face perhaps a little longer than she should, unable to look away from the beard stubble on his face, which gave him a rugged sexy appearance. When she glanced back at his eyes she saw that he'd lifted one eyebrow at her.

She dropped his hand and rubbed hers on her jean-clad leg. *What the hell was wrong with her today?*

"Oh, like that little mouse in *Ratatouille*," she said. Her niece loved that film and after they'd watched it together Louisa had insisted on having ratatouille for dinner.

"Ratatouille? The vegetable dish?"

"No," she said. "The Disney-Pixar movie. It's about a chef who is lost and finds his culinary way with the help of a little mouse named Remy."

"Um...no like my great-uncle," he said. "I don't watch animated movies."

She shrugged. "It's cute. You should give it a try."

She stepped further back to look at him. "Sorry again about bumping into you."

"No problem. I get messier in the kitchens," he said. "I'm just thinking about cooking today."

"Me, too," she said with a half-smile. "I'm the co-owner of Sweet Dreams, a cupcake bakery in San Diego."

"The cupcake girl," he said. "I read over the profiles of the other chefs this morning."

"Cupcake girl? My partner and I own a very profitable bakery...I'd rather not be referred to as the cupcake girl." She wished she'd thought to read the profiles as well, maybe then she'd know more about Remy. But as she'd been running late she hadn't had time.

Now he was the one to step back and gave her a low bow. "My most humble apologies, baker."

"Where do you work?" she asked.

"I'm sort of between gigs right now but I've worked in the best kitchens in New Orleans."

"I suspected as much," she said.

"How?"

"That slow Southern drawl of yours gave you away."

He gave her a slow steady smile that made her pulse kick up a notch. She couldn't put her finger on what it was but there was something familiar in his smile. Also something so damned sexy that she wondered if she should just get off at the next floor.

Some women were into men in uniforms, others into men with power and money but for her it had always been the earthy sensuality of a man who could cook.

"Do you like it?" he asked, his drawl even more pronounced than before.

She grinned back. "Maybe."

He arched one eyebrow at her. "Most people find my accent charming."

"Really?"

He gave her a measured look and then winked at her. "Cupcake girl, it's a big part of my personality," he said. "Some people underestimate me based on it, but I use that to my advantage in the kitchen. I can be very demanding."

She knew he was talking about cooking but a part of her was thinking he'd also be demanding in the bedroom. She cleared her throat.

"I am, too," she said. Running the bakery with Alysse was hard work and they'd only become successful by making sure the bakery always came first.

"Cupcake girl—"

"If you call me *cupcake girl* again I'm not going to be so nice."

"This was you being nice?" he asked.

And though the tone was still there in his voice she glanced up at his eyes and saw a hint of a sparkle. She liked him and looked forward to kicking his butt in the kitchen.

"Guess you're not the only one who is more spice than sugar," she said.

The door opened and they were met with a long line of folks waiting to sign in.

"I'm surprised to see so many people here today," she said.

"I'm not. The prize money is going to bring out everyone from executive chefs to prep cooks," he said. "I'm going to wash up. See you in the kitchen."

She watched him walk away before giving herself a mental slap. She wasn't here to repeat the mistakes from her past, but to fix them. This time she was going to do it right and that meant no falling for another chef even if he did have a killer smile, sexy ass and a charming accent.

REMY CRUZEL HAD GROWN up in one of the most famous kitchens in New Orleans. Gastrophile—the three Michelin starred restaurant that raised the bar and set the new standard for American Creole cooking. His grandfather and great-uncle had shocked the culinary world by getting three Michelin stars—something hard to achieve outside of Paris and even harder to do when you weren't French by birth. But the Cruzel brothers had done it and then passed that expertise on to their children.

Everyone quieted down as three men walked into the main room. He recognized Hamilton Ramsfeld, a popular American chef who his father said was a pompous ass who'd lost his love of food in his quest for notoriety. But then his old man was a hard man to impress.

"Hello, chefs, I am the head judge Hamilton Ramsfeld and the other judges in this competition are Lorenz Morelli executive chef and owner of a string of successful high-end Italian restaurants and Pete Gregoria, the publisher of *American Food* magazine."

"We look forward to tasting the dishes you prepare for us," Lorenz said in his heavy Italian accent. "Everyone on the left side of the room will come with me," Lorenz instructed. "Everyone on the right will stay here with Hamilton."

"Good luck to you all," Pete said.

The field of chefs here today was as diverse as he'd expected it to be and he wasn't surprised when the judges immediately divided the room in two.

He saw Cupcake Girl go with the other group and gave her a mock-salute. She was cute and funny but he wasn't here to flirt with women, he was here to prove he had the cooking chops to take over as Chef Patron at Gastrophile in New Orleans. His family name was legend in the food world and it wasn't Stephens. He'd lied on his application.

It was hard to know how much of the praise heaped on his head was due to his last name and how much was due to his skills. So Remy Etienne Cruzel had become Remy Stephens. He didn't know how long he could keep up the ruse, but on his side was the fact that none of the celebrity chefs were friends of his father and Remy had kept a rather low profile at the Culinary Institute of America and while working at Gastrophile.

"Welcome to *Premier Chef—the Professionals* Audition. A love of food has brought you here today but we will only be accepting those of you who have real skill and ability in the kitchen. You might be the king of the kitchen back home, but here in this competition you will have to earn everything. Every new day will bring another chance to prove yourself and at the end of the 12 weeks if you have what it takes you will be the new Premier Chef," head judge Hamilton Ramsfeld said.

Remy nodded knowing this was exactly what he needed to hear.

"Chefs, each of you will prepare a dish from our pantry in 15 minutes that demonstrates your culinary point of view. When the time is up your dish will be judged and only half of your number will make it onto the show."

"Yes, chef," was chorused by the cooks waiting to get in the kitchen. They'd set up a line of tables in a big circle around the room and Remy was anxious to get to his station and start his *mis en place*. He knew what he could cook well in 15 minutes and already he was prepping in his head.

Remy didn't really care who the judges were as long as they scrutinized him for his dishes and not his pedigree, and by lying about who he was he'd ensured they would. They called start and the chefs all ran to the pantry to gather ingredients. It reminded Remy of a game his grandfather used to play with him when he was little. Hiding ingredients in the cupboard and then making him wear a blindfold to see if he could sniff out the items.

He had an image of Cupcake Girl in a blindfold and little else as he directed her around his kitchen back home. He shrugged off that thought and forced his mind back to the competition. It'd be embarrassing if he were sent home before filming even began.

He gathered his ingredients and prepared his dish, cooking easily under the pressure of the clock.

"Dude, this is intense," said the shaggy blond guy next to him. "I'm used to working under the gun but not with this many people around."

"It is crazy, but I think they do that to rattle you," Remy said.

"It's not shaking you," the guy said.

"I've worked under some shouters in my day so it takes more than this to rattle me," Remy said, thinking of his father who didn't let blood temper his tongue when Remy screwed up.

"Me, too. I'm Troy, by the way."

"Remy." He didn't want to chat but needed to get his

dish finished and plated. A quick glance at the clock confirmed that he was right on schedule.

Troy kept up a constant stream as he cooked and Remy had worked with talkers before and had to be honest and admit he didn't like them. The kitchen was for cooking not for talking. He didn't trust a chef who was busy rattling on instead of focusing on his dish.

"Time."

Remy put his hands up and stepped back from his station. The judges came around to taste and he wiped his sweaty hands on his pants, as they tasted his dish. He couldn't remember being this nervous since his first day at the CIA.

"Good. Nice balance of sweet and heat. I like it," Hamilton said.

"Thank you, chef."

The other judges also complimented him. And he realized he was good. He'd known it, but it was nice to hear it from someone else.

They called names of the contestants going home. Troy didn't make the cut and gave Remy a wave as he walked out the door. Remy wasn't surprised. This was a serious competition meant for those who were serious about their work. The other group rejoined them and he noticed Cupcake Girl in the center of the pack.

She was cute with her pixie haircut and her delicate features. Her hair was jet black and her figure petite but curvy. As Hamilton started talking to them again Cupcake Girl's cute ass and the way her jeans fit distracted Remy.

"...teams," Hamilton said.

Dammit. He should have been listening instead of staring at the woman. He had a feeling his sweet tooth was going to be his downfall. "What'd he say?" he asked the man next to him.

"We're going to be put on two person teams and will cook against the other teams, at the end of the round half of us will go home and the remaining chefs will be going onto the show."

"Thanks."

"Come forward and take a knife from the cutting block. There are 15 teams, you will be given a number and A or B. The A knife is the head of the team. You will have thirty minutes to plan your dish and then an hour to execute it."

Everyone moved forward to take a knife and Remy drew 7B. "My lucky number."

"Mine too," a soft feminine voice said from behind him. "And I get to be in charge. My fate has definitely changed since the elevator."

"Cupcake Girl," he said. "I hoped you'd make it through. I think I should be in charge since I'm a trained chef and you are a baker."

"Southern boy, I'm the leader on this mission you can either follow me or perish in flames, but either way I'm not about to screw up a challenge."

He liked her spunky attitude, but he wasn't about to risk going home because of her. He'd let her think she was in charge but no way was he putting his fate in her hands. "What did you have in mind?"

"Well, I'm from LA and you're from the south so I was thinking some kind of taco-po-boy combo. The dishes both have their roots in common street fare. Working class food that we can elevate to fine dining," she said.

"I like the idea. Can you make your own tortillas?" he asked.

"I can," she said with a grin.

"I'll make the filling a shrimp and andouille sausage blend with some vegetables in it."

She nodded. "Sounds good. What do you think of a hint of lime in the tortillas?"

"Yes, that's what we need. But we're still at street food level with this," he said.

She looked over at him with those large chocolate brown eyes of hers. "We can do it three ways and have a plate with three different tacos on it."

He could see that she was here to win but he still wasn't sure she had the cooking skills needed to execute her plan. They discussed the other two tacos and then went into the pantry to gather ingredients. Staci talked to everyone she met and joked. She was easy going and that concerned him.

Could someone so laid back win? He wasn't too sure about trusting her instincts on the dish. He'd seen other chefs going for lamb and beef.

He started working the dish allowing his experience and instincts to take over. He changed a few things from her original suggestion and felt her at his shoulder one time. She reached over and put her finger in his bowl.

"What are you doing?"

"Tasting. It's all about layers. Thought you'd know that, Southern man."

He did know that but he'd been busy trying to make sure he got everything done in the allotted time. She brought her finger to her lips and her small pink tongue darted out to taste the sauce on her finger. He mentally groaned as all thoughts of cooking took a back seat. She was damn sexy and he had the feeling she knew it when she winked at him.

"A little spicy, but then I like things hot," she said, walking back to her station.

He watched her for another second before someone called out that they only had ten minutes left and Remy forced his mind back to the competition and off his sexy competitor. He had to stay focused or everything he wanted to prove would be lost. He only wished that Staci wasn't such a distraction.

2

DESPITE WHAT SHE'D SAID about being in charge, Staci knew that Remy had done some of his own things. But since this was a competition and neither of them wanted to go home, she gave him a pass. Plus, his additions were delicious.

When they started plating their dish, he reached around her to adjust the garnish on the middle taco and his arm brushed hers. Staci took a deep breath, forcing herself to ignore the man and focus on the chef.

"Not bad, but you didn't do what I said."

"I've been cooking a long time, *chère*, I don't necessarily follow instructions."

"If we go home you'll wish you had," she said. "I didn't take a ninety minute bus ride only to be sent home today."

"I'm not planning on going home which is why I simply perfected your idea."

"You're cocky," she said, not at all impressed with his attitude. She tried a bit of the filling left over from the plated dishes. Dammit, it was good. Better than she'd anticipated because she hadn't thought, she sheepishly admitted, that someone who looked like he did could cook.

"Well?" he asked, lifting one eyebrow at her.

"It'll do."

That startled a laugh out of him and she caught her breath as he smiled at her for the first time since they'd met. Really smiled so that his whole face lit up.

"Oh, it will more than do. Let's see if you are up to snuff, *chère*."

She knew the flat bread she made was the best that he'd ever taste. "Angels weep because they can't get my bread in heaven."

He quickly tore off a piece of the bread still on the tray and popped it in his mouth. He chewed slowly and she found herself watching his mouth. She wondered how his lips would feel on hers.

"It'll do."

"I know," she said. She glanced around and noted that the judges were getting closer to their station. They had been directed to stand back from the table until the judges approached them.

Hamilton was the first judge to reach them. He motioned Staci and Remy forward with an arrogant wave of his hand. Staci remained where she was before Remy nudged her with his foot. She hated arrogance in a man. It was okay to be proud of what you accomplished but it was something else entirely for a person to act like such a jerk.

"Your dish looks interesting," Hamilton said. "A little plebian."

"Our taste is anything but," Staci said.

Remy elbowed her. She glared at him.

"Once the camera crew is in place we will ask you about your dish, then taste it," Lorenz said coming over.

The cameraman got into place, a make-up person arrived and brushed something off of Staci's cheek. "What was that?"

"Flour," she said, then with a final whisk of her make-up wand she walked away.

Great, Staci thought, she'd been standing there looking like a messy little girl with flour on her face. She wished she'd known...but then it was a good thing she hadn't. It might have affected how she'd acted toward Remy and Hamilton and she didn't want that. She was serious about her food and this competition and she wanted to let the boys know she'd come to win.

"I think we are ready," the director said. "Go."

"Tell us a little about yourselves," Pete invited them. "Staci, you're a baker?"

"Yes, I co-own a cupcake bakery in San Diego called Sweet Dreams. I was trained at Le Cordon Bleu in Paris."

"And Remy?" Lorenz asked in that sexy Italian accent of his.

"I'm from Nawlins," he said, combining the two words into one with his smooth southern accent. "I learned to cook at my granddad's elbow. I've been working down there but am currently between gigs."

"Staci, you were the leader on this dish, tell us what you prepared for us."

"We combined what makes both of our culinary influences so great. A mixture of street food from the Big Easy and So Cal. Its a trio of po-boy tacos."

"Remy, what did you make?" Hamilton asked as Lorenz cut the first taco into thirds.

"The filling," he said.

"What's in them?" Pete asked.

"Shrimp and andouille, lime crusted tilapia and Portobello mushrooms Vera Cruz style."

"Sounds interesting," Lorenz said. "We are going to taste now."

All three men sampled the tacos and Staci felt her heart in her throat as she waited for them to give their critique. She'd tried the food. She knew that she and Remy had put together a good dish but now she was so nervous. She reached over and grabbed his wrist, as the silence seemed to grow.

Hamilton glanced at Lorenz and than at Pete.

"I really enjoyed this. The mixture of spiciness with the lightness of the bread. Well done," Pete said.

"I liked it too," Lorenz said. "The sausage was delicious and the seasoning layered and complex."

"Well that's three of us who'd come back for more of this. You two worked well together," Hamilton said.

With that the judges moved on, Remy's hand turned in her grasp and he briefly held her hand before dropping it. She wanted to jump up and down but Remy didn't seem to think it was time to celebrate.

"What's the matter? You look almost nervous."

"I'm hardly that. I just don't believe in counting my chickens before they're hatched."

"Um…all three judges liked our food. It's a safe bet that we'll be asked to stay," Staci said.

"I want to hear what he's saying to the others. This is a competition. Just because we made a good dish doesn't mean the other competitors didn't as well," Remy said.

She nodded. And for the first time really looked at the other chefs and the dishes they'd put together. Everyone wanted this chance to make it to the next level. Everyone wanted to win and she had to remember that.

The chefs next to them had made a dry rubbed brisket that they had sliced thin and steamed. "Sounds iffy to me," Staci said. "Brisket needs to be slow cooked."

"I agree, but Pete seems like he's enjoying it."

She had to admit the restaurant critic did seem to be enjoying the meat. But Hamilton made a face and spat his portion back out. "Dry."

"It is dry," Lorenz agreed. "But it's admirable that you tried to do a brisket in the time allotted and I love the spice combination in the rub. Whose recipe is that?"

"Mine," the tall, skinny chef said.

"Good job, Dave. It really flavors the meat and to be honest makes up for the dryness," Lorenz said.

"I enjoyed it," Pete said. "The barbecue sauce you made covers up the lack of moisture in the meat."

"Thanks," Dave said.

The judges finished up their tasting and they were all told to clean up their stations while a final decision was reached. Remy was introspective as he worked quickly and efficiently. She watched him moving and then realized what she was doing.

She always had the worst timing in her infatuations

and it seemed the worst taste in men. She'd let a man ruin her cooking career once. Was she really going to let that happen again?

"Don't worry, *chère*, whatever happens today, you can cook and no one can take that from you," he said. "I enjoyed working with you today."

"Me, too," she said.

They were all told to move back to their stations as a final decision had been reached. Remy stood next to her and this time he squeezed her hand as Hamilton started talking.

"We've sampled some truly fine dishes given that we asked you to work with a chef whose style was different from yours and gave you a time restraint. We know you can all cook; this competition is designed to take you beyond that. Therefore the winners of this challenge and staying in the competition are…"

"Staci Rowland and Remy Stephens," Lorenz announced.

Remy tugged her close for a victory hug but he held her a little longer than he should have and when she pulled back there was a new awareness in his eyes.

REMY MADE SURE HE WASN'T in the same Escalade as Staci when they left the studio and were driven to the Premier Chef house in Malibu. They were in a luxury home that overlooked the Pacific.

The water was bluer than his beloved Gulf of Mexico but the scent of salt in the air reminded him of home. There were production assistants in the house when they arrived. And they were all directed where to go in the eight-bedroom house. They'd be sharing two to a room to begin with and the producers had already assigned them into pairs. Remy was in a room overlooking the ocean with Quinn Lyon.

"Dude, do you mind if I take this bed?" Quinn asked.

Remy shrugged. "That's fine. Where are you from?"

"Seattle. I'm the executive chef at Poisson...one guess what our specialty is?"

Remy smiled. There was an easy-going nature about Quinn and he reminded Remy of one of his Cajun uncles who was a shrimper. "Fish, right?"

"Hell, yes. Your accent says you're from the south—where?"

"Nawlins'," he said.

"Where do you work?"

"Currently, I'm between jobs," he said. It was sort of the truth since he'd taken a leave of absence from Gastrophile.

"That's cool. I saw you working today, you keep a neat station," Quinn said.

"I began cooking with my dad and he's a tyrant in the kitchen."

Quinn laughed. "My old man was a logger, didn't know anything about food."

"How'd you come to be a chef?"

"Dropped out of high school," Quinn said. "Started as a dishwasher and worked my way up. I never thought I'd be a chef when I was a kid. I mean, girls cooked where I came from, you know?"

"No, I don't. The women in my family can cook but the kitchen has always been filled with men. I can't remember a time when anyone thought I'd be anything but a chef."

"What's your family think of you being unemployed?" he asked.

"Not too fond of that. But getting on this show will probably help ease their minds," he said. The truth was his parents didn't know where he was right now. But he figured that Remy Stephens's family would be happy that he was cooking with the chance of employment at the end of the show. "What about your family?"

"My wife's great. My dad moved to Alaska so he's not that involved with my day-to-day life," Quinn said. "I don't know if I should unpack or not."

"I am," Remy said. "My *grandmère* is superstitious and she's always said that if you believe you'll succeed you will and vice versa."

"Ah, that's confidence not superstition," Quinn said, unzipping his suitcase and starting to unpack. "But I think you're right. Better to act like I'm here for the long haul."

"Definitely," Remy said.

Quinn had a picture of his wife and one of him with his dad holding up the biggest fish that Remy had ever seen. Quinn kept up a quiet conversation while he moved around the room and Remy learned the other man was thirty-eight and was contemplating an offer to become the chef owner of Poisson. Something he wasn't too sure he wanted to do.

Remy didn't give the other man any advice. He'd learned that decisions that significant had to be made intuitively. Otherwise doubt and resentment followed.

Quinn's cell phone rang and he smiled. "It's the wife."

"I'll leave you alone," offered Remy.

The bedrooms were all on the second floor of the house, which sat, nestled on a cliff overlooking the Pacific ocean. Remy went downstairs and saw that several contestants were on the balcony smoking. But he didn't see Cupcake Girl. He wasn't looking for her, he thought, but part of him knew he was.

She'd been good in the kitchen today and he was happy enough that her direction had resulted in a win, but there could only be one winner of Premier Chef—The Professionals and he needed to be that winner.

His future hinged on it in his mind. He envied Quinn and his easy relationship with his father. The older Lyon hadn't pressured and bullied Quinn into cooking. In his early twenties, Remy would have been happier to make up his own mind and to find his own path. Instead, it had been done for him. Hence his doubts now.

Remy headed toward the kitchen for a bottle of water. Quinn would be tough to beat in any seafood challenge but Remy had grown up on the Gulf so he wasn't too worried, but he wanted to get an idea of what else he was up against.

"You smoke?" a heavily tattooed man with a Jersey accent asked him as he reached the bottom of the stairs.

"No," Remy said.

"Good. So far everyone who's come downstairs is a smoker. I'm Tony. Tony Montea," he said, holding out his hand.

"Remy Stephens," he said shaking the other man's hand. "I'm guessing you're from New York or Jersey."

"Jersey—born and bred. But I work in Manhattan. You'd think I'd cook Italian but my grandmother is French."

"Mine too...well, French Creole," Remy admitted.

"Cool. Did she cook?"

"Yes," he said. "Yours?"

"Yeah. She's the one that taught me to cook. But you can only go so far in a home kitchen," Tony said.

"True. Do you have any formal training?"

"CIA," he said with a smile. "This might be the only place where I don't have to explain that it's the Culinary Institute of America not the Central Intelligence Agency. Though to be honest there are a few from my hood that think I'm with the government."

Remy laughed. "Where do you work?"

"Dans La Jardin," he replied, naming one of the most popular French restaurants in the city.

"Head chef?"

"Nah, junior, but I'm hoping to learn some skills here that will give me a leg up when I get back home."

"Not here to win?" Remy asked.

"Sure I want to win, but I have heard of some of these other chefs," Tony said. "They might be hard to beat."

"They might be," Remy agreed, writing Tony off as a nice guy but not much competition. Anyone who was more concerned about what would happen when he got home versus what needed to happen here wasn't going to win it. And Remy was definitely here to win.

"You're not worried?" Tony asked.

"Nah, but I have been around celebrated chefs before," Remy said.

"Me, too," a tall thin girl with skin the color of cappuccino said, joining them. "I'm Vivian Johns."

"Tony Matea," Tony said. "This is Remy Stephens. Whom have you cooked with?"

"Troy Hudson," Vivian said flashing them both a grin. "I work at The Rib Mart in Austin and he came down there for one of his cook offs."

"How was it?" Remy asked.

"Interesting. He's a solid cook but a lot of his talent gets lost in filming the show. He had a staff with him for the challenge," Vivian said.

"Did you win?" Tony wanted to know.

"Hells to the yeah," she said. "It's hard to beat Austin ribs in Austin but my dish was good. *Really good.* It's interesting how people act around celebrity chefs. Who've you cooked with, Remy?"

"Alain Cruzel," he said. His grandfather was one of the most famous chefs to come out of New Orleans.

"Yeah, I've heard of him. He's one tough guy in the kitchen."

"Yes, he is. He doesn't tolerate mistakes," Remy said. "However, sharing the kitchen with him made me realize even the greatest chefs make mistakes some times. That's why I'm not worried about anyone's reputation."

"You don't have to," Tony said.

"What do you mean?" Remy asked wondering if he'd somehow given away his real name and pedigree.

"You won today. I think that means most of the participants will be gunning for you."

"Not just me," he said. "Cupcake Girl was pretty impressive as well."

"I don't think she's going to take kindly to being called that," Vivian said with a grin.

He didn't think so either but Remy would do whatever he had to in order to avoid the chemistry between them. And to preserve some kind of edge over her. The nickname bothered her so he'd keep using it.

"We need everyone gathered in the living room," the director said.

Everyone moved into the spacious room that had a big screen television on one wall and three long sofas and a number of assorted armchairs casually placed into conversation groups. He saw cupcake girl across the room and forced himself to look away from her.

"The winners of today's challenge are going out to dinner tonight at Martine's where they will have a private tour of the kitchen and talk with their chief sous chef. The rest of you will be participating in a grilling workshop."

Remy shook his head. The last thing he wanted was more time alone with Staci. If he were as superstitious as his grandmother he'd believe that fate was pushing them together.

But he wasn't.

Really.

DINNER ALONE WITH REMY and Chef Ramone wasn't what she'd anticipated when she'd started the day off by spilling tea all over the hottie in the elevator. However, she was happy enough for it now. She got dressed in the one nice dress she'd brought with her.

The instructions for *Premier Chef* were pretty explicit. She'd had to bring her cooking gear but also jeans, a dress, a skirt, a bathing suit and a number of other expected items. Still, it was the specific clothing that had struck her as funny.

She knew it was a television show and that they'd want them all to look a certain way but beyond that she hadn't given what she wore much thought. Now that she was heading to one of the LA areas nicest restaurants she was glad she'd gone shopping with Alysse last weekend.

She enjoyed spending time with the co-owner of Sweet Dreams, especially since Alysse was so busy—engaged to be married and busily determined to expand their cupcake business. Staci had decided to take a break from the day-to-day running of the bakery to get ready for this show. Staci was the first to admit her dreams lay in a different direction now.

The bakery had saved her sanity when she'd first come back to California but that was a long five years ago and given that she was almost thirty, Staci felt it was time to figure out what she wanted from life. And she couldn't until she made up for her past mistakes. Until she resolved her lingering doubts about her abilities as a chef. This show was her chance to do that.

She did a double check of her make-up, although she knew that the production person would re-apply it and make it heavier for the television cameras.

"You look good," her roommate Vivian said.

"Thanks. I wasn't sure that I'd be wearing this dress on TV. Do you think it's too low cut?" she asked. She'd tried it on in the store but had been wearing a sports bra so she hadn't noticed how much cleavage it revealed.

"Not at all. Sex sells, baby. It also distracts. If Remy is staring at your chest it should give you an edge over him."

She sighed inwardly. It was a contest after all. She wanted Remy distracted and off his A game. But at the same time using her body to win, well, why not? Remy hadn't hesitated to use his sexy southern accent to distract her.

She grabbed her handbag and made sure she had her moleskin recipe journal in there. The journal had seen better days and was bulging with pages and photos she'd added. She never went anywhere without the journal. She liked to make notes about the meals she ate and she found eating out always inspired her palate.

"Knock 'em dead," Vivian said.

"I hope so," Staci replied as she left their room. She was used to living alone, cooking alone and spending most of her time by herself, so this living with the other contestants could be a strain.

Remy was waiting in the foyer with Jack, the director and one of the producers. She almost missed a step on the stairs staring at Remy. His thick black hair was slicked back. He wore a white dress shirt left casually open at the neck and a navy dinner jacket and gray pants. He glanced at his watch and then at the stairs, his mouth dropping open when he saw her.

She gave herself a mental high five and forced herself to smile at him in what she hoped was a casual way. To be honest, he was oozing sexiness in his dinner wear, so she wasn't entirely sure what impression she gave off.

"Now that you are both here we will head over to the restaurant. We won't be filming until we are there so you can relax."

"Thanks," Remy said. "Will we be driving ourselves?"

"No. We have a production assistant who will take you and pick you up. During the course of the show you will always be in our hands. Chef Ramone doesn't like cell phones and he has requested you leave them with us."

"Okay," Staci said, opening her handbag to retrieve her phone, which she handed to Jack.

"What's that book in your bag?" the producer asked.

"Just my food journal. I like to write down the meals I eat."

"I'm sure that will be fine. Though we will check with the chef before you arrive and if it's not, you'll have to give it to one of our staff at the location."

She didn't like the thought of letting anyone else have her journal but she wasn't going to argue about it right now. Jack directed them out the door and into a Mercedes sedan.

"How many vehicles do you have?" Remy asked.

"Enough. In this case Mercedes is sponsoring one of the upcoming challenges and giving away this car as a prize."

"Nice. I hope I win," Staci said. "I've been riding the bus for too long."

Remy laughed. "Ah, without the bus I wouldn't have that great first impression of you."

She shook her head remembering how she'd landed in his arms. "I could have done without that."

Soon they were both seated in the backseat and being whisked across town toward the famous restaurant. Instead of thinking about the evening or even the contest, Staci's thoughts hadn't drifted any further than the man sitting next to her.

She wished she'd made a better first impression on him but she knew that her skills in the kitchen had made up for her stumble. And if she were honest, she wouldn't trade their first meeting for anything.

"Nervous?" he asked.

"A little. But not really," she said. "You?"

"No. I'm curious to see his techniques. I haven't cooked much outside of the South."

"I was trained in Paris," she said.

"Really? Pastry?" he asked.

"Yes and everything else," she admitted.

"Then why are you the co-owner of a cupcake bakery? You should be working in the finest kitchens in the world."

"That is a long story," she said.

"Well, we do have a long drive ahead of us," he replied.

3

THE WARMTH OF THE CAR'S interior felt like an intimate cocoon and it would have been easy for her to forget that Remy was her competitor. Yet, this situation was so far removed from what she knew life to be like. Remy might be an out-of-work chef but he was clearly used to luxury. He sat relaxed next to her in his expensive clothes.

What was his story? Did she want to know? A lot of people said it was better to know your enemy but given her personality flaw regarding men, she thought a little mystery was probably in order.

"You were going to tell me how a Cordon Bleu chef ends up owning a cupcake bakery," he said in that sultry southern way of his.

It would be easy to dismiss him as an innocent were it not for the shrewd look in his eyes. She didn't have to guess to know that he was one of those who subscribed to the know-your-enemy theory.

"Was I?" she asked, turning toward him. The fabric of her skirt slid up her legs and she waited to see if he had noticed.

He had. But he arched one eyebrow at her to let her know that he knew she'd done it deliberately. She shrugged and he smiled.

"It's clear that neither of us is going to forget this is a competition," he said.

"I'm here to win," she said. "I have to assume you are too."

"Indeed. Why else would I travel across the country with just my knives and culinary training?"

"Where did you train?" she asked, turning the tables back to him.

"CIA. But we'll learn about that during the competition. I want to know more about you. The things you aren't going to reveal in front of the camera," he said, as he shifted to stretch his arm along the back of the seat. His fingers just inches from her shoulder, she felt the heat of his body against her skin.

"But those facts aren't ones I'll give up for nothing. What are you going to offer me in return, what secrets do you keep, Southern Man?"

She realized that the attraction ran both ways and that Remy wasn't afraid to turn the tables on her. She cleared her throat.

"Show me yours and I'll show you mine," he said.

"That hardly seems fair unless I know what you're offering to give up," she said.

"Okay, tell me how you got started cooking. Where did your culinary journey begin?" he asked, running his finger along the side of her cheek.

She turned her face away from his touch. "And you'll do the same?"

"Oui, *chère*," he said.

She rubbed one finger along his beard-stubbled jaw just to try to keep him off-balance and because she was longing to know what it felt like. He seemed to just reach out and touch her whenever he wanted to.

"Good. I grew up in here in southern California. I'm an only child and was always in the kitchen with my grandmother who practically raised me," she said. "Your turn."

"I grew up in Louisiana. Though I live and work in New Orleans now, I spent a lot of time in the bayou as a young boy with my grandmother's people. I learned to shrimp and cook off of what we found each day. I didn't realize how great a gift that would be as a chef."

"I bet. My grandmother used to buy whatever was on sale at the grocery store when we went. She never had a menu and when we'd get home she'd combine the ingredients in different ways."

"Sounds like we are similar in our upbringing," he said.

"Maybe. You seem very comfortable surrounded by luxury," she said.

"Do I?"

"Yes. This is probably the nicest car I've been in unless you count the limo I took to prom. I don't think that's the case with you."

He laughed. "Who did you go to prom with?"

"A boy who thought he loved me," she said.

"Why did the boy think he loved you?" Remy asked.

She was not about to start talking about her rocky

past and the loves that might have been. "Don't avoid the question."

"What was the question?"

She frowned at him. "You're difficult and cagey. What exactly are you hiding, Remy Stephens?"

"I believe that some things shouldn't be spoken of. But you are right, I did grow up in a comfortable home financially. However, that's not as interesting as a boy who thought he loved you. Didn't you love him?"

"I'm not talking about that," she said. She hadn't allowed herself to really care about anyone when she'd been younger because she'd had big dreams of leaving California and going to Paris. She was going to be the next Julia Child.

"What about emotionally? Was your home as comfortable in that way as it was financially?" she asked. She'd met more than one person who hid behind evasion and had grown up in a difficult home. Having money didn't always mean that someone had an easy upbringing.

"It was good. My family are all Cajun or French so there is a lot of passion and tempers flaring, but I always knew I was loved." His voice revealed the truth of those words. And she thought about how he'd been in the kitchen. There was something very controlled about Remy. She doubted he'd be the sort of man who'd let passion for a woman interfere with his desire to win.

She needed to remember that.

"Spoiled?" she asked.

"A little. But I can't blame my parents for that. I just like to get my way," he said.

"Like you did in the competition this afternoon. Doing what you thought was best instead of what I told you."

He shrugged again. "I have to give my all in the kitchen. Even if that means making other chefs mad."

"Is that why you are between gigs right now? Do you have a hard time taking orders?" she asked.

He rubbed the bridge of his nose and pulled his arm off the back of the seat to his lap. She guessed that she'd asked a question that cut too close to whatever he was hiding from her. Whatever his emotional vulnerable point was. *Interesting.*

"Perhaps," he said. "Mostly it's that I have been praised for my cooking but by those who've known me my entire life. I want to know if I'm really good."

"Why? Did something happen to shake your confidence?" she asked.

"Did something happen to you?" he asked, focusing that intense blue gaze of his on her. "I bet it did. No one goes from Paris to a cupcake bakery without a big event forcing the change."

"True. I guess we both have our secrets," she said. "But I will tell you this, I've never doubted my ability to put a good dish on the table. I know when I'm done cooking that the person eating my food is going to be blown away."

"Do you?"

"Yes. I think you must be the same," she said. "Otherwise why would you come here?"

"Why indeed," he said.

She leaned back against the leather seat and looked

out the window again. This time the answers she sought had nothing to do with her, but with him. "You want external praise."

"Don't you?" he asked.

"I guess. Really I want a chance to get back what I once had," she said, speaking from the heart.

As much as the success she'd had with Sweet Dreams validated her as a chef and businesswoman, she wanted to know that she had the chops to go head-to-head with the best cooks in the world. She'd competed years ago to get that original role in the kitchen of a top Parisian chef, and then she'd thrown it away for love. No, that wasn't right. There hadn't been love between them, but there had been passion and danger, she thought. It had been very dangerous to give in to her passions.

Yes. That was what had been missing from her life. That was what she was afraid she'd never find again. Her passions for living and for cooking. It was only when she embraced both, that she really did have balance. Yet that was the very thing that frightened her the most.

"You look like you just solved the problems of the world," he said.

"Nah, just the problems of one woman. It's funny how you find answers when you didn't know there was a question," she said.

"What did you figure out, *ma chère*?" he asked, lifting his arm against the back of the seat again and touching the side of her face.

No way was she sharing the truth with him, but she knew that if she were going to reclaim her passion in the kitchen she'd have to reclaim it in her life as well.

She needed to figure out a way to balance her personal passions with her professional ones and a part of her felt like maybe she could do that with Remy. But another part of her warned that the last time she'd attempted this she'd been burned. Could she survive another dance of passion with a chef?

REMY HAD COME TO COOK but he found most of his time so far had been taken up with thinking about the sexy little woman seated next to him. Her perfume was elusive but tempting, and he found the scent distracting as they worked next to Chef Ramone in the kitchen. Remy shook his head, forcing his attention back to the cutting board in front of him. The executive chef moved off to take care of an emergency on the other side of the kitchen and Staci moved closer to Remy.

"He's so low-key I almost don't believe he could prepare these spectacular dishes."

"I know what you mean. I've never met a chef who doesn't yell," Remy said. "Certainly never worked with one who didn't."

"Me either. Even Alysse and I yell back and forth at the bakery."

"That's your partner?" he asked.

"Yes. She's funny. Usually we're just telling each other stories from the night before or I'm bossing her around," Staci said.

"Do you do that a lot?" he asked. He'd finished dicing the vegetables he'd been assigned to work with by the chef. Staci still had half her pile to go. He reached over and took the carrots from her.

She smiled her thanks. "Yes, I do boss her around a lot. But not just her, anyone who needs my advice."

"Do I need it?"

"I don't know. A part of me wants to say yes, but I don't know you well enough. You're wicked with that knife."

"Knife skills are one of the best weapons in a chef's arsenal," he said.

"Yes, they are, Remy," Chef Ramone said returning to them.

"You've done well with the task I assigned you. Ready to assemble our dish?"

Remy found the same comfort of working in the kitchen with Staci and Chef Ramone as he did working in his own kitchen back home. It was telling he thought that this was home for him even though he was thousands of miles from New Orleans.

And he wasn't sure he could find his own way. Staci messed with his concentration and that intrigued him. He'd had affairs before, he was too passionate and his sexual drive too high for him not to. But he'd never allowed himself an affair with another chef. It seemed to him that life was best served by keeping his personal and professional lives separate.

Now, he wasn't sure. He watched her dip her spoon into the sauce she was preparing and stared at her full lips and saw her eyes sparkle. He suppressed a groan. In his mind he moved closer and leaned in to taste the sauce but not from the spoon, from her.

"Want a lick?" she asked.

He snapped back to the present and nodded. He

wanted way more than a lick but that would be a good place to start. She held the spoon out to him, but instead of taking it from her hand, he wrapped his hand around her wrist and drew her to him.

He brought their hands up and then he leaned down to run his tongue over the sauce, keeping eye contact with her the entire time. Her lips parted and her tongue darted out again, just as it had before. Her pupils dilated and there was a rosy flush that climbed up her face.

"Delicious," he said, letting his hand drop and stepping back to his station.

"Thanks," she said, her voice thready, husky even and he knew that in the game of flirtation, he'd just won the round.

It was at that moment that he knew he wasn't leaving California without taking Staci Rowland to his bed. He'd thought that she'd distract him from cooking but he was coming to realize that if he didn't have her, it would be more of a distraction.

She was temptation incarnate and he was from The Big Easy. He'd been raised to indulge his passions in the kitchen and out and even though this would be the first time that he combined the two, he found the anticipation exquisite.

"Remy?" she asked.

He glanced over at her and saw the confusion in her eyes. And for a second he wondered if he'd misjudged her but then she licked her lips again and he smiled. He knew that he hadn't.

Staci seemed as if she were dealing with some issues in this competition, much like the rest of them.

And though tonight it was just the two of them, he knew that whatever knowledge he gleaned about her would be useful for the rest of the weeks ahead.

He closed the gap between them. Put his hands on her shoulders and leaned down as he drew her closer. He brushed his lips over hers and tasted the buttery sweetness of the sauce but also the indescribable taste of Staci. It was unique, mysterious and so addictive he didn't want to stop kissing her.

Yet he knew he had to. He stepped back and saw her watching him with an unfathomable expression. He'd shocked her. Hell, he'd surprised himself because he'd thought the young impulsive man he'd been was gone forever. But he was glad that he was back.

He thought he needed to be a little impulsive if he was going to find the right path forward for himself and for Gastrophile.

He had an idea of a seasoning to add to the dish and turned away from Staci and returned to his station. Cooking with renewed enthusiasm, when he was done and they both presented their dishes to the chef, he knew he'd prepared something different.

Something unique and something that he couldn't have come up with if he hadn't kissed Staci. It was as if she were a muse.

She was quiet and stole sideways looks at him, but he didn't face her. He waited for the verdict on the dishes, unsurprised when his was pronounced the winner.

He felt a balm of satisfaction and realized that he owed Staci a big thank you, but more than that he wanted to keep cooking with her by his side. Earlier today he'd been resentful of having to listen to someone else in the kitchen but tonight he acknowledged that only with outside input could he move to the next level.

Chef Ramone stepped away again and Staci put her hands on her waist as she turned to him. "What was that about?"

"What?"

"Kissing me like that. I thought we were both professionals," she said.

"We are," he admitted. "That kiss had nothing to do with our cooking and everything to do with the fire burning between us. I thought it would be distracting..."

"Wasn't it?" she asked. "It was for me."

"No," he said. "It wasn't distracting. It was inspiring."

He leaned over and kissed her again. "Thank you for that."

She semi-glared at him and he felt her displeasure. "You're welcome, I guess. I don't want you doing that again."

"I'm not making any promises," he said.

STACI KEPT HER DISTANCE from Remy for the ride home. She'd thought flirting with him would give her an edge and it had surprised her how easily he'd flipped the tactic on her. But as she watched him moving easily around the living room of the house and talking to the other competitors she knew there was more to it than that.

There was something about Remy that was shaking her to her core. She had to tread carefully. Where kissing her had spurred him and inspired him to make a creative and unique dish, it had floored her and made her put up something mediocre. She was lucky that tonight hadn't been a judged cooking session that counted. She was lucky that it had merely been a learning experience. She wasn't going to forget it either.

"How was it?" Vivian asked, coming up next to her and handing her a glass of wine.

Staci took a swallow of the dry white wine as she weighed what to say to Viv. They were roommates so the impulse to share what had happened was strong, but she also knew from watching these kinds of reality television shows that close personal relationships often backfired. Even friendships.

"It was fantastic," she said. She also knew that she wasn't going to ever say anything negative about anything.

"I knew it. I'm going to win the next challenge," Vivian said.

"Are you?"

"Hell, yes. I wouldn't mind being whisked away for a private dinner with dreamy Remy."

"He might not be the runner up," Staci warned.

"Why? Did he show you some weaknesses tonight?" Vivian asked.

No, she thought. She'd shown herself some weaknesses and she knew that she had to figure out how to turn that into a strength. She could do it. She just had to remember…what? She had no idea how to handle Remy and she knew it.

She'd known it from the moment she'd crashed into his arms in the elevator. He rattled her and she'd thought that by being her usual bold self she could gain the upper hand, but he'd turned that against her. How had he known that would work? But she thought maybe he hadn't known for sure and had only chanced upon…wait, a second, she thought. He didn't realize he'd thrown her. He'd been too engrossed in what had been going on with himself.

She had to remember how her grandmother had admonished her many times when she'd been growing up. Not everything was about her.

"So?"

"Sorry, Viv. He's a great chef and it's going to take a lot of skill to beat him," she said. "He took the chef's dish and made it taste even better. You know that's saying a lot."

"Dang. Well, I will tell you that Dan doesn't have any butchering skills. He made a mess of the fish tonight. He couldn't get a steak out of a salmon. I mean that's first year skills, right?" Vivian asked.

"Yes, it is. But he did make that rub that Lorenz liked. We might have to watch out for his flavors."

"True. I'm ready for the individual challenges but the team ones worry me," she admitted.

"Me, too," Staci said. "I hate having to depend on anyone other than myself."

They chatted a while longer about the competition until slowly everyone got ready for bed. Vivian put in her iPod headphones and switched off her light. She drifted off to sleep a little after midnight, but Staci was still wide awake.

Questions ran through her head and images of the dishes she'd eaten that night flashed through her mind.

She took her journal and got out of bed. Pulling on a sweatshirt, she then walked through the quiet house to the deck that overlooked the ocean. The moon was full, lending some light to the evening and she sat down on one of the padded deck chairs, letting the soothing sound of the ocean ease her confusion.

She opened her notebook and started writing about what she'd eaten and cooked that night. She wasn't too surprised to see that Remy featured in her notes. She focused on him, finding the part that made sense and the many things that didn't. Her sauce had been her downfall. Kissing him...no, that had been the thing that had knocked her off her game. Until that moment she'd been fine.

She'd teased him and it had backfired. But only because she hadn't been prepared for him to be as bold as she had been. And that had been a mistake she wouldn't make again.

"Can I join you?"

She glanced around to see Remy standing in the doorway. He wore a pair of faded jeans and a long sleeved black t-shirt that molded his upper body. He held a mug in his hand and had bare feet.

She nodded and gestured toward the chair next to her.

He sat down, leaning against the back of the lounge chair and saying nothing for a long minute or two. He sipped his hot drink and she felt that he was toying with her, but when she looked over at him she saw he wasn't.

Not everything is about you, she reminded herself again.

"Why can't you sleep?" she asked.

"Quinn snores," he said. "But I'm too restless from cooking tonight. If I was home I'd be in the kitchen trying all the different dishes that are in my head."

"Same here. It was inspiring to see what Chef Ramone had done. I mean he started from really humble roots."

"Yes, he did. My grandfather says all good cooking comes from the heart," Remy said.

"Was that what inspired you tonight? I've never tasted that combination of spices before."

He shrugged and took another sip from his mug. "I think I was inspired by something a little lower than my heart."

That startled her and she stared across the space between them trying to ascertain if he was telling the truth or not. And she saw in his eyes that he was. He wanted her.

She put down her notebook, stood up and moved over to sit facing him.

"Are you trying to say that your groin inspired the dish?" she asked, putting her hands against the back of the chair on either side of his face.

"Yes, I am. There was something fiery in that kiss I stole from you," he said. "My dish was a pale imitation of it." He leaned up, tunneling his fingers through her hair and drawing her head down to his and this time when their lips met, she opened her mouth over his, running her tongue along the seam of his lips before thrusting it teasingly into his mouth.

He moaned, angling his head to the right to deepen their kiss. His hands slid down her shoulders to her waist and he drew her closer to him. She straddled his lap, tried to taste more of him. God, he was addicting.

And addictions seldom were a good thing, she tried to remind herself but for the moment, logic wasn't in control and she wanted more of the passion Remy inspired.

4

A HOT WOMAN IN HIS LAP wasn't what he'd anticipated tonight but to be honest there was nothing he wanted more. He was high on the exhilaration of the dish he'd created. He felt as if everything inside of him had been pushing toward this interlude. He didn't have all the answers he'd been seeking but thanks in part to Staci he'd found a few of them.

Sliding his arms up and down her back, she shifted to accommodate him, her hands still framing his face. Her fingers were delicate and cool against his beard-stubbled chin; he rubbed his face against her hands breaking the contact with her mouth.

She exhaled a long drawn out sigh as she shifted her weight to settle back on her ankles.

"What am I going to do with you?" she asked.

But he could tell she wasn't really expecting an answer from him. It was more of a question that he'd bet she wasn't even aware she'd muttered out loud. He smoothed his hands over her back, she felt so ethereal in his arms. Like the fairies his little sister collected when they'd been children. Staci didn't belong in this world, yet there was something very real about her.

He felt like the wrong move would send her skittering back into the house and into a permanent retreat.

He wasn't much for being tentative. It went against his hot-blooded Cajun nature. But he was willing to do what was necessary to keep Staci here tonight. He needed her. He wasn't sure how or why but he knew that she'd inspired him tonight and he wanted to keep that energy going.

"Kiss me again," he said as the breeze off the Pacific stirred around them.

She tipped her head to the side. "You'd like that, wouldn't you?"

"Hell, yes, I'm a guy after all."

She smiled at him but the expression didn't reach her eyes and he sensed there was a feeling of sadness in her. He remembered the boy she'd mentioned who'd believed he'd been in love with her.

Remy wanted to know more about Staci. He needed to, yet at the same time he recognized that if he was going to win, and prove to himself what needed proving, he couldn't let her be the first one to make him back down from a challenge.

Yet that very action was impossible. There had been other women in his life but none of them had ever inspired him to cook the way he had tonight. There was no denying it. He could only hope that he'd be able to control his need for Staci. He knew that men who played with fire did get burned.

"But you'd also like it because we're competitors and

you saw the way that you threw me in the kitchen tonight," she said.

He didn't have to feign surprise. He genuinely had no idea that their embrace had rattled her. But now that he did, he filed that information away for later. "No, I didn't."

"Truly?" she asked, tracing her fingers along his five o'clock shadow.

He closed his eyes and tipped his head to the side enjoying her touch as sensation spread throughout his body. His blood seemed to flow heavier in his veins before pooling between his legs. His erection hardened and he almost canted his hips forward.

"Yes. I was inspired by our kiss. There was something so hot in that embrace with you I thought I'd explode right there in Chef Ramone's kitchen but then I channeled it into the dish…I've never done that before. I always cook from a place of history. Dishes made the way they've always been made."

"Why?" she asked, running her hands down his neck and over his shoulders and warmth started to flow through him. Not unlike what he'd felt earlier in Ramone's kitchen. This woman—Staci—made him feel things that he knew would complement their situation. He should put her from his lap and walk away…but he knew he wasn't going to do that.

He took her wrist and drew her hand lower, rubbing it over his chest and pectorals. Her hands were small and petite as she was. Staci called to the wildness in his soul and he was powerless to ignore it. He wanted her, but more than that, he wanted to be the man who chased the shadows from her eyes.

She stretched her fingers out and then he felt the bite of her nails through the fabric of his shirt.

He reached around her, she was as hot as the spiciest pepper in his garden and one taste was simply not enough.

He held her hips, bringing her down into contact with his erection. She sighed. The sound of his name on her lips made him shudder. He liked it. He wanted to hear it again when she was breathy and on the cusp of pleasure.

He thrust up against her as her fingers continued to caress him. How he wanted this woman.

Tonight, with only the moon and the sea as his witnesses, he felt free to give in to his desires. He needed to claim her—his muse. He tangled one hand in her short hair and drew her mouth back to his. Her kisses were addictive and he was hungry for more of them. He rubbed his lips over hers until her mouth parted and he slipped his tongue inside her mouth. He was desperate to find that elusive taste that had so intrigued him earlier.

She shifted again, her tongue toying with his. He couldn't get enough of her. He wondered if she'd be both his savior and his downfall. But pushed the thought aside. Only a fool dwelled on thoughts when he had a woman like Staci in his arms.

For tonight she was a gift sent from the gods to inspire him and there was no step he could take that would be out of line. She was his, he thought. Just another element of the new knowledge he had gained on the first step of his journey.

He found the hem of her shirt and slid his hands underneath and up her back. She wasn't wearing a bra, which made him even harder than he already was. Her skin was so smooth he just kept stroking her as he devoured her mouth. She was rocking on his lap, her own hands finding the hem of his shirt and pushing it up under his armpits.

The first brush of her fingers against his bare skin made him burn for more. He pushed her shirt up and she lifted her mouth from his, staring down at him. She pulled her shirt up and off tossing it on the ground next to their chair. He did the same with his shirt and adjusted her on the lounge chair so that he could pull her closer to him. Her center was nestled close to his groin, the tips of her firm breasts brushed against his chest.

Her nipples were hard and pointed, pushing against him and he kept his hand on her back right between her shoulder blades so that he could enjoy that feeling. She lifted her head toward his and her hands were on his face again, pulling him down until their mouths met.

The kiss this time was blatantly carnal and he wanted it to never end. He let his hands explore her body the way his tongue did her mouth. Slowly, with long languid sweeps. It felt as if they had all the time in the world. As if this moment would last forever.

He brought one hand to her backside and urged her to brush her pelvis against him. She did. The slow movement echoed their tongues. He felt a feathering of sensation down his back, surprised at how quickly she was getting to him. He hadn't felt this near to the edge from a little petting since he'd been a randy teenager.

She rubbed her breasts against his chest and he brought his hand from her back around to cup her and tease her nipple with his thumb. She gripped the back of his head, pressing her mouth passionately, fervently to his.

Her hips started to move more rapidly on him and he knew she was on the cusp of orgasm. He scraped his nail around her areola and felt the goose bumps spread, then suddenly she stilled.

She jerked her hips forward and he grabbed her butt as he lifted his hips and held her, his erection right against her center, until she groaned. He was sure she came as she collapsed against his chest, resting her head on his shoulder.

He hugged her in his arms, wanting more but happy for this moment just to hold her. To pretend that he'd captured his muse and that she'd never leave him. His senses were alive as he stroked her hair and whispered softly into her ear.

STACI FELT TOO LANGUID to move and yet she still wanted more. That orgasm had been nice but nothing would truly satisfy her until she felt his hard, hot length inside of her. His hand rested on the crown of her head, her back, then her waist. His fingers dipped beneath the waistband of her pajama pants.

She rubbed his chest, tracing the line of hair that tapered slowly down his midriff disappearing beneath the waistband of his jeans. She mirrored his movement, her fingers beneath his waistband and felt the tip of his erection.

"I'm guessing you liked that."

"Not as much as you did," he said with a wicked grin. "But yes, I definitely liked it."

She shifted around on his lap until she could undo his jeans. He shifted his hips and his cock was thrusting up at her. She wrapped her hand around him and began stroking from root to tip. He shivered and she tightened her grip.

He ran his hands over her torso and rekindled the fires that had been merely banked but not extinguished by her first orgasm. He cupped both of her breasts but she kept her grip in place, moving so that he could touch her the way she liked it.

She extended her shoulders back and watched as he leaned forward. She felt the warmth of his breath against her skin, then the sweep of his tongue. He circled her nipple once, twice, closed his mouth over her and suckled her deeply.

She stroked him slowly, then sped up until she felt his hips lift toward her in counterpoint to her hand. He groaned and his mouth left her breast. He held the back of her neck and brought her mouth to his this time his tongue thrusting so deeply into her that she thought they'd be joined together forever.

He tugged at the fabric of her pajama pants and she slipped them down her thighs and stepped free of them. Immediately, his hands were there on her hips, drawing her down against his cock. She didn't remove her hand except to enable the tip of his erection to enter her. Just the tip as she kept that tight grip on his shaft.

"Put me inside of you."

"You are," she said.

"All of me."

She accommodated him and he muttered a Cajun curse under his breath. She smiled to herself, reveling in both the feel of him and at her power over him. But then he lifted his head and teased her nipple in his mouth again, and she shuddered.

The time for playing the little game she'd been indulging in was over.

She leaned down and whispered dark, intimate words in his ear. Telling him how exquisite he felt and how much she loved what he was doing to her. A second later he filled her completely.

She rocked her pelvis forward trying to take him deeper but he was already as deep as he could go. His hands found her bare buttocks and he rocked her forward. God, she loved the feel of those big hands against her ass. He parted her cheeks and she felt one finger sliding along her furrow and she squirmed closer to him.

Every ounce of her being craved more of his touch. His mouth slid from hers, nibbling down her neck and tempting her without restraint. She shivered as she'd done before and felt everything in her reaching once again toward a climax. But she didn't want it to happen too soon. She wanted this to last as long as it could.

The roughness his stubbled jaw against her cheek tipped her closer to the edge. She dug her fingernails into his shoulders as she rocked her hips harder against his and when he called out her name, she melted. Her orgasm rushed over her as she continued thrusting forward.

His hips moved in sync with her, then she felt him stiffen and eventually relax. Over and over he whispered her name. She, in turn, couldn't stop pressing against him, as she nursed her second orgasm.

Softly panting, his breathing tingled over her sensitized nerves as she fell forward. He wrapped one arm around her shoulder and the other around her waist. She shivered now from the cold and he reached down to grab his shirt, which he draped over her.

She didn't want to move or to face him at this moment. She wanted to pretend that nothing had changed and she'd still be able to view him as just another competitor. And she almost had herself convinced about doing just that until he kissed her gently on the forehead.

That sweet gesture should have meant nothing, instead it made her heart beat faster and there was a hope that maybe this was more than mere lust. She didn't want it to be. Embracing her passion was one thing but falling in love with a competitor would be a disaster and a mistake.

One she wasn't willing to make. She shifted out of his arms and off his lap. She pulled her pajama pants on and tossed his shirt at him while she put hers back on.

"Um...I'm on the pill, not that you asked, but we should be covered."

He nodded as he fastened his jeans and stood up next to her. "I wasn't thinking about anything but you."

His words brought out goosebumps on her arms, but she steeled her heart against them. It was almost as if he knew the exact right words. To make her forget. To distract her. He was playing her.

And she'd have no one but herself to blame if she didn't heed this warning and walk away.

REMY WATCHED HER WALK away knowing that Staci thought this had been a mistake. He rubbed his hand over his face and didn't follow her into the house.

"Am I supposed to say I'm sorry?"

"No," she said, glancing over her shoulder at him. "I should know better."

"Better than what?" he asked. Regret came hard to him and he didn't want to apologize even though he knew he should. He'd taken her because he wanted to, and she wanted him to. And yes, he'd tasted something new and inspiring in her passion, but he'd also hurt her. Something he'd never wanted to happen.

"*You* kissed *me*," he pointed out softly.

"I know," she said. "I don't regret it. I'm mad at myself. I keep making the same mistakes."

"Like what?"

She shook her head. "I think you've seen me naked enough tonight."

She headed into the house and this time he could only watch her go. What had she meant by that? He would figure it out another time. Tonight he had his hands full figuring himself out. At the balcony railing, he pulled his shirt on. He'd always had a clear-cut path in front of him until last year when he'd overheard a restaurant critic saying that this latest generation of Cruzels were slackers.

That one comment had shaken his confidence and made it seem as if he'd taken everything for granted.

Now he was here and tonight he'd felt a little like his old self again but at what cost, he thought. His new confidence had been earned at the expense of Staci. She was battling her own demons, he knew that, but he still didn't like the way that feeling sat on his shoulders. He was in part to blame for what was going on with her.

And he truly didn't want that. More than anything he needed some advice. Despite the late hour, he went inside and came across Dan in the main living room.

"I thought I was the only one up at this time of night," Dan said.

Remy felt lucky that Dan hadn't come up earlier when he'd had Staci in his arms. He shouldn't have been surprised that he hadn't thought of getting caught when he'd had her. All he'd been able to think about was Staci.

"Seems a lot of us are having trouble sleeping tonight," Remy said.

"Yeah." Dan rubbed the back of his neck. "I was the last one to make it in today…I'm excited and nervous about tomorrow."

Remy nodded. That was exactly the way he felt. Each new phase was going to challenge a preconceived notion he had of himself in the kitchen. While he looked forward to finding out what he was made of another part of him worried that he'd made another mistake.

Sleeping with Staci had been a colossal one. He didn't want her to have the impression that he was the type of man who'd use someone to get what he wanted.

"You? The judges practically wept when they tasted your dish," Dan remarked.

"Not quite. Besides that was a team challenge. What will they think of a dish I make on my own?"

"Are you really nervous?" Dan asked.

"No. A little. To be honest, tonight at Chef Ramone's I made a dish that was probably one of the best I've ever prepared. Not sure I can keep up that standard. There are a lot of good chefs here."

Dan smiled. "I can't work as well as I thought I could under pressure. I mean in my own kitchen I can work a dinner service like a pro but going up against the clock and preparing something new…that kind of threw me off," he said.

Remy relaxed as he talked cooking with Dan. It was then that he realized that the guilt he felt at Staci's reaction earlier was easing, too. He hadn't been manipulating her. Twice now she'd initiated something sexual with him and twice he'd been blown away by his own reaction to her.

Remy studied the other chef. Dan was younger than him, probably in his mid twenties. "Don't think about it too much. When we get to the kitchens tomorrow just be cool and imagine you're preparing a meal for someone you love."

"Good idea. But what if the ingredients are weird."

"They probably will be. But it's your knife skills you should be thinking about."

"You heard about that?" Dan asked. "I never went to cooking school. Just learned from working in the kitchens."

"That's no big deal. Just understand your weaknesses. Everyone who goes up against you will be thinking they can butcher better than you can. If it were me, I'd be in the kitchen every second working on them."

"Can you show me how to cut a fish up?" Dan asked.

"Yes," Remy said. "Want to do it now? The fridge is stocked with everything."

"Okay," Dan agreed. "Uh, Remy, why are you willing to help me?"

"Because you're a good chef I'd hate to beat you on a technicality."

Dan laughed and followed Remy to the kitchen. Remy glanced up the stairs to where the bedrooms were and an image of Staci naked invaded his mind. He tried to conjure her curled up under her blankets. He knew she wasn't sleeping and he felt bad about that. She'd invigorated him tonight. He wanted to give her back something. But time would tell what that would be.

He spent the next hour showing Dan the proper way to debone a fish and how to cut it into steaks. The younger man was an attentive student and Remy knew he'd made the right decision to help him out. Two hours later he headed up to his bedroom, smelling of fish, and went straight to the shower. Staci's scent lingered on his skin, too, and he couldn't get the image of her in his arms out of his head.

It wasn't until the water ran cold that he groaned, turned off the shower and dried himself. Eventually, he drifted off to sleep only to be plagued by images of himself in his father's kitchen trying to prepare a dish that would please his father while a naked Staci kept stealing his attention. He woke up in a state of frustration. He hoped the day would bring another new revelation in the kitchen but his dreams had showed him what he already knew.

His doubts and fears were still firmly rooted inside of him and no matter what he discovered here about himself, until he figured out how to accept his own capabilities he'd never find peace.

The odd thing was that in his head his peace was now tied somehow with Staci. It was a mess. She was the last one who'd help him out after last night and to be honest he couldn't blame her. What had felt so right under the moonlight didn't seem very smart in the bright sunlight of morning.

5

STACI WANTED TO FALL right to sleep but she couldn't with all that was on her mind. She'd come here for a very specific reason and tonight it seemed clear that she was capable of letting herself be distracted. What was wrong with her?

Part of her knew it was because she'd never had a positive male role model. She didn't need her shrink to tell her that when she met powerful men she was always drawn to them. And it seemed the more power they had over her dreams and her future the more lethal her attraction was.

But Remy…he had no real power over her other than the attraction. She pulled her cell phone from her bag and texted Alysse. She knew the other woman would be awake and was probably in her kitchen baking because Alysse's fiancé Jay was on an assignment. The retired marine worked for a private security company. And while most of his jobs kept him in the Los Angeles area, he'd recently accepted an assignment in D.C. that had him away from home.

Staci: Can you talk?

Alysse: Yes. Give me a sec. Brownies going in the oven now.

Staci: Great. I won the first challenge and got to go to an amazing restaurant tonight.

Alysse: Cool. I don't think you are supposed to tell me all this.

Staci: Oh. You're right. There's a guy here who—

Alysse: Cute?

Staci: Yes though that's not the problem. He really bothered me in the kitchen tonight. I'm worried. What if I screw this up?

Alysse: Maybe he got to you because you just didn't expect it. See what happens tomorrow, you know?

Good advice, Staci thought.

Staci: I'm so unsure and that's not like me.

Alysse: Stop it. You're the most powerful, kick-ass girl I know. You need to get him out of your head and you into his head.

Staci smiled to herself. It was a little late at night for Alysse's crazy outlook on life but she knew her friend's logic was sound.

Staci: Thanks. Heard from Jay?

Alysse: Not since yesterday but he said I wouldn't. I hate that he might be in danger.

Staci: He's coming back to you. And you both know it.

Alysse: Yeah. You okay now?

Staci: Yes. Thanks. Enjoy your brownies.

Alysse: I'm thinking of eating them all. :)

Staci: I suspected as much. Night.

Staci put her phone down and rolled over. The coolness of the air-conditioning circulated through the room making her feel as if she were on vacation. She and her grandmother didn't have air conditioning in their old fashioned ranch house. It had been built in the 50s and her grandmother had come to it as a young bride. The kitchen was the only thing that had been updated religiously by the women in her family.

Her grandpa had been killed in Vietnam, her father... well, she'd never known him.

The Rowland women had a weird legacy of being left behind by their men. She scrubbed her hand over her eyes and rolled over again.

"Hey, what are you the princess and the pea," Vivian grumbled from her bed.

"Sorry," Staci muttered. She'd never had to share a room with anyone. And she'd liked it that way.

The only way she'd have a room to herself was to out-cook everyone else. She forced her mind to cooking and the dishes she'd eaten tonight. Food had been her ticket out before and it would be again. WP24 was heavily Asian influenced and the tastes were familiar to her having grown up here on the West Coast. It was silly but she dreamed of food and cooking the way some women dreamed of shoes and purses.

What, she wondered, did Remy dream about? Was he like her and couldn't sleep when something new had been introduced to his palate? And why did it matter? She rolled over and heard Vivian sigh.

"Put your headphones in," Staci whispered. "I'm a very restless sleeper."

The other woman grumbled as she took her iPhone headphones and put them in her ears. Staci grabbed her food diary as she thought of the night wind and the moonlight and the hot way that Remy had held her, touched her. She channeled that passion into food.

She heard the sea and tasted in her mind a new dish with seafood and spices but not from Mexico as she usually went to, but from China instead. There had been a wealth of new spices and tastes that had been brought to her tonight and now they were alive in her mind.

She wrote down ingredients, sketched in variations and maybes and then in her mind started to cook. She drifted to sleep with the pen in her hand and the notebook open on her lap. In her mind she was in the kitchen preparing her fresh ingredients. She smelled sesame oil heating up in a wok and glanced over to see Remy standing there waiting.

He'd chopped the garlic. "Let's cook together. I can help make this dish stronger."

She nodded and started telling him what to put in and he did exactly what she told him to do. They moved together in the kitchen, which, she noticed from the picture of her, her mom and her grandmother next to the stove, was her kitchen. He was talking and smiling in a way he hadn't when they'd cooked earlier and she started to resist the dream. This wasn't real.

She shoved him out of her kitchen and out of her mind waking up to find her flashlight and notebook on her lap. She didn't want or need Remy Stephens cooking with her. In real life or in her dreams, she needed instead to find her strength on her own. It was something she knew very well that she could do.

She closed the notebook and rolled over on her side to watch the shadows on the wall. She drifted in and out of sleep but it wasn't restful and in the morning when everyone started waking she was still tired.

She got dressed and hung out with the other women. Drinking coffee and talking about what they thought the challenge was going to be that day. She almost fooled herself into believing that she could handle Remy and that last night had meant nothing to her. However, when they piled into the cars to go to the studio, she ended up sitting right next to him and she knew she'd been lying to herself.

He smelled good. She hated that. She didn't want him to be one of those men who made her want to lean closer and breath more deeply.

"We have to talk about last night," he said quietly under his breath.

"Not now," she said. "We have to cook."

He nodded, but she knew he wasn't going to let it go for long.

"Hello everyone, I'm Fatima Langrene and I will be the host for the show. Each week we will start with a Quick Cook challenge," she said as they'd all been wired for sound and had their make-up done.

Fatima had mocha-colored skin and almond shaped eyes. He noted she also had a pretty smile and as she outlined the rules for this phase of the game, he knew he should pay better attention and did with one part of his mind.

But another part wanted to get some closure to what had happened with Staci. He needed to know that he hadn't hurt her. And that despite the timing, he wanted to see more of her.

"Our guest judge this week is Marcel Roubin, food critic from the *LA Times*. Mercedes is sponsoring this challenge so the winner will receive the keys to a brand-new M Class sedan. I'll let Marcel explain this challenge."

Marcel was skinny and wore all black clothing from the tips of his shining dress shoes to the color of his black dress shirt. His skin was pale in spite of the bright California sun.

"I knew it," Dan said under his breath, "He's a vampire."

Remy smiled.

"We all know you can cook with fresh ingredients and a well-stocked pantry but many in America are forced to create dishes for their family with only packaged and processed foods. Many families need new ideas to create something healthy and filling for their families from these ingredients," Marcel said, Taking the cover off a table that was laden with bags of frozen meats and vegetables.

"I mentioned Mercedes is sponsoring this Quick Cook challenge and they will be making a donation in the winner's name to the local food bank in your home town. You will have thirty minutes to create a main meal from these ingredients. Your time starts now."

Remy hadn't cooked with frozen ingredients ever but held hope there'd be some shrimp he could create a dish from. When he got to the table he saw that most of it was breaded or coated in seasoning already. He tried to think how to turn these mundane ingredients into a winning dish.

"My grandma used to make these fish sticks once a week," Staci said.

"Mine, too," Vivian added. "I don't know how I'm going to make them taste different but I'm starting there."

Staci smiled as she grabbed her choices and then, when she caught him staring at her, she winked. "Better get a move on, southern man. I'm planning to beat you today."

"Challenge accepted, cupcake girl," he said. He liked that they could still banter in the kitchen. That was how it should be. The personal stuff would have to wait for now. He grabbed some frozen shrimp and scallops, as well as a bag of frozen ravioli and went back to his station. The pantry was open but the shelves almost bare, except for dried herbs, butter, milk, and eggs. There were no fresh veggies so his idea for a Florentine pasta dish started to fade until he remembered there was frozen spinach. He grabbed what he needed and then ran back to pick up the spinach.

Ten minutes had already gone by and he hadn't even started removing the breading from the frozen seafood. He saw the other chefs around him similarly struggling, but a few of them were already cooking. Including Staci. He thought of her background, how she'd talked about cooking with her grandmother and realized that the key to this challenge was in something he'd never experienced before. He'd cooked from fresh and local ingredients because they were the best sources for good food. Staci had done that because they'd been the quickest and likely the cheapest.

He threw away everything he'd learned in the kitchen and carefully considered the ingredients before him. He needed to make something simple, healthy, yet tasty. A Florentine dish was still his goal but he needed to streamline it. He changed his main plan and discarded the fish, opting for a single dish lasagna instead. He heated up the prepared tomato sauce, which tasted too bland so he went back to the pantry to get more spices until the seasoning tasted as he wanted it. He layered the heated sauce into the pan with the ravioli and the spinach and then crumbled some cheese on top and put it under the broiler to heat through and brown.

He pulled the dish out with two minutes left on the clock. He sampled it and realized the dried spices and processed cheese had yielded something that was very tasty. He had never felt so free in the kitchen. This wasn't something his grandfather, father or uncles had ever done and as the timer sounded and he glanced at the other stations he felt a certain confidence in both himself and in his dish.

Marcel and Fatima started three stations down from him and he glanced around the room, noting some interesting takes on the frozen food challenge. The sense of pride he felt didn't wane. He knew his skills and the dish he'd put together met the challenge requirements.

Marcel didn't like the dish that Max, who was at the station next to him, had prepared. "This shows little imagination. It's like you dumped the package on a cooking tray and prepared them per the instructions. I expected better from you."

"Everything is well cooked and I really liked the spices you added to the potatoes," Fatima said.

Now they were at Remy's station, staring at his dish. "What have you prepared?"

"A Florentine style lasagna, using prepared tomato sauce and ravioli."

Marcel didn't look like he was expecting much and Fatima just smiled at him. Remy realized that this was his first big cooking challenge all on his own. The world wouldn't end if he screwed this up, but then he'd never be more than the sum of his family. He'd never—

"Delicious," Fatima said. "What did you add to the sauce?"

"Spices and garlic," he said.

"It really is good," Marcel agreed. "I see you have seafood on your station why didn't you use it?"

"I was going to take the breading off and then I thought if I've worked all day and have hungry kids to feed, the last thing I'm going to want to do is take the bread off of some frozen shrimp. I want to feed the kids quickly and nutritiously. I would have wanted fresh spinach, but the frozen does still offer lots of nutrients," Remy said.

"Yes, it does." Marcel nodded.

The chef and host moved on to the next station and Remy caught Staci looking at him. He winked at her and she frowned at him. When the judges had tried all the dishes Remy, Staci and Conner had the top three meals.

"Our top three produced some really good and healthy dishes and all three will be presenting them at an LA Food Fair later this week. But today's winner is Staci."

Everyone clapped and Remy felt a pang of resentment that he hadn't won, but the smile on Staci's face made up for it. He wasn't happy to lose but he did like seeing her happy. Next time though he wanted her to have to be satisfied with second.

THEY TOOK A BREAK FROM filming after her win was announced. And the studio was cleared. Staci wanted to share her news with someone. Though as Alysse had reminded her last night, she wasn't supposed to share any details from the contest. All of the episodes were being taped to air once the entire competition was over.

"Another winning dish. Looks like you might be the chef to watch," Quinn said coming up to her. Quinn had been at the station next to her during the Quick Cook challenge and had made a faux risotto from boil in a bag rice. It had sounded pretty good but there hadn't been enough time to cook the rice and it had stuck together.

"I think each new challenge is going to up the stakes. So far they've been up my alley."

"Lucky," he said. "I wonder what the elimination challenge will be this week."

"From watching the show I thought they'd have told us already but I guess not," she said. She noticed Remy standing at the back of the room talking to Marcel. She'd heard—well everyone had—how much Marcel had enjoyed his dish and Staci was surprised that she'd beaten him.

"What's his story?" Quinn asked, gesturing toward Remy.

"Out of work New Orleans chef. I wonder if it's an effect of Katrina. I know that was years ago but I've heard from friends there that the city still hasn't recovered."

"Who knows? He's good," Quinn said.

Staci was getting a little annoyed at the way Quinn was talking about everyone else's skills and not his own. "Everyone's good or they wouldn't be here. You earned a spot just like everyone else. Shake off what just happened and focus on what you'll be doing next."

He gave her a half smile. "Sorry. I didn't sleep well last night. I don't like having to share a room."

"I don't either," Vivian said, joining their group. "The Princess and The Pea over here tossed and turned all night. But it didn't seem to affect your cooking."

"I don't need a lot of sleep," Staci said. "I've always been able to function on five hours."

Remy was lingering at the edge of the group. She tried to ignore him, wanted to show him he meant nothing more to her than any of the other chefs in the competition, but her heart beat a little faster and she found herself staring at him when she thought he wasn't looking.

"What's everyone's thoughts on the elimination challenge?" Remy asked.

"Well, I'm guessing an offsite test," Vivian said. "I

saw that they were bringing the cars around front for us. Plus they always start with that on the show."

"Do they?" Staci asked. "I've only watched a few episodes."

"Not me. I've been addicted to the show from the beginning. Love everything about it." Vivian smiled.

"Maybe we just have to go shop for our ingredients," Quinn suggested.

"I was hoping for a mystery basket," Staci said. She had done well with the first blind challenge after all.

"Doubt it after the Quick Cook," Vivian said.

"I don't care what it is as long as we start soon," Quinn said. "The waiting is hell."

The rest of the chefs continued talking and Remy took her arm and drew her away from the group. "Congratulations on your win."

"Thank you," she said. "I wasn't sure I could beat you. You had Marcel eating out of your hand."

"I was surprised. Critics don't usually go for easy comfort foods."

"No they don't but that was the spirit of the challenge," she said.

"Your mac and cheese looked good," he said.

"Thanks. Family recipe," she said with a quick grin.

"I gathered as much. Listen, Staci, I want to learn more about you. I like—"

"For the contest?" she asked.

He shook his head. "For me. I...I like you."

She backed away from him. "Not now. I said I don't want to talk about anything personal while we're here.

I need to stay focused on what I'm doing. Last night proved it to me. And I'm here to cook."

She wondered what he was hoping to find in her expression and then if he found it because he seemed to nod and take a step away. "All right, but when we get back to the house I want you to go for a walk on the beach with me."

She didn't want to commit to doing anything with him. She wanted to put distance between them but then remembered her dream last night. Remy was tied to her cooking now and she knew it. That passion he'd kindled in her last night was the fire that drove her whether she wanted to admit it or not.

"Fine. Let's get back to the others," she said.

They soon found out that Vivian was right. It was an Off-Site Challenge and they were headed to the UCLA college campus to serve lunch for the hungry students. They'd have to shop for their ingredients and then prepare them in two hours.

Staci tried to think of what she could make that would please the college students and the judges. But her mind was blank. She was thinking about Remy again and she had to wonder if that was his strategy. He'd certainly done a good job of distracting her. Ugh, she thought. She had to stay away from him. From now on when he walked over to her, she'd walk away.

They were driven to Whole Foods and everyone was shouting and running around like crazy people trying to find what they would need to create their dishes. Staci felt lost and she knew that after her win she was the one to watch so she took a second and pushed her trolley away from the crowds. She closed her eyes and thought about her grandmother, Alysse and all her friends back home in San Diego. She concentrated on them, but it wasn't calming her down.

"You okay, *chère*?" Remy asked coming up behind her with his buggy.

Suddenly she had an idea of what to cook and a new fire in her belly. She wasn't going to collapse in on herself. She was determined to win and to beat Remy again. She wanted him to see her, to know she was a good chef and she needed him to know that she was strong in the kitchen and out of it.

She gave him her sexiest grin. "I am now."

"Good. I'd hate to beat you if you aren't on your A game," he said.

"Ah, Southern Man, you're going to have a hard time beating me," she said. "That's a promise."

"Sounds more like a challenge," he said. "One I'm happy to accept. Whoever does better this afternoon—the loser has to cook dinner for them."

"Deal," she said. "I'm ready for you to have to cook for me."

"Pride goes before the fall," he said, pushing his trolley away.

And she just laughed as the dish finally coalesced in her mind. She didn't want to assign too much importance to Remy and instead decided that like a secret spice he was the key to her cooking. She realized that wanting to beat him and prove herself worthy in his eyes made the competition personal and that was what she needed.

6

SHE WON AGAIN AND AS SHE sat in the Escalade for the return trip to the Malibu house she was in a sort of stunned shock. While Staci knew she was capable of cooking, the win was confirmation that she had a real talent like her grandmother used to say. It was bittersweet though because she realized what she'd thrown away for "love".

"Congrats," Vivian offered. "I thought I had you at the last minute there when that pork you took off the grill was a little pink."

"Same here. I mean Austin barbecue is hard to beat. Everything was just flowing for me today," she said.

"I could tell. I tasted your dish and as much as it pains me to admit this, it was delicious."

"Thanks, Viv. Yours was good too," Staci said.

"I'm surprised Dave was in the top three," Vivian said. "Someone sure helped him with his butchering skills or he was sand-bagging last night…do you think he's clever enough to do that?"

Staci didn't know. She shrugged and pulled out her food journal to make a few notes about the dish she'd prepared. Because of the nature of the show she hadn't had time to make notes as she was cooking. With only an hour to cook there just wasn't time to analyze as she went along. One thing she had observed was that Remy had fallen back on another New Orleans taste that had cost him points in the final round according to the judges. She'd made an Italian flavored dish, which was very different from the food she'd been putting up before.

Beating Remy felt good of course because he challenged her and she wanted him to notice her and see her as the one to beat. But he'd looked angry and upset with himself after they'd announced she was the winner. That was something she didn't want for him.

Losing was hard. She'd certainly done it enough times when she and Alysse had been competing against each other in bake-offs. Staci would never have thought so at the time but that rivalry with Alysse had helped prepare her for this moment.

"I can't believe Quinn is in the bottom three. That was a shock," Vivian said. "Last night he put up a great dish."

"It's different cooking against the clock," Staci said still making notes in her journal. She didn't want to talk about the other chefs. Really the only one she was interested in had a slow southern drawl. She felt like maybe he hadn't been at his best today.

Had last night thrown him more than he wanted to admit?

She hoped so. She didn't want to think she was the only one who was making bad decisions and suffering for them. Yet at the same time she really hoped he wasn't affected by her. She wanted—no needed Remy to be a carefree kind of relationship. That would make it easier when they went their separate ways. To write off their encounter as just lust.

She turned to stare out the window and focused on the fact that all that training in Paris had been worth it. She'd have never guessed she could win a Mercedes by cooking, granted she'd achieved a lot in baking and even started her own business, but these were skills she'd avoided using since she'd left Chef Renard's kitchen all those years ago. Skills she'd associated with her poor decisions and resulting heartache. It was gratifying to know that sex with Remy didn't really feel like a mistake.

Even though she had absolutely no plans to do it again, she didn't regret it. Hell, she thought, glancing back down at her food journal, if sleeping with Remy raised her cooking to this level she might have to figure out how to sleep with him and not let her emotions get involved.

They got back to the house and all piled out of the Escalades. Staci tried not to watch for Remy but she couldn't help it. A part of her wondered if he still wanted to meet up with her this afternoon. But she knew he would. If she'd learned one thing about Remy in the short time since she'd met him it was that he never said anything he didn't mean.

"I guess you've got the judges where you want them," Quinn said. "Hard to believe a little cupcake baker is beating all of us."

"I'm—"

"She's a skilled chef, Quinn. You can talk trash all you want but it's the dishes that we are all being judged on," Remy said in that quiet southern way of his. "She wouldn't have won if she hadn't deserved it."

"Whatever," he said, storming away from them.

Vivian lifted both eyebrows at her as if to ask *why's he defending you*? Staci just shrugged. She really didn't have a clue why he had, but there was a part of her that really liked what he'd done.

"Thanks," she said, as they climbed the steps into the house.

"Remy's right," Dave said.

"You did well today," Staci remarked to the other man.

"I just relaxed like Remy suggested. Stopped hearing the ticking of the clock in my head and I could think about the food," Dave said.

"Look at you, Remy, giving advice and defending chefs…."

Remy didn't say anything but entered the house and walked to the open-concept living room and specifically the bar. "I don't see the point in winning something if everyone's not playing up to par."

"I agree," Vivian said as she joined Remy pouring herself a gin and tonic. "What about you, Stac? What does our winner want to drink?"

"Diet Coke," she answered.

"And rum?" Vivian asked with a grin.

"No," she said. She still had to face a talk with Remy about last night and she would need all her wits about her. Everyone broke into groups as they discussed what they would make for dinner. It had a bit of a summer camp feel to it.

Because of her win everyone wanted to be around her and the afternoon passed in a blur as she chatted with all the chefs. Finally, most of the contestants went off to their own space while a few others left to walk on the beach or go surfing. Remy came over to her where she was sitting on a deck chair.

"Ready for that talk?" he asked.

No, she thought. At this moment she was at peace. The chaos in her mind was calm and she was enjoying the fact that she'd done the kind of cooking her grandmother would have been proud of her for doing. But she knew she had to deal with Remy and last night.

"I guess so."

"I'm not planning on torturing you," he said with a wry grin.

"I know. It's just at this moment...never mind. I'll sound silly if I say it." She got to her feet and started to lead the way down to the shoreline.

"There's nothing silly about you, Staci. I underestimated you, that's probably due to your size."

"Everyone always does. But as Shakespeare once said... Though she be but little she is fierce."

"He had it right. It's always funny to me how much of 17th century wisdom applies to life today."

"Do you know much Shakespeare?" she asked.

"I do. My mother is a high school English teacher and my father said that women like to hear a man read sonnets to them."

"And you believed him?" she asked.

"Well, he had at this point proven himself right about a few other things. I have never let him know that fact though. He has a big ego."

She laughed at the way he said it. She could tell from his words that he and his parents had a close relationship. She shouldn't be surprised, he had the persona of someone who had it all. A man who was very used to getting what he wanted. So what exactly did he want from her.

"Do you remember any sonnets?" she asked him as they reached the beach and started walking along the water's edge.

"Not any more," he said. "But I didn't want to quote Shakespeare for you. I wanted to discuss last night."

Of course he did. "What about it?"

"DO YOU WANT IT TO HAPPEN again?" he asked.

She stopped abruptly and turned to look up at him. "We aren't here for sex."

"No we're not, but there is something between us," he said.

She nodded. "I know you said that kissing me made you cook better in Chef Ramone's kitchen…"

"What are you trying to ask me? If I want to sleep with you again to cook better?" he asked, insulted that she'd think so little of him as a man. But then he realized that she didn't know the real him.

She bit her lower lip and then took an aggressive step toward him. "That's exactly what I want to know."

Remy saw bravado in her expression and knew despite the way she was playing it nonchalant that last night had meant more to her than a casual hook-up. The last thing he'd intended was to get involved with any woman during this competition. He was making a life-changing decision during his time in California and he needed to stay focused on that.

But he also knew that life had a way of nudging him in the direction he needed to go in and he wasn't sure exactly why he was so turned on by Staci Rowland, he only knew there was no denying it.

"I don't need sex to cook well," he said to her. "I've been cooking my entire life, but I've yet to find a woman who knocks me out of my comfort zone in the kitchen the way you did today."

"Really?" she asked, taking a step back and seeming to not notice the surf, which curled around her ankles and soaked the bottoms of her jeans. "I'm sorry."

"Don't be," he said, reaching for her hand and taking it in his, he started walking again afraid to say too much more. But he'd already revealed more than he should have given they were competitors. Yet lying about the attraction he felt for her wouldn't have sat well with him. "I just wanted you to know I'm not toying with you."

She took a deep breath. "I'm glad. I have to admit I was a little afraid that might be part of your strategy. Though to be honest it seemed to backfire on you today. What happened when you were cooking?"

"I don't know," he admitted. "I just fell back on my familiar tastes and dishes."

"And the judges didn't want that. I think they want us to grow…you know you owe me a dish. You have to cook for me."

"I know. What do you want me to make for you?" he asked.

"I don't know. Something that will make me forget everything I know about you. Make me a dish that will force me to see you in a different light," she said. "Like the tidbit about Shakespeare did."

"You liked that, didn't you?"

"Yes," she admitted. "You have a very nice voice I wouldn't mind hearing you recite a few sonnets for me."

"Maybe our next bet will involve that," he said.

She shook her head. "You don't want to hear me stumble over old English."

"Maybe I'll have you read something a little racier to me. I think there'd be nothing sexier than listening to you talk about your fantasies."

She flushed and shook her head. The wind stirred the short hair of her bangs. "I'm not...that is to say I don't—"

He laughed as he realized that the unflusterable Staci Rowland was uncomfortable talking about sex. She was flirty as hell and took what she wanted when they were intimate but there was a part of her that was shy when it came to the words.

"I can't believe you don't have fantasies," he said.

"Of course I do," she said. "Everyone does, but that doesn't mean I want to talk about them."

"I do."

"I'm not surprised. Despite what your father told you about sonnets you are still a man. Why is it men like to hear women talk like that?" she asked.

"It's sexy," he said. "And it's not every woman's fantasies I'm interested in."

She turned away again to glance out at the sea. He wondered, despite the fact that they were together here for six weeks, whether he'd ever really get to know all of her secrets. The core of Staci was very private. Would he be able to find out more about her through her cooking and her dishes? He doubted it. It felt to him like she was hiding herself away not only from him but from the world. She let him see what she thought he wanted to see.

The shyness with talking about sex was probably one of the first real things he'd been able to find out about her. She was all boldness and nerve but underneath there was a vulnerable woman.

He was being honest when he said that he wanted her and it had nothing to do with the competition but he saw now that that very fact made their relationship complicated. Did she even want to give him a chance?

"How do you feel about getting to know each other during the competition?" he asked. "I'm not trying to manipulate you."

She turned back to him her gray eyes as stormy as the Gulf of Mexico when a hurricane was blowing. "I don't know. I want to say no. I'm here to prove something to myself and to win. And I know it's the same for you."

"That's right. We both are cooking for our futures," he said. "I think everyone here is."

He noticed that she hadn't answered his question. Not really. He had the feeling that if he let her she'd never answer it. "I'm not going to ignore us, cupcake girl. I want you, but more than that I want to get to know you."

"I get it, but I'm not sure what to say. It doesn't matter if I say no and ask you to leave me alone. You're already under my skin. Dammit, I shouldn't have said that."

He laughed and tugged her off balance and into his arms, leaning down he kissed her with all the pent-up frustration he'd been feeling all day. When he lifted his head and stepped back her lips were swollen and her eyes half-closed. He wanted to carry her someplace private and make love to her. But he knew the next time he and Staci made love it would change things between them and there would be no going back.

"There's something between us," he said.

"I know. I wish it was just cooking," she admitted. "I have always had bad taste in men."

"Maybe your taste is changing," he said reluctant to let her lump him in with the other men who'd come before him.

I hope so, she thought. "I've been hurt in the past and I don't want to make the same mistake again, but then I always was a slow learner."

"What mistake?"

She shook her head. "That's not a story I'm willing to tell you."

"Just give me the Twitter version."

"A hundred and forty characters?" she asked, but she smiled at him.

"Yup."

"Thought that fairytales could come true and believed every word he said at hash tag shouldhaveknownbetter."

"What kind of fairytale?" Remy asked.

"That there is one guy out there for me. One man who could make me complete and give me my happily-ever-after. But that's not realistic. I can't ignore the truth about the Rowland women.

"What truth is that?"

"We live alone," she said.

"What about your dad?"

"Never knew him or my granddad. None of the women in my family ever knew their fathers...do you know what that means, Remy?"

"I'm not that type of man."

"Are you making me promises?" she asked.

She wouldn't believe him if he did. Promises after all were just words and Staci needed, no, deserved action.

"No."

STACI WAS A LITTLE SURPRISED that he'd been so honest with her. A part of her had to respect his honesty. But the little girl inside of her who still wanted to believe in fairytales was disappointed that he hadn't stepped up. "I guess that's that."

"It is," he said. "I won't waste your time making you promises when you probably wouldn't believe them anyway. I'll just have to convince you that I'm not like the other men who've passed through your life."

She held her breath and her heart skipped a beat. Was he serious? Or was this just a ploy to make her believe...

he'd have to be cruel to say that type of thing…to get her hopes up only to plan to dash them later.

"Okay, prove it."

"I can't do it right now, can I?"

"No," she said. Thinking he probably never would. She wasn't going to pin any hopes on Remy. He was here for his own reasons, as was she. There was no point complicating things any further.

"We should be heading back."

"Not yet. I want you to show me around LA."

"Um, why?"

"We have the afternoon free and if I'm preparing a meal for you, I need to know more about you."

"Ha," she said. "How is walking around a city with me going to help?"

"I was thinking we'd go to the LA farmer's market."

"The good produce will already be gone. Besides it's more of a shopping center with permanent merchants."

"Then show me something that says LA to you," he said.

"I'm farther south," she said. "Los Angeles isn't really my town."

"I don't think the producers will let us drive to San Diego," he said with that half-grin of his that made her breath catch.

There was no denying he was a very attractive man. Even standing on the shore with the breeze ruffling his thick, black, curly hair just made him sexier. His eyes were shadowed by the sun. His T-shirt complemented his broad chest. His faded jeans hugged his legs and when he turned she let her gaze linger on his butt. She wanted to reach out and touch him but didn't. She had to keep control of herself. Until he proved to her that he wouldn't love her and leave her.

"Well?"

"Well, what?" she asked. Distracted by his body. She wished she'd gotten to see more of him last night.

"Where can we go that says LA to you?" he asked. "What are you thinking about?"

"Nothing," she said. Johnnie's in Culver City jumped to mind. It wasn't that far from where they were and the sandwiches were…well not really LA more New York Jewish Deli. The kind of thing that could transport the diner to another place. It was perfect to demonstrate what she'd said to him earlier.

"I've got an idea. I'll talk to Jack and see if we can get a car."

"Very well. I think we'll probably have to take others with us," he said. "I can't see the producers allowing just the two of us to go off on our own."

"I agree. That's okay, Remy. You'll figure out how to woo me even with others around."

"That's right," he said.

They walked back to the house and she was happy to finally be in the midst of the other competitors. There was a tension in the house probably because those in the bottom three would be cooking tomorrow to stay in the competition. She was glad that the only thing she had to think about tonight was Remy and not going home after the first week of competition.

She found Jack and asked him if they could make a trip to Johnnie's. Twenty minutes later he confirmed they could and seven of them headed to the Escalades. She was surprised that Quinn came with them. Thinking he'd want to stay behind and work on his knife skills like Christian and Frances who were also in the bottom three.

She was squeezed in the back seat between Remy and Quinn. She tried not to notice that she still loved the scent of Remy's aftershave. "Have either of you been to Johnnie's before?"

"Not me," Remy said. "This is my first time in Los Angeles."

"I've been here before but I tend to frequent the high-end restaurants," Quinn said. "I'm not surprised you like a walk-up diner."

"What's your problem with me?" she asked Quinn.

He shrugged. "I just don't see how someone with your tastes could beat me in the kitchen."

"My tastes? Quinn food isn't for the epicureans out there all the time. Today's challenge was to cook for college students. Do you really not get where you went wrong? It doesn't matter how obscure your ingredients are if the customer doesn't like it…that's cooking 101."

"She's got a point," Remy said. "I tried to introduce a new dish at my last restaurant and the clientele revolted. They wanted the dishes they'd come there expecting."

Quinn nodded. "I guess I wasn't seeing the big picture."

Staci smiled.

"I said I was wrong," he admitted.

"I don't want you to be wrong, just to stop blaming me because you didn't win."

He didn't say anything else on the drive and when they pulled up to the roadside diner on Sepulveda and everyone piled out of the vehicles, Remy took her hand and stopped her.

"What?"

"I just wanted us to be together when we go up there. What is it about this place that speaks to you?"

"The tradition of it," she said. "And it reminds me of a trip I took with my mom and grandmother to New York City. We ate in a diner there…it was a good trip. The only real vacation I had with my mom since she was working all the time. When I take a bite of the pastrami sandwich here I remember that day and her laughter."

Staci feared she'd said too much but Remy just nodded. "For me it's beignets at Café du Monde. My dad and I used to walk down there every Sunday morning and I'd sit while he read the paper. It was just the two of us…"

"Food should do that every time," Staci said. "I can't always capture it but that's why the traditional recipes are important. Finding that familiar flavor and taking it some place new."

"Yes," he said.

But Staci could tell that he was lost in his own thoughts. She wondered if she'd given away too much by bringing him here but then she had learned over the years that most people only saw what they wanted to in her and in themselves. Remy wouldn't realize how important food was to her and her past or that it was the key to all her secrets. He'd have to have been listening to what she hadn't said to figure that out. And he was after all just a man.

7

REMY KEPT HIS DISTANCE from Staci as they both returned to the house. He did some shopping in the pantry and started cooking. The contest seemed a little more real to everyone when faced with the fact that tomorrow one of them would be leaving.

That knowledge that any one of them could leave in a moment made Remy determined to make the most of his time with Staci. So he cooked for her remembering what she'd said about her mother and New York City. While he'd never been to Los Angeles before, New York and he went way back. One of his uncles owned an exclusive cooking school there and Remy had spent three weeks every summer in the meatpacking district honing his chef skills.

There were others with him working in the kitchen now but none of the jovial talking of the night before. The competition had gotten serious today. Christian, one of the chefs in the bottom three, was tirelessly going over the same sauce he'd made earlier in the day. The sauce that had netted him horrible reviews.

Christian had a carefully trimmed beard and dark brown eyes that seemed to view the world wearily. He was tall but not as tall as Remy's six-foot-three frame and a little bit stocky. He moved almost awkwardly when he wasn't at his station. But once he had a knife in his hands his skills came to the fore.

"Have you figured it out yet?" Remy asked, when he noticed the chef had stopped scribbling in his notebook.

"Just about. I have no idea what they are going to throw at me tomorrow but sauces have long been my weak point. I can muster a buerre blanc but that's about it. I should have known better than to try one today."

"You did what you had to in order to win."

"Did I?"

"Yes, you have to push yourself. That's what I realized today. I can't just do what I've always done," Remy said. It was nothing less than the truth and he wished he'd figured that out earlier. More than likely that was part of the reason for his reluctance to take over as Chef Patron of Gastrophile. He had tried to introduce new dishes but today he'd realized he'd done that in the wrong way. There was a way to put his stamp on the restaurant without eviscerating what had gone before. And that was the key.

"True enough. I'm in the same boat. Cooking was always easy for me when nothing else was. This is the first time I've flat-out failed. I don't like it."

Remy laughed. "I don't either. I'm too used to winning."

Christian smiled over at him. "I'd take third over bottom three."

"I bet you would. Next time we'll both be in the top three."

"Next time, I'll be number one," Christian said. "I'll leave you to your cooking."

Remy finished his dish and then put everything in plastic containers and packed it in a cooler he found in the pantry. He left it sitting on the counter and went to find Staci. She was sitting on the edge of her bed with her notebook open reading over her notes. He stood there for a long minute just staring at her. Though it had only been a few days his impression of her had changed radically from that first moment they'd met and she'd spilled tea all over the both of them.

Yet one thing hadn't changed. He still wanted her and would continue to want her he suspected no matter how many times he had her. There was something almost elusive about the woman. Something that he just couldn't shake no matter how many times he tried.

He noticed the way her jet black hair was tucked behind her small ear and the long curve of her neck. The t-shirt she wore hugged her breasts and then her tiny waist. Her legs were curled under her in a position that he doubted he'd be able to make if he tried for hours.

"Like what you see?" she asked, a hint of humor in her voice.

"You know I do, *chère*," he said, taking his time and letting his gaze slide back up her body. She shifted on the bed, uncurling those shapely legs and standing up.

"Your dinner is ready," he said, bowing slightly.

"Great. I'm interested to see what our field trip this afternoon has inspired in you."

It wasn't the food that was inspiring him and he knew that now. If he'd had this new knowledge and his wits about him during the UCLA challenge he wagered he'd have won today. But he hadn't. He could only use it to make sure he kept himself in the top three and moving forward with each week of competition.

"I hope you will be surprised," he said.

"I'm sure I will be. It's rare that I've had a man cook for me," she said, following him down the hall to the kitchen.

Given the little he knew of her personal history that wasn't a real surprise. "The men you've known haven't been chefs."

"One of them was," she said almost beneath her breath.

He lifted the cooler and led the way through the open living room to the back patio. "We can eat here…or down on the beach where we will have more privacy."

"I vote for the beach," she said. "I don't want everyone to know that we are dining together."

"Why not?"

"People will talk," she said. "It doesn't matter that there are no rules against fraternizing, I know how unkind gossip can be. I think we'd both fare better if we keep this private."

He nodded. He thought so, too. Besides he didn't want to share Staci with anyone else. There was something intense about his attraction to her. He wanted to know more about her and it occurred to him as they walked down the beach to find the perfect spot for their picnic away from the other beach goers that he had created a dinner tonight to seduce her. He should have guessed.

Food was one of the most sensual experiences for him. He spread out the blanket he'd taken from the linen closet and watched as Staci sat down in the center of it. He set the cooler next to her before sitting down.

He opened the cooler to take out the bottle of wine that he'd wrapped in a chilled towel and had positioned on the cool side of the cooler. He deftly opened it and then took out the two stemmed glasses and poured them each a glass.

Staci took one from him. "I'll say this for you, you picked the perfect place for dinner. Light breeze, setting sun…I'm almost seduced just sitting here."

"Almost is the key word, by the time this meal is over you will be totally seduced."

"I'm not too sure about that, but I like your confidence."

"I like yours as well," he said. If there was one quality that always shone through in Staci it was her belief in herself. He admired her for it. He knew she'd worked hard for that, unlike himself, who'd had it assumed of him that he'd be good just because of his DNA.

"A toast to confidence and ego and hoping there's room enough in the kitchen for both of ours."

He smiled and lifted his glass toward hers. "To confidence."

He noticed that she kept eye contact when she took her first sip of the wine. It was something that his father said only people with great gumption did. The wine was dry and cold just the way he liked it.

"Ready to be impressed."

"Always," she said.

He pulled out the dishes he'd packed and the containers. "While I'm getting our dinner ready why don't you tell me something about the other chef you mentioned."

Her hand shook as she was taking a sip of her wine and a drop of it spilled onto her lip. She stared over at him and he wondered what he'd said that upset her. "I assume it was just another man who didn't cherish you."

The last thing that Staci wanted to talk about was the past but today Jean-Luc Renard seemed to be everywhere. But she knew she had to at least say something. Remy had gone to more effort with this meal side-bet they'd had than she'd expected.

Her hand trembled again. Was she seriously thinking they might be a couple? She thought of how she handled her relationship with Alysse and they had a business contract as a safety net to ensure that Alysse lived up to her side of the bargain. Though now that she knew Alysse she understood the other woman would never leave her hanging.

But she hadn't known that at first. And weary of being hurt again she'd done everything she could to protect herself. She'd come away from Sweet Dreams Bakery with the belief that she could trust women but not men. Now she was looking at Remy and wondering if she could trust him.

She wanted to.

"Are you going to take the plate or simply keep staring at it?" he asked, his voice quiet as if he sensed she was dwelling on deep thoughts.

She wanted to scream at frustration with herself. Any other woman would just enjoy the night and the romance of it but she was weighing his every move against her tender heart and trying carefully to get to know him while protecting herself. It was harder than it should be because she felt as if she could believe him.

She wanted Remy Stephens to be just what he appeared to be—an out-of-work chef who could cook like nobody's business and charm her socks off.

"Yes, I'm going to take it. The food smells delicious," she said.

"I hoped you'd like it. Why don't you save your story of past loves for another night?" he suggested. "I don't want you thinking about another man while savoring my dishes."

She nodded. She didn't want to think about Jean-Luc either. And one thing that made it easier to ignore her past lover was the fact that three-star Michelin chef that he was, he'd never cooked for her. That should have been her first clue that what they had wasn't real…

"What have you prepared?"

"New York City," he answered with that rogue's grin of his. "You said your happiest memories were associated with your mother and that city."

"You know New York?" she asked. "How does someone from New Orleans become familiar with a big city like that?"

"I do get out of the bayou occasionally," he said wryly.

"I didn't mean it like that. Sorry, it's just you seem very rooted in the South," she explained. "It's a surprise that's all."

"Well taste it and tell me if it's a good surprise or not," he said.

She shook off the mantle of the past and instead concentrated on the now. Remy hadn't proven himself to be anything other than a white-hot lover, first-class chef and a really nice guy who liked her. She set her wine glass down on the tabletop Remy had made with the cooler lid and took the heavy silver fork he'd passed to her.

Carefully she arranged a bite of the meat, which was breaded and had a sauce on it, the creamy risotto and lifted it to her mouth. It smelled incredible and her mouth was already watering. When she opened her lips she noticed that Remy stared at her mouth. She let her tongue dart out to taste the food before taking the first bite.

His eyes narrowed and suddenly she was lost in the food as the feeling of New York City was on her palate. The food had that warm comfort that Staci had always gotten from her mother, but also the edge that she'd felt when in New York. She closed her eyes and forgot about everything and admitted that if he cooked like this next week then she and the other contestants were out of the running.

"It's good," she said at last, well aware that her words were faint-praise for the dish she'd just sampled.

He nodded. "Thanks. I won't let all the effusive praise go to my head."

"Like you need me to tell you that you're good," she said. "The dish is New York, but my experience there. How did you do that?"

He leaned over and touched the side of her face. As if she could ever not pay attention to Remy Stephens.

"I listened to you," he said. "Everything that you said this afternoon about food memory made me realize I was missing a powerful spice in my chef's kit. And it was the personal experience."

"Memo to self—stop giving Remy advice if you want to win this competition," she said with a rue grin.

He laughed as she'd hoped he would but it didn't lessen the tension inside of her. Somehow she knew it was the mere mention of her lover in Paris that cast a damper over her spirits. She'd thought that almost six years would be long enough to dull not only his memory but his hold over her but she was realizing it wasn't.

She guessed there were some wounds that cut too deep. But she also knew that there were so many elements in this very situation with Remy that were similar to how she'd fallen for Jean-Luc. The food, the passion for cooking...that very Gallic outlook on life that they both shared.

"I think you'll do just fine. You have some of the best cooking instincts I've ever seen. My grandfather would have loved to have you apprentice in his kitchen."

"Who is your grandfather?"

Remy bit his lip and looked away from her and down at his plate for a minute. "No one really, just an old chef who said to me that cooking comes from the soul but until I heard you talk about it I never got what he meant."

"So you're saying I remind you of your grandpa?" she asked.

"Not in the slightest. But you do have the same gut instincts he does. I think he'd be very impressed by you," Remy said.

"Are you impressed?" she asked. She wanted to groan after she said it but she also really wanted him to like her. To see all of her talents and none of her flaws. Dammit, she thought. She was already starting to hope that he could be the man she saw tonight. A man who had the same goals, the same soul as she did. It was something that she really needed to work on if she was going to have any chance of protecting herself from falling for Remy.

"*Chère*, you've done nothing but wow me since the moment you fell into my arms," he said.

They both finished up their dinner and then Remy stowed the dishes back into the cooler. She noticed that he kept everything as neat and tidy as he did his mis en place when they were cooking. "You are very neat."

"That's a good thing in a chef," he said.

"Yes, but even away from the kitchen. Why is that?" she asked. It might be nothing but then again it could be the key to figuring out Remy.

"My father said a man who lacks the discipline to keep himself tidy lacks the discipline to run a kitchen."

"And that was your goal?" she asked.

"It was my heritage," he said.

There was gravitas in his voice and she wondered what kind of expectations his family must have put on him. The disappointment they'd feel that he was out of work now. He needed this win, she thought, almost as much as she did.

"From your Creole family?"

"Most definitely," he replied.

She took his hand in hers. "You're a great chef, Remy. No one can take that from you and no matter if you are the head chef in New Orleans most famous restaurant or the purveyor of street food in New York you're still honoring your talent."

REMY WAS FLATTERED BY what she said and it was a sentiment his grandmother would have echoed but his father, his grandfather and his uncles they had a different plan for Remy and his future. They wanted him to take up the mantle of Chef Patron and continue the tradition of the kitchen that had won three Michelin stars. And for the first time, Remy understood that he might not want that path.

He'd come here with seemingly one goal, one objective, yet from the second he'd met Staci all of that had changed. It didn't matter what he'd told himself in the past, there was something in this moment that felt like truth. It felt like his life was changing and he hadn't experienced that outside of the kitchen before.

He moved around on the blanket until he was positioned behind Staci and drew her into his arms so that her back was pressed to his chest. She sat stiffly at first. So all the seducing he'd done with his food hadn't made her relax with him. Sex, he thought, might have created more barriers between them than he'd thought.

For all her tough-girl attitude there was a soft inner

core to Staci that she protected like a fierce warrior. His intuition told him it was because she'd been hurt before...disappointed by people in general. But more than that. He remembered what she'd said about no man in her life having stayed. No father or grandfather. No boyfriend.

And though he knew his intentions were honorable there was a part of him that knew he had to be very careful. He had no idea if this attraction was just the excitement of being in a new place and meeting a type of woman he'd never encountered before. He was old enough at thirty to know himself and what he wanted but he had no idea if he could tame Staci and convince her he was a staying kind of man.

Or if he wanted to. The fact was he was lying to her by not telling her his real name and background. And a part of him knew he should say something to let her know but he couldn't risk anyone else knowing who he was. And the secret was his burden. If at some point his true heritage in cooking became known he didn't want her to have to pay the price for not coming forward sooner.

His reasons all sounded good to him but another part of him knew that as long as he kept his secret this life, this idyllic time with Staci could continue. He didn't have to try to figure out the logistics of falling for a woman who lived on the West coast. He didn't have to face the fact that his life was always going to be in New Orleans and she was as deeply entrenched here. He kind of enjoyed the freedom of being Remy Stephens instead of Remy Cruzel. Remy Stephens could stay.

"Do you see that constellation?" he asked.

"Yes. Orion, right?"

"Yes, the hunter. It's the most visible of all the constellations, you can see it anywhere in the world. When I was young, my father had to travel for a few years and every night he'd tell me to look up at this constellation and know that he was doing the same. That we were together even though we were miles apart."

She relaxed against him as he told her more about the night sky. He didn't know much but he'd already figured out that with Staci sharing parts of himself was the key to getting past her barriers.

"My mother and I did that with the moon. She'd send me a kiss to the moon and I'd retrieve it when I went to bed…" she said, her voice wobbled a little. "I've never told anyone that before."

"It's okay. Your secret is safe with me," he said.

She shifted around to look at him. "I want to believe that but the past has taught me that a secret is only safe if you keep it."

He had just thought the very same thing and he knew that a man who was busy trying to cover up something had no ground to stand on. He leaned down to kiss her because it seemed a better thing to do than to make promises he knew he couldn't keep. He wanted to tell her he'd never lie to her but since he already was…

Angry at himself for not being able to be the man he wanted to be with her, he slipped his tongue deep into her mouth. Trying to show her the truth the only way he could at this moment. He wanted her but more than that he liked her, he respected her, he was in awe of her.

He wanted her to be the woman in his life despite the fact that they were both competitors and going after the same prize.

While he wasn't ready to throw in the towel and concede victory to her he knew that if she won, he wouldn't be as disappointed as he might have been a mere week ago. He'd already learned more about himself in the last few days then he had in the last four years of doing the same thing every day.

He put his hands on her waist and hugged her close to him as he lifted his head. Her lips were swollen and her eyes closed. "That nearly got out of hand."

"Did it? I thought that might have been your plan for the evening," she said.

"No. I want to get to know the real Staci Rowland so the next time, when I take you to my bed…and it will be my bed and I can have the time to explore your body, we both understand it's more than just attraction."

She turned in his arms and put her hands on his shoulders leaning down close to him. "You keep saying the right things…"

"Is that a problem?" he asked, keeping his hands on her waist even though he wanted to slide them around to her ass and draw her in closer to him. He wanted to feel her straddling him and claim another kiss to stir the passion that was between them.

"No. But I've heard it all before. The lies, the lines. And a part of me wants to believe you are different, Remy, but you're a guy."

"Yes, *chère*, I am. And one you've never known before."

She shook her head. "You've got a point but in my experience every man is hiding something and my gut says you're the same."

He swallowed hard and knew that if he told this lie it would hurt him later but he decided he could make up for it. Staci needed him to be a man she could believe in. She needed a man to prove to her that there was more to a relationship than sizzle and he was determined to be that man.

She turned back around and he held her in his arms but this time as she settled back against him he didn't feel the peace of the night or the need to share past memories. Instead his mind was active with the thought that sooner or later he was going to have to tell her who he really was. But when?

8

THE HOUSE WAS A BEEHIVE of activity when they returned from their walk on the beach. Though things had gotten hot and heavy they hadn't made love and Staci felt unnerved by that. She was also feeling what she knew was the first flush of love. She couldn't help smiling every time she looked over at Remy as they sat in the living room with the other chefs.

Some of the contestants were already clearly working on a strategy by talking about their own skills and pointing out the weaknesses of others. It wasn't as if she didn't expect it from them. After all they were being taped all the time they were in the house and it was a television show so some tension was a good thing. But she wasn't interested in that side of the game.

She was more focused on winning by cooking and if she were being completely honest Remy.

"Next week will be interesting. Staci, you're the one to watch. What do you think the next challenge will be?" Viv asked.

"Not sure. I've been as surprised as you guys so far," she said.

Staci preferred to do all of her talking in the kitchen rather than speculating on what might be coming up. Whatever it was, the challenge would be to keep her cooking fresh. She glanced over at Remy. After eating the dinner he'd prepared tonight she knew he was probably her toughest competition.

"They change it up every season. I really want a mystery basket," Dave said.

Conversation flowed around her as everyone discussed his or her favorite type of cooking. Christian, Quinn and Frances were all quiet no doubt dwelling on the fact that the next day they'd be cooking to stay in the competition.

Slowly, everyone got up to go to bed and she left after Remy did. There were too many people around for a private goodnight and Staci was okay with that. Since they were in the house now they weren't a couple. Were they anywhere else?

But she knew that they were. At least in her eyes. She wondered if her mother had felt this way with her father. Staci had always wondered why her mom hadn't seen the signs that her father wasn't going to stay. But the feelings swamping Staci now made her realize that love came whether it was wise to get involved or not.

Staci could only hope that she had chosen better than both her mother and grandmother. She was still feeling not exactly happy with her new feelings for Remy when Vivian walked in.

"I noticed you and Remy were getting cozy tonight,"

Vivian said after she'd washed up and they were both sitting on their beds.

"Yes. I...he and I had a bet and he had to cook me dinner since I won the challenge."

"Did you learn anything you can use from his cooking?" Vivian asked.

"I did. But that's not why I did it."

"It should be. Unless you're not here to win. And given the way you are cooking I'm pretty sure that's the only reason you are here."

"You're right, but I think..."

Vivian shrugged. "I'm the last one to give another woman advice on a man but you should watch your back. Everyone here is playing an angle."

"Even you?" Staci asked.

"Hell, yes."

Was Remy still playing an angle? It would be easier for her to believe in that than to trust him. But it almost felt like it was too late to stop the feelings that were welling up inside of her. She didn't want to be a fool again.

She needed to keep her distance. Starting tomorrow she'd back away. It was the only smart thing to do.

"What's *your* angle?"

"Don't give away my strengths," Vivian said. "Not even to you, girlie!"

Staci smiled at her. "Come on, Viv. You can trust me."

"Is that what Mr. Man said to you?" she asked. "I'm not trusting anyone. I like you but when it comes down to it, there can only be one winner and I'm going to be champion."

Staci realized that what Vivian said was true. But there was more to life than winning. In five weeks the prize would be handed out and either way, win or lose, she was getting on with her new life. She'd already started pulling out of the day-to-day running of Sweet Dreams so she could pursue new directions. This show…her time here was supposed to help her decide where to go next. Would that be enough though?

Her new feelings for Remy could influence where she ended up but truly was she going to follow a man she'd met on a cooking show? She knew she had to figure out her priorities. She'd already decided to put some extra distance between them and as of this instant she understood that it wasn't just a good strategy for the game but also for her life.

The only person she'd ever truly trusted had been her grandma and when Rosalyn had died Staci had been alone in the world. Her mother, albeit kind hearted, had never been emotionally stable enough for Staci to lean on and she had to remind herself that the only one she could count on was herself.

That didn't mean she regretted anything with Remy. It simply meant that she was going to remember the truth behind every emotion. He was doing what was right for him. She had to do what was right for herself.

"Well, I hate to break it you, Viv, but I'm going to do my level best to beat you and if today is any indication I think I'm off to a good start."

"You are, girlie, but the judges now expect a higher standard from you. You'll have to keep cooking up to it."

Staci wasn't worried, even brokenhearted and alone

she'd always been able to keep a clear head in the kitchen. This would be no different.

"We will see next week, won't we?"

"Yes, we will," Vivian said. She got under her covers and curled up on her side. "I hope I didn't speak out of turn saying what I did about Remy. It's just I don't want to see a chef as good as you go home because of a man."

She got under her covers too and reached over to turn out the lamp on her nightstand. She'd already thrown away one chance because of a man, she didn't want to let it happen again.

"Me, either," she said rolling over and punching her pillow but it didn't relieve the frustration flowing through her. She'd started to believe that Remy was different but listening to Vivian was like talking to herself. She knew that men lied. It made sense that he'd be playing an angle. They were competitors after all. But the man who'd held her tenderly and told her about his father and the constellation…that man she wanted to trust.

Promising herself she was smart enough not to make the same mistake twice. Promising herself that she'd be cautious where Remy was concerned. Promising herself that she'd weigh everything he said to her and not just trust him blindly.

Vivian slept restlessly and her dreams were tortured visions of the kitchen in Paris. Remy and Jean-Luc were both there watching her cook and then tasting her dishes and judging them to not be good enough.

And a part of her woke to the feeling that she was determined to prove that this time she was going to be the one who judged them. This time she'd walk away the winner. This time she wasn't going to risk her heart so easily.

REMY HAD SUSPECTED THAT things wouldn't be as easy as they'd seemed that night on the beach, but he hadn't anticipated Staci ignoring him or how he'd react to it. Frances had gone home and the next week of competition had pitted the men against the women in a restaurant challenge. Each team had to choose a captain, plan a menu and then run a pop-up restaurant for one night. The diners ate in both restaurants and voted on their favorite dishes. Whichever team had the most votes would win the team challenge and whichever chef produced the favorite dish would win the individual prize.

The men had chosen Christian fresh off his win in the bottom three challenge to be the leader. The women had chosen Staci. Remy wasn't surprised but he did wonder how the mantle of leader would sit with her.

He tried to steal some time alone with her but she was careful to keep her distance from him. Perhaps he should be doing the same thing instead of trying to catch her attention. He focused on his dish. Remembering everything he'd learned in the previous week and in a lifetime of cooking. He created a dish to please his palate. Not being in charge of the team meant he could stand back and just cook. Which turned out to be a good thing because there was a lot of testosterone in the kitchen. He stayed clear of Conner and Quinn, who were in a battle to prove each was a bigger egomaniac than the other.

Christian did his best to lead but it was clear to Remy

that the other man's strength was really in the creation of the menu and the front of the house. He charmed every patron who entered their restaurant and it wasn't long before Remy believed that they would win.

Until he heard the laughter and compliments coming from the women's side. Just that was enough for Conner and Quinn to put their egos aside and start working together. No one wanted to lose this challenge.

"The judges are here," Christian shouted, coming into the kitchen. "I've just seated them. Chefs, we need your very best!"

They all cooked and plated their food and there was no time to wait for feedback from the judges as other customers were waiting to be served, but they sent back the appetizer that Conner had prepared. Which didn't sit well with the other man. It worried Remy since he knew the dish had been well prepared until he learned there was a shell in the seafood pate that Conner had created.

An error, Remy thought. That was something that Conner should have caught before the dish was sent to the floor.

But the other man had been too focused on other things…just as he Remy had been with Staci in the Quick Cook. The only way to win this, and that was still his objective, was to do as Staci was doing and put her from his mind.

But that was harder than he'd anticipated. His dreams had been filled with steamy visions of Staci in his arms on the beach. He'd been tormented by the memory of her soft warm body wrapped around his.

"You're up, Remy. Three mains."

He started cooking, remembering making love to Staci and when he plated his dish he knew he'd created something that had its roots in what they had both experienced together. He sent the dishes out with the waiter and tried not to stand there like a first time chef.

None of the dishes came back and the rest of the night passed in a blur. Soon they were back in the *Premier Chef* kitchen. There was a tension in the stew room as they waited to be called in front of the judges. Staci jotted notes frantically in her journal. Others drank water like it was cheap vodka. Finally Fatima entered the room.

"We're going to do individual judging first and then teams. We'd like to see Vivian, Remy and Gail."

Remy got to his feet more nervous than he wanted to be. He knew he'd cooked a great dish but he hadn't exactly hit a home run with the judges thus far.

"Now it's time to see if we're the winners or the losers," Vivian said. "But if we're the bottom three then there is something wrong with them. I know I didn't screw up today."

"We will just have to see," Remy said.

"Yes, we will."

They entered the judging room where a long table sat with the three judges behind it. Fatima took her spot next to them and Jack, the director gave them all marks to stand on. In this moment he really resented the fact that this was a TV show. He wanted them to just deliver the news—good or bad. But they had to be set up and then wait.

Eventually, the production crew were in their spots

and Fatima smiled at them. "Congratulations, the three of you had the top dishes."

"I know that," Vivian muttered.

Relief coursed through Remy. He was very happy to know that he'd made a good showing today. A part of him, just a tiny part felt bad that Staci wasn't in here. But perhaps being the leader of her team had distracted her from cooking.

The judges all took turns telling them why they liked their dishes before Fatima announced that Remy had won the challenge.

"From the first dish you put up, we knew you could cook," Hamilton said. "But tonight you showed us something fresh and new. Good job."

"Thank you, chef."

"You're welcome," Hamilton said.

"We need you to send back a few of your colleagues."

"Certainly," Remy said.

They asked to see Tony, Ashley and Conner. Remy had a feeling that Conner might be going home. Although he had no idea how bad Ashley's dish was. Tony's dessert hadn't set right but Remy had tried it and presentation aside it had tasted really good. He was thrilled they didn't ask to see Staci. He wanted her to stay in the competition. He wondered if their date had been a distraction for her. And decided he'd keep his distance as she clearly wanted him to.

They returned to the stew room and sent the three chefs to see the judges after Remy announced he'd won.

"I heard them raving about your dish," Staci said when he sat down.

"The judges?" he asked.

"No. The diners. There wasn't one who didn't talk about the main and how delicious it was. I thought that must be Remy's dish. Did you make them what you made for me?"

"No," he said. "That was just for you, *ma chère*. But I did use the advice you gave me. By talking about food and memories you reminded me that there is more to cooking than technique."

Staci smiled. "Given that you won, maybe I should have kept my mouth shut."

"Maybe you should have."

"I'm glad I didn't," she said.

"Why is that?" he asked.

"Now that you've upped your game everyone has and the competition feels more unpredictable. These challenges really shake us up and force us to focus on the food. That gets lost in the day-to-day working of the kitchen, you know?"

"I do indeed," he said.

The three chefs re-entered the kitchen and they were told that Conner had the least favorite dish and was going home.

"They want to see the rest of you," Conner said. "The cook-off will be between the bottom three on the losing team. Good luck, guys."

Everyone said goodbye to Conner and then they all went back to the judges room. The comments started out harsh but then ended on an upbeat note. The contestants were given a chance to defend themselves but everyone owned up to their mistakes. The women lost the round and Staci, Kristi and Whit were the bottom three.

STACI WON HER QUICK COOK with Kristi going home, but the next week was back in the bottom three again. A part of her wanted to blame Remy but he'd kept away from her which was all she'd wanted. They had a free day and Staci knew she should be in the kitchen practicing but she had the feeling her head was getting in her way. It was as if she'd forgotten all the things she really knew about cooking.

Remy walked up to her where she sat in the living room watching Sponge Bob with Dave.

"Pack your bathing suit and meet me out back in ten minutes."

"Um...why?"

"Because it's our day off and we need to talk and to get out of this house."

Remy had won the last two weeks and he was clearly hitting his stride at the right time. "You don't owe me anything."

"Go get changed. The clock is ticking," he said.

She wasn't sure that going out with him was a wise idea but ignoring him hadn't exactly been working for her either. She pushed to her feet and went to change. Putting on her black bikini and covering it up with a pair of denim shorts. She grabbed her sunglasses and put on a pair of Roxy flipflops before heading out back to meet Remy.

He'd swapped clothes for a pair of blue board shorts and left his shirt off. Oh, the man was ripped. His chest muscles drew her attention and she didn't want to look away. It was the first time she'd seen his chest. She'd touched him, true enough, but now she knew what he looked like. She understood why he'd said the next time they made love it would be in a bed. She wanted the chance to explore his body, too.

He glanced over at her as she approached, his gaze skimming over her body. "Ready?"

"Yes," she said. "What are we doing?"

"You'll see. I arranged for us to go sailing."

"I'm not really that proficient on a boat."

"That's okay. I hired a crew."

"Can you afford that?" she asked.

"Let me worry about that," he said. When they got to the beach he directed her toward the pier where there were a number of yachts tied up. Suddenly she was feeling a bit underdressed in her bikini top and denim shorts but Remy took her hand in his and led the way to a large yacht.

He helped her onboard and directed her to a padded bench in the back of the boat. "I'll be right with you."

"Um…where are we going?" she asked.

"Away from the world," he replied disappearing below deck. She took a seat where he'd directed her and tried to relax. It was harder than she'd expected because she felt unsure of what Remy was up to.

He'd been keeping to himself for weeks, now they were on a luxury yacht. She took out her cell phone and texted Alysse.

Staci: You'll never guess where I am.
Alysse: Where?

Staci: On a yacht...with Remy. Is this a mistake? Tell me to jump overboard and swim for shore.

Alysse: Ha. Stay there and enjoy your time with him. The competition is just heating up and he must like you if he's wooing you."

Staci: I'm scared.

Alysse: Men are like that. Remember how afraid I was to trust Jay.

Yeah, but Jay loved Alysse. Jay had come back to town to win her friend's heart and make a new life with her. This was totally different. She heard footsteps and glanced up to see Remy approaching with a champagne glass in each hand.

Staci: TTYL

Alysse: Like I said, relax and enjoy it.

Staci doubted that was going to happen. She'd let Vivian's words and her own natural reticence take over and she knew that it was going to be hard to be calm around Remy. She didn't know if he was sincere even though he did seem to be. But then she'd never had a good radar to judge when a man was lying.

She put her cell phone back in her bag as Remy sat down next to her and handed her the champagne. "I realize we should be dressed more formally but I didn't want to give my surprise away."

"And what exactly is your surprise?" she asked as the boat's engines were fired up.

"A day out at sea, just the two of us. I took the liberty of securing permission with Jack for us both to be gone until ten tonight."

"All day at sea?" she asked.

"I thought we could go swimming and sunbathe. And just have a chance to get to know each other away from the house. A chance to take a break without thinking about the competition," he said.

"You know the water in the Pacific is cold unlike the Gulf of Mexico," she warned him.

"I do. I have wet suits for us both. Have you ever tried spear fishing?" he asked.

"No. Have you?"

"Yes. In the Bahamas with my grandfather. I'd like to show you," he said.

In for a penny, in for a pound. "Why not? Given the way I've been cooking I could go home next week and then I wouldn't see you again, would I?"

"At least not until the competition is over. I can't think beyond that but I do know that I want to enjoy every moment with you," he said. "And I think you want the same. That's why ignoring each other isn't working for us. We need to pay attention to this part of ourselves. You are constantly on my mind and my body aches for yours, *ma chère*."

"You seem to have done a good job of ignoring your desires and cooking up a storm," she said.

"That's an illusion," he said. "I've missed you."

She didn't know what to say to that. A part of her had missed him too but she really had her hands full. All of her energy either went to cooking or ignoring him. Maybe he had a point about why that wasn't working.

He handed her the champagne flute and lifted it to her. "To new beginnings."

"New beginnings," she said, taking a sip of the

champagne as they sailed farther away from the shore. "Where exactly are we going?"

"Trust me," he said. "The captain said we have a thirty minute ride to where we will try fishing. Why don't we sunbathe?"

"Okay but this is nice."

"It is but I want to see all of you," he said.

"All of me?" she asked, realizing he was talking about her denim shorts. "And maybe help me put on some sunscreen?"

He laughed. "I'm obvious, aren't I?"

"A little."

"It's true I relish the thought of running my hands over your curvy body. You need to relax. I've never seen anyone more tense than you are with each passing day."

"I'm struggling to find some balance. And it's hard to always be on your guard around all the contestants."

"Do you miss your roommate?" he asked.

Recently, Vivian had been the eighth chef to be sent home. "I do. She was funny and I could count on her to lighten the mood. I'm not looking forward to being alone in my room."

"If this afternoon goes well, perhaps I'll ask to be your new roommate."

"You will do no such thing. I don't want to be gossiped about."

"Why does gossip bother you so much?" he asked. "That's the second time you've mentioned it."

"It bothers everyone. No one wants to hear their name whispered behind their backs."

"We aren't doing anything wrong," he said.

"I know. But I'd rather keep it private," she said. "Between us." She couldn't help but admit that if for some reason her track record with men held true and Remy ended up breaking her heart and leaving her, she didn't want the cast of *Premier Chef* to know she'd been burned by love. Again.

9

Remy needed a break from the intense competition but he also needed time alone with Staci. He'd been cooking at the top of his game, although that was due more to the fact that she made him happy. She made him want to be a better man and a better chef. He cherished the moments they had spent together.

Like on a Quick Cook when they had brushed hands while reaching for the same bunch of basil. Or when he'd met her gaze as she'd turned to put a pot on the stove. Or a million little instances that had been not enough for him. He wanted to see if it were simply the fact that he couldn't have her that was making everything about her seem so enchanting.

And this day was for them. He'd had to use his credit card to book the yacht and though he didn't like leaving a trail for his parents to follow and perhaps find him, he'd needed to do it for himself and for Staci. He wanted to show that he was more than an out-of-work cook and this type of a day was something he could offer her.

Staci stretched out on one of the loungers to tan and

he stood next to her his hands actually tingling as he anticipated touching her back. She handed him the sunscreen but all he could do is stare down at her. The black bikini bottoms hugging the curve of her butt beckoned him. He sat down next to her on the bench, stroking his hand down her left leg. She lifted herself on her elbows and glanced over her shoulder at him.

"I don't feel any lotion," she said.

"Are my hands too rough? I know I have calluses and scars. You should be touched by something as soft as you are," he said.

"Your hands are fine. I was teasing you. Touch me if you want. But I will burn so I have to put lotion on."

"I'll make sure you're covered. I never burn," he said.

"Thanks to your olive skin. I wish I had it. I'm so pale. I could stand in the sun for hours and never get any color other than red."

He smiled at her. He wouldn't change anything about her body. The soft pale skin was part of Staci. He poured lotion onto his hand and warmed it by rubbing his hands together and then stroked his hand down her left leg. He started at the curve of her butt and then worked his way slowly down the back of her thigh. She giggled when he reached the back of her knee.

"Ticklish?"

"Not normally. I think I'm nervous to have you touching me while I just lie here."

"Surely you must have some fantasy of being massaged by a man who has to put only your pleasure first," he said. He was having a few fantasies of being just such a man for her.

"Well, yes, but is that what you're doing?"

"Yes. I am. I told you the sex we had was nice but it left me craving more. I still don't know your body or you." He kept moving his hand in tiny circles on the back of her knee. She shifted a little to turn and face him.

"I don't know you either," she said.

"I promise you will." It was impossible to learn a woman the way he needed to know her without revealing at least something of himself. And though he was a man living a lie he knew he wanted her to know him. He needed that kind of sexual honesty between them now and, he suspected, for the future.

"Okay. I'm going to lie here and let you be my personal masseur."

"Perfect," he said. He put more lotion on his hands and finished moving slowly down her leg. He took a minute to massage her calf knowing that being on her feet all day would make those muscles ache. It wasn't guesswork; he'd had the same aching legs at the end of a long day cooking.

"That feels good," she said. "Last year for Christmas, Alysse and I went to the Spa at the Hotel Coronado and had massages…"

"How do I measure up?" he asked, letting his hands slide between her legs and sweep up to the apex of her thighs.

"You are a bit more…intimate," she said.

"I should hope so," he said, not liking the thought of another man's hands on her. He knew that jealous wasn't noble and tried to shove it aside but he wanted Staci to be his. And his alone.

There was something about Staci that made him possessive. Maybe it was that he was away from Gastrophile, which consumed every second of his life when he was home. Or maybe it was just Staci. It was too early in knowing her to make that determination. He only knew that there was something about her that had captured him.

He poured more lotion in his other hand, starting at the top of her right thigh and slowly moving his way down to her feet. She had tiny feet. And delicately painted toe-nails, he lifted her leg and rubbed the lotion into each foot before caressing his way back up the inside of her legs. He admitted to himself that caress was for himself, but noticed that she shifted slightly, parting her legs, and he guessed she liked his touch, too.

"I'll do your back and then you roll over and I'll do your front," he said.

"Hmm...mmm...."

He couldn't tell if it was sleepiness that made her mutter that sound or just the simple enjoyment of being touched. He poured more lotion on his hands and starting at the waistband of her bikini bottoms placed his hands on her back. He spread his fingers wide and moved them in slow circles upward. He noticed that one of his hands could span her waist as he rubbed his hands over her.

There was a small mark in the middle of her back just above her waist and he leaned closer to check out the strawberry colored mark, brushing hands over and over it. Some sort of birthmark, he thought.

"The only part of my back that has color," she said. "I can't wear low cut dresses."

"Why not?"

"Everyone always thinks I have something on my back," she said.

"Everyone or men?" he asked, knowing that if he saw her in a slinky dress and noticed a mark on her back he'd be desperate to touch it and her.

She thought about it and then shrugged. "Mostly men."

"Yeah, they want to touch you, *ma chère*."

"I don't let them," she said. There was something very private about her. He imagined that was because she didn't let people in very easily. He wanted to be let in, he thought.

"I'm glad," he said and meant it.

He caressed the centerline of her spine, careful not to rub too hard. Finally he reached the back fastening of her bikini top and he deftly undid it as he continued to massage her back. He really liked touching her. He couldn't believe they'd made love and this was the first time he was seeing her beautiful back and really taking the time to enjoy touching her.

"Um…what are you doing?"

Turning himself on, he thought, shifting his legs as his erection grew. "Making sure you don't burn," he said. "Your top could shift while you are lying here and I did give you my word that I wouldn't let you burn."

"Yes, you did," she said. "Your word means that much to you."

He shifted around so he could see her eyes because

there would be a time when she might doubt it, yet his word meant everything to him. "It does."

She looked at him intently and then reached over to touch his lips with her forefinger, tracing the lines of his mouth. "I want to believe everything you say but it's hard, Remy. It's not that I can't trust you...I can't trust myself."

FOR SOME REASON SHE DID trust Remy. Maybe it was the way he seemed to take everything in stride or maybe it was the fact that so far he hadn't been anything but honest with her. Or maybe it was those stupid feelings in her stomach that made her want to believe that he really cared for her.

She knew it was too soon to be love. But she also knew she was lying to herself. She'd never felt this way before. And maybe that had been why her cooking had suffered. All she thought about was Remy.

His hands on her back were turning her on but it was really just him stoking a fire that was already smoldering. A fire that had been growing with every slight touch in the *Premier Chef* kitchen. Each night as he slipped into her dreams. Every single morning when she saw him over coffee and regretted that they hadn't passed the night in each other's arms.

His hands moved smoothly over her back and down to her sides, his big fingers caressing the sides of both of her breasts, massaging gently but there was no way she'd confuse him with a masseuse and they both knew it. She savored every intimate second of it. Until she remembered that there was something almost too good to be true in Remy. She wanted to believe him—really there was nothing she wanted more in the world.

When he slipped his hands up to her shoulders and kneaded them she closed her eyes and wished she didn't have her past.

"You're tensing up."

"Sorry."

"What are you thinking?" he asked.

"That you can't be real. So far you haven't done anything wrong," she said.

"I lost the first two rounds," he said.

"Not in the competition," she said. But maybe that was what she should be thinking about. It was clear that his mind wasn't really on this peaceful afternoon away from the show. Though the sun was warm and his touch on her back even hotter, she felt a cold chill overtake her.

"Oh. Well in that case, I would have not slept with you that first night. I wish I'd waited until now so I could really know you."

"That's not a misstep. I wanted you to."

"I know that, but by taking you I let you believe I'm like every other man you've ever known. I made our getting to know each other even more difficult than it should be. Relax and let me make it up to you."

She wanted to. Finally she just ignored her nagging conscience. She was going to enjoy this time with Remy. Even if he turned into a two-headed toad after this she'd have these moments. And she'd cherish them. No man had done this for her. No man had cooked for her. No man had treated her the way Remy did.

That had to count for something. She felt something

warm and damp tease her neck and realized he was kissing her. Goose flesh spread out from the place where he was nibbling on her shoulder. Her breasts felt heavier and her nipples tightened.

She felt his mouth moving along her back in the same path his hands had taken. He lingered over her shoulder blades and then he encouraged her to move her arms above her head. He shifted over her and she felt his chest hair against her back.

Then she felt the tender warmth of his breath. He touched the curve of her breast. His other hand caressed her nipple. Her hips jerked and his hand slid down to her butt, to one cheek.

His mouth slowly left a trail of nibbling kisses. "You're so beautiful, *ma chère*. I love touching you."

She wanted to say she loved being touched by him but the words stuck in her throat. Ultimately, she didn't want to reveal to him what she felt. She was more afraid of him in this moment than she had been in any other. There was something scary about letting him see how much he affected her. She didn't want him to know that he had this kind of power over her. But she knew it was more than likely too late to stop it.

He kissed the side of her right breast and he did that thing where he swept his finger under her body and over her nipple again. She moaned his name. Hoping she appeared nonchalant but knowing there was no way to hide her body's reaction to him, especially when he sweetly stroked between her legs.

She was determined to appear cool and in charge, even though she knew she wasn't cool at all. She was sizzling in the summer sun. And there was nothing that was going to make her cool off.

When he reached her feet he licked the arch of one foot then the other before again working his way up the inside of her leg. Oh, God, his mouth moved closer to her center and everything inside of her clenched. Afraid of what he might not do, or where he might not go.

At her very core, he left a little kiss and started his journey down that leg.

She was a mass of quivering nerves and barely aware of when he put his hands on her waist and rolled her to her back.

"I think we made sure you are not going to get burned on your back…now to make sure your front is okay."

"You are taking this seriously," she said, not at all surprised that her voice sounded husky and low.

"That's the kind of man I am. How are you liking your massage so far?" he asked.

She tried to seem calm when she shrugged but the fabric of her loosened bikini top started to slide and she had to grab for it. "It's good."

He smiled at her. "I'm glad."

He poured lotion in his hands and started again at the top of her thigh working his way down to her feet. This time was worse because she could see his face as he touched her body. He did seem to enjoy every inch of her skin. And there was a part of her that knew she'd never forget that look.

It was easy to believe that he was as involved in her as she was in him except for the rapt way he looked at her body. He glanced up and saw her watching him.

"What?"

"I just didn't believe you really wanted me...I mean in more than a sexual way until now. Any other guy would have been after his own satisfaction, but not you."

"Oh, I intend to have satisfaction and much more, but you're a mystery to me, *ma chère*, and I'm not going to rush one thing with you."

REMY WASN'T USUALLY A patient lover. That was when it hit him that this was nothing like those vacation flings he'd had in the past. Yes, he was away from his normal life and he had the sun on his back. But Staci was the woman lying in front of him. He had never wanted a woman more. Her taste was on his lips, the imprint of her body was on his fingers and he longed to rip off that brief bikini bottom and bury himself hilt deep inside her.

She stared up at him with those clear gray eyes of hers and he knew that he didn't want to disappoint her in any way. There was vulnerability in her gaze that he knew she'd hate if she knew it was there.

He put his hands on her waist and leaned down to kiss her because he didn't want to face that clear gaze of hers for another second. He lingered over her mouth. Slowly, he pushed his tongue over her lips and teeth and tasted the hidden recesses of her mouth. Her taste was addictive. He couldn't imagine a time when he wouldn't want to be able to taste her. He needed her like a dying man needed to breathe.

Her hands came up to his shoulders and she clung to him while their tongues dueled and her body lifted toward his. He was ready for her, ready to take her but he'd meant what he'd said about wanting them to be in a bed the next time they made love, so he lifted his head and got to his feet.

"I think we've had enough sun for now," he said, his voice was gruff, his mind full of images of the two of them entwined on that big bed down in the stateroom. He'd made sure everything was ready for them before they'd left the marina. When he made love to her he wanted everything to be perfect.

She nodded, nibbling on her lower lip. He wanted to groan and couldn't help but steal another deep kiss. There was something about this woman that he couldn't get enough of.

"Definitely enough sun."

He lifted her into his arms; she was so slight that he carried her easily across the deck and down the few stairs to the stateroom. He closed the door behind them and placed her in the center of the queen-size bed. The light streamed through the sheer curtains on the porthole windows.

She stretched her arms and legs out, letting the richness of the satin duvet caress her skin. The bikini top shifted around her breasts, showing him more of the pale white globes that he wanted to touch. She noticed his eyes stayed on her breasts and she reached up to undo the top knot behind her neck.

"Like what you see?" she asked. Her thick black bangs, falling in a heavy wave toward her eyes.

"You know I do," he said.

The fabric was still there just draped over her and he pushed his swim shorts to his ankles freeing his erection. He noticed that her gaze tracked down his body and paused on his masculinity. He took her ankles in his hands and drew her legs apart, before placing one knee between them. He reached for her bikini bottoms and pulled them down her legs, tossing them on the floor next to his swim trunks. Then he started kissing her legs again, starting at her feet this time.

He wanted to go as slowly as he had up on deck but his body had different ideas. He liked foreplay because the longer he drew out their coming together the more intense the feeling was when finally he was inside her body. But this was Staci and he felt as if it had been ages since he'd had her in his arms.

When he reached the top of her thighs he settled between her legs and parted her intimate flesh. With his tongue he flicked at the swollen bud there as her hips raised off the bed and into his touch. He kept flicking his tongue over and over that spot until she reached for him. The taste of her was spicy and he couldn't get enough of her. He teased and tempted her center until he felt her hips moving more quickly and her heels dug into the bed as her orgasm washed over her.

He was so hard he felt as if he were going to explode and when she reached down and took him in hand he almost did. He pulled her hand from him and drew her arm up and over her head.

He pushed aside the bikini top that revealed her hard pink nipples. Her breasts were small but curvy. They fit her tiny frame. He rubbed his hips over hers, letting the tip of his manhood settle into her while he suckled one nipple. He swirled his tongue over her engorged flesh until she shifted her shoulders and dug her hands into his hair to hold his head to her breast.

She chanted his name under her breath, the words were music to his ears, inflaming his desire and pushing him over the edge. He could barely hold on when he shifted to kiss and suck her other breast.

Her fingers tightened around his hair, but he wouldn't be hurried. Now that the end was so close he wanted her to enjoy every second of it. This time felt more real than their hurried coupling on the balcony had. This was what he'd been waiting for since he'd met her.

He stopped to look up at her. Her lips were parted, her eyes were half closed. Her hands flung above her head with abandon and her skin was covered in a dark pink flush. He memorized her in this instant before he thrust a final time into her.

She cried out as they climaxed together. She wrapped her legs around his waist and kept him buried inside her.

He wanted to give Staci everything he had. And he realized that she was more important to him than any other woman he'd ever been with.

He rolled to his side, keeping their bodies joined but held his weight from crushing her. A sense of peace and belonging overcame him, although he knew that it wouldn't last because no matter what he'd been trying to tell himself this wasn't real. He wasn't even the man she thought he was.

10

STACI STRETCHED, ROLLED over and curled against Remy. There was no confusion about where she was or whom she was with. And for the first time since she'd left Paris all those years ago, she felt as if she hadn't made a mistake in trusting a man. She snuggled closer to him, breathing in the woodsy scent of his aftershave, the lingering smell of sea breeze on his skin and the subtle fragrance of sex.

He squeezed her tight and rubbed his hand down her back in a long languid stroke. It occurred to her that if they stayed here at sea for the rest of their lives everything would be okay. It was only when they got around others that they'd encounter problems. But her grandmother had always warned her about hiding from the truth.

There was a reason she wanted to hide and that was… she didn't know. Maybe she was scared or too attached to Remy. Maybe she didn't want him to know that he could make her feel as good as he had. Because she still was afraid to really trust him. She might feel good now, but her mind was getting active and her doubts floated to the fore.

Tension settled over her and stole her sunshine as sure as clouds could on a summer's day.

"What are you thinking about?"

"Getting up," she said, because that was the safest answer.

"Yeah, right. Come on, what are you really thinking? You owe me that."

She realized he had a point. She just wasn't sure she could tell him. She just didn't know if she could drop her baggage at the door and be the woman that could make a relationship work with Remy.

"If you could see your face," he said.

"What would I see?" she asked.

"A woman who's afraid."

Exactly as she feared but she'd always known she didn't have a poker face. She didn't have it in her to be false with people once she started caring about them. No matter how much she wanted to deny it, she did care for Remy.

"I keep circling around and coming back to the same spot about trusting you," she said. "But right now I have to protect myself—"

"No you don't. We're in this together, you and me. We don't have to protect ourselves from each other."

She pulled the sheet up with her as she sat next to him. Tucking her hair behind her ear, she stared at him through narrowed eyes. "I can only assume you've never had a broken heart."

He shrugged in that Gallic way of his and it wasn't so

charming to see his casual attitude when she was feeling everything way too intensely.

"I tend to keep things casual because that's my way. My job is pretty demanding."

"Yes, but you're between gigs now. So what's keeping things so low-key this time?" she asked.

"We're away, in a different place," he said. "It's not the norm."

She arched both eyebrows at him and he shook his finger at her. "Don't get your back up. You know damned well you wouldn't have looked twice at me if we weren't trapped here together. This show is giving us a reprieve from our everyday lives. It's your chance to trust in a man and mine to slow down."

"What happens when this reprieve is over?" she asked, fearing she already knew his answer. Remy was the kind of guy who could move on. She had to remember his words. They weren't in the real world right now. She couldn't fall in love with a man who was enjoying a vacation from his life.

"I don't know, *ma chère*. I don't have all the answers. I didn't expect to meet you or to feel the way I do about it, but there it is whether I want it or not. If I could walk away from you then the last two weeks would have been a stroll in the park."

She didn't say anything.

"For both of us. Denying it won't change the truth. There is something between us that we can't deny. You know it's true or you wouldn't have been so tense the last two weeks."

He had a point but she hated it. She didn't want him

to be right or for this situation to be out of her control. Yet it had been since she'd tripped over the threshold of the elevator and fell into his arms.

He'd caught her and she had to wonder if that's why she thought she could trust him. If that's why she really wanted to make this work.

She hated the weakness inside her that made it impossible for her not to hope that…well, that this would last. "Let's stop talking about it."

"Why? You'll keep worrying over it, won't you?"

"Yes. But talking isn't making it any better," she said.

"It is, *ma chère*. It's letting you know that you're not alone. I'm unsure, too," he said.

"Renting a yacht and seducing me on the sun deck doesn't seem unsure to me."

He tugged her off balance and back into his arms. "I wanted to show you I was more than just a one-night kind of guy."

She had to laugh because there was no way that she'd ever have thought that about Remy. Even their first intense lovemaking hadn't felt casual. Nothing did with him and she knew if she didn't want to go crazy she would have to start forgetting the fear that he wasn't a man of his word.

After all everything he'd done since they'd met had proven to her that he wasn't lying about his feelings.

"What else do you have planned for today?"

"I was hoping we'd cook together in the galley. I've ensured that we have state-of-the-art appliances. Then we'll eat on the deck under the moonlight, maybe dance to some Cajun rock and then I'll seduce you again before we go back to the house."

"I can see you've given this some thought."

"I have," he said. "I wanted…I still want to get to know the woman behind all these defenses, Staci. I care about you. I can't make myself stop thinking about you."

She understood what he was saying; he was verbalizing what she felt. She knew if she kept her guard down then she could enjoy the rest of her time with him. And to be fair it would probably be easier on him; he could stop worrying that he wasn't living up to her needs.

"Okay but I'm in charge in the kitchen."

"Like you were the first time," he said.

"Ha. This time you take orders and act as my sous chef," she said, standing up and reaching for her bikini bottoms.

"As you wish," he said.

"As if. You'll let me think I'm in charge, won't you?"

"You bet," he said with a grin. "Let's shower and I took the liberty of stocking some clothing for you."

"You did?" she asked. "Who does that?"

"A man who wants to impress his woman."

His woman. Was she really Remy Stephens's woman? Did she want to be? She knew she did. That was why she was laboring over everything he said and did. She wanted this to be real. More real than she'd wanted her father to show up when she was a kid. It was wrong in a way that a man still held the key to her happiness and she was afraid to let him see how much he meant to her.

"Well, I'm impressed," she said. "Are we showering together?"

"No, I'll let you have the facilities first. I need to check with the captain and tell him we won't be fishing," he said.

"I doubt you ever really intended for us to do that," she said.

"Why?"

"I think you said it so I wouldn't be wondering if you were going to make a play for me."

"You're right. I wanted you to relax. And I think I succeeded."

He had done that all right. "Thank you, Remy."

"For what?"

"The massage, the understanding. I know it's been difficult—"

"Nothing worth having comes easily," he said, before he pulled on his swim trunks and walked out of the stateroom.

STACI REGAINED HER equilibrium in the kitchen while Remy showered. She chopped vegetables, letting the sounds of her knife on the cutting board sooth her. The captain and crew were still staying out of sight, which Staci truly appreciated. She felt raw and exposed after making love with Remy and needed to put herself back together.

She was used to always being the strong one, the one who was tough and made everyone else feel better. Even Alysse let her be the tough one. It was Staci who always dealt with difficult small business loan officers, overzealous customers and one time a would-be burglar.

At this moment she felt entirely incapable of doing anything but working in the kitchen.

"What can I do?" Remy asked as he came and stood beside her.

He wore a pair of jeans and a white linen shirt that he'd left unbuttoned at the neck. His hair was still damp from the shower and the white linen made his skin tone seem even deeper. Seeing him now she wondered how a man as together and successful as Remy could be out of work. He seemed more like a wealthy restaurant owner.

"I wasn't sure what we were making so I'm just chopping vegetables," she said. "I already made some cupcakes for dessert...they're baking in the oven."

"Cupcake girl, I'm flattered," he said, and dropped a kiss on her neck. "Face me so I can see if the dress I ordered looks as lovely on you as it did on the model."

She put her knife down. She thought this was part of the problem, too. She normally wore jeans and a T-shirt. The dress was a simple sundress that tied at the back of her neck. The skirt fell to her knee and wasn't full or flowy, something which would have made her petite frame seem shorter. He'd chosen well, she thought. But now that he was standing there waiting to see how she looked she was nervous.

To heck with it, she thought. She'd never been a nervous Nelly why was she behaving like one now?

She turned toward him and put her hands on her hips, staring up at him in challenge. "What do you think?"

He tipped his head to the side and peered at her for what seemed like an eternity. "Exquisite. But why are you angry?"

"I don't know. This isn't me. I'm jeans not fancy dresses. And this place is nice but it's outside my comfort zone."

"I'm sorry. I thought you'd enjoy a vacation from everything."

"The house in Malibu is that as well. I feel like this is just one more illusion," she said. Knowing she meant her feelings. There was something inside of her that was so scared and unsure. And every move that Remy made just reinforced how out of control she really was.

"This is real," he said. "Even though I'm out of work right now I have money."

That knocked her back. Yet it made perfect sense. He was totally at ease in any situation. It was something that she'd noticed in wealthy friends before. "Oh, okay."

"Staci, we are getting to know each other in carefully measured steps. You and I are creating a new dish and every time we get something right and try to move onto the next ingredient we have to readjust."

She agreed. "I'm not wealthy, but the cupcake business has been good to me and Alysse. We have an investor interested in expanding Sweet Dreams into a chain of stores. If that happens, we'll both be millionaires."

"Good to know. Are you going to do it?"

Staci shrugged. "I'm not sure. I have been considering doing other things, but we're both just so used to bakery…what would we do without Sweet Dreams."

"I'm sure any new investor would love it if you both stayed on and worked there," he said, coming over next to her and taking over chopping the vegetables.

"But we would be working for someone else. That doesn't seem right."

He laughed at her and she smiled back. "I know I'm bossy, what can I say?"

They worked together making a seafood gumbo that she'd been dying to try and with his input she thought it tasted very nice. When the cupcakes had cooled she set them on the countertop next to the icing she'd prepared.

"So we can decorate our own or decorate one for each other," she said.

"I vote for each other. What do you have here?"

"Buttercream frosting, fondant, colored sugar…the usual suspects," she said. Handing him an offset spatula.

"Is there a theme?" he asked.

"I think you've been a *Premier Chef* too long. It's a dinner date, southern man. You make whatever you want," she said.

"You're right. Okay, prepare to be amazed," he said.

"I've been amazed all day," she admitted. "I think I was so grumpy earlier because I'd thought I'd figured you out, but once again you've made me re-evaluate you."

"Good," he said. "You're still a big ol' mystery to me, *ma chère*. No matter how much I think I know you I keep realizing I don't."

She was glad. She didn't want to think that Remy had uncovered too many of her secrets. There were parts of her that even she didn't want to know. They each took a cupcake to the galley table and sat down at opposite ends. She worked with food coloring and the different frostings to do an image of Remy on top of her cupcake. She'd won several awards for her artistic designs and she thought he'd be impressed. She used an upside down bowl to hide the cupcake, so he couldn't see the finished product until dessert time.

He took another bowl and put his cupcake in it. It had been hard but she'd resisted the temptation to look over at him several times while he'd been working. Finally they cleaned up the galley. Remy's watch pinged and he glanced down at it.

"It's almost time. I'll get the crew to finish prepping our dinner and bring it up to the deck while we have a cocktail and watch the sun set."

"Sounds good," she said. And it did. Everything Remy said sounded just right. Soon they were on deck French martinis in hand, the Chambord flavored cocktail just right as a light breeze stirred around them.

She shivered and Remy wrapped an arm around her shoulder. They sipped their drinks as the sun slowly drifted down and disappeared beyond the horizon. The deck wasn't dark for a second as twinkle lights came on and she heard the footsteps of the crew bringing their dinner up on deck.

It was a simple meal but she had seldom enjoyed one more. Remy talked to her more about his travels and the people he'd met. But he did it in such a way that she didn't feel envious or jealous. They talked about Paris and Staci felt that bittersweet pang she always did, but it faded as Remy and she compared favorite sites and meals they'd had there.

She was afraid to admit it even to herself but she knew as the meal ended and the slow, sexy music began, that she was falling in love with him. He pulled her into his arms and danced her around the deck under the moon. She rested her head on his shoulder, sure that this one night she could let him see that she wasn't always a tough cookie.

Sure that she could allow herself to enjoy the moonlight, the man and the memories that felt as if they'd last forever. But being Staci she couldn't help but worry that tomorrow there would be another surprise like his wealth. That niggled at the back of her happiness, stealing a little of it. What if the next thing she found out about him wasn't as pleasant as this one?

REMY WAS RELUCTANT TO leave the yacht. He wasn't a man who normally hid from life, so today had been a refreshing change from the persona he'd been maintaining for the last few weeks. But he also knew that showing Staci he was a wealthy man was a far cry from telling her the truth about who he was.

He was doing all he could to prepare her for the truth once it came out. The more he cooked and the way things had gone lately, he was pretty sure he could win this thing. And when he did, and the episodes started to air his real name would be revealed.

"Thank you for a wonderful day," she said, wrapping the Hermès scarf he'd given her around her shoulders.

"You're welcome." He felt so sure of himself with her that if it weren't for the lie of his identity, he'd already have swept her off to his Garden District mansion in New Orleans.

Even if that were possible Staci wouldn't blindly go

where he wanted her to go. He admired her strength and independence. A part of him feared these six weeks in Malibu might be all the two of them ever had together.

"We haven't had dessert," she said.

"You are right. I'm having coffee brought up and then we can sit on the deck and enjoy our dessert."

The staff brought a silver coffee service and placed a cup in front of each of them. Then their dishes with cupcakes were set on the table. Remy was the first to admit he didn't know anything about decorating cakes. They had a head pastry chef at Gastrophile—his cousin Helene who was a genius at desserts, but he'd wanted to impress Staci.

Did he always? There was something about her...or maybe it was something about him and the fact that he knew he couldn't be totally truthful with her, that made him strive to always impress her.

She smiled as she handed him her covered cupcake. "Open it."

"Okay," he said, and then sat staring at the cupcake. She'd captured his likeness on the small dessert. It was amazing and a little bit unnerving. "I'm supposed to eat my own face?"

She laughed. "I know it's weird. You can lift the fondant off and save it, if you can't do it."

"Why haven't you made a dessert in the competition?" he asked. "You have a lot of talent."

"I know I do. But there hasn't been an appropriate task for it yet. If there is, I'll try my best to win."

"I'm pretty sure you will win hands down," he said.

"Now, open mine. Keeping in mind I'm not a pastry chef."

She gave him one of those enigmatic looks of hers from under eyelashes. "Are you nervous? Say it isn't so, southern man. I thought you had ego to spare."

"I do, but I'm also a realist and let's face it I don't have your skills at dessert."

She raised the makeshift lid and caught her breath. She slowly lifted the cupcake out and set it on the plate in front of her. "You made me a water lily."

"Yes, I did. It wasn't until dinner that I learned you liked Monet. So I think we are going to have to put this down to really good chemistry between us."

She reached over and took his hand as she looked up at him with those pretty gray eyes of hers. "It's perfect. And I don't think you should worry about any dessert rounds in the competition."

"As long as I can do something simple I'll be okay," he said. But he didn't want to talk about *Premier Chef*. He wanted this day and night to be about them. "Do you really like it?"

She lifted his hand to her mouth and kissed his knuckles before letting it go. "Yes, I do."

They ate their desserts both of them lingering over them.

"Why did you do my cupcake like that?" he asked.

"Something to remember me by," she said, glancing over at him.

He met her gaze. It seemed as if time itself was standing still. He wasn't a romantic, not really, but tonight he thought he could be. "I'd rather have you instead of having to remember you."

Something flickered across her face and she looked away before turning back to him with a tight smile. "But we both know I won't last. With you."

"Why?" he asked, afraid he knew the answer. Still, he wanted to hear it from her own lips. He wanted to have a chance to defend himself. To show her he was different from the other men in her life. But then he was afraid that no matter how different he was his outcome in her life might be the same. He was determined it wouldn't be.

"You said it earlier. The *Premier Chef* house is an illusion. Win or lose we are both going back to our real lives. And I live here. My friends and family are here and I'm not sure I'd ever really trust you enough to give that up."

"What if I were the one who gave up New Orleans?" he asked.

"Would you?" she asked. Then she shook her head. "I don't know. That's a lot to put on a relationship. If you moved out here and things didn't work out...I think it's more likely that this is a sweet affair that will end when the competition does."

He sat back in his chair and crossed his arms over his chest. He knew he should say something to lighten the mood. He didn't want the day to end on a sour note, but he couldn't accept her version of things. He knew she was right, he thought, that was why it made him so angry that she had put it so plainly. Because she didn't know who he was and that leaving New Orleans was impossible for him.

"I never pegged you for a quitter. I've seen you bring dishes back from the edge that should have been thrown away," he said. "Why would you live your life with less passion?"

She put her napkin on the table after folding it carefully. "Food hasn't ripped my heart out."

"I haven't either," he said.

"Not yet," she said, getting to her feet.

He almost let her go but he couldn't. And that was the part that bothered him. He wasn't willing to say this was just an affair, a part of him wanted more with this complex and sexy woman.

He stood up quickly, knocking his chair over in the process. She stopped and turned back to him.

"Remy—"

"Don't say it. I'm not going to hurt you. I've promised you I wouldn't. True, there are things about me you don't know. But everything I have shown you…it's more than I've given any other woman. I'm not playing a game with you, Staci."

He picked the chair up and stood to see if she'd left but instead she'd come back to his side. "You frighten me. I can't be as open to this as you are. I know that's not fair but that's what life has taught me."

He tugged her into his arms because he was very much afraid no matter how well he prepared her now, when the truth was revealed about him it would hurt her greatly. If he was a stronger man—a better man—he knew he would have let her walk away.

And since he only had these six weeks in Malibu he was determined to make them the best six weeks of her life.

11

WHEN THEY ARRIVED AT the house, there was no time for a long goodbye, which was fine, Staci thought. Jack was waiting in the living room with two of the other finalists, Christian and Will.

"What's up?" Remy asked as they settled into chairs.

"A special announcement," Jack replied. "We're waiting for the last few contestants to show up. By the way, did you enjoy your day off?" Jack asked them.

Staci would have liked to have gotten changed and been in her normal jeans and T-shirt in front of the other competitors. She didn't want them to see her dressed up and it was making her uncomfortable.

"It was very nice and relaxing," she said, hoping she was playing it cool. "Can I go change?" she asked the producer.

"No, I'm sorry you can't," Jack said.

"Just be glad you weren't skate boarding all day and smell like sweat," Christian remarked.

Everyone laughed at the way he'd spoken. Staci noticed Remy's hands resting on his knees. She so wanted to reach out to him to remind her of his touch.

Eventually, the rest of the group arrived and when they were all seated in the living room Jack stood up. "Now that we've reached the halfway point in the contest we will be upping the stakes. Cars will be here for you at six tomorrow morning. You will all need to pack your bags and bring along your formal wear—men that's suits and ties for you, ladies that's dresses. We are taking you to New York City. I suggest you get a good night's sleep because you will hit the ground running with a Quick Cook as soon as you land."

"How long will we be in New York?" Remy asked.

"One week. We'll fly back here for Judges Table and Elimination on Friday night," Jack said. "So you don't have to pack everything."

"Will there be any guest judges?" Christian asked.

"Yes. But I can't give you any names. I will say this, there is more than one guest judge and they are both world famous. Any other questions?"

A million but none she thought she'd get the answers for tonight.

"Good. We'll see everyone in the morning. As always, good luck."

Jack left the room and as soon as he did there was muttering from everyone.

"New York…have you been back since the visit with your mother?" Remy asked her.

"No. Unless you count a stop-over when I flew to Paris. But I didn't leave JFK so I don't think anyone would count that," she said. She wondered who the guest judges would be but now that Jack was gone, she wanted to get back to her room and have some time alone.

"I was just there before I came out here to audition. Should be nice to be back there," he said.

"I'm sure it will be. I'm going to pack and get ready for bed," she said.

"I'll walk up with you."

She shook her head. "Gossip."

"Everyone here knows you two hooked up," Sarah called out. "It's no big deal and kind of sweet."

Staci groaned. "Fine. You can walk up with me."

Remy laughed but she knew his mind wasn't on this house. "Are you worried about New York?"

He shook his head. "Just not sure who the guest judges will be. It bothers me that they didn't tell us who they are."

"Why?"

"There are some chefs I'd rather not see," he said.

"Bad blood?" she asked. The gourmet cooking world was full of its share of…well, divas for lack of a better word. Prima donnas who'd always been told they were the best and had rarely heard the word no. In a way that was what Jean-Luc Renard had been. But Staci had been young and he'd been so passionate that she'd easily mistaken lust for love.

She was only now realizing how mistaken she'd been about her ex. The feelings that she had for Remy were a hundred times more powerful than those she'd had for Jean-Luc.

That should upset her more than it did. Remy seemed

distracted as he sat quietly in her room. Something was obviously bothering him.

"Sort of," he said at last. "I just don't know if I'm imagining trouble where there will be none or what."

That sounded vaguely ominous. She wondered what kind of trouble he was talking about and reminded herself she only knew about Remy based on what he'd told her. She wanted to believe he was the man he'd shown himself to be but what if he was doing something to fool her.

"Want to talk about it?" she asked. "I'm told that I am a really good listener."

"I can see that. One of the things I've noticed about you during the competition is how adept you are at helping the other contestants. And that comes from paying attention to people."

"Thanks for the compliment," she said. "That's also how I know what is going on with people. If you pay attention to people they can't shock you."

"Truly?" he asked. "Does that work?"

"Usually...so do you want to talk about whatever is on your mind?"

"No."

"Well that was definitive," she said. "I'd say that you are afraid of something or someone. Am I right?"

"Perhaps," he said. "But if that were true I'd never admit it to the one chef in this competition who could actually beat me."

"You think I could win?" she asked, interested to hear what he thought unguarded about her cooking. It was the one thing that she thought really defined her.

"Yes. You know you could, too."

She knew better than to get cocky. "Do you think you might lose?"

He sighed and ran his hands through his hair, tousling it and making the curls spike up before he smoothed them back into place. "I'm not sure, but I just don't like not knowing."

"I agree it's unnerving, which is probably why they did it. It's probably some chef who's friends with Hamilton," she said. "It'll probably be someone with a show on this network. You know how incestuous these things can be"

"Why are you so calm about it?"

She smiled at him. "Because you're not. Anything that rattles our current champ has to be good. Sort of levels the playing field for me."

"Brat," he said.

"Whatever. There is one thing I'm not looking forward to," she said, as her gazed strayed to Remy. It was hard to concentrate on anything other than him. He sat on the bed that had been Vivian's and though they were talking as friends, she could still sense their underlying physical chemistry.

"What is it? That we'll get stopped at airport security for trying to carry through our knives?" he asked, smiling.

"No, but that would be funny. You should totally go and tell Jack to consider it. We could cross promo with the cop show." She could just imagine Jack weighing the idea as if it were a serious option. She'd learned the producer spent most of his time analyzing ratings and trying to figure out how to get a bigger share of the audience. Hence him letting them leave the house for the day.

Remy laughed. "You're learning that this is all about ratings."

"Aren't you? It's all that they seem motivated by. The judges are here for the food and the cooking but the producers obviously want good TV."

"Yes, they do," Remy said, getting up and coming over to sit down next to her. "You were about to tell me what you weren't looking forward to."

That's right, she was. "Um...I kind of like having the upper hand on you. "

"I won't tell anyone whatever it is that's bothering you," he said.

"I don't like flying. Normally I'd take a travel sickness pill that would knock me out, but since Jack said we'd be doing a quick cook when we land..."

Remy reached for her hand and held it in his. "I'll be there next to you."

The words shouldn't have been as soothing as they were but she knew that if Remy were beside her she could succeed at anything.

REMY HELD STACI'S HAND as they sat next to each other on the bed and knew that it was time for him to tell her the truth about who he really was. He knew there was a pretty good chance that the guest judge in New York could end up being his uncle or one of his other assorted relatives.

He also had the feeling that he should go and talk to Jack about it, too. He didn't want his uncle to be waiting at the Quick Cook, see him and reveal who Remy actually was. He knew that good TV aside, that type of thing would really hurt Staci and probably his chances of winning the show.

But she curled next to him tucking her head on his shoulder and the very last thing he wanted to do was to disturb her. Yeah, right, he thought. Since when did he start lying to himself? Maybe this new persona was having a bad influence over him.

"Everyone was nice about us being a…"

"A couple?" he asked.

She nodded, but didn't say anything else. God, this woman with all her skepticism and trust issues needed a man who was honest with her. She couldn't even say they were in a relationship because it possibly wouldn't last and he was…well, he was just holding her and staying silent because he knew that if he mentioned his last name wasn't Stephens he'd lose her.

It was that simple. He could pretend that he'd told her enough truths about himself to make up for the one lie and that lie had been told before he'd ever even met her, but he knew that he was making excuses for himself. And they were excuses she wouldn't buy.

He shifted around on the bed so that he was leaning against the headboard with two pillows stacked behind his back and drew Staci into his arms. He couldn't help but notice that she actually let him and that she cuddled next to him so trustingly.

"Thanks for today."

"You already thanked me," he said. This day was going to be one he cherished for the rest of his life. In his mind this was the day he first made love to Staci. It had been more than sex and had changed him in many different ways. Prior to today he would have been able to keep up the illusion that he was just an out-of-work cook, but now he wanted her to know everything about him. Truly, he needed her to.

Because as he held her in his arms he acknowledged that he wanted her to be by his side for the rest of his life. Inside a part of him that had never been alive before awakened and he realized that he loved her.

Sleeping in here tonight, holding her in his arms, might be something he needed but another part of him knew that if he did that he'd lose all hope of protecting a part of himself that he'd never known was vulnerable before.

Until he came clean with Staci and told her all about Gastrophile. Until she knew everything about him and he about her he couldn't let her know how he felt. He wasn't completely sure if she'd return his emotions. As wary as she was of the opposite sex, a big part of him believed she'd never be able to forgive him.

And he had to figure out how to let her know who he really was and convince her that he hadn't really been lying to her the entire time they'd known each other. He shoved his newly realized feelings to the back of his mind, knowing that people who made decisions based on anything other than logic often regretted them.

When he left her room he'd call Jack and start the process of revealing who he really was.

"What are you thinking about?" she asked him.

"Cooking," he said and it was partially true. "I've never met anyone like you before."

"I didn't want to trust you, Remy, but a part of me can't help it. Every time I start to think you're lying to me about something you prove that you aren't..."

Her words were like a dagger in his heart and he knew if he were a braver man, a stronger man, he'd confess then and there. But he wasn't. He'd never seen this particular look in Staci's eyes before and when she gazed at him with all that trust and devotion, he couldn't help but want to bask in it. To want to pretend he was the man she thought he was.

Hell, he thought he was that man. At least, he had been until the show.

"You make me want to be better than I am."

"You've already proven yourself to be a man of honor," she said, touching his cheek softly and then leaning up to kiss him.

He deepened the kiss trying to show her with actions how much she meant to him and how deeply he cared for her. Even though he knew how he felt for her, the words were far away and hard for him to say.

"Please don't," he said at last.

"Don't what?"

"Make me sound like something I'm not," he said.

"What do you mean?" she said, pulling away to face him. "What is it that you aren't?"

He searched for a way to answer her. He knew that he was on shaky ground. "I'm not anything more than who I am."

"That's very zen of you," she said.

He sighed and rubbed his hand over his eyes. "I think I'm a bit tired."

"I know I am," she admitted. "What is it that you're trying to tell me?"

He took her hands in his and lifted each one to his mouth. He kissed the back of her hands and then drew her into his arms and squeezed her close. He didn't want to see the look in her eye right now because she seemed to see through the subterfuge and to the very heart of him.

"I care about you, *ma chère*. More than I have any other woman and that frightens me."

She squeezed him back, dropping a soft kiss on his neck before she glanced up at him.

"I care more for you than I have for any other man. In fact the only one who comes close almost ruined cooking for me. That's why I've been so recalcitrant with you."

"Recalcitrant? Really?" he asked, focusing on her personality instead of the fact that he might be responsible for doing the same thing to her and her passion for food. If he did ruin cooking for her, he'd never forgive himself.

"Okay fine, I've been stubborn and difficult. Alysse would say that's the only way I know how to be."

He could easily believe that. Since her nature was just contrary. "I think you're passionate."

"Ha. You say that now because I'm lying in your arms but I bet the last two weeks you thought of me differently."

"You're right, I did."

"See? But you've won me over. I can't help myself. I'm tired of fighting the both of us. If you can call us a couple, well, I guess I can, too."

He hugged her close as she stared up at him and he knew he needed to say something. Though the only words he had would be lies, so he kissed her and made love with her until the wee hours of the morning when she at last fell asleep and he snuck back to his room. He didn't call Jack or talk to anyone about his secret, but he felt like time was running out for him. And he only hoped he'd done enough to convince Staci that even though he'd been playing at being another man, the one he truly was adored her.

STACI WOKE ALONE AND that seemed to set the tempo for the entire morning. There was something distant about Remy though he was good to his word and held her hand during the flight take-off and landing. When they exited the flight and were out of the airport Fatima and Jack met them with two Escalades.

The crew were waiting for them as well and soon they were all miked and had make-up applied.

"Okay, guys, I hope you're all ready for some fun in The Big Apple," Fatima said. "You will be taken to the Time Square Marriott Marquis where you will drop your bags at the desk and have one hour to shop for food that represents the excitement of this trip and how you feel about having made it to the last half of the show.

"You will then have thirty minutes to cook your dish in the Marquis's convention kitchen. Are you ready to go?"

"Yes!" Staci shouted along with the other remaining contestants.

They were divided into groups, Remy in a different opposite one than she and then they headed to Times Square. They had been given directions to a Whole Foods market and sent to buy their ingredients. Staci tried to get close to Remy but he was in competition mode and she decided she should be, too.

She hadn't let him influence her this much since the first week of competition and she had decided that for the rest of the competition she would go back to making cooking her priority. She let the essence and vibe of the city sink into her soul as she walked to the grocery store and back. When she was in the kitchen and directed to her work station she started preparing her dish in her head. Going over each step in her mind since she'd only have thirty minutes to actually cook.

Fatima and Jack were there as they were all once again made presentable for the cameras and told to get ready to meet the guest judge. Staci hoped it was Bobby Flay or someone equally famous. She couldn't have been more shocked than when Jean-Luc Renard entered the kitchen. The guest judge was definitely someone she'd heard of.

She felt all the blood rush from her body and literally felt faint. Oh no, why hadn't she anticipated this?

Everyone was talking and she quickly raised her hand. "Jack, I need a minute."

"Cut," the director yelled.

Everyone was staring at her. She knew there was no

graceful way to do what needed to be done. Jack came over to her station but Jean-Luc had already noticed her.

"*Ma petite*, Staci. Good to see you again," he said in his slightly accented French.

"You know Chef Renard?" Jack asked.

"Yes. I'm sorry I wasn't sure if you needed to know that before we started cooking for this challenge," Staci said.

"Thanks for letting us know. I will talk to the other judges and our producers and get back to you. Everyone please go to the temporary green room," he said.

They all filed out of the kitchen and Staci was careful not to meet anyone's eyes, but as they reached the doorway, Remy took her arm and drew her to a halt.

"That's the man from your past?"

"Yes," she said.

"Why didn't you say?" he asked. "I was thinking your ex-lover was some—"

"Why does it matter?"

"Now I understand more what you meant by how he ruined cooking for you. Are you going to be okay cooking for him?"

"Yes," she said and realized it was true. A few weeks ago her answer might have been different but now all Jean-Luc was to her was an old boyfriend, nothing more. He didn't have the effect on her that he had previously. "I really am."

"Good. I'm still going to beat you," he said gesturing for her to enter the green room.

"I don't think so, southern man. I've got a dish planned that's going to blow the judges away."

"That's all well and good, Staci, but how do you know Chef Renard?" Quinn asked. "Doesn't seem fair if you have the advantage."

"I worked under him at his restaurant in Paris almost six years ago. We had a brief fling and I left," she said. It was easier for her to talk about the past if she just dealt it out in facts. No one would know that Jean-Luc had broken her heart when he'd dumped her to start an affair with the new pastry chef. Or at least, she hoped they wouldn't. It was hard enough to be on her A-game cooking against Remy—who she definitely had feelings for and knowing she'd be judged by Jean-Luc.

"Well, that's interesting," Whit said. "I guess you had more of a surprise than the rest of us when he walked through the door. I didn't even know who he was."

"He's one of the best chefs in the world," Staci said.

"Figures they'd get someone French. I think the next competition is going to be working in Ramsfeld's restaurant here," Christian said. "He's the only judge with a kitchen here. And his new menu is French cuisine inspired."

The door opened before anyone could comment and Jack stood there. "We need to see you, Staci."

She got up and followed Jack. She hoped they weren't going to penalize her for this. But really how could she have known that Jean-Luc would be asked to judge. She had noted on her experiences that she'd worked in Paris before opening her own bakery.

"Am I in trouble?" she asked.

"Not at all," Jack told her. "Chef Renard was a surprise and you couldn't have anticipated it. Fair enough.

The judges just want to talk to you before the Quick Cook."

She entered a small office where Fatima, Hamilton, Pete and Lorenz all waited. They gestured for her to have a seat.

"We've talked to Jean-Luc and he feels that he will not be biased against you in any way. Do you feel as if you could cook for him?" Lorenz asked.

"Yes. I don't feel as though having him for a judge will influence me one way or the other. It was a shock to see him," Staci acknowledged. "I just wanted to make sure you all knew that I'd worked for him."

"You did the right thing," Fatima said. "We will reveal the fact that you worked for him in a voice-over during the edited version of the show. How long has it been since you've seen him?"

"A little over six years," she said.

"Good. I think we're ready to get on with the competition," announced Hamilton. "Unless you have any further concerns, Chef Rowland?"

"I don't," Staci said.

"Good," Hamilton repeated. "Please go back and wait with your peers."

She nodded and did what he asked her to. The hallway was empty and Staci paused while she was still alone. Her bravado had seen her through this, but a tiny part of her felt betrayed all over again.

It made her appreciate Remy all the more. She was lucky to have him in her life. She stood a little taller as she walked down the hallway determined to put up a dish that made Chef Renard realize what a good cook she was, and possibly regret forcing her out of his kitchen all those years ago.

Her mind was focused on food as she re-entered the temporary green room. Remy waited just inside the door and took her hand in his, immediately squeezing it. Instantly she let go of all thoughts of the past instead focused on what was her future. She didn't need to cook to prove anything to Jean-Luc, she needed to cook for the joy of it. Cook for the new life that was waiting for her when this competition ended.

12

REMY DIDN'T MUCH CARE for the way that Chef Renard was preoccupied with Staci's dish. He knew the girl could cook, but Remy was a guy and he saw that the other man was flirting with Staci and perhaps regretting letting her go the way he had. He hoped the other man continued to regret it.

Staci appeared as if nothing was bothering her but Remy had felt her sweaty palms when they'd first entered the stew room after she'd seen her old lover for the first time. Frankly, Remy didn't admire Chef Renard. He'd been to his restaurant in Paris and his father Alain could cook a lot better than Jean-Luc.

"What have you prepared for us?" Fatima asked.

Remy described his dish and then stood back to let them taste it. He saw the other chef's eyes widen as the spice he'd used hit his palate. He knew that he had the other man in the palm of his hands. That he, Remy, had created a dish that was surprising the more experienced man. And in that moment, Remy knew that he wanted to best Chef Renard. To prove to Staci that he was the better man in every way.

But he couldn't do that as Remy Stephens. Remy Cruzel, however, cooked on the same level as Chef Renard.

"Very good. The taste is familiar to me," Renard said.

Remy just shrugged.

"Chef Stephens is from New Orleans and it is probably those seasonings that you are tasting," Fatima suggested. "Very nice."

Chef Renard gave him a quizzical look as they moved on to the next station and Remy wondered if he'd finally found a dish that would give him away. But then he knew he was tired of hiding. He wanted to come clean with Staci and the show so that he wouldn't feel like a liar and a cheat.

He was ready to claim his legacy now; he knew he could live up to his family's reputation whether or not he won the competition.

The reasons why he'd come, the need to show that he was ready to take on the role of Chef Patron had been assuaged. The last three weeks he'd cooked dishes in new ways and learned a lot about himself as a chef. He was proud of the cooking he'd done.

Fatima, Chef Renard and the other judges were back in the center of the room and as they looked over the stations, Remy couldn't help but notice that Renard avoided making eye contact with Staci.

"Okay, cut. Judges, you may go confer over your decision. Chefs, clean your stations."

They all started working and Remy cleaned his quickly and went to find Staci. He had some questions he wanted answers to. Not the least of which was what exactly had happened to end things between her and the other chef.

"Jack, how long is the break?"

"Fifteen minutes. The smokers are headed outside," Jack said.

"I'm going to take Staci up to the atrium for a chat," Remy said. "Is that okay?"

"Yes, be back on time," Jack warned.

"We will be."

"Who will be, what?" Staci asked coming up behind him.

"You and me back on time," Remy said, taking her hand in his and leading her away from the kitchen.

"We've got fifteen minutes, cupcake girl, and I want some answers," he said.

"Answers to what?" she asked. "I think I've done enough explaining about my past for the day. To be honest I'm ready to really put it behind me. I can't believe Chef Renard is going to be here all week."

Remy waited until they were alone on the escalator heading to the atrium. "Exactly what happened when you and Renard broke up?"

"Why does that matter?" she asked as he led the way to a padded bench hidden in a private alcove.

"I think he regrets it. Were you the one who ended things?" he asked as they were seated. He couldn't stand the thought that she might have ended it and now Renard might try to win her back.

She nibbled on her lower lip and looked up at him with an inscrutable gaze. She had her chef's coat on and because of the TV cameras she had on stage make-up, but underneath all that was the woman he knew very well. And he hated to see her looking so unsure.

"Why does that matter?" she asked.

"It matters because…," He hated this feeling, these emotions that made him feel vulnerable and ache inside. He wanted to just take her in his arms and never have to let her go. "Staci, he was looking at you like he was interested in rekindling your romance. So I want to know if that's a possibility?"

"No, Remy," she said. "There isn't a chance of that happening."

"Why not?" he asked. "If I lost you…well I'd always try to get you back."

"Really?" she asked, looking up at him this time with a very caring expression and he wondered if she had fallen for him too. He knew that she cared about him. She admitted that in spite of her fear of being lied to, she had started to believe in him.

"Yes," he said. "Did you really doubt it?"

"All I know is what I'm feeling," she said. "I know that you called us a couple, but I'm still not sure of myself to believe that this can last. So when you say things like that I'm a bit surprised."

"Why? You have to know what a lovely woman you are. Haven't I done enough to show you that?"

"You've done more than that, but it's my issue," she said. There was a wariness in her tone that told him she was exhausted from her past and how heavy a burden it must be for her to keep carrying it around. He wanted to take it from her but he wondered if he were really the man who could.

A part of him felt like she used the past as a wedge to keep him from getting too close and to keep her from really falling for him.

"Maybe it's time you let it go. Just because you've had a few bad relationships—"

"It's more than that, Remy. You asked me what happened with Jean-Luc and the truth is he moved on to another woman. I came into work one day and caught them together. That was it, he never said a word to me other than to say chefs had big appetites. I gave my notice and left."

"I'm sorry," he said.

"It's not your fault," she said, reminding him.

But he knew Staci. Proud, tough, confident Staci who had been hurt by that one incident. She'd been telling him all along that trust was going to come hard for her, but until now he hadn't realized just how hard. He had thought that he could just fix her hurt for her by showing her that a real man was tender and caring. But he saw now that the kind of betrayal she experienced, well…

Her past and his lie were pretty much kindred spirits and he knew, even though he'd been reluctant to admit it, that when the truth came out—and it would—Staci was going to walk away from him as surely as she'd left Jean-Luc Renard and Paris all those years ago.

STACI WON THE QUICK COOK, which made her feel satisfied. She knew she'd cooked well but more than that she was happy to know that Jean-Luc's praise meant nothing to her. It wasn't like the painful time when they'd been lovers and she'd waited and waited for some words of praise from him.

The fact that her reaction was no reaction showed her how much she'd moved on. Though she was used to keeping the past between her and Remy, she knew now that she was over it and really she only had one person to thank and that was her current lover.

The man who'd come in second in today's challenge. He winked at her across the studio when she'd been announced the winner and she knew he was proud of her achievement. What she liked about Remy was his own ability to give praise and not feel as if it stole anything from him. Jean-Luc hadn't been like that at all.

They were all told that Staci would have an advantage in the following day's elimination challenge and were sent one-by-one to record their video diaries about the day and the trip to New York. That night there would be a group dinner at Hamilton's restaurant, Ramsfeld East, and Staci suspected that Christian had been correct when he'd guessed that's where their challenge would be the next day.

They had the afternoon free.

"Want to go sightsee?" she asked Remy.

"That's the first time you've asked me on a date," he said.

"It'll be the last time too unless you answer correctly," she warned.

"Then, yes, I'd love to go with you. Where did you have in mind?" he asked.

"I've never been to the top of the Empire State Building," she said.

"You didn't go with your mom?" he asked, he'd hit all the touristy spots long ago with his parents and his cousins. And he hadn't been to the Empire State Building since he'd been twenty. As he stood there, thinking of all the places they could go, he finally realized that going back to New Orleans and cooking at Gastrophile was the only thing he really wanted.

"Mom was afraid of heights. Grandma and I decided we'd see a show with her instead of going up. But if you're game…"

"I am," he said. "Let's go."

When they got down to street level, Remy hailed a cab and gave the driver their destination. They sat in the back seat with the summer sun shining down on them.

"I can't believe you beat me today," Remy said. "I guess getting you to relax was a good strategy for you."

"It seems as if it was," she said with a cheeky grin. "To be honest. It's not being relaxed that is really the thing that made me win today," she said, full of mystery.

"I want to know what it is, but we're getting out at the end of the block," Remy said.

The cab stopped and Remy paid the driver. They followed the signs up to the ticket booth and then took the elevator to the viewing platform. Remy linked their hands together, realizing that even doing this type of thing was fun with Staci. He knew he needed to stop ignoring the truth that needed to be said but he couldn't.

"Okay, so tell me what made you win today," he said

after he'd led them to a spot away from most of the tourists.

"The truth?"

"Isn't it always about the truth with you?"

"Yes, it is," she said. Then she sighed and the breeze ruffled her short black hair. "It was knowing that you were the man you are…that sounds silly, doesn't it? But it was you and the way you made me feel. I channeled that into my cooking.

He was glad to hear it, he wanted to give her as much as he could so that she'd remember the good times with him when the bad inevitably came. Today's circumstances had made him realize he needed to step forward before a chef that could recognize him came through the door, like Chef Renard had done.

"You did a good job with that, *ma chère*."

"I did. I don't want to talk about the show though. Thank you for being so supportive about everything. It was nice to look over and know that you were on my side," she said.

"No problem."

She ambled over to the rail and studied the City and beyond. "It's easy to forget that we're a part of something so huge. I've seen more people here today than I normally see in my neighborhood in a year. I mean I like my quiet little life. Is New Orleans like this?"

"The French Quarter is busy all the time. It's a bit like New York, but the Garden District…that's where I live, it's quiet like the little neighborhood you described."

"Do you think you'll head back there when the competition is over?" she asked.

"I don't know," he said, but the truth was yes. He had so many new ideas for Gastrophile. But he couldn't share them with Staci. And that drove home the fact that this wasn't as real as he'd been pretending it was.

"Really?" she asked. "I'd think you'd have some idea of what your next move will be."

There was something in her tone that bothered him. It was as if she were questioning his honesty and okay, he knew he wasn't being up front with her. He knew that everything he felt and worried over stemmed entirely from the fact that if he were being honest he'd tell her all about Gastrophile and ask her to move home with him.

Frankly, he was tired of running.

"Sorry, it's just that you might sell your interest in Sweet Dreams and then we'd both be without a job. Where would that leave us?"

She stepped away from him and he knew without being told that he'd said the wrong thing. "I guess that pretty much sums it up. Why didn't you just say when the show is over, so are we?"

"Because I don't want that to be the case," he said, feeling trapped and knowing he had no one but himself to blame. If he'd been a different sort of man he wouldn't need external praise to know he was good at what he did. But he wasn't. And this show had been the only way to know if he was the same quality of chef as his father, uncles and grandfather.

He wanted to be worthy of their name, he needed to know his place in the culinary dynasty had been earned and not given, but today seeing the hurt and disappointment in Staci's eyes, he acknowledged, he'd give it all up if he could find a way to smooth over everything with her without having to reveal what he'd done.

But he was a realist and knew that would never happen. So he had to make a decision of what to tell her and he knew that the more of his soul he laid bare now the easier it might be for her to forgive him later.

"I do want you to come to New Orleans with me," he said. "But I was afraid to say that."

STACI GUESSED SHE SHOULD be careful when she pushed Remy. He always did something that was unexpected and inviting her to come to New Orleans was no exception. Even though he hadn't really invited her to come with him. He'd just said it was what he wanted.

"Why didn't you just ask me then?" She didn't see why it would be hard for him. He had nothing to lose. Or was he not sure that she'd accept him. He didn't have a kitchen to return to. "Listen, if you're worried about not having a gig, it's not a big deal. Once this show airs everyone in the country is going to be beating down your door. You'll be able to choose your assignment."

He reached over and rubbed his thumb over her lower lip before kissing her so sweetly that she felt wrapped in some emotion she was afraid to name.

"Thank you. Your offer means everything to me. But I don't think it's fair to ask you to give up your family and friends to move across the country with a man you aren't committed to."

"I understand. Just so you know if you asked me to move to New Orleans and give our relationship a real try, I'd say yes."

She felt braver than she had been in the last five years. Since she'd talked Alysse into starting Sweet Dreams with her. It had been so long since she'd risked anything, which was why she'd signed up for the show and it was Remy that was the challenge that made her feel alive. Remy and the way he inspired her to cook better. She had never felt this completely into another person before.

She was dancing around naming the emotion because once she said it, she'd be just like her mother and grandmother. She'd have fallen in love with a man and Staci wasn't entirely sure she knew him and could trust him.

"Then I'm asking," he said. "At the end of the competition, will you move to New Orleans with me?"

She took a deep breath and held it. All the rash decisions she'd made in her life flashed before her eyes and she knew that this one was the smartest one of all.

"Yes," she said. "But I reserve the right to change my mind."

"No," he challenged her, shaking his head. "No matter what happens, you and I have made a deal to give each other a try. I asked and it was hard to do. You're either in this with me or not at all."

"I'm in it," he said.

He smiled and kissed her again. "This calls for a celebration!"

"It does?" she asked, but then realized what she'd said. "I mean, it sure does. What should we do? We're already pretty close to the top of the world."

"I know a place I think you will like," he said. "Do you trust me?"

"I wouldn't be moving to New Orleans if I didn't," she said. Hearing the words out loud warmed her. She wondered how different leaving home would be this time. When she'd moved to Paris she'd been scared but so sure of herself. This time she wasn't scared or as sure of herself. She'd wager her grandmother would say that was age giving her some wisdom.

"That's right. Okay," he said, taking her hand in his. "Follow me."

She followed him through the gift shop where he stopped at the jewelry counter and bought her a bracelet with an Empire State Building charm on it. "This is so you'll always remember this visit."

"I don't think I'll be forgetting it any time soon."

"I hope not," he said.

They took the elevator to the lobby and Staci was full of such a feeling of love. There she said it, she thought.

"Remy?" a man called to them.

Staci heard Remy curse under his breath as he turned. The man who'd spoken looked vaguely familiar to Staci. He was about as tall as Remy and had salt and pepper-colored curly hair. His eyes were dark chocolate brown and he eyed them both intently. The woman at the man's side was slightly taller than Staci and had reddish brown hair that was perfectly coifed. She wore a Lily Pulitzer sundress and looked altogether way more chic than Staci could ever hope to.

"Do you know them?" she asked under her breath.

"Yes," he said. "They're my parents."

"Mom and Dad, this is Staci. Staci, this is my mom and dad."

"Hello," Staci said holding out her hand to the couple who each shook it in turn.

"I'm Alain," his father said. "This is Betsy."

"It's so nice to meet you. Remy has told me a few things about you," Staci said.

"That's good to hear," Alain remarked. "We know nothing of you."

"I suspect that's because we're not supposed to make any calls home," Staci said.

Remy seemed as if he wanted to run away. She gave him a what's up look, which he ignored.

"Why ever not? Most boys who run away from their responsibilities aren't forbade from calling home," Betsy said. "Unless the world has changed."

"What are you talking about?" Staci asked, dropping Remy's hand. Clearly there was more going on here than she understood.

"That our son walked out of his job and has been missing for the last three months," Alain explained. "Not a single word in that time."

She faced Remy and demanded, "What are they talking about? I thought you lost your job."

"Not exactly," he said.

"Then what is the exact story?" she persisted. "Because the picture I'm getting is of a man who hasn't been honest with me."

"I'm sorry, my dear, but who did you say you were again?" Betsy asked.

"Staci Rowland, Mrs. Stephens. I'm a competitor on a cooking show that your son is also participating in."

"Mrs. Who?"

Staci swallowed hard as the truth slowly sunk in. This wasn't one lie but something much bigger. And this guy had some serious problems if he thought...what did he think?

"Isn't that your last name? Remy has presented himself as an out of work cook from New Orleans...Remy Stephens."

"He's not out of work," Alain said. "He was promoted to Chef Patron at Gastrophile and his last name is Cruzel."

"Wait. Staci I—" Remy began.

"Too late!" Staci blurted. "Stay here and explain it all to your parents. I'm going back to the hotel. I'll give you until tonight to inform the judges of your duplicity."

"Staci!"

"No. I don't want to hear any more of your carefully concocted stories. To you they might seem amusing, but to someone who had believed them, I can assure you they aren't."

13

REMY RAN AFTER STACI but she'd disappeared into the crowd and he couldn't find her. He knew as soon as she'd turned ashen that all the joy of the day had been lost. He had tried to reach for her but Staci was small and quick and determined. Determined to put as much distance between her and him as she could.

His parents were right behind them; his dad put his hand on Remy's shoulder. He didn't want to have a conversation with them right now. Everything had come undone and in the worst possible way. He needed to sort the mess out in his head so he could do what he needed to in order to win Staci back. If that were even possible.

Without Staci cooking meant nothing to him. He was looking forward to returning to New Orleans with her by his side. Not by himself. Now that he'd found love he didn't want to go back to his old life.

"We need to talk." His father's tone was solemn.

"I know we do," Remy said. "I know, it's just I have to go after her and…"

He'd seen that look in her eyes and he knew that if

he didn't get to Staci quick everything with her would be gone. And he couldn't accept that.

"I'm sorry, dear," Betsy said, "but what was that all about?"

Remy cursed under his breath and spoke to his parents. "I can talk to you both later. I'm staying at the Marquis in Times Square."

"We want some answers now," his father repeated.

"We've been worried to death about you," his mother said.

"You'll have to wait. I've made a hell of a mess, Dad, and I have to clean it up first." He went over to his mother and hugged her and gave her a kiss on the cheek. Then did the same to his dad.

"I'm sorry," he apologized.

"This girl *must* be important," his mom said.

"More important than you know and I think I just hurt her in a way I'd been hoping not to. I've got to go," he said, waving goodbye to his parents and heading out the door. He hailed a cab and as it drove through the streets, Remy carefully scanned the crowds for a glimpse of Staci, but she wasn't to be found.

As soon as he entered the Marquis, he called Jack. This disaster was entirely of his making and maybe if he did everything he could now to mitigate it he'd still be able to save his relationship with Staci. Though he knew it wouldn't be easy.

"It's Remy. There's something I need to tell you."

"Is it something that will make our ratings soar? I know you've been dating Staci—what do you say to an on-air proposal," Jack said. "I'm actually in the bar with the judges right now and some of the other production team. Come and meet us."

Remy agreed, though completely ignored Jack's suggestion about Staci. He doubted she'd say yes to anything involving him right now unless it was his head on a platter. And he couldn't blame her. Now that he knew his secret was out he regretted not telling her sooner.

When Remy entered the bar Jack waved him over and Remy ordered a Fosters from the bartender.

There was a round of greetings from everyone and Remy sat down next to Jack and turned to the producer. He took a deep breath.

"You okay?"

"Yes, I haven't been up front with who I really am."

"What? You're kidding me, right?" Jack said. "We've got three weeks of shows in the can, Remy. Please tell me you are joking."

"I'm not. My last name isn't Stephens it's Cruzel."

Everyone in the group stopped talking when he said that and stared at him.

"Are you related to Alain?" Hamilton asked.

"He's my dad."

"Why would you do this?" Lorenz asked. "A pedigree like yours should be celebrated."

"Yes, it should," Remy said. "But I've spent my entire life being told I could cook because I'm a Cruzel. And I did because that was what was expected. Even at the CIA I was treated like a star pupil and I never knew if it was because of my skills or my name."

"You decided to try an experiment to prove you had

the Cruzel talent," Pete said. "It's an interesting idea but you've lied to us all."

"I know. I'm sorry," Remy said. "At first I wasn't even sure if I'd make it to the second round so it seemed a challenge for myself more than for you. And I wanted you all to judge my dishes, not look at me and think of my father and grandfather's cooking."

"I understood that," Hamilton said. "But what does that mean for our show?"

"I'm thinking," Jack answered. "We're going to have to talk it over, Remy. I'll let you know our decision as soon as I can. Has anyone else heard about this?"

"Staci," he said.

"Ah, is she the reason you mentioned it?" Lorenz asked.

"Yes. That and the fact that the guest judges could be anyone. I know my father won't do television but my Uncle Pierre would jump at the chance to come on. I didn't want to have another shock for you guys like Staci's today."

"That's very kind of you," Fatima said.

But he could tell as they all looked at him that they were as disappointed as Staci had been. They'd become a family on the show and Remy had been lying to them all the entire time. He knew his reasons were solid but now he just felt guilty and selfish for doing it.

"What should I do now?" Remy asked. "I'd like to find Staci."

"Is she lost?" Lorenz asked. The other man leaned forward in his seat staring over at Remy.

Remy shook his head. He felt like an idiot at how he'd handled this entire situation. But he wasn't hiding anything any more. "She didn't take the news very well and we split up. Now that you guys know the truth my priority is finding her."

Hamilton watched him through narrowed eyes and then nodded. "Go. We will text you when we need you back here."

"Thank you," Remy said.

He had signed a contract with these people and though he'd read the fine print and knew there was no reason why Remy Cruzel couldn't have entered, he wondered if they'd penalize him for misrepresenting himself.

He didn't know and honestly at this moment didn't care. He'd go on to cook again when this was done but he knew deep inside his soul that there was only one woman for him and that was Staci.

He also knew that getting her back would be the hardest thing he'd ever done. It had been hard enough to woo her the first time. Although now that the truth was out he could be Remy Cruzel. He had nothing to hide and it was time that he stopped ignoring the truth of his emotions and made Staci aware of them.

Remy Stephens had had to lie low, but Remy Cruzel didn't have to and he fully intended to take advantage of that. He strode from the hotel onto the bustling sidewalk at Times Square and for the first time let himself admit that his heart ached at the thought that he might not be able to fix this and win Staci back.

STACI RAN AS HARD AND as fast as she could. When she finally stopped she realized that she'd been crying. Not silent ladylike tears, but belting sobs.

She'd had it all for a few brief seconds, she thought.

She had protected herself for so long, figured she'd been smarter this time by making Remy...what? She hadn't done anything right. She'd fallen in love with the wrong man as surely as her grandmother and her mother had done. It was sad really that another generation of Rowland woman had followed the same pattern.

She should have stayed to herself. She should have just focused on her cooking.

"You okay?" a stranger asked.

She nodded and started walking. She probably looked like something from a zombie apocalypse movie. She'd had on the camera-ready make-up, which was thick, and now it had to be ruined by her tears.

She found a Starbucks and went into the bathroom. Once she locked the door she stood in front of the mirror.

She hated the raw pain on her face, but forced herself to keep staring so that she'd always remember the real thing that Remy had given her. It was heartbreak. She needed to never forget what this felt like.

The worst part of learning that Remy had lied about everything he was from the second they met—was that she still loved him.

She buried her head in her hands and let the sobs out. She cried for all the half-formed dreams that had been floating around in the back of her mind. She cried for the little girl inside of her that had for a brief instant thought that maybe all those books she'd read as a kid had been right and that a girl like Staci could be truly happy.

She cried because she knew when she left this bathroom she'd never let herself be this weak again.

The logical part of her mind was trying to take over but the weepy woman inside her couldn't let go. Staci kept replaying the scene with Remy and his parents over and over again in her head.

She pulled out her phone and called her one true friend.

"Sweet Dreams, home of the incredible red velvet dream cupcakes. This is Alysse speaking, how may I help you?"

"It's Staci," she said. Her voice sounded deeper than normal and so rough that she was surprised by it.

"What's wrong? Where are you? Do you need me to come to Malibu?" Alysse asked.

Staci felt the love immediately from Alysse, her sister of the soul. "Everything's wrong. I'm in New York, in a bathroom…Remy has been lying to me all along."

"Is he married?"

"What? No. I mean, I don't know. I have no idea," Staci blurted. The lies that he'd told her now took on even more disturbing connotations.

"Okay, start from the beginning and tell me everything," Alysse said.

Staci took a deep breath. Just having Alysse there made things a little easier.

"Remy is part of the Cruzel family. He's been lying about who he is on the show."

"Why?"

"I don't know," Staci said.

"He could have entered the competition as Remy Cruzel, so why make up a fake name?" Alysse asked. "You have to find out."

"He lied to me," Staci said. "I can't see beyond that. I don't care what his reasons were. He told me he was a man of honor."

"He's a dirt bag," Alysse said. "I'm making you a tray of brownies and sending them to you."

"You can't. I'm not even supposed to be talking to anyone back home. I just don't know what to do. I think I love him, Aly. For the first time I thought I'd met a man who got me, you know?"

"Oh, honey, I do know. I'm so sorry."

There was only silence on the line. She couldn't help but feel like there was no hope for her and Remy. "Everyone knows we've been dating."

"I'm sure they will all be kind to you," Alysse said.

"You always were so trusting of others," Staci said. She knew that having Remy's lie exposed in front of the others was going to be hard. She didn't want their sad looks.

"I want to run away."

"If that's what you think you should do, but you're not someone who lets their problems drive them into hiding. You're a fighter, Staci Rowland," Alysse said. "Don't forget that."

She wanted to believe what her friend was telling her but a part of her, a really big part of her, was scared. She didn't know how to make this work. She didn't know how to move on from what had happened.

"What should I do?"

"I'd go back to the show and hold your head up high. You still have a competition to win, right?"

"Uh…"

"Listen," Alysse said. "I don't know how you're doing in the competition but if it were me I'd channel all that anger into kicking his butt in the kitchen. Show him and the others that you're stronger than anyone, Remy included, ever expected."

Staci liked the sound of that. She checked herself in the mirror and this time she saw the woman that Alysse had just described. Staci had been fighting her entire life and she certainly wasn't going to let Remy steal this from her. He'd shaken her faith in men. To be honest he'd probably delivered the death knell to her faith in herself.

But that was okay, she knew the way back and she'd succeed or put every last ounce of her sweat and skill into the fight.

"Thanks, Aly."

"You're welcome, honey. You know I love you. And text me later to let me know what happened."

"I will if I can. I'm going to win this thing. At least cooking is something that's just for me."

"Your cooking is for the world," Alysse said.

"You're right."

Staci hung up the phone and left the coffee shop, feeling a million times better. As she walked back to Times Square and her hotel, she felt the weight of that bracelet Remy had given her. At the concierge desk, she slipped the bracelet off her wrist and put it in a envelope to be delivered to Remy's room.

She wasn't over what had happened by any means but she was in control again and she knew that she was headed in the right direction.

Two hours later Remy got the text he'd been waiting for. He hadn't been able to find Staci anywhere in the city and he suspected that when he did find her she wasn't going to be in a mood to listen.

Which put him in a really bad mood. But he tried to shake it off as he walked upstairs to the meeting room where he found Jack waiting outside.

"What's the verdict?"

"The judges want to talk to you," Jack explained. "If they agree to let you stay I'll need some extra filming time with you and I'd like to include an interview with your father."

"Why?"

"He's the reason you were pretending to be someone else, right?" Jack asked.

"Yes, but I don't think that has anything to do with the show. My parents didn't even know where I was. I needed to disappear."

"And you did, which was great for you and of course our good luck that you can cook but you still misrepresented yourself," Jack said.

"My dad won't do it, Jack. I know the man and he doesn't think much of reality TV," Remy said.

"Okay, go and see the judges. I'll try to think of an angle…but your dad disapproving of what we're doing might work."

Remy just shook his head. The room he entered was a board room with a large dark wooden table in the middle and several large armchairs set around it. On the wall were black and white photos of iconic New York City landmarks.

"Have a seat, Remy," Hamilton said from the head of the table.

Lorenz and Greg were seated on either side of him. The men were all dressed in suits and had very serious expressions. As they should, Remy thought. He pulled out a chair at the end of the table directly across from Hamilton and sat down.

"We've had a long talk and we can see why you did it," Hamilton said. "To some extent we even admire it."

"Thank you, Chef," Remy said.

"It's our decision that you can remain in the competition," Lorenz said. "We haven't spoken to the rest of the contestants yet. You will have to go on camera and explain what you were doing and why. Jack will have Fatima explain that we're giving you a second chance."

"Thank you so much," Remy said. "And again I'm sorry for what I did."

"We accept your apology. If you will move down here by us, we are going to call the rest of the contestants in for you to explain the situation to them. We have to give them a chance to adjust to this news before we all go to Ramsfeld's tonight."

"Do you think it will affect the competition and the elimination challenge?" Remy asked.

"Not on our part but we want your peers to have a chance to hear the news and discuss it. Then we can move on."

Remy nodded. He was as ready as he'd ever be to face the remaining chefs. "Is Staci with them?"

"Yes, she is," Hamilton said. "She said it didn't matter to her what name you used, she was still going to beat you."

Of course she did. Leave it to Staci to pull her defenses back around her and start showing the world her game face. He wished she would have at least let him explain privately what had been going on, instead of just assuming he was lying to hurt her.

Pete got up and left the room and Remy could only assume it was to get the other *Premier Chef* contestants. He hadn't expected to feel nervous but his palms were sweaty and he realized he'd rather have a cook off against every single one of them than have to tell them he'd lied to them.

He suspected more than one of them might want him kicked out of the competition. "Why did you decide to let me stay?" Remy asked.

"Your skills," Lorenz said. "We started this competition to find the best chefs in the country and highlight them. We've been surprised in each series how many good chefs there are around the country. To a certain extent you are the epitome of that."

"What do you mean?" Remy asked.

"The Cruzel family doesn't cook outside of New Orleans but brings Michelin judges to their part of the world. You're the head chef at a three-starred kitchen, that counts for a lot. And you didn't have to go to France or Britain or New York."

"My father thinks everyone deserves to have a fine dining establishment wherever they live," Remy said.

"I agree," Hamilton said. "That's why I do so many shows. I want audiences to know they don't have to settle for the same menu and the same dishes each time they go out for a meal. There are more choices, but unless people know about them then often the small, truly creative places close."

"I agree," Remy said.

Jack entered the room with a camera crew and placed one cameraman at either end of the room and then made sure they all had microphones on. "I might not use this but I thought it could be useful later."

The door started to open and Remy watched as his peers filed into the room. Dave and Christian on one side. Erin, Whit and Staci on the other. Staci wouldn't meet his gaze but even from this distance he could tell she'd been crying.

He felt a rush of emotions so strong that it was all he could do not to go to her. Those emotions were quelled when she finally did look at him and he saw how cold and glacier-like her gaze could be.

"There is no easy way to say it other than to tell you that Remy Stephens is not this man's real name," Greg said. "He is the son of famed Michelin starred chef Alain Cruzel. I'll let Remy explain his reasons to you and then we will listen to your comments. We have already conferred and agreed that he may remain in the competition. Remy."

Remy looked at each of the chefs remembering all the time they'd spent together in the kitchen, but it was when he looked at Staci that he felt the real need to explain. "I know we all have different reasons for entering a cooking competition, some of us are doing so to prove something to ourselves, others to prove something to the world.

"I'm in the former category in that all my life I've been treated like I was a master chef simply because of my last name. I have prepared dishes that were developed by my father and grandfather and won praise for them. But I never knew how much of the praise was because of the Cruzel name and how much of it was due to my skills.

"My father has asked me to take over as Chef Patron of Gastrophile—our family's restaurant in New Orleans. But I didn't feel ready to take on the task until I knew for certain that I was worthy of the title.

"To find out, I left New Orleans and cooked my way across the country. And when I heard about this competition and read the terms and conditions I knew I could enter and use the Anglicized version of my middle name as my last name. In truth I wasn't lying too much, I am Remy Etienne or Stephen but that's neither here nor there.

"I can only say I'm sorry that I deceived you, but I wanted a chance to be treated like everyone else and to have to prove myself one dish at a time."

14

Staci never heard a more eloquent definition of a lie than the one that Remy had told. She wanted to believe that he was merely trying to recover lost ground but there was a truth to his words, she admitted. To some extent she even understood his reasoning. But her heart was a lot slower to forgive.

Remy looked as if he'd been up all night and even though it had only been a few hours since she'd seen him, he seemed tired and tense. A part of her was worried about him until she remembered that he'd lied to her. He'd known what he was doing the entire time.

She didn't have anything she wanted to say to him. She was following Alysse's advice and focusing on cooking and winning. She'd go home and lick her wounds, not to mention celebrate.

"Why are you coming clean now?" Christian asked.

Remy cleared his throat and looked directly at him. "Staci and I ran into my parents while sight-seeing and the truth came out. I also had a feeling today that Chef

Renard might have recognized me and I thought before this went any further I should step up and clear the air."

"Did you know about this?" Whit asked under her breath to Staci.

"Not until his parents said their last name wasn't Stephens."

"Oh, man, I would have been pissed," Whit said.

"I was."

"Still are, if your body language is any indication," Whit said.

"Ladies, please ask your questions to the room," Pete directed them.

"Sorry, Pete," Whit said. "My fault entirely. I don't have any problems with him staying in the competition."

"Good. Does anyone have any concerns?" Pete asked.

There were a few concerns but mostly everyone seemed to agree that by not using his legally registered name Remy had leveled the playing field. Dave thought that it had given Remy an unfair advantage but since Christian and Erin both were executive chefs in well known restaurants everyone else agreed that Remy was fine.

"If that's everything then we have a few housekeeping type items and then you can all go get dressed for dinner at Ramsfeld's East tonight. Jack, do you want to handle that?"

"Yes," Jack said. "Starting tonight please refer to Remy as Chef Cruzel, rather than Chef Stephens. We will reveal his identity as we film this week's episode and each of you will be asked to tape a special entry in your private video journals discussing the news and how it affected you."

"Will we have to do it now?" Staci asked. She didn't think she was ready to talk on camera about Remy's lie. Maybe once she had a few days to clear her head.

"No. When we get back to Malibu we'll do it at the house. Any other questions?" he asked.

There weren't any and they were all dismissed. Staci went immediately to the express elevator but the line was long and by the time she got on Remy was standing next to her.

"We have to talk," he said.

"I don't see why. I'm cool with everything for the show," she said as they were squeezed together along with a large group of conventioneers and a family of four. Remy was pressed right against her.

Her heart started to beat so fast and it was all she could do not to reach out and hold onto him. But then she remembered he wasn't the man she thought he was and no matter how she looked at it or how he tried to justify it, she honestly didn't know Remy Cruzel.

She pulled back and wrapped her arm around her waist. And tried to put more distance between them in spite of the crowded elevator. Remy remained still.

Here, she'd made up her mind to ignore him and now he wasn't letting her. Which just added to the anger building inside of her. When they reached their floor, she and Remy stepped off the crowded elevator.

"I'm being as civil as I can be right now, Remy," she said. She had heard his explanation and while she could buy it, she didn't want to. At least, and not right now. She felt betrayed and brokenhearted today.

"I don't want you to be civil. We need to have this out. We need to get it all sorted so we can move on. I asked you to come and live with me," he said. "That invitation still stands."

She shook her head. "And I tried to console you because you didn't have a job. Wow, that must have made you chuckle."

"I'm not that kind of man, *ma chère*—

"Don't. Do not use any endearments. We are competitors, that's all."

The elevator dinged and people got off the elevator. Remy took Staci's arm, leading her down the hall to his room. "We need to be some place private."

"Fine," she said. Agreeing that she didn't want anyone to hear the things she had to say to Remy. And now that she'd started talking to him, she had a lot to say to him.

She'd promised herself she wouldn't get upset and she was determined to keep her word.

He opened his door and gestured for her to enter. His room was set up similarly to hers with a king-size bed and two chairs over near the desk. She sat on one of them as he took the other.

"Staci, I want you to know that everything I said to you was the truth. All of it."

"Really, Remy?" she asked. Feeling that wave of emotion roiling up inside of her only this time instead of shocked tears it came out as anger.

"Do you have a job?" she asked.

"Yes, but—

"Is your last name Stephens?" she interrupted to ask him. Hurt overcoming her patience.

"No, but—"

"Would you really give it all up and move to San Diego to live with the co-owner of a cupcake bakery?" she asked. And this was the one that bothered her the most. The one she knew he'd hate to have to answer honestly.

"No, I wouldn't."

"So you kind of proved my point," she said. "You lied about the important things. The foundational things. And you said things to me that you never should have. Not until you were free to be who you really are," she said.

"If you'd give me a chance to explain then I will. I didn't lie to *you* per se I—"

"That's not helping," she said.

"Truthfully," he said. "I wasn't sure I would go back to Gastrophile. What if I'd lost all the challenges and had it proven that I wasn't the cook I thought I was. Then I wouldn't go back there and take over the restaurant. Technically, I was out of work."

"It's not the same thing and you know it."

"I do know it, which is why I'm sitting here trying to explain. I knew from the first that you were trouble."

"Don't do that," she said.

"Don't do what?"

"Make it seem like I was special. I was just gullible and bought every lie you told," she said.

THIS WASN'T GOING AT all the way that Remy had hoped it would. He saw that Staci was trying to mask her pain over his betrayal. It should have made him be more conciliatory, instead, it frustrated him.

He'd fallen in love with her. He'd invited her to come and live with him and she acted as if it were all for nothing. That he'd done it just to make a fool of her.

"If I could go back and do things differently, I would. But I never planned on what happened between us. And you've got to believe me, I never lied to you about my feelings. In fact I was more honest with you than I have ever been with a woman. Since I couldn't share my real last name with you I wanted to share everything else."

He didn't think she'd ever understand how badly he now felt about the entire situation. Their flirtation had started out so intensely. "I never meant to make love with you that first night, but there has been this overwhelming attraction between us, and I'm not sorry I didn't ignore it."

"Why not?"

"Because then I would have missed out on you and me. And I wouldn't have wanted that. Deep inside I hope you can forgive me."

"I don't know," she said.

Staci had left behind a promising career once and reinvented herself because of a doomed love affair. More than likely she'd do it again.

But he could only say he was sorry so many times and then the rest was up to her. Could she forgive and forget? Could. Staci get beyond the things he'd said and done to see the man he was underneath.

"I know that saying trust me isn't going to win you back, but if we can move past this—"

"I can't. I might be able to at some point but today I just can't do it. I'm sorry, Remy. I wish we'd come into each other's lives at another time. Though to be honest I can't imagine it ever happening."

She stood and he knew she was leaving. There would be no getting her back now and no chance of working things out any further. This was it.

And so it seemed that his vacation affairs had been the smart way to go. He had thought that this romance when he was rediscovering his love of cooking and who he was, and finding this woman were meant to be.

"Before you leave, will you answer one last question for me?" he asked her.

She was standing in front of the door with her back toward him but she turned to face him. "Sure."

He looked right into her eyes and took a few steps closer.

"I know that you will never believe this, but I was taking you to my cousin's cooking school in Manhattan to show you the truth about me. I wanted you to see it and I wanted to do it in my own way."

She stepped back and reached for the door handle.

"Remy, by your very silence you took the easy way out. I'll admit I've made some bad decisions in my life but this one has cost me the most."

"I care about you, Staci," he said. "We can figure this out, make it work."

"Maybe it was because we were trapped together in the house and there was that spark between us," she said. "Because both of us should have remembered that lust isn't love. And we're both adult enough to know that affairs like this do end."

"It wasn't being trapped with you in the house. I know my feelings a lot better than that. Please believe me that I didn't set out to hurt you. The only thing I've wanted for you was a chance at happiness."

"I'll remember that," she said and then opened the door and walked away.

STACI KNOCKED EVERYONE'S socks off and won the next two weeks of challenges. She kept thinking about what Remy had said to her. It was impossible not to think about it or about him. After all she was living in the same house with him. They'd returned to Malibu but everything was different now. Especially as they entered this last week of competition and everyone had been eliminated except for her, Christian and Remy.

A part of her was glad Remy was still here because she wanted him to see that he hadn't broken her spirit. But another, secret part of her was just glad he was still around because even though it made her ache a little inside she knew she'd miss him if she couldn't see him every day.

It was Sunday and starting tomorrow they'd have an intensive cook-off where they'd be judged and earn points every day. At the end of the week the two chefs with the most points would go up against each other in a three-course meal.

Staci stiffened her spine and met the others in the living room. She took a seat at the opposite side of the room from Remy.

"Staci, that's not necessary," he said.

"Just trying to be smart," she said. "I'm hoping to win this by next week."

"I hope you do, too," he said quietly.

Christian arrived and then a moment later Jack did. "Good news, guys, tonight you will be dining at Hamilton Ramsfeld's house. He and Lorenz are fixing dinner for you. They've invited some special guests along and instead of making you wait until we get to Hamilton's place I've brought the guests here to meet you."

Jack went back outside. Staci looked at Remy and Christian and they both shrugged.

"At least they aren't taping this," Christian said, glancing around to confirm that there weren't any cameras.

"That's one small blessing," Remy agreed.

They heard the door open and then the sound of footsteps on the marble foyer. Jack's voice was a low rumble as he gave directions to whomever he had with him. The next minute a group of three people were standing before them. In the middle was Alysse.

Staci was so happy to see her best friend she almost started crying. She noticed that Remy's dad stood next to Alysse and a tall, thin woman with mocha colored skin stood on the other side.

"Everyone this is Alexi Montrell, Christian's wife. Alysse Dresden, Staci's best friend and Alain Cruzel, Remy's father," Jack announced. "You have the rest of the afternoon free. Be back here in the living room dressed casually at five."

Jack turned to leave as Christian rushed to Alexi's

side and lifted her off the ground in a big hug. Watching them made Staci wish that things had turned out differently for her and Remy.

"Hey, girl. I've missed you," Alysse said, catching her in a warm hug.

"I've missed you, too," Staci said, welcoming her friend.

"I brought brownies with me. Want to go somewhere and chat?" Alysse asked.

"May I interrupt?" Alain asked. "I'd really like the chance to speak to you, Staci."

The last thing she wanted was a heart-to-heart with Remy's dad but she had to admit she was intrigued. "All right. If Alysse doesn't mind."

"Oh, I don't," Alysse said. "I've got a few things I'd like to say to Chef Remy."

Immediately, Remy looked worried.

Staci half smiled at that and followed Remy's dad into the next room where there was a seating area.

"I'm sorry for butting in just then but we never got properly introduced," he said. "And I really wanted to talk to you again."

"I'm Staci Rowland," she said. "I hope you will forgive the way I acted in New York. You and your wife were a surprise to me. The entire thing with Remy was a mess."

"Yes, it was. Betsy and I both feel to blame for how things happened that day," he said. "Please accept our apologies for everything."

"You have nothing to apologize for," she said. "Remy is responsible for all this."

"Yes, he is. I understand that he felt pressured by me to do something he wasn't ready for."

"I don't know what Remy told you about us, but he had shared certain stories with me. I think the expectation of always living up to or rather cooking up to your reputation took its toll on him. I was just in the wrong place at the wrong time."

"I don't know about that," Alain said. "Maybe you were in the right place."

"How do you figure?"

"Remy told me that you and he were involved," Alain said.

"He did?"

"Yes and his mother and I were happily surprised that you were. We've never met anyone Remy dated," he said. "But yourself."

"You technically didn't meet me either," she said.

"We would have. Remy said he invited you to move to New Orleans."

The words still caused a pang in her heart. She had relived that moment every night in her dreams. Except the ending was always different. She knew that she was still hung up on Remy.

It was what had convinced her that her feelings for him were genuine.

"Yes, but that's not in the cards now," she said.

"It could be. I want you to come to New Orleans and work for me when the show is over. Give yourself a chance to get to know Remy again," Alain said.

She smiled at the older man because she remembered the father that Remy had described and she knew that Alain was here to do whatever he could to ensure his son's happiness. And she guessed hers as well. But Alain couldn't invite her to New Orleans. Remy had to.

And it was only then that she'd know if they had been in the right place to meet each other.

"That is a very kind offer," she said.

"But you are going to turn it down," he finished for her.

"Yes I am. I don't want to go there unless Remy and I resolve things. My home is San Diego. I don't have many blood relatives living there but I have my friends."

"I understand," Alain said. "I had to ask."

"Why?"

"Because our son has never been in love before and we wanted to meet the woman who inspired such devotion in him."

Alain made to leave. Could this be real?

"How do you know that? Did he tell you he felt that for me?"

"No. He told us by what he didn't say."

Staci wanted to believe him but she'd already been played for a fool. Except that if Remy loved her and she knew she loved him didn't they deserve the chance to be together?

15

STACI'S FRIEND AND BUSINESS partner, Alysse, was anything but sweet or dreamy when she cornered him on the balcony. Remy accepted her hard glare. He knew he deserved it.

"Okay, you had your reasons, Remy, but really, lying to Staci…it was the worst thing any man could do to her. And she thought you were different," Alysse began. "I told myself I'd be civil. Promised Jay that I wouldn't threaten you with bodily harm, but I want to. How could you?"

"I'm glad you're angry on her behalf, you should be. She's your friend. I didn't mean to hurt her," Remy said. "I wish I'd done things differently."

"You still care about her," Alysse said.

"Yes, I do. I am not going to let her keep me away. I've been giving her some space because of the competition but I intend to convince her that she belongs in my arms as soon as this is over," he said.

"Fine. I can live with that," Alysse said.

"You can?"

"Yes. I thought…well, some not nice things about you, but I am pretty good at telling when someone is being sincere and you are," she said. "Want a brownie?"

"Aren't those for Staci?" he asked.

"They were but I see now that you and I are going to have to plot and plan and come up with an excellent way for you to make it up to her."

Remy was surprised at the way she said it. "We're a team?"

"Yes, of course we are. Staci's been alone, independent for so long. We have to stick together. She's a tough nut," Staci said.

"She sure is. What'd you have in mind?" Remy asked. He liked Staci's friend and he could see why the two women would work well together. They were nothing alike, total opposites in looks and temperament but there was a good solid core in both women. A determination to get things done.

"It'll take a big gesture on your part. Staci's not going to believe it unless you do," Alysse said. "Plus, you did break her heart."

"I know that. I don't know about big gestures," he said. It wasn't his style. Still, for Staci he'd do anything it took.

He thought if he could get close enough to get her into his bed he could show her how strong his feelings were for her. They had a bond between them that even this kind of mess couldn't weaken.

"It doesn't have to be writing her name in the sky or telling her how you feel on a Jumbotron. A big gesture just has to come from the heart and it has to be at the right time."

Intimate thoughts of Staci led him to recognize that he was going to have to tell her how he felt first. Suddenly, it seemed so easy.

He'd never told Staci that he loved her. He'd done everything but that because he'd been afraid to risk getting hurt. But by being afraid and keeping her in the dark, he'd isolated her. He'd made her feel like he didn't care for her at all. He knew what gesture she needed and he had the perfect solution for when to make it.

"I've got an idea. And it will only work if we both cook our hearts out this week and make it to the finals."

"I hope you do," Alysse said.

"Staci's waiting for you inside," Alain said as he joined them on the patio.

"Thanks." Alysse stood. "Good luck, Remy. With everything."

For the first time since New York he felt a surge of hope. He now knew how to win Staci back and he would use every skill he had to ensure it happened. He'd show her in a big way.

"You look very serious, son," Alain said.

"I am, Dad. For once I think I understand why you want to retire and spend more time with Mom," Remy said.

Alain laughed. "Glad to hear it. Tell me about the cooking you've been doing. Do you have new ideas for the restaurant?"

Remy did tell his father about the new ideas he had but his mind wasn't on Gastrophile. It was on Staci and the future that he craved. He knew now that there was nothing he wouldn't do. Nothing that could stand in the way of him winning her back.

Dinner that night was uneventful. Remy watched Staci all night long. He couldn't help himself. He desperately needed her back in his arms.

"Why are you watching me like that?" she asked, when Christian and the others were preoccupied.

"Because I want you and I'm hoping to talk you into meeting me on the balcony like you did the first night we were in the house," he said.

She wet her lips with her tongue and he wanted to groan as he could think of nothing but how she tasted and just how long it had been since he kissed her.

"Sex won't make everything better," she said.

"It can't make anything worse." He frowned. "Sorry, I've missed holding you in my arms."

"I've missed that, too," she said, "But this is the last week of competition and I don't want to mess anything up. Maybe we can talk about this next week."

He smiled, knowing that by this time next week he'd have won her back if all went according to plan.

THE NEXT SEVEN DAYS WERE the most intense of Staci's life. Even though nothing had changed between her and Remy, Staci felt more positive toward the chances of them having a relationship when the competition was over. She sensed that he wanted to start again and she knew that she did. But that was going to have to wait until they were done cooking.

On Wednesday both Christian and Remy were in the

lead but on Thursday it was a dessert cook-off and she overtook them both and claimed the lead. Remy edged out Christian to claim the second spot in the final.

Friday morning dawned bright and sunny in California and as she and Remy entered the *Premier Chef* studios and went up in the elevator they both looked at each other remembering their first day here.

Remy hit the stop button on the elevator.

"What are you doing?"

"Giving us the chance to start over."

"Truly?"

"Yes."

"Okay, hi there, I'm Staci Rowland."

"Ah, the cupcake baker. Nice to meet you, cupcake girl," he said.

She shook her head and smiled at him. It had been so long since he'd called her that. She missed it, she realized.

"I'm Remy....Remy Cruzel," he said. "I'm the Executive Chef at Gastrophile in New Orleans."

"Of the famous Cruzels?" she asked.

"One and the same. I'm here to prove I can cook but now that I'm meeting you…cooking is actually the farthest thing from my mind."

"I didn't see that in your bio," she said.

"That's because I'm keeping my true identity a secret but I have a feeling I can trust you."

"Trust is a big thing for me," she said.

"I can understand that," he said. "I—"

She fake stumbled into him and he caught her. She gave him a quick kiss on the cheek but he turned his head and kissed her full on the lips instead. He held her tenderly in his arms. She had missed the feel of his arms around her, too. He drew her closer to him.

"That's what I wanted to do when you fell into me that first time," he said.

"I would have called the cops," she said.

"Would you have?" he asked. "My kisses are pretty good. Maybe you've forgotten."

He leaned down and kissed her again slowly and passionately and she wrapped her arms around him, wanting to hold him close. But the elevator doors opened and they sprung apart.

"Ladies first," Remy said.

Heading down the hallway to the studio, they entered and found that the entire cast had been invited back. Staci had a quick catch-up with Vivian and then it was time to get ready for the taping.

They were both miked and had stage make-up put on and then sent to their stations. Staci had been practicing her menu in her mind since the beginning of the week. The dishes they'd prepared throughout the week would be the ones they'd make today. She knew she had to improve on her appetizer course, which she'd lost to both men.

"Welcome, Chefs. It seems like a long time ago when you first stood in this room and now we're down to two would be Premier Chefs left standing before us. Chef Rowland and Chef Cruzel," Hamilton said.

"You two have impressed us by winning Quick Cooks and challenges but mostly you've won us over with your fabulous dishes," Lorenz said.

"Today is your last chance to out-do the competition and claim the title of Premier Chef," Pete said.

"Chefs, it is time to start cooking," Fatima chimed in. "The cameras are rolling. We'll begin with appetizers and you will each have thirty minutes to prepare them. Your time starts now."

Staci cooked her heart out but Remy's dish won five points and hers only four. The next round was a tie with them both scoring five points each. Staci was nervous and so afraid she might lose but then she thought, as she watched Remy cooking, that she'd gained more the last six weeks than she'd ever expected to.

At the dessert round, she was completely focused and felt confident. Remy went first, presenting his dessert to the judges and after a few minutes they asked for hers. The judges tasted her Crème Freche Torte and sent her and Remy to the main studio to await the final results. There, Remy quickly pulled her into his arms away from the cameras and the audience.

"Now it's time for me to do what I should have done in New York when we were at the Empire State Building. In my heart I knew then that I loved you more than life itself. I wanted to tell you but was scared that if I did and you later found out about my lie you would never believe in our love.

"And while it's too late to change the past," he said, staring into her eyes. "The future is ours and I mean to spend the rest of my life with you. Will you give me another chance at being the man of your dreams?"

"Yes, Remy," she said. "I will. I love you, too and

can't think of anything I'd like better than being with you."

When it was time, Remy and Staci re-entered the studio holding hands.

"So perhaps we have something else to celebrate?" Hamilton asked.

"Yes," they said in unison.

"Good, now maybe we can get on with our show," Hamilton said smiling at both of them.

Fatima announced, "The dessert round has been the toughest yet and the hardest to judge but after much deliberation we are happy to announce that Staci Rowland is our winner!"

Staci turned to Remy who hugged her and kissed her and lifted her off the ground. "I knew you could do it."

"Not without you," she said with a smile, knowing she had truly found it all. Now that she had the Premier Chef title and had put the past behind her, her future was filled with love, and the man of her very own sweet dreams.

* * * * *

Give a 12 month subscription to a friend today!

Call Customer Services
0844 844 1358*

or visit
millsandboon.co.uk/subscriptions

* This call will cost you 7 pence per minute plus your phone company's price per minute access charge.

MILLS & BOON®

Why shop at millsandboon.co.uk?

Each year, thousands of romance readers find their perfect read at millsandboon.co.uk. That's because we're passionate about bringing you the very best romantic fiction. Here are some of the advantages of shopping at www.millsandboon.co.uk:

* **Get new books first**—you'll be able to buy your favourite books one month before they hit the shops

* **Get exclusive discounts**—you'll also be able to buy our specially created monthly collections, with up to 50% off the RRP

* **Find your favourite authors**—latest news, interviews and new releases for all your favourite authors and series on our website, plus ideas for what to try next

* **Join in**—once you've bought your favourite books, don't forget to register with us to rate, review and join in the discussions

Visit **www.millsandboon.co.uk**
for all this and more today!

The World of
MILLS & BOON®

With eight paperback series to choose from, there's a Mills & Boon series perfect for you. So whether you're looking for glamorous seduction, Regency rakes or homespun heroes, we'll give you plenty of inspiration for your next read.

Cherish

Experience the ultimate rush of falling in love.
12 new stories every month

Romantic Suspense INTRIGUE

A seductive combination of danger and desire
8 new stories every month

Desire

Passionate and dramatic love stories
6 new stories every month

nocturne

An exhilarating underworld of dark desires
2 new stories every month

For exclusive member offers go to
millsandboon.co.uk/subscribe

The World of
MILLS & BOON®

HISTORICAL

Awaken the romance of the past
6 new stories every month

MEDICAL ROMANCE

The ultimate in romantic medical drama
6 new stories every month

MODERN™

Power, passion and irresistible temptation
8 new stories every month

By Request

Relive the romance with the best of the best
12 stories every month

Have you tried eBooks?

With eBook exclusive series and titles from just **£1.99**, there's even more reason to try our eBooks today

Visit www.millsandboon.co.uk/eBooks
for more details